Narratives of Disability and Illness in the Fiction of J. M. Coetzee

Narratives of Disability and Illness in the Fiction of J. M. Coetzee

Paweł Wojtas

EDINBURGH
University Press

Edinburgh University Press is one of the leading university presses in the UK. We publish academic books and journals in our selected subject areas across the humanities and social sciences, combining cutting-edge scholarship with high editorial and production values to produce academic works of lasting importance. For more information visit our website: edinburghuniversitypress.com

© Paweł Wojtas 2024, 2025

Extracts from *Dusklands*, Copyright © J. M. Coetzee, 1974, 1982; *In the Heart of the Country*, Copyright © J. M. Coetzee, 1976, 1977; *Waiting for the Barbarians*, Copyright © J. M. Coetzee, 1980; *Life & Times of Michael K*, Copyright © J. M. Coetzee, 1983; *Foe*, Copyright © J. M. Coetzee, 1986; *Age of Iron*, Copyright © J. M. Coetzee, 1990; *The Master of Petersburg*, Copyright © J. M. Coetzee, 1994; *Boyhood*, Copyright © J. M. Coetzee, 1997; *Disgrace*, Copyright © J. M. Coetzee, 1999; *Youth*, Copyright © J. M. Coetzee, 2002; *Elizabeth Costello*, Copyright © J. M. Coetzee, 2003; *Slow Man*, Copyright © J. M. Coetzee, 2005; *Diary of a Bad Year*, Copyright © J. M. Coetzee, 2007; *Summertime*, Copyright © J. M. Coetzee, 2009; *The Childhood of Jesus*, Copyright 13 Infirmary Street *The Schooldays of Jesus*, Copyright © J. M. Coetzee, 2016; *The Death of Jesus*, Copyright © J. M. Coetzee, 2019; *Doubling the Point*, Copyright © 1992 by the President and Fellows of the Harvard College; *As a Woman Grows Older*, Copyright © J. M. Coetzee, 2004; *Cripplewood*, Copyright © J. M. Coetzee, 2013; 'The Old Woman and the Cats', 'Cripplewood', Copyright © J. M. Coetzee 2014; 'A House in Spain' in *Three Stories*, Copyright © J. M. Coetzee 2014; 'He and His Man' © The Nobel Foundation 2003; *The Good Story*, Copyright © J. M. Coetzee, 2015 (with respect only to the exchanges written by J. M. Coetzee)

Edinburgh University Press Ltd
13 Infirmary Street
Edinburgh EH1 1LT

First published in hardback by Edinburgh University Press 2024

Typeset in 11/13pt Adobe Sabon by
Cheshire Typesetting Ltd, Cuddington, Cheshire

A CIP record for this book is available from the British Library

ISBN 978 1 3995 2257 1 (hardback)
ISBN 978 1 3995 2258 8 (paperback)
ISBN 978 1 3995 2259 5 (webready PDF)
ISBN 978 1 3995 2260 1 (epub)

The right of Paweł Wojtas to be identified as the author of this work has been asserted in accordance with the Copyright, Designs and Patents Act 1988, and the Copyright and Related Rights Regulations 2003 (SI No. 2498).

Contents

Acknowledgements	vi
List of Abbreviations	viii
Introduction: Towards the Embodied Fiction of J. M. Coetzee	1
1. Disabled Textuality: *Dusklands* and *In the Heart of the Country*	17
2. Scopic Regimes, Haptic Commitments: Countering Ocularnormativism in *Waiting for the Barbarians*	41
3. Eco-Ability and Narrative Violence in *Life & Times of Michael K*	76
4. Mute Letters: Against Phonocentrism in *Foe*	101
5. Impossible Modalities, Ailing Selves: Illness, Metaphor and Selfhood in *Age of Iron*	125
6. Disability Ethics and Gothic Form in *The Master of Petersburg*	148
7. Dismodernism and Forms of Dependency in *Slow Man*	175
8. What is the World Coming to? Senility, Illness and Irony in the *Costello* Fictions and *Diary of a Bad Year*	198
9. Negative Capabilities: Illness Narrative as Bibliotherapy in the *Jesus* Novels	230
Epilogue: Positive Incapabilities	266
Works Cited	273
Index	296

Acknowledgements

I would like to express my heartfelt thanks to the Kosciuszko Foundation for funding my research fellowship at The Harry Ransom Centre, The University of Texas at Austin. I am also indebted to the staff of both institutions for their invaluable support and guidance throughout my research visit at Austin. My warmest thanks also to the Faculty of 'Artes Liberales', University of Warsaw, for funding my postdoctoral research at the Humanities Research Centre, University of York, as well as to the staff of both of these organisations for helping me throughout my research. I am grateful to J. M. Coetzee – as well as Peter Lampack Agency and David Higham Associates – for generously granting me permission to quote from his published works and unpublished materials. My thanks are also due to Penguin Random House, for giving me permission to quote from J. M. Coetzee's published novels, and to The Nobel Foundation for kindly permitting me to quote Coetzee's J. M. Coetzee's speech at the Nobel Banquet in full.

I would like to extend my very special thanks to David Attwell for his immense and generous support, guidance and encouragement during my research at York and throughout the various stages of drafting of this book. I would also like to thank Derek Attridge, Jerzy Koch and Liliana Sikorska for their kind and helpful words of advice. My warm thanks are extended to Matthew Foley and Stuart O'Donnell for their valuable feedback on selected chapters.

My gratitude goes to Maria Kalinowska for hosting a group discussion dedicated to my book project, as well as to Jerzy Axer, Ewa Róża Janion and Agata Zalewska for offering their useful remarks on the project's outline. Sincere thanks also to Robin Berghaus, Klaudia Ciesłowska, Bryan W. Davies, Wojciech Drąg, Ruth Evans, Krzysztof Fordoński, Robert Kusek, David Rudrum and Piotr Urbański, all of whom have supported me and this project in various ways. I would also like to thank my students from the Faculty of 'Artes Liberales' for sharing their inspiring ideas during class discussions as well as for their enthusiasm and interest.

I am grateful to my family, friends and colleagues for their generous and untiring support and encouragement. My thanks are to Katarzyna Skąpska for kindly allowing me to reproduce her artwork on the cover of this book. I have also been greatly helped by the editors and reviewers of Edinburgh University Press, who have expertly guided me through all stages of drafting and production, for which I am immensely grateful.

Finally, parts of Chapter 1 comprise a revised version of my article originally published in 2018 in the *Journal of Literary & Cultural Disability Studies* (12 (1): 71–87), under the title '"Form follows dysfunction": Coetzee's Narrative Ethics of Disability'. I would like to thank David Bolt, the journal's editor-in-chief, for allowing me to reproduce these fragments in this book.

List of Abbreviations

Works and Materials by J. M. Coetzee

Novels and memoirs

AI – *Age of Iron*
BH – *Boyhood*
CJ – *The Childhood of Jesus*
DBY – *Diary of a Bad Year*
DG – *Disgrace*
DJ – *The Death of Jesus*
DL – *Dusklands*
EC – *Elizabeth Costello*
F – *Foe*
HC – *In the Heart of the Country*
MK – *Life & Times of Michael K*
MP – *The Master of Petersburg*
SJ – *The Schooldays of Jesus*
SM – *Slow Man*
ST – *Summertime*
WB – *Waiting for the Barbarians*
Y – *Youth*

Short stories

HHM – 'He and His Man'
HS – 'A House in Spain'
L – 'Lies'

OWC – 'The Old Woman and the Cats'
WGO – 'As a Woman Grows Older'

Collaborations

CW – *Cripplewood-Kreupelhout*
DP – *Doubling the Point*
GS – *The Good Story*
HN – *Here and Now*

Archival material

HRC – The Harry Ransom Centre

Introduction: Towards the Embodied Fiction of J. M. Coetzee

When the Belgian artist Berlinde de Bruyckere invited John Coetzee to curate her exhibition at the Belgian Pavilion for the Venice Biennial of 2013, she asked her writer-friend to accept rather unconventional terms of his curatorship: 'Not to assist me during the working process or to help me make any decisions, but as a source of inspiration' (CW 29).[1] In response to the invitation, Coetzee complied by sending her his unpublished short story about an elderly woman discussing with her son her reasons for looking after unwanted cats.[2] The fruit of this 'inspiration' was *Cripplewood/Kreupelhout*, a large sculpture made from barkless tree branches wrapped in linen, reminiscent of '[a] crippled body in need of support' (43). But what sort of inspiration did Coetzee act as exactly? Or, in de Bruyckere's words: 'And where is J. M. Coetzee in this story?' (32). As '[t]here are no literal references to' Coetzee's fiction in her work, his position as the Belgian artist's muse of sorts is awkward (32). The answer lies, it turns out, in Coetzee's ability to utter '[t]he unspeakable' through a text that yields a 'different meaning with each reading' (32). This approach to reading Coetzee's narratives will cause '[t]he compelling empathy that you cannot but experience' (32). What follows from this is that the empathy-generating qualities of Coetzee's text depend on certain formal operations that provoke meditation on the vulnerability of the body, even if this theme does not define the story or is omitted from it.[3]

De Bruyckere's intuition about the prevalence of intrinsic narrative processes, which are evocative of certain reading effects, over the intricacies of the story in Coetzee's fiction echoes Coetzee's own reflections from his private notebooks about his experience of writing: 'I have no interest in telling stories; it is the process of storytelling that interests me' (HRC 33.3, 17-10-1977). In his preparatory notes for *In the Heart of the Country* Coetzee further expounds on his writing strategies: 'I am interested in the project not of "writing" a book but of "reading" a book' (HRC 33.3, 30-10-1974).[4] These endeavours are to produce a 'reading-novel, a feminine novel of things <u>done to</u> one without the thrust of story' (HRC 33.3, 8-10-1975).[5] Coetzee's intention to write a 'reading-novel' aims to contravene the familiar associations of writing that heavily depend on the masculine injunctions of agency, action, completeness and closure for their operation. He intends to write a novel whose evasions make up 'holes in the text', which are 'her holes, characteristic of her, and therefore of a piece with the text' (HRC 33.3, 28-1-1976). In favouring feminine hole-ness over masculine wholeness as an operative principle of writing, Coetzee places his text in a position that privileges reception, fragmentation and incompleteness, concepts that resist the triumphalist narratives of normalcy.

Rephrasing de Bruyckere's words quoted above for our present purposes, one may ask: and where is disability in this story? Or, most importantly: and where is disability in Coetzee's story? In their foregrounding of incompleteness, Coetzee's 'reading-novels' show a systematic narrative pattern that Michael Bérubé calls 'disabled textuality', which 'cannot be attributed simply to any one character's mental operations' (2018, 15). Instead, as I attempt to show in this book broadly, and in Chapter 1 in particular, the disabled textuality of Coetzee's fiction consists in the ways in which his narratives reproduce – through the formal strategies of fragmentation, temporal disruption, deferral of closure, ambiguity, structural incompleteness, and so on – mechanisms that are commonly associated with the normative notions of disability experience. But Coetzee does not place his text in the position of lack in order to uphold the normative assumption about disability as a marker of deficiency, but, conversely, to decentralise the narratives of normalcy that consign disability to a marginalised status and discredit authentic disability experience. Put differently, the disabled textuality of Coetzee's fiction frustrates the non-disabled position's totalising claims for superiority, completeness and normalcy; a sentiment that is consistent with Coetzee's sustained critique of the oppressive forms of power and authority in his fictions. Privileging female receptivity over male action, Coetzee's 'reading-novels' challenge the reader to call into question their ableist biases and overcome the prejudicial stance towards fictional representations of non-normative bodies which Ato Quayson calls 'aesthetic nervousness' (2007, 19).

Some of these hermeneutic effects of Coetzee's text are obtained through a staging of the formal signifiers of disability. The sudden disruption of realism through an unsolicited arrival of the quasi-author-figure of Elizabeth Costello in *Slow Man* creates a rupture in the story that echoes the process of Paul Rayment's coming to terms with his physical impairment. Along similar lines, the formal experiments and narrative unreliability of *Dusklands* and *In the Heart of the Country* aim to reproduce the protagonists' mental anxiety caused by their exposure to violence or psychological abuse. Undergirding fictional representations of disability, these formal operations partake in Coetzee's critique of oppressive injunctions of normalcy. Such productive affinities between form and representation in Coetzee's text engender what Adam Zachary Newton refers to as 'hermeneutic ethics', denoting 'the ethico-critical accountability which acts of reading hold their readers to' (1997, 18). Coetzee's ways in which he employs signifiers of disability to elicit an ethical response from the reader involve – as I discuss in Chapter 2 – forms of subverting the primacy of sight-centred representational regimes through encouraging non-ocularcentric habits of reading, which Laura Marks refers to as 'haptic visuality' (2002, 2). Similarly, as I argue in Chapter 9, Coetzee's illness narratives, in their fostering of defamiliarising and decelerative reading strategies,[6] prompt forms of affective engagement that can have therapeutic effects on the reader.[7]

But Coetzee's interest in disability transcends the formal operations of his fictions. On the representational level, Coetzee's novels are inhabited by protagonists with acquired psychiatric disorders (Eugene Dawn), disfigurements (Michael K), physical impairments (Paul Rayment, the barbarian woman), sensory impairments (the barbarian woman, Marianna), and those facing disabling symptoms of senescence or terminal illness (Elizabeth Curren and JC as well as David in *The Death of Jesus* and Witold in *The Pole*). With textual ambiguity being a trademark of Coetzee's poetics, the tally includes characters whose disabilities are implied rather than stated explicitly or, conversely, stated but questionable. Such is the case with Magda's psychological disorder, Friday's muteness, Michael K's learning difficulties and John's (from the *Scenes from Provincial Life* trilogy) autism.[8] Textual ambiguity is also in operation when the disabling states of the protagonists are subsumed into the work's allegorical make-up. When Elizabeth Curren's contemplation of her experience of cancer fosters the novel's indictment of the self-destructive politics of apartheid in *Age of Iron*, or when Dostoevsky's epilepsy chimes with the theme of falling as a harbinger of his betrayal of Pavel, the protagonists' experience of the symptoms of illness in these works is indivisible from Coetzee's sustained interrogation of ethical aporias.

After Coetzee's critique of reason, which he holds responsible for enabling modern forms of violence and warfare,[9] has taken a new quasi-transcendental turn in the *Jesus* novels, the rhetoric of indeterminacy has continued to inform disability representation. The problematic intellectual status of David in the *Jesus* trilogy, one extended between atypicality and super-ability,[10] takes an active part in Coetzee's resistance to ethical rationalism.

Considering Coetzee's famous formulation 'All autobiography is storytelling, all writing is autobiography', it is worth noting the autobiographical underpinnings of fictional representations of disability in Coetzee's works (*DP* 391). Coetzee's personal notebooks from 1993 show the author taking stock of his life in South Africa and bemoaning the heavy psychological toll his homeland took on him: 'Deformation. My life as deformed, year after year, by South Africa. Emblem: the deformed trees on the golf links in Simonstown' (HRC 27.2, 11-5-1993). Seeing Coetzee frame the devastating effects of South African politics in disability figures and tropes suggests that the use of cancer metaphors in *Age of Iron*, a novel published three years prior to writing this note, to berate the evils of apartheid may not be fortuitous. Apart from employing illness metaphors as markers of his affective and psychological states, Coetzee had some of his later characters, such as Elizabeth Costello, Paul Rayment and JC, share the aspects of his own personal experience of ageing. In their other guises, autobiographical parallels involve the events or themes in Coetzee's fiction that are inspired by the experience of illness and its disabling symptoms by Coetzee's family members. All of these works can be read as examples of Coetzee's fictionalised 'autogerontography' and, more broadly, disability life writing.[11]

Following Coetzee's permanent relocation from Cape Town to Adelaide in 2002, it has become customary among Coetzee scholars to periodise his fiction along this divide, thus distinguishing between the early or South African fiction and late or Australian fiction. While Coetzee has been committed to interrogating the vulnerability of the body consistently throughout his oeuvre, it could be argued at the risk of oversimplifying the matter that the evolution of disability representation in Coetzee's works also partially yields to this pattern of periodisation. The witnessing of atrocities committed by the apartheid state authorities in South Africa compelled Coetzee to contemplate the implications of political violence visited upon the marginalised social groups under authoritarian regimes. As a result, in his early fictions Coetzee is preoccupied with what Jasbir K. Puar calls 'the biopolitics of debilitation' (2017, xiv), denoting the state's tactical subjugation of the non-conforming subjects by means of violent practices that are calculated to reduce one's body to the position of vulnerability and docility. In these fictions, Coetzee is interested in the disabled body in the sense of the body being rendered disabled by the state's oppressive measures, such as torture, mutilation, persecution, segregation, imposed restriction of mobility and other forms of injustice – themes variously explored by other anti-apartheid writers of Coetzee's generation, including Alex La Guma, André Brink, Mongane Wally Serote, Breyten Breytenbach, Nadine Gordimer and others.[12] Such early novels as *Dusklands*, *In the Heart of the Country*, *Waiting for the Barbarians*, *Life & Times of Michael K*, *Foe* and *Age of Iron* show characters whose physical and psychological states are a direct consequence of the biopolitics of debilitation at the hands of those occupying the position of power.

Like his South African fiction, Coetzee's works of the Australian period remain attuned to the denigration of disability experience. This time, however, Coetzee seeks to debunk the myths of the culture of disability inclusion characteristic of neoliberal states, Australia included. Such works as *Slow Man*, *Diary of a Bad Year*, and some *Costello* novels and short stories interrogate the ways in which liberal societies accommodate disability while perpetuating various forms of ableism. His later works, which I discuss in Chapters 7 and 8, can be read as an indictment of the ways in which western societies produce disability: not through political violence, as in the earlier fictions, but by creating the debilitating mechanisms of exclusion while upholding the façade of the culture of inclusionism. In this sense, Coetzee's later fiction echoes the main assumptions of the 'social constructionist model' of disability which maintains that 'disability' is not a form of functional limitation (which is better described by the term 'impairment') but is produced by social and architectural barriers, such as lack of accessible spaces and facilities for non-normatively embodied people or prejudicial attitudes (Hall 2016, 168). This model has emerged as a critique of the 'medical model' of disability which 'tends to consider disability as a deficit: a problem or pathology that needs to be treated, concealed or dealt with through rehabilitation' (ibid., 166) – a position of which Coetzee has been suspicious since his earliest works. In refusing the rehabilitative measures imposed by medical officials to correct their physical impairments, such characters as Michael K and Paul Rayment epitomise a critique of the medical model's commonplace that every physical or psychological divergence from a medically established norm is in need of a cure or correction.

While, as suggested above, Coetzee has addressed some concerns foregrounded by the social model in his indictment of the neoliberal forms of social exclusion and countered the medical model's pathologisation of non-normative forms of embodiment, his works refuse to exhaust themselves in a straightforward endorsement of the former and refutation of the latter approach. Although alert to the justified concerns of the social model of disability, Coetzee's fiction, in its sustained linking of social discrimination with the complexity of embodied experience, echoes an implicit critique of this model's 'disembodied notion of disability' (Hughes and Paterson 1997, 330), as well as its failure to account for 'the complex interplay of individual and environmental factors in the lives of disabled people' (Shakespeare 2017, 202). Coetzee's notions of embodied understanding are in tune with the 'interactionist perspective' which takes account of the social constructionism of disability while retaining its focus on the materiality of the body (Hall 2016, 27). Along these lines, some of Coetzee's works anticipate some assumptions of 'neomaterialism, nonnormative positivism, or posthumanist disability theory', which mark an attempt 'to think more deeply about materiality's agential capacities without continuing to consign disability to a reductively pathologized and thus wholly human discursive fate' (Mitchell, Antebi and Snyder 2019, 4). Michael K's wilful retreat from social spaces and dietary habits in favour of chthonic habitation result in a recalibration of his physical state and abilities in keeping with the pressures of the natural environment. As I propose in Chapter 3, K turns into a figure of 'eco-ability', one that redefines the anthropocentric and humanist conceptions of materiality of the body as well as social and medical parameters of ability (Nocella 2017, 141). Similarly, Coetzee's refusal, as I argue in Chapter 4, to position Friday in *Foe* as either a mute man or wilfully silent colonial subject presents a liminal position that serves to dislodge the prevailing notions of sensory experience, beyond the established ability–disability binary. This liminal ontological status of certain characters often arises out of formal operations that foreground ambiguity, thus precluding facile formulas of identification or closure. Such is the case in *In the Heart of the Country*, where, as I venture to argue in Chapter 1, the novel's textual strategies provoke questions about Magda's mental state while refusing to provide a definitive answer.

By creating characters whose physical and intellectual states do not accord with the cultural and medical notions of normalcy, Coetzee destabilises norms that define and sanction the perimeters of disability. In so doing, he anticipates certain ideas that are the subject of debates among Disability Studies scholars. These include Rosemarie Garland-Thomson's deconstruction of the term 'normal' through drawing attention to the constructionist underpinnings of the socially privileged 'normate' position, as she calls it (1997, 8), or Lennard J. Davis's notion of 'dismodernism', which purports that the postmodern subject's dependence on technological solutions compromises her claims for completeness. It is, therefore, disability, not ability, that defines our common identity and determines the norm. In Chapter 7, I read *Slow Man*'s resistance to the rehabilitative injunctions of neoliberal culture along the lines of dismodernism's radical recharting of postmodern body politics. But Coetzee's questioning of the narratives of normalcy as well as condemnation of social injustice is often inextricable from broader, or intersectional, issues around identity. For instance, regarding Coetzee's earlier works, it is impossible to discuss Magda's psychological state without considering her domestic containment and exposure to the patriarchal culture of apartheid South Africa. Similarly, while the barbarian woman's physical impairments and Friday's possible mutilation are inextricable from their status as colonial subjects, Michael K's social ostracism due to his facial disfigurement is compounded by his marginalised status as a working-class 'coloured' man living in South Africa.[13] Finally, Coetzee's later fictions contemplate their character's physical and intellectual symptoms of ageing as well as the debilitating effects of social discrimination, in its various guises of ableism, ageism and lookism, which is inherent in the neoliberal culture of bodily perfectibility and hyperproductivity.[14]

As this study takes account of Coetzee's fictionalisation of disability, it also examines the representations of the disabling symptoms of illness. Some disability scholars warn against conflating disability and illness on the grounds that this perspective 'is in line with a purely medical approach to disability' (Kudlick 2018, 110). The point is that, just as a disabled person should not think of her disability as an 'illness' that is in need of a cure, a person who has an illness need not be or see themselves as 'disabled' by her illness. This way of framing disability and illness in negative discursive patterns serves to reinforce stereotypical presuppositions about either position. While I agree that such precarious equations risk perpetuating the narratives that label disability as a pathology or deficit, I think there are costs incurred in overlooking the productive affinities between these terms, too. When David in the *Jesus* novels experiences physically incapacitating symptoms of a mysterious illness or when JC in *Diary* of a Bad Year confronts the physical effects of Parkinson's disease, Coetzee uses illness and disability to acknowledge the complex materiality of the body, and ethical implications thereof, beyond the negative ascriptions of cultural metaphors or biomedical narratives. Similarly, when Michael K's severe emaciation helps him reframe the ways of interacting with the environment or when Dostoevsky's epilepsy prompts a rethinking of the metaphors of seeing, the questions of the ailing body become inextricable from those of ability and its limits. For fear of overlooking these fruitful correspondences between representation and figures of illness and disability, I often discuss these terms in tandem.

Although the amount of scholarship on disability in the works of Coetzee is relatively modest compared to the immense critical and scholarly attention that Coetzee's works have garnered in general, the complexity with which Coetzee approaches the various inflections of disability representation adumbrated above has attracted some interest from Disability Studies scholars. One of the chief publications on the subject is Ato Quayson's 2007 book *Aesthetic Nervousness: Disability and the Crisis of Representation*, which focuses on Coetzee's earlier works and specifically on the ambiguities of the representation of autism in the *Life & Times of Michael K*. Also focusing on Coetzee's early fictions, *The Secret Life of Stories* (2016) by one of the leading Disability Studies scholars Michael Bérubé persuasively discusses how Coetzee's, among others', depictions of intellectual disability can influence the reader's understanding of narrative. The most comprehensive publication on disability in Coetzee's later fiction is Alice Hall's immensely illuminating *Disability and Modern Fiction: Faulkner, Morrison, Coetzee and the Nobel Prize for Literature* (2012b), in which the author examines the ethical and formal demands that Coetzee's narratives of ageing and disability make on their readers.[15] Among the more recent monographs, the scholar of postcolonial fiction, Christopher Krentz explores the link between disability metaphors and human rights in Coetzee's South African fiction in his *Elusive Kinship: Disability and Human Rights in Postcolonial Literature* (2022). Also, on top of these book publications, Coetzee's interest in disability has been discussed by both disability and Coetzee scholars in a number of articles and book chapters.[16] While building on these important publications, the present book intends to be broader in scope. Considering that, as argued above, Coetzee's depictions of disability have evolved in tune with the changing social and political circumstances of the author's life and times, this book attempts to study all of Coetzee's novels to date[17] to demonstrate the extent to which the author's multifaceted depictions of disability offer a sustained critique of the ableist implications of political violence and biomedical discourses of postmodernity across all periods of his writing life.

For these reasons, the chapters of this book follow the order of publication of the novels or series of novels under discussion rather than their themes. To examine the ways in which the 'disabled textuality' of Coetzee's fiction counters prevailing discourses of normativity, each chapter considers disability or illness themes in the light of the narrative challenges that Coetzee's text presents to the reader as well as the ethical implications of these textual operations. Drawing on Adam Zachary Newton's concept of 'narrative ethics', Chapter 1 demonstrates how the ethical implications of social or political oppression in Coetzee's works are inextricable from the formal and meaning-making devices of his fictions (1997, 17). Coetzee's characters with disabilities demonstrate the ways in which the disabled body makes problematic an affirmation of the wholeness and authority of normative subjectivity. Similarly, many formally experimental devices of Coetzee's fictions serve to debunk the normative myths of textual completeness and closure. Therefore, this chapter attempts to test the extent to which Coetzee's first two novels, *Dusklands* and *In the Heart of the Country*, stage the complexities of mental and physical disabilities through their deployment of formal modes of textual disruption as a way of subverting hegemonic and normative discourses.

The subsequent three chapters are centred on the counter-ableist implications of Coetzee's fictional accounts of sensory disabilities. Chapter 2 attempts to determine how Coetzee's third novel, *Waiting for the Barbarians*, challenges the sight-centred habits of thinking. Reflecting on the notion of 'haptic visuality' (Marks 2002, 2), I examine the ways in which the haptic triad of touch, feel and grope undermine the dominance of vision-centred discourses and their 'ocularnormative' implications in Coetzee's works (Bolt 2016, 5). I focus on the ethical effects of Coetzee's use of haptic narrative devices and linguistic forms as well as his implicit critique of ocularcentrism through a self-reflexive use of visual metaphors. In my analysis of *Life & Times of Michael K* in Chapter 3, I contemplate the ways in which the titular protagonist's disabilities and disabling conditions, such as facial disfigurement and body emaciation, collude with ecological themes and terms to account for his elusive ontological status. Drawing on Alison Kafer's term 'cripped environmentalism',

I demonstrate the extent to which Michael K's disabilities, which are a product of socio-political factors, are reframed through the novel's challenging of anthropomorphism (2017, 204). The interlocking of ecological and disability vocabularies takes the analysis deeper into the narrative construction of the novel. Here I consider K as an object of other characters' and narrators' acts of 'testimonial injustice' and his agency in countering such forms of narrative violence (Fricker 2010, 9). I also examine Coetzee's term the 'poetics of failure' to take account of the novel's crisis of narrativisation, both on the part of the author-narrators and focalisers, as well as study the implications of the use of this term in relation to disability (*DP* 87). Chapter 4 interrogates Coetzee's representations of silence and muteness in *Foe*. Drawing on the titular concept of Jacques Rancière's *Mute Speech: Literature, Critical Theory, and Politics* (2011), it begins with a discussion on the divide between the conceptual couplings of speech-writing and silence-muteness. I further look into the ways in which writing pairs with muteness to examine the complex ways of giving voice to those that refuse or are unable to operate within accepted linguistic protocols, or those to whom access to dominant language and forms of writing has been denied. I argue that Coetzee's interlinking of the metaphysics of writing and materiality of the disabled body has the capacity to unsettle allegorical depictions of disability that are symptomatic of traditional literary representations.

The following two chapters take as their focus the figurative signifiers of illness and disability in Coetzee's works. Chapter 5 interrogates the link between the ethics of subjectivity and contemplation of the ailing body in *Age of Iron*. Focusing on Søren Kierkegaard's notion of 'sickness unto death', I attempt to show how the philosopher's ethics of inwardness anticipates Coetzee's representation of the suffering body of the narrator-protagonist (2004, 48). I further explore Coetzee's use of cancer as a political metaphor by studying the implications of the metaphorisation of disability in literary texts. I finally show how Coetzee's ethics of subjectivity resists traditional impulses for allegorising the ailing body. Chapter 6 then probes the extent to which the imbrication of the vocabularies of disability and Gothic aesthetics in *The Master of Petersburg* informs the ethical commitments of Coetzee's works. I argue that through the interlacing of Gothic and disability themes Coetzee refuses to acknowledge the limits between fictional representation and factual accuracy. The part that follows studies ethical implications of Coetzee's representation of specular metaphors and vocabularies in the light of Jacques Derrida's concepts of 'hauntology' and 'specter'

(1994, 9, 46). In the closing section of this chapter, discussing the problem of instrumentalisation of disability in *The Master of Petersburg* and, by comparison, *Disgrace*, I propose that Coetzee's fiction's resistance to affirmative modes of disability representation challenges normative notions of morality.

An analysis of Coetzee's Australian novels begins with Chapter 7 where I look into the double meaning of Lennard J. Davis's term 'dismodernism' (2002, 27). The first meaning presupposes disability as symptomatic of the postmodern culture of dependency. The second one, based on the etymology of the prefix 'dis-', gestures towards resistance to cultural and formal practices of modernism and late modernity. The novels of J. M. Coetzee are committed to practising a rebranded form of modernism, one that both embraces and defers modernist formal tactics. I, therefore, propose that through some formal devices deployed in the novel *Slow Man*, which disrupt the illusion of textual wholeness and verisimilitude, Coetzee mounts a critique of neoliberal injunctions of normalcy. I also attempt to show the ways in which Coetzee's text formally reproduces the structure of the culture of dependency. Finally, I contemplate how these formal tactics complement Coetzee's representation of physical disability in relation to the ethical aspects of care. In Chapter 8, I explore the relationship between irony and senescence in Coetzee's fiction of the first decade of this century. The opening section offers a theoretical introduction to the cultural constructions of senility and its links to the notion of irony. In the second section, I read the novels and shorter fictions that include Elizabeth Costello as a character (mainly *Elizabeth Costello*, 'As a Woman Grows Older' and 'The Old Woman and the Cats') to probe the intersection of what I refer to as the 'ironic dialogism' of Coetzee's Australian fiction and the ethical aspects of senility. I later analyse *Diary of a Bad Year* to examine the ways in which two forms of irony, formal and overt irony, aid Coetzee in mounting a critique of neoliberal biopolitics and prejudicial discourses around senescence. I also introduce the term 'ironic autogerontography' to focus on the links between Coetzee's fictional representations of old age and his own experience of ageing.

Centred on Coetzee's trilogy of novels, *The Childhood of Jesus, The Schooldays of Jesus* and *The Death of Jesus*, Chapter 9 aims to investigate the psychotherapeutic effects of Coetzee's illness narratives. I will seek to demonstrate the extent to which Coetzee's illness narratives lend themselves for bibliotherapy despite failing to meet the standards of traditional books for prescription. The *Jesus* trilogy prompts meditation on the relationship between fiction and self-understanding as well as the therapeutic effects that this self-understanding elicits. A fiction so constructed contains within itself a certain capacity to trigger the reader's self-searching habits by withholding its textual meanings. This problematic 'capacity' of fiction is coupled with the complicated ontological and fictional status of the protagonist, David, together with the boy's understanding of his (dis)abilities as well as a sense of self in illness (1994, 232). In the closing section of this book, I trace the parallels between Coetzee's *Jesus* novels and his fictionalised memoirs, *Scenes from Provincial Life*, in terms of their representations of illness and disability. I propose to read both trilogies as unusual examples of disability life writing.

Although this book mostly analyses Coetzee's published works, it also makes references to the early drafts of his novels, private notebooks and diaries which yield fascinating insights into the development of depictions of disability or disabled characters in his works. Since the acquisition of Coetzee's private papers by The Harry Ransom Center at the University of Texas at Austin in 2011, the archival research of these materials has marked, in the words of David Attwell, 'a turning point in Coetzee studies, the effects of which will be felt for generations' (2016, 374). This 'archival turn' has produced a number of important studies aiming to reread Coetzee's oeuvre through a vast body of handwritten drafts and typescripts, private and business correspondence, research and related materials which shed a fresh light on the complexities of Coetzee's creative practice (Easton, Farrant and Wittenberg 2021b, 2). Focusing on the autobiographical underpinnings of Coetzee's novels, David Attwell's seminal publication *J. M. Coetzee and the Life of Writing: Face to Face with Time* (2015) set these debates in motion. Similarly, Jan Wilm's *The Slow Philosophy of J. M. Coetzee* (2016), Robert Kusek's *Through the Looking Glass: Writers' Memoirs at the Turn of the 21st Century* (2017), Anthony Uhlmann's *J. M. Coetzee: Truth, Meaning, Fiction* (2020) and the edited collection *J. M. Coetzee and the Archive: Fiction, Theory, and Autobiography* (Easton, Farrant and Wittenberg 2021a) centre their analyses on the archival research of the Coetzee papers at The Harry Ransom Center.[18]

The present book draws on archival material to complement its discussions on Coetzee's published novels, which remain the core subject of its textual analysis, and in doing so does not purport to be as thoroughly engaged with the Coetzee papers as the above publications. That being said, it is hoped that this book will reveal that studying Coetzee's unpublished materials offers penetrating insights into his narratives of disability and illness. The progression of the early iterations of such characters as Michael K, Anna K, Friday or Harry (a minor character from *Dusklands*) reveals Coetzee's strategy for deliberately constructing certain characters as figures of 'narrative prosthesis'[19] to self-reflexively report on how literary authors tend to instrumentalise disability for narrative purposes and acknowledge his own complicity in this process, thus questioning the reliability and authority of the author.[20] Whereas some of these developments – such as when the prototypes of Michael K and Friday gradually progress from non-disabled to disabled characters across the drafts[21] – arise from the transformative dynamic of the writing process, others appear to directly reflect authorial intentions recorded in Coetzee's meticulously dated private notebooks and writer's diaries which serve as companion pieces to the drafts. Likewise, Coetzee's private papers hint at the parallels between certain characters' physical or intellectual states and Coetzee's life experience.[22] These insights into works in progress profoundly illuminate textual operations involved in the process of storytelling and help expose affinities between the mechanisms underlying forms of 'disabled textuality' and the ethical – which includes therapeutic – effects of Coetzee's 'reading-novels'.

Notes

1. See Kusek and Szymański (2015) for further information about 'the cooperation between Coetzee and the Belgian artist Berlinde De Bruyckere which has so far resulted in one installation and two art books co-authored by Coetzee and De Bruyckere' (13).
2. This short story, 'The Old Woman and the Cats', was published in *Cripplewood/Kreupelhout* (2013) among materials comprising the record of the artistic collaboration of De Bruyckere and Coetzee, including their correspondence related to the exhibition of the *Cripplewood/Kreupelhout* sculpture and a number of photographs of this installation.
3. In his *J. M. Coetzee and the Ethics of Reading* (2004), Derek Attridge provides a sustained analysis of the ways in which Coetzee's text, through its formal effects, makes ethical demands on the reader.
4. The abbreviation 'HRC' denotes archival materials accessed from The Harry Ransom Center, University of Texas at Austin. The numerical order in the citations follows this pattern: HRC, number of container, number of folder, date of entry or page reference as specified by J. M. Coetzee. This pattern will be used throughout this book.
5. Underscores as in the original. When I quote from Coetzee's handwritten manuscripts or typescripts I try to follow, if possible, the original

punctuation here and throughout this book, including deletions and underscores.
6. These strategies are called by Jan Wilm 'slow reading' (2016, 16) and by Eva Maria Koopman and Frank Hakemulder 'stillness' (2015, 80).
7. The suggestion that Coetzee's fiction lends itself for bibliotherapy rests on these ameliorative, as I see them, hermeneutic qualities rather than on the supposition that Coetzee's text can or should be used for curing certain psychological disorders.
8. I discuss the controversial psychological status of those characters in Chapters 1, 3 and 9, respectively.
9. See Woessner (2010; 2017) for further information on Coetzee's critique of rationalism.
10. In Chapter 9, I examine the possibilities of John Keats's term 'negative capability' to address this liminal position in relation to disability (1994, 232).
11. In Chapters 8 and 9, I focus at length on the ways in which Coetzee's personal experience of impairment, illness and ageing inspired the construction of some of his characters. Also, in her article 'Autre-biography: Disability and Life Writing in Coetzee's Later Works' (2012a), Alice Hall provides a very insightful account of these biographical parallels.
12. See Coetzee's own discussion on the representation of torture in South African fiction in his essay 'Into the Dark Chamber' (republished in *Doubling the Point*).
13. I use lower case when referring to the ethnic identities of South Africa to denote racial categories used under apartheid.
14. See Stuart Murray's 'The Ambiguities of Inclusion: Disability in Contemporary Literature' (2018) for his analysis of neoliberal forms of disability discrimination. For Coetzee's critique of neoliberal culture more broadly, see Andrew Gibson's recent book *J. M. Coetzee and Neoliberal Culture* (2022).
15. See also Hall's 'Autre-biography: Disability and Life Writing in Coetzee's Later Works' (2012a) for the autobiographical aspects of Coetzee's late fiction and her *Disability and Literature* (2016) for a discussion on the ethics of dependency and care in Coetzee's *Slow Man*.
16. Another prominent disability scholar Stuart Murray examines the ethical implications of Coetzee's early and late fiction in his articles 'From Virginia's Sister to Friday's Silence: Presence, Metaphor, and the Persistence of Disability in Contemporary Writing' (2012) and 'Allegories of the Bioethical: Reading J. M. Coetzee's *Diary of a Bad Year*' (2014). The articles that address the link between disability and power or disempowerment in Coetzee's early works include Ayobami Kehinde's 'Ability in Disability: J. M. Coetzee's *Life & Times of Michael K* and the Empowerment of the Disabled' (2010), Saloua Ali Ben Zahra's 'Masculinity, Disability, and Empire

in J. M. Coetzee's *Waiting for the Barbarians*' (2021) and my own contribution 'Disability and the Modalities of Displacement in the Early Fiction of J. M. Coetzee' (Wojtas 2021b). Also, Coetzee's novel *Slow Man*, especially in terms of its affinities between disability ethics and literary form, has attracted much scholarly attention. Apart from Hall's publications quoted above, see, for instance, Dolcerocca and Ergin's 'Crippling Story: Disability and Storytelling in J. M. Coetzee's *Slow Man*' (2017) and Shadi Neimneh and Nazmi Al-Shalabi's 'Disability and the Ethics of Care in J. M. Coetzee's *Slow Man*' (2011). Also, A. Marie Houser's article '"There, there": Disability, Animality, and the Allegory of *Elizabeth Costello*' (2020) is a contribution to the intersectional debates about disability. Finally, Coetzee's accounts of ageing and disability have inspired some comparative studies, which include Alice Hall's analysis of ageing in Coetzee's *Diary of a Bad Year* and Philip Roth's *Exit Ghost* (2014) and my own reading of disability ethics in the fictions of Coetzee and E. M. Forster (Wojtas 2021a).

17. While *Disgrace* is the only novel by Coetzee that has not been given an in-depth analysis in this book, I discuss some aspects that this novel dramatises which are pertinent for the present purposes, such as elective silence, instrumentalisation of disability and senile irony, in Chapters 4, 6 and 8, respectively. Although the novels are the main focus of this book, the shorter fictions that feature Elizabeth Costello, such as 'The Old Woman and the Cats' and 'As a Woman Grows Older', are also discussed as they continue to fictionalise the protagonist's experience of ageing, which is one of the central themes of the *Costello* novels. Similarly, the semi-autobiographical trilogy *Scenes from Provincial Life* is referred to when it alludes to or inspires the autobiographical aspects of Coetzee's novels.

18. Other shorter publications based on the archival research of the Coetzee papers at The Harry Ransom Center include Jan Wilm's 'The J. M. Archive and the Archive in J. M. Coetzee' (2017) and Andrew Dean's 'Lives and Archives' (2020).

19. 'Narrative prosthesis' denotes a form of instrumentalisation of disability in literary texts. When literary narratives depend on disability 'for their representational power, disruptive potentiality, and analytical insight', they use it for prosthetic purposes (Mitchell and Snyder 2000, 49).

20. 'What emerges' from Coetzee's self-effacing tactics, as affirmed by Marc Farrant, 'is a conception of the authority of the literary author as defined by a lack of authority' (2021, 168). Coetzee's insights into the limits of authorial authority or complicity in reinforcing cultural stereotypes, which will be discussed in Chapters 1–4, implicitly take to task another kind of author, the author of this book, for his complicity in instrumentalising and objectifying disability. Indeed, if unchecked, academic discourse about disability, this book not excluded, risks

perpetuating forms of 'epistemic injustice' about disability representation (Fricker 2010, 1). Although a wider discussion on the problem of the appropriation of authentic disability experience in academic discourse falls outside of the purview of this book, I think it is vital to mention that the self-reflexivity of Coetzee's works has the capacity to inspire debates about the limits of agency and reliability of scholarly accounts of disability, an issue that merits a debate of its own.

21. Or, conversely, when some characters who were initially conceived as having certain disabilities turn into non-disabled characters. See, for example, the closing part of Chapter 6 for details about the progression of David Lurie from a character with acquired impairments to a non-disabled character in Coetzee's preparatory notes for *Disgrace*.

22. These include correspondences between Coetzee's allusions to his autobiographical counterpart's neuroatypicality and the character construction of David from the *Jesus* novels. I discuss these autobiographical references in Chapter 9.

Chapter 1

Disabled Textuality: *Dusklands* and *In the Heart of the Country*

The cultural position of disability is ambiguous. On the one hand, it has been traditionally subjected to various forms of discrimination and denigration. The prevalence of biomedical narratives that define disability in terms of deficiency (along the lines of the medical model of disability) has reduced disabled people to a marginal position, which has enabled the so-called normal or non-disabled majority to configure the social spaces and facilities in keeping with their needs. Consequently, modern western societies maintain social and structural barriers that exclude non-normatively embodied people from normal functioning. As emphasised by the social constructionist model of disability, it is these barriers, and not the specific qualities of their bodies, that disable them and render them vulnerable.[1] On the other hand, disability has the capacity to subvert the cultural narratives that both reduce it to the state of exception and mark the non-disabled body as complete. But disability is a much more flexible and capacious category than this distinction allows for. Disabilities can be short-lived, invisible or acquired in the course of one's life, especially as one approaches the stage of senescence. A normate,[2] in other words, is always potentially disabled or 'temporarily able-bodied' (see Hall 2016, 6, 168). If the western subject's claim for cultural supremacy hinges on the notions of white, able-bodied and intellectually superior masculinity, this status is undercut by the fluidity of ability as a cultural category. As a result, the position of vulnerability is not exclusive to the marginalised – in terms of gender, ability, ethnicity and so on – groups to whom it has been traditionally ascribed.

The early fictions of J. M. Coetzee interrogate the ambivalence of ability in relation to other forms of identity. While impairment in these works is often a symptom of a physical debilitation of the cultural other at the hands of those claiming the position of power, it is also staged to force those in the position of authority to confront the vulnerability of their own bodies. So positioned, disability in Coetzee's works is inextricable from ethical concerns.[3] But in Coetzee's works the ethical implications of social or political oppression link with the formal and meaning-making devices of his fictions. His characters with disabilities demonstrate the ways in which the disabled body makes problematic an affirmation about the wholeness and authority of normative subjectivity. Similarly, many formally experimental devices of Coetzee's fictions serve to debunk the normative myths of textual completeness and closure. Therefore, this chapter attempts to test the extent to which Coetzee's first two novels, *Dusklands* and *In the Heart of the Country*, stage the complexities of mental and physical disabilities through their employment of formal modes of textual disruption as a way of subverting hegemonic and normative discourses.

The Narrative Ethics of Disability: *Dusklands*

Some disability scholars have argued that the literary canon has been complicit in reinforcing ableist narratives and stereotypes. As famously stated by Lennard J. Davis, 'the novel as a form promotes and symbolically produces normative structures' (1995, 41). Traditional literary forms, in their adherence to normative discourses of power as well as reinforcement of representations of corporal normalcy, have aided and abetted the cultural side-lining of the non-normative body. The dominance of literary realism, with its claims for mimetic veracity, structural coherence and transparency of language, has been instrumental in endorsing this negative cultural coding of social others. Although the novel can indeed reinforce negative cultural assumptions about disability, it can also counter them. Rather than fundamentally homogenising, the novel depends on oppositional and heterogeneous rather than conventional textual strategies. 'Literature' is, in this sense, 'a frontal assault on our sensibilities or our linguistic expectations', and as such it has the agency to unsettle normative and dominant reading habits (Attridge 2015, 121). As argued by Wolfgang Iser, 'all thought systems are bound to exclude certain possibilities, thus automatically giving rise to deficiencies, and it is to those deficiencies that literature applies itself' (1978, 73).

A literary work is also a fertile venue for a dramatisation of ethical complexities. It is enacted on the representational level in the fictional encounters between literary characters. Where there are characters, there is a relationship that calls for an ethical interpretation of their encounter. However, a fictionalisation of ethical choices of literary characters marks only one way of engaging with the ethical in a literary work. Derek Attridge claims that literature at large, and modernism in particular, demands from the reader an ethical response through a foregrounding of its aesthetic operations and narrative self-reflexivity (2004, 6). It is therefore both in fictional representations of literary characters and hermeneutic modes of the reader's response that a literary work manifests its ethical potential. Along similar lines, Adam Zachary Newton proposes a triadic structure of what he refers to as 'narrative ethics', which includes:

> a narrational ethics ([. . .] signifying the exigent conditions and consequences of the narrative act itself); (2) a representational ethics (the costs incurred in fictionalizing oneself or others by exchanging 'person' for 'character'); and (3) a hermeneutic ethics (the ethico-critical accountability which acts of reading hold their readers to). (1997, 17–18)

In typologising this narrative structure of literary ethics, Newton suggests a reciprocal dependence between ethics and the narrative modes of the literary text. Newton's typology is important for the present purposes because the ethical implications of disability representation are inextricable from the formal and narrative operations of Coetzee's works, as shall be demonstrated in the analysis of *Dusklands* to follow, as well as in further chapters.

Coetzee's first novel, *Dusklands*, consists of two seemingly unconnected narratives. 'The Vietnam Project' recounts a story of Eugene Dawn's engagement in a project on psychological warfare in the Vietnam War commissioned by the US government. Narrated as Dawn's first-person account, the story charts the narrator's gradual descent into psychosis, partly caused by his exposure to war atrocities and the underhand psychological operations of the American war machine, which culminates in his attempted murder of his son. The other story, 'The Narrative of Jacobus Coetzee', takes place in eighteenth-century South Africa and relates the expedition led by Jacobus Coetzee into the interior. The story centres on Jacobus's encounter with the Namaqua tribe. Initially on friendly terms with the locals, Jacobus falls into disrepute with them, which ends in his subsequent expulsion and a punitive revenge expedition against the Namaqua people.

Dusklands relies to varying degrees on both realist (considering the specialist language of the project report and narrative of realist travelogue) and experimental (narrative fragmentation, a multiplicity of linguistic registers, unreliable narration and metafiction) narrative modes. This formal tension inflects fictional representations of disabled characters as well as the language of disability. As the language and narrative are mediated by narrators who occupy the positions of power, the rhetoric of disability is employed to both subvert and reinforce supremacist and normative narratives conveyed by realist literary conventions. As regards the latter, in his account of Klawer's death, Jacobus asserts, 'If he had believed in me, or indeed in anything, he would have recovered. But he had the constitution of a slave, resilient under the everyday blows of life, frail under disaster' (*DL* 146). What Jacobus introduces here are the notions of biopolitical supremacy. Physical survival is reserved for the master; the 'frail' body of the slave, on the other hand, is condemned to oblivion. Jacobus's first-person narrative, related in keeping with the conventions of realist travelogue, endorses the claim of a biopolitical control over the body of the other (who is doubly stigmatised by physical infirmity and racial otherness) through a regurgitation of the vocabularies of western domination.

Such racist and ableist discourses, which are conveyed by the language of the realist novel, are undercut by the novel's modernist formal effects. It, however, does not follow from this that modernism was conceived to remedy supremacist biases. Quite the opposite, 'a large part of modernist writing was insensitive to the otherness produced by patriarchal and imperialist policies and assumptions' (Attridge 2004, 6). Nor is it productive to think of Coetzee as a hard-line modernist himself. Coetzee may practise a form of modernism, but it is in one of its 'post'-modernist varieties. David James claims that *Dusklands* is 'a deliberate meditation on the political implications of reviving modernist aesthetics' (2011, 39). If correct, Coetzee's revisionism may derive from his understanding of modernism as an exploration of 'artistic conscience', as he writes in his master's thesis on the works of Ford Madox Ford, rather than formal experimentation (as quoted in James 2011, 43). Coetzee's modernism depends on the formal devices of undermining received conventions and unexamined discourses: his formal experimentation is mediated by its own foregrounding of the ethical through self-conscious narrative strategies. Coetzee seems thus to have fully absorbed the idea that 'politics, ethics and aesthetics [are] fundamentally intertwined, connected through the concept of representation' (Hall 2016, 1). In a related argument, Derek Attridge suggests that Coetzee's literary strategies rely heavily on the subversive formal and fictional methods of interrogating authoritative narratives and resisting the normalising impulses of realism (2004, 17). This compulsive questioning of the text's devices exposes certain formal instability that is antithetical to realist narrative conventions. Along these lines, Hall intimates that in Coetzee's fiction 'instability become[s] absorbed into the narrative technique itself' (2012b, 98). Coetzee's fictions capture the aesthetic operations of the literary text itself, which in a foregrounding of its formal processes creates the space for contemplating and embracing the disruptive modes it depends on, revealing in this way structural incompleteness as a meaning-making device.

Coetzee has been committed to questioning traditional literary devices since his earliest novelistic endeavours. The opening part of Coetzee's *Dusklands*, 'The Vietnam Project', is an inverted Bildungsroman that charts a journey of Eugene Dawn from experience to innocence. This inversion of the law of the novelistic genre depends for its effects of mirroring the narrator's gradual mental deterioration on Dawn's first-person unreliable narration. Dawn's introduction is telling: 'My name is Eugene Dawn. I cannot help that. Here goes' (*DL* 1).[4] The telegraphic rhythm and fragmentary quality of the opening line underpins a language of vulnerability registered in the narrator's rhetoric of resignation. This is followed by Dawn's account of his superior, named Coetzee, whom he 'fear[s]' and 'despise[s] his blindness' (1). Working on the project, 'hunched and shifty' (3), Dawn is painfully aware of his neurotic body sabotaging the process of writing: 'As I write this moment I catch my left fist clenching, [. . .] a sign of depression' (6). His body is a failure, a site of 'anxiety': 'I am vexed by the indiscipline of my body. I have often wished I had another one' (7). He thinks his body so 'revolting' that the vocabularies of bodily dysfunction mingle with Gothic imagery: 'organs [. . .] squelching against one another like unborn octuplets' (11). He muses that the 'Vietnam report has been composed [. . .] in a mood of poignant regret (*poindre*, to pierce)' (9–10). Accepting that staging disability in a story is conventionally contrived to disrupt narratives of normalcy, Dawn explores the meanings of words to challenge their semantic familiarity. The word 'poignant' might carry positive associations (moving, passionate, emotional), but Coetzee tactically navigates the meanings of words to mirror the narrator's deteriorating mental state or anticipate narrative events: with '*poindre*, to pierce' ironically prophesying Dawn's mutilation of his son later in the novel.

The subversive quality of the vocabularies and metaphors of disability is most pronounced in the narrational and structural strategies of the novel, often evinced in the metafictional devices of Coetzee's text. Dawn's hospitalisation presents one such example: 'Everyone agrees I am a classic example of the sudden breakdown, the aberration' (*DL* 74). He seems to pledge unconditional obedience to the authorities by accepting his state as *aberrant* and approving of institutionalisation and treatment. Eugene at this point self-consciously comes to terms with his role as a character who is at the mercy of exploitative powers of his author; just as a hospitalised patient depends on the dictates of the authorities ('I approve of the enterprise of exploring the self' [74]). His unreliability as a narrator helps activate some hermeneutic modes of narrative ethics by drawing attention to the ways in which socially disenfranchised groups absorb hegemonic narratives that are instrumental in their marginalisation. Dawn's unreliable narration, which makes no claims for rational explanation or ethical integrity, lends itself for communicating the themes of the capitulation of reason (the narrator's descent into psychosis), suspension of traditional ethics (the attempted child murder) and internalised ableism. Dawn constructs an internally disruptive narrative that invites the reader to put into question the narrator's credibility. It is in this ability to compel the reader to critically interrogate the narrator's unwarranted pronouncements that Coetzee's text reveals its ethical potential.

Nor does Coetzee's linking of self-reflexive mechanisms with biopolitical control exhaust the narrative potential of his works. In their other varieties, metafictional devices inform the politics of disability representation. After a brief introduction of his microcephalic colleague, Harry, Dawn curtails his narrative account: 'I am sorry there is no more of him in my story' (*DL* 9). Dawn self-consciously exercises his narratorial authority over the construction of his story. The tactical removal of Harry from further plot development acts as an ironic metafictional commentary on how literary texts tend to instrumentalise characters with disabilities. Coetzee's drafts of *Dusklands* reveal that Dawn's self-referential remark: 'I am sorry there is no more of him in my story' appears only in the later versions of the novel.[5] This, together with the fact that the character's name changes from Ewart[6] to Harry,[7] may suggest that Coetzee's meditation on this marginal character's role developed with each draft. By removing Harry from the plot, Coetzee may be said to employ a character with a disability as a figure of 'narrative prosthesis', that is a figurative 'crutch upon which literary narratives lean for their representational power, disruptive potentiality, and analytical insight' (Mitchell and Snyder 2000, 49). In this sense, Harry seems to inhabit the text to legitimate the other characters' normative status. After all, he seems to confirm some stereotypes about people with intellectual disabilities, such as that he regularly masturbates at work, is pitied by the narrator on the grounds of his disability, is passively bullied by his colleagues, and so on. However, through the self-referential remark, Coetzee seems to draw the reader's attention to the complicity of literary authors (himself included) in reinforcing the ableist structures of the novel. In doing so, Coetzee does not so much attempt to recuperate the textual autonomy of the disabled subjects as to bring his fiction to bear on the hegemony of discourses of normalcy. Coetzee does not wave a banner of identity politics; he merely offers a venue for a rethinking of unexamined structures of power.

In 'The Narrative of Jacobus Coetzee', Coetzee practices a different kind of narrative unreliability. While Dawn epitomises an epistemological crisis conveyed by the narrator's lapse into mental illness, Jacobus Coetzee embodies the self-assertion of reason undercut by the insubordination of the body. Drawing on the convention of the realist travelogue, which is characteristic of the style of western colonial explorers, the story attempts to self-consciously establish itself in keeping with the western hegemonic structures of power, with Jacobus as an overbearing leader of a colonial expedition into the heart of darkness of the African inland. Faithful to the literary genre it imitates, the narrative only exposes an illusion of realistic pastiche in the staging of the dysfunctional body that for the narrator becomes a site of suspension of his unexamined certainties. The uneven exchange of power develops through a self-legitimising narrative that creates an illusion of objective certainty in its projection of cultural assumptions on the other. In his first-person account, Jacobus relentlessly denigrates the cultural otherness of the locals: 'For they are not like us, they don't look after their aged, when you cannot keep up with the troop they put down a little food and water and abandon you to the animals' (*DL* 90). However, Jacobus's one-sided narrative of cultural otherness is tested the moment he finds himself on the receiving end of social marginalisation, and his disempowerment comes through bodily dysfunction. Plagued by bouts of fever, Jacobus is relocated to a hut 'for menstruating women, who during their flux are permitted to congress with neither husbands nor cattle' (110), which doubles up as a carceral space of subjugation of the female body and a locus of social control of disability. The menstruation hut is a space of a biopolitical control of the disruptive body (Flaugh 2010, 296). At this point, patriarchal consciousness colludes and overlaps with ableist narratives to police and side-line social otherness. It is only when the narrator, an embodiment of the western mindset, assumes the place of the disabled other that the narrative displays its disruptive agency. At this juncture, Jacobus occupies a position of vulnerability which is profoundly gender-coded. If vulnerability figures as feminine in western cultures, to position Jacobus as disempowered and disabled by his disease and skin condition is to make problematic the dominant pattern of white hypermasculinity reinforced by colonial adventure stories. Just as the forced hospitalisation of Dawn leaves him in the state of utter docility, submission and emasculation (in a way that echoes the fate of Randle McMurphy in *One Flew Over the Cuckoo's Nest* by Ken Kesey), Jacobus's experience of the ailing body mixed with his consignment to a space reserved for women undermine his claims for masculine power. At this point, disability representations partake in Coetzee's critique of the narratives of masculine triumphalism that are responsible for upholding racist, sexist and ableist biases.

Similarly, the novel's mediation on sensory experience serves to further destabilise the discourses of authority:

> In the wild I lose my sense of boundaries [. . .] [T]he five senses stretch out from the body they inhabit, but four stretch into a vacuum. The ear cannot hear, the nose cannot smell, the tongue cannot taste, the skin cannot feel [. . .] Only the eyes have the power. (*DL* 121)

Ill, delirious, immobilised, Jacobus, a figure of colonial-normative consciousness, must again come to terms with his vulnerability. Sensory deterioration serves as an auto-commentary of western colonial experience told from the position of inferiority. Curiously, although most senses fail, the sense of sight is intact. This is telling because western epistemology depends on the sight-centred 'scopic regimes', that is, modes of visibility that oversee the social construction of disability and otherness (Davidson 2008, 17). Sight – coded as an instrument of oppression of western reason, via which it monitors and controls the colonised – is tactically preserved to recuperate the western normative consciousness as authoritative. Such a use of rhetoric and metaphors of disability exposes narrative disruption that tentatively undermines the colonial discourse of power from within. Coetzee's narrative ruptures are spaces of contingency that refuse to exhaust themselves in the discourses they attempt to unsettle; nor do they succeed in unsettling these discourses completely.

By situating disability themes in the colonial context, Coetzee risks 'imposing a hegemonic model of disability' (Barker and Murray

2010, 228), thus universalising that which should remain culturally specific. However, while exploring the instruments of western reason, Coetzee's attention to the cultural and political complexity of early South African colonialism serves as a tactical sabotage of colonialist and normative narratives and assumptions through the use of disability metaphors.[8] Clare Barker and Stuart Murray propose that '[w]hile disability is frequently used, problematically, as a metaphor for the "damaged" or abject postcolonial body politic, there are many semantic permutations to disability representation' (2010, 233). Unexamined, disability metaphors may lend themselves as prostheses on which to reassert reductive discourses of normalcy.[9] What makes Coetzee's enactment of such metaphors nuanced is his commitment to ethical complexities registered in representations of the characters' singular bodily experience. Jacobus's moments of critical self-consciousness are precipitated by his coming to terms with his ailing body, as revealed in the scenes in which the narrator suffers from a skin infection, an anal carbuncle causing him pain and relief alternately. Those fluctuations of pain (caused by sickness or disability) and relief (evacuation of bodily fluids) shape the narrative in keeping with the rising and falling rhythms of the factual travelogue's dramatic structure. Jacobus's self-inflicted penetration of the carbuncle near the riverbank performed in public in an undignified position is followed by a disruption (he is taunted by the local children during the humiliating act) and resolved by his counterattack on one of the young assailants. His body undergoes ordeals ('Ants, ants raped from their nests [. . .] their little pincers scything and their bodies bulging with acid, descended between my spread buttocks, on to my tender anus' [*DL* 140]) which are further aggravated by the assaults committed by the enraged inhabitants of the village, culminating in his retreat into himself: 'Beyond rage, beyond pain, beyond fear I withdrew inside myself and in my womb of ice totted up the profit and the loss' (141).

The mediation of the body in pain is further strengthened by another representation of physical debilitation: the self-preservation mechanism of the Zeno beetle that does not flinch even when its legs are gradually being severed from its body. However, for all Jacobus's self-searching impulses, the suspension of the western mindset though introspection is only tentative:

> In each case the challenge was to undergo the history, and victory was mine if I survived it. The fourth game was the most interesting one, the Zenonian case in which only an infinitely diminishing fraction

of my self survived, the fictive echo of a tiny 'I' whispered across the void of eternity. (*DL* 153)

Jacobus's demise forces him to reassert his superior position vis-à-vis the Hottentots. He intuits that for the recovery to be complete, he must reduce his body to the point of vanishing. Ironically, the reassumption of imperial power comes symbolically through a radical diminution and humiliation of the body. This point is made more pronounced in the earlier drafts of the novel. After the public humiliation and mob lynching meted out by the locals, resulting in the crippling of his arm, Jacobus makes a resolution: 'It was at this moment, with darkness closing in, that all the heat left me and I began to live only for revenge' (HRC 1.5, 24-01-1970). And, as if to fulfil the demands of the colonial adventure novel genre, Jacobus does avenge the dissenters for his humiliations, thus bringing his bloody quest to its logical conclusion. If representations of the aching body are used to affirm certain novelistic conventions, they become part of Coetzee's project to induce the reader to question the narrator's assertions. In this sense, writing about the body energises the self-reflexive devices characteristic of Coetzee's fictions.

Although many Coetzee's novels rely strongly on self-reflexivity, Coetzee has expressed his scepticism about the effects of this narrative technique: 'Writing-about-writing hasn't much to offer,' he divulges in an interview with David Attwell (*DP* 204). Rather than in self-denial as to his own metafictional interventions, Coetzee brings it to our attention that narrative self-reflection, in its forestalling of the text's meaning-making processes, fails to exhaust the text's hermeneutic capacities. Linda Hutcheon, on her part, would reject the assumption that 'self-informing narrative' is 'a mark of crisis, of the asphyxiation of fiction by an overworked critical intellect' (1980, 18). Rather than a marker of exhaustion, metafiction has the ability to rescind the illusion of a text's completeness and activate the subversive rather than totalising qualities of the text. Despite Coetzee's apparent disapproval of metafictional devices, 'there remains a powerful – even abysmal – strand of self-reflection and self-reflexivity in Coetzee's own writings' (Farrant 2021, 171). Striking in *Dusklands*, for instance, are the iterations of the name Coetzee, which the author assigns to various characters and narrators of his fictions (for example Coetzee, Jacobus Coetzee, JC, John). In the first part of the novel, Dawn laments his uneasy relationship with a Coetzee – his superior – whose insidious presence and high-handedness are factors in the narrator's mental deterioration.

Through the metaphors of disability ('I fear him and despise his blindness' [*DL* 1]) and idioms connoting subjugation ('I am under [Coetzee's] thumb' [1]), Coetzee, the supervisor, assumes the role of a detached, erring, yet all-powerful author-figure. Dawn's assessment of Coetzee as an overbearing man 'utterly without vision' (1) is in line with J. M. Coetzee's overall critique of the literary author's perpetuation of oppressive structures of power. By investing the fictional Coetzee with the signifiers of authorial power, Coetzee submits himself to his own criticism. Metaphors of impairment again serve to counter the accepted totalising notions of authorial or narratorial omniscience. In this sense, Coetzee furnishes his narrators with 'idiosyncratic verbal habits which also serve as clues to unreliability' (Nünning 2005, 103). Further on, the first-person narrative of the other Coetzee character of *Dusklands*, Jacobus, epitomises the pre-modernist centrality of the author figure. It should also be mentioned that the second narrative is loosely based on the historical account of the expedition of Coetzee's ancestor, Jacobus Coetzee, whose venture into the South African interior was recounted in his *Relaas*.[10] It is not accidental that the novel's historical setting, amply represented by early novelistic conventions of literary realism, should appropriate metafictional modes that hint at the conventional notions of authorship. This is what David Attwell calls 'situational metafiction', 'a mode of fiction that draws attention to the historicity of discourses' (1993, 21).

If authorial self-reference is what binds these two seemingly unrelated narratives together, other metafictional devices act in tandem in both parts as well. As argued above, while Dawn's refusal to include his disabled colleague further in the story precipitates a narrative auto-commentary on the instrumentalisation of disabled characters in literary works, 'The Narrative of Jacobus Coetzee' offers its counterpart to this episode:

> 'Klawer, old friend,' I said, 'things are going badly with you. But never fear, I will not desert you ...' 'No, master,' said Klawer, 'I cannot do it, you must leave me.' [...] 'Goodbye, master,' he said and wept. My eyes were wet too. I trudged off. He waved. (*DL* 147)

Bearing in mind that after this episode no further mention of the fate of his servant Klawer is made by Jacobus, the reader will likely wonder about the narrative status of this character. Attridge suggests an answer: '[T]he final dialogue between master and servant sounds, as we say, as if it came out of a book' (2004, 21). Like Dawn's colleague, Harry, the ailing Klawer is doubly abandoned by Jacobus, first literally and later narratively; a reminder that his existence in the text is a function of a literary convention. Klawer figures in the text only to fill in the gap of the social other on whom the western subject relies for sustaining his illusion of supremacy. That is why Klawer's departure from the plot can only be expressed with platitudes characteristic of pre-modernist realist novels. Harry and Klawer are in that sense the figures of narrative prosthesis, but ones whom Coetzee strategically constructs as such to foreground the literary authors' involvement in perpetuating racist and ableist narratives.

Disruptive Uncertainties: *In the Heart of the Country*

In his second novel, *In the Heart of the Country*, Coetzee does not part his ways with unreliable narrators. As in *Dusklands*, he continues to chart an interlocking of narrative and formal effects, ethico-political issues and mental disorder (or the possibility thereof). As regards the latter issue, however, while *Dusklands* is specific about the various forms of its characters' mental and physical conditions (microcephaly, rectal abscess and psychosis), in *In the Heart of the Country* the ambiguity around Magda's mental health (as she demonstrates possible symptoms of psychosis and schizophrenia) connects with the fiction-making strategies that the novel dramatises.

Coetzee's second novel is narrated by Magda, a white unmarried woman who lives with her domineering father on a South African farm. Two narrative aspects of the novel reveal themselves at its outset. First, the novel is divided into 266 numbered sections: a strategy that draws our attention to the textuality of the story. Second, the first-person narration gradually descends into a self-contradictory and unreliable account. In section 26, for instance, Magda claims to have killed her peremptory father with an axe; in 116, the father is killed again by his daughter, this time, however, with a gun; but in 262 the protagonist ruminates on the passing of time accompanied by her living but senescent father. These anti-realist narrative effects could be accounted for in two ways. Magda is either a playful narrator who intentionally bends the conventions of realist verisimilitude to play up the fictionality of storytelling; or else – if one is inclined to cling to the text's realism – she shows symptoms of a psychological disorder. The latter is most forcefully hinted at in the scenes where she repeatedly kills her father (or fantasises about doing so), thereby displaying symptoms of psychosis; or when she claims to communicate with extra-terrestrial beings, as auditory hallucination is a common symptom in people with schizophrenia:

> The voices speak [...] They accuse me, if I understand them, of turning my life into fiction, out of boredom. They accuse me, however tactfully, of making myself more violent, more various, more racked with torment than I really am, as though I were reading myself like a book, and found the book dull, and put it aside and began to make myself up instead. (*HC* 140)

For all its prefiguring of symptoms characteristic of psychotic disorders, this passage makes problematic such a diagnostic reading of the novel. If we know about Magda as much as she is willing to reveal in her narrative, it follows that we are lured into the process of the narrator's 'making up of herself' through the text. In other similar passages, Magda appears to demonstrate her demiurgic fiction-making powers by way of resisting the imperatives of narrative reliability, linearity and objectivity typical of realist fiction. What remains unclear, however, is why a suspension of realist effects should be presumed to bolster Magda's narratorial self-assertion. In the end, all that Magda wants is for her 'story to have a beginning, a middle, and an end' (46). Nevertheless, her involuntary entanglement in social metanarratives and injunctions (those of colonialism, patriarchy and normalcy) forestall her aspirations to obtain closure and authority over her story.

Bearing in mind Davis's point that the novel has consistently served to reinforce normative social structures, as well as Attridge's argument that formal modernist devices are intended to counter the hegemonic effects of rationalism, the formal experimentalism of *In the Heart of the Country* highlights the novel's involvement with ethical concerns through its resistance to the discourses of reason. As stated by Jane Poyner, since Magda falls victim to prevailing rationalistic metanarratives, 'understanding Magda's plight entails addressing a "hierarchy" of oppressions, those of women and of colonized peoples, as well as that of the lunatic as other' (2016, 36). Although Poyner seems to subscribe to the mental disorder hypothesis about Magda, she is correct in pointing to the intersectional nature of Magda's sense of oppression as her primary source of anxiety. Along the lines, Magda's alleged psychosis and schizophrenia would be inextricable from her double domestication brought about by the joint forces of colonialism and patriarchy. Her cloistered life in the Karoo with her overbearing father is an aftermath of the racial segregation policy enforced by the apartheid regime, which led to the rupturing of social bonds along racial lines. Her relationship with the servant Hendrik and his wife, Klein-Anna, is indicative of such severance of social ties.

A linking of mental and physical disability with the plight of the colonial subaltern counts among the well-traversed themes of postcolonial literature.[11] Many such novels reveal how disabled people are forced to negotiate their position between the pressures of colonial oppression and social exclusion. While offering an indictment of British colonialism, Chinua Achebe's novels condemn various forms of tribal ableism inherent in local Nigerian communities. In Salman Rushdie's fiction, set at the juncture between magic and realism, the disabled characters' supernatural powers, as in *Midnight's Children*, epitomise the hidden capacities of the victimised groups to overturn the oppressive political order.[12] Also, while retaining his focus on postcolonial forms of debilitation, Wole Soyinka's interest in the link between disability and ritual in his plays probes the paradoxical position of disability as a site of victimhood and resistance – a position explored by Coetzee in his *Life & Times of Michael K* and *Foe*.[13] Other postcolonial writers have also interrogated the affinities between ableism and male domination. The argument that women have been 'disabled by patriarchal oppression' has been well documented in the annals of modern women's literature (Schalk 2018, 172). Resonating with the main plot of *In the Heart of the Country*, Anita Desai's *Fasting, Feasting*, for example, explores an intellectually disabled daughter's struggle with paternal control.

The question as to whether Magda does show symptoms of mental illness remains controversial. Like Poyner, Caroline Rody explicitly refers to Magda in terms indicating mental disorder, such as a 'crazed white heroine', 'mad, reclusive writer' or 'mad, white colonial daughter' (1994, 168–9). Other commentators suggest further alternatives. David Attwell, for example, talks about Magda's 'obsessive interior monologue', when describing her experience as an oppressed diarist, thus refusing to accept unexamined biomedical terms in relation to her complex state (1993, 58). Ato Quayson, similarly, attributes Magda's monologues to her acute 'sense of narrativity' rather than mental instability (2007, 158). Derek Attridge goes as far as to argue that the reader might miss much by unwarrantedly attributing the character's narrative unreliability to insanity or 'psychological derangement' (2004, 24). To my mind, the figuring of Magda's mental state should be considered in the light of the text's flaunting of its formal effects rather than a demonstration of the debilitating consequences of the colonial oppression of the other alone. The disruptive narrative devices undergirding Magda's story show that she is more than a palimpsest of intersectional cultural otherness. In resisting the impulse to pathologise Magda's mental state, Coetzee goes against the grain of the prevailing assumption reinforced in literary texts, which is that 'madness is the only reasonable response for women to the strictures of a patriarchal society' (Schalk 2018, 172). As argued above, in *Dusklands*, the exclusion of Harry, the character with microcephaly, from further plot development marks Coetzee's implicit critique of instrumentalising characters with disabilities by literary authors. In *In the Heart of the Country*, the ambiguity around Magda's psychological state through form serves to countervail stereotypical assumptions across the gender and disability divide – ones that are both misogynistic and ableist.

Assuming that the inconsistencies of Magda's first-person account can be explained in other ways than by offering a medical diagnosis of her mental state, the question remains by what means the novel invites such interpretative short-hands. The answer lies partly in the popular conceptions about the presumed affinities between modernity or modernist aesthetics and psychological disorders. The modernist investment with 'hyper-self-consciousness and alienation' marked a significant intellectual shift from the Romantic model of creative inspiration and the cult of feeling (Sass 2001, 55). The development of the modern city, industrialisation and warfare led to the development and categorisation of such psychological states as post-traumatic stress disorder (formerly known as shell shock), hysteria, neurasthenia or agoraphobia, among others (Davidson 2018, 75). As a result of the political and cultural transformations, 'paranoia' became 'a psychological response to the conditions of modernity' (Bukowski 2014, 3). Also, the buzzwords associated with modern subjectivity and aesthetics, such as hyper-consciousness, dissociation, fragmentation, alienation, pessimism, anti-traditionalism, became loosely associated with psychiatric disorders such as neurosis, paranoia, schizophrenia, depression, autism or amnesia.[14] The recruitment of the metaphors of mental disability has reinforced a pathologisation of modern experience. This 'cultural logic of disability in modernism' has resulted in a production of social metanarratives that privileged the normative body and mind in modern societies (Davidson 2018, 86). It may be argued that such a reductive use of disability metaphors denoting aesthetic innovation was inconsequential in comparison with other forms of denigration of the disabled body in modernity, such as eugenics, mass sterilisation or the extermination of people with disabilities in Nazi Germany. Even so, the metaphorisation of disability experience helped fuel the ableist ideas about the cult of perfectible body and mind, which were adopted by the adherents of eugenics of the early twentieth century. Speaking of the ableist roots of modernism, it should be noted that many imminent modernist intellectuals were in favour of the eugenic ideas promoted by Charles Darwin's cousin Francis Galton. Among them were W. B. Yeats, Gertrude Stein, Virginia Woolf, T. S. Eliot, D. H. Lawrence and Ezra Pound, among many others (Davidson 2018, 76).

Following this thread, Coetzee's deployment of such narrative devices as unreliable first-person narration, fragmentation, non-linear narration or narrative implausibility might lead the reader to question the character's sanity. However, rather than enlisting the trope of madness to unlock its formal complexities, Coetzee's second novel seeks to disrupt traditional forms of communication and narration that are responsible for legitimising medical metanarratives, including those of psychological and psychical normalcy. For Dominic Head, the reader's coming to terms with narrative implausibilities depends on her grappling with a dynamic between the narrated events and the construction of the character's identity. Once this is established, what Magda tells us about the narrated events is secondary to what these events 'tell us about Magda' (Head 1997, 56). In this way, our coping strategies against narrative implausibility expand (while the suspension of disbelief shrinks) the moment we align our perspective with the one of the storyteller. Consequent upon these effects is also our grasping of the nature of storytelling itself; namely, that 'our encounter with human lives, thoughts, and feelings is to take place against the background of a constant awareness of their mediation by language, generic and other conventions, and artistic decisions' (Attridge 2004, 21).

Ato Quayson views Magda as a 'sceptical interlocutor' of her story, engaged in an ongoing revision of her account (2007, 158). 'For Magda,' he goes on, 'these interruptions emanate from an insistent sense of narrativity, that is, both the excitement to narrate and the fact of being narrated through her diaries' (ibid., 158). A prerequisite for Magda's tireless self-questioning ('I am having second thoughts about everything' [*HC* 64]) is her profound, yet troubled, sense of self-consciousness. She is mindful of her impossible ontological position as an embodied being and a textual artefact: 'Am I, I wonder, a thing among things, a body propelled along a track of sinews and bony levers, or am I a monologue moving through time [...]?' (68). She is a self-proclaimed 'poetess of interiority', one whose sceptical interlocution cannot, however, eschew the materiality of embodiment. Fighting migraine, 'focussed on the kernel of pain, I am lost in the being of my being' (38). Inseparable from her ontological ruminations is also the old Cartesian question of cognition as the underlying warrant of existence: 'How can I be deluded If I think so clearly?' (137).

Through Magda's self-interrogation – 'Is it possible that there is an explanation for all the things I do, and that that explanation lies inside me [...]?' (*HC* 67) – Coetzee implicitly asks us the bold question: what does it mean to be a textual artefact? This question also resonates from Magda's self-inquiring broodings: 'I create myself in the words that create me' (8). Coetzee's heroine of the later Australian-based period, Elizabeth Costello, will echo similar sentiments by challenging her audience to put themselves in the mindset of non-human beings through 'sympathetic imagination' (*EC* 80). In his essay 'Fictional Beings', addressing the challenges of reading a narrative of Benjy Compson, a man with cognitive disabilities from William Faulkner's *The Sound and the Fury*, Coetzee deliberates on what it takes for the storyteller to enter the minds of fictional characters of her creation. He admits that the storyteller's claim to 'inhabit real beings and represent them from the inside' and 'create them out of nothing and turn them into real beings' may be paradoxical, 'but it does appear to be a position of some importance to human societies' (2003b, 134). The challenge that Coetzee poses in *In the Heart of the Country* is, however, more subtle: how to construct a disembodied textual consciousness that self-consciously presumes her embodiment while, by virtue of this very capacity for self-consciousness, being unable to discard the sense of textuality of her existence? Would such a consciousness 'yield to the spectre of reason?' by expressing itself in the familiar languages of rationalistic binarisms? (*HC* 150), or does this ontological aporia render it psychologically unbalanced as a matter of course? Magda's account appears to disconfirm either of these solutions. By withholding diagnostic prescriptions about Magda's mental state, Coetzee prompts a meditation on the character's conscious and embodied experience, which he places on the broad continuum of cognition and ability rather than relegating it to the reductive extremes of reason and madness.

The question of Magda's mental breakdown is linked with her role as a woman in a male-dominated society. As some passages from the handwritten first draft of the novel forcefully show, Magda is aware that her unwilling subjection to male-centred rules has taken a heavy toll on her mental well-being: 'Lunacy? Why is it that I can never act but in the name of lunacy? I have spent a lifetime on this farm communing with myself, telling myself the story of myself, but going about my duties like a good child, punishing no one but myself for the oppressions of my father' (HRC 3.2, 26-9-1975). '[B]orn into a language of hierarchy', Magda uses ableist and ageist metaphors that expose her internalisation of triumphalist discourses of power (*HC* 106). She often, for instance, refers to herself as a 'crazy old lady' (*HC* 6), 'mad hag' (8), 'witch-woman' (39), 'mad old woman' (86), 'crazy old queen' (150) and 'loony as a hatter' (HRC 33.3, 31-8-1975). This last simile is adopted from Coetzee's preparatory notes for the novel. At these early stages, Coetzee considered rendering his female protagonist 'older [...] a mad old tramp-woman, a rural beggar' (HRC 33.3, 15-12-1974) – a role that the Magda of the first draft envisions for herself to counter the socially and mentally debilitating effects of patriarchy to which she has been exposed: 'Either I must remain imprisoned in this stiff young woman, play out the role for which she was designed [...] or I must literally annihilate myself and rise from the ashes as this cracked old rural beggar who attracts me (I confess) more and more' (HRC 3.1, 17-12-1974). Although Magda's invocation of the mad old woman myth is all but stereotypical, it also reveals a remedial agency of non-normative mental states. Shackled by the constricting forces of male rationality, Magda contemplates madness, which marks the other of reason, as a force or a resource that promises liberation through total self-cleansing.

Curious in Magda's narratorial self-staging is also her penchant for playing up the effects of uncertainty and inconsistency. These narrative devices are usually presented with the use of the conjunction 'or'. For example, as mentioned above, Magda either intermittently contradicts her previous versions of the events she recounts or else changes her mind about them. Such retrospective revisions are often conveyed with the use of the recurrent phrase 'or perhaps'.[15] Elsewhere, the word 'or' figures as a grammatical disjunction marker used to signal Magda's critical interlocution or ontological anxiety: 'or am I a monologue moving through time [...]?' (68); 'or am I going to yield to the spectre of reason and explain myself to myself [...]?' (150). On a larger scale, the sentential connective 'or' helps grasp the narrative strategies employed in *In the Heart of the Country* in particular, and Coetzee's fiction-making strategies in general. In conjunction with the function word 'or', used for indicating an alternative, the section numbering device of the novel suggests that scenes are merely alternative versions of themselves. In this sense, the transition from, for instance, section 1 to section 2 is based on an alternative conjunction (as in 'either/or') than sequential coordination ('and').[16] The laying bare of these numbered versions – some of them following from each other sequentially while others standing for independent alternatives – seems to suggest that we are following a work in progress, whose erratic scenes and unreliable narratorial accounts are open for revision. The only difference is that the revision is in the reader's, rather than the author's corner.

The implied alternative conjunction of the novel's numbered sections seems strangely redolent of Coetzee's own creative strategies. Attwell's research of the drafts and manuscripts of Coetzee's works reveals Coetzee to be a conscientious editor and rewriter of his works. The writing process often involves more than a dozen revised drafts of a work prior to its completion. 'Such methods', Attwell reports, 'are built on absolute faith in the creative process, on tenaciously working through the uncertainties [...] towards a distant goal until an illumination arrives, providing direction and momentum for the next phase' (2015, 20). It could be argued that in a sense *In the Heart of the Country* exposes what Coetzee's other works attempt to conceal, that is, that the writing process heavily depends on overcoming its blind spots and inconsistencies. Confronted with a text that lays bare its internal methods, the reader is enjoined to partake in these processes.

The implications of such methods are not only textual but also ethical. Søren Kierkegaard, through his pseudonymous author of the second volume of *Either/Or*, emphasises the ethical force of the act of choice: 'That which is prominent in my either/or is the ethical. It is therefore not yet a question of the choice of something in particular, it is not a question of the reality of the thing chosen, but of the reality of the act of choice' (1946, 149). For Kierkegaard, a choice based on the logic of the alternative conjunction 'either/or' is paradoxical, as it leads the chooser to regret her decision either way. What recuperates the choice from a contradiction is the meaningfulness of the subjective stance that the individual takes in the process of choosing, regardless of the potential futility of the outcome of the act.

In *In the Heart of the Country*, Coetzee points to the inability of the conjunction 'either/or' to offer a satisfactory solution. Magda's recurrent litanies of 'or' reveal her profound suspicion of structuring her story in keeping with the reason-centred epistemes or binary oppositions. Although 'or' entails uncertainty and contradictions – she openly admits that 'there are inconsistencies in [her story]' (*HC* 52), or that she is 'full of contradictions' (43) – Magda does not give up on searching for alternatives. She creates herself by negotiating the uncertainties and constantly revising her complicated position as a narrated and narrating subjectivity. Conscious of being narrated, she comes close to occupying a role of what Coetzee refers to as a figure of a 'poetics of failure', which he defines as a consciousness that fails to assert her autonomous position due to the inconsistencies posed by the self-reflexive text of which she is part (*DP* 87).[17] When Magda claims to 'seem to exist more and more intermittently' (*HC* 87), she provides a description of a character's/narrator's experience captured in the process of being written, such as when she is left at the whim of the writer's work schedule, with 'whole hours, whole afternoons go[ing] missing' (87). These passages show Magda as a figure of the critical inquirer who is struggling to navigate her subjectivity amid the contradictions of the text she inhabits, rather than pandering to the either/or axiomatics of reason and unreason.

Finally, the possibility of Coetzee's fictional staging of psychiatric disorders entails questions about the instrumentalisation of disability. It could be argued that Coetzee deploys madness in *In the Heart of the Country* as a prosthesis with which to prop up his critique of rationalism. However, as revealed in Coetzee's preparatory notes for his second novel, the author was fully aware of the precarious allurement of fictionalising madness: 'Why the attraction of/to craziness?' (HRC 33.3, 25-11-1975). The apprehensions registered in Coetzee's self-critical remark are substantiated. If unchecked, madness all to easily turns into a prosthetic device that reduces disability experience to a mere narrative function. Coetzee, therefore, admits elsewhere that, while Magda 'may be mad', she is rather 'passionate in the way one can be in fiction (I see no further point in calling her mad)' (*DP* 61). Coetzee seems to be suggesting here that the representation of his protagonist's mental status resists the pressures of verisimilitude or biomedical narratives. This way Coetzee shows that a fictionalisation of the protagonist's psychological state can open narrative and representational vistas that operate beyond accepted social stereotypes and medical lexicon.

It is also possible that the reader's assumption that Magda is mentally ill might be little else than a symptom of their 'aesthetic nervousness', which denotes disruptive and defamiliarising effects that a character with disabilities has on the reader in the process of reading (Quayson 2007, 19). In that regard, the text holds up a mirror to the reader's cultural biases which are entrenched in normative metanarratives around mental disability. Coetzee's deployment of ambiguity around the fictional status of disability thwarts the short-hand readings of the role of disability in the novel, such as that madness functions as a key to grasping the formal complexities of the novel. Textual ambiguity, alongside other narrative and formal devices the novel deploys, acts as an impulse for the reader to pursue meanings beyond those permitted by normative metanarratives. Coetzee's figuring of formal effects in relation to disability representation partakes in a sabotaging of systemic ableism that is deeply entrenched in cultural narratives. These effects help show the shifting modalities of embodiment and consciousness that elude diagnostic or stereotypical portrayals of the character's mental states. As such, Coetzee places Magda's psychological state on a continuum that eludes binaries of normative descriptions and medical diagnoses alike.

The ambivalence around Coetzee's pairing of the tropes of mental disability and textual operations, a phenomenon that Michael Bérubé refers to as 'disabled textuality', has the capacity to provoke the reader to confront the points of uncertainty (caused by formal disruption or unreliable narration) and consequently question her biases around physical and intellectual normalcy (2016, 15). As mentioned in the Introduction above, in his notes for *In the Heart of the Country*, Coetzee writes: 'I am interested in the project not of "writing" a book but of "reading" a book' (HRC 33.3, 30-10-1974). The result of this preoccupation would be a 'reading-novel, a feminine novel of things done to one without the thrust of story' (HRC 33.3, 8-10-1975). Coetzee's 'reading-novel' is one that in eluding triumphalist protocols of masculine action and storytelling produces the hermeneutic effects of receptivity and response. This writing programme is perhaps best summed up by Magda in the novel's first draft: 'My medium is the endless monologue of consciousness, not the crises and resolutions of drama' (HRC 3.2, 15-12-1975).[18] Her text is one that generates 'holes': a hole symbolically ascribed to femininity, 'characteristic of her', and one created by the text's 'evasions' (HRC 33.3, 28-1-1976). In this sense, Coetzee's project of a 'reading-novel' is of a piece with the notion of disabled textuality which through its foregrounding of incompleteness, uncertainty and passivity undercuts the illusion of wholeness, reason and power distinctive to both normativistic and patriarchal narratives.

The pressures of Coetzee's disabled textuality extend to the author's own torturous relationship with his text. In a notebook for his next novel *Waiting for the Barbarians* Coetzee confesses, in what seems like a moment of creative impasse, that 'I can get nowhere unless the whole story turns into a drama of consciousness a la *In the Heart*. But I cannot face the project of writing at that hysterical intensity again. Once is enough' (HRC 33.3, 10-10-1977). It transpires from Coetzee's notes that a construction of a character experiencing extreme mental states takes a toll on the writer's own psychological state. Coetzee's affective engagement with his text complicates a traditional divide between authorial and fictional consciousness. But it also casts a light on the fiction-making mechanisms more broadly. If writing fiction is a process in which a person constructs alternative versions of reality, is writing not a symptom of an atypical mental state, or a product of a passionate or troubled state of mind? Seen in this light, for Coetzee writing is a kind of experience that unhinges traditional habits of thinking and typical psychological states. The essence of Coetzee's disabled textuality lies thus in a proximity between (meta)textual operations and literary constructions of disability.

Conclusions

As Coetzee divulges in one of his notebooks, 'I have no interest in telling stories; it is the process of storytelling that interests me' (HRC 33.3, 17-10-1977). Following this line of reasoning, I have argued that disability in Coetzee's early novels manifests itself in its relation to textual operations rather than as an element of representation alone. Furthermore, Coetzee's formal techniques that reproduce the experience of disability have the capacity to subvert normative conceptions of narrative construction as well as narrative constructions of intellectual normalcy. For all his preoccupation with the ethics of otherness, Coetzee eschews didactic or prescriptive discourses that endeavour to vindicate the other (Tegla 2015, 249). Mike Marais goes as far as to state that it is in Coetzee's refusal to give voice to the other that his fiction claims its ethical currency (1998, 45). Coetzee's commitment to disability is ethical in narrative modes that absorb the structures of lack and deficiency as their operative condition; that is, in those varieties of modernist aesthetics that evince a commitment to challenging hegemonic injunctions of wholeness as a symbolic template of normalcy, be it narrative or bodily.

Coetzee's narratives of disability help override modes of affirmation while eliciting from the reader an ethical commitment to alterity. Coetzee's first novel, *Dusklands,* presents itself as a compelling case in point about how normative societies sanction the rules of social functioning that produce categories, disability being one of them, which relegate non-able-bodied people to the fringes of society. Complicit in this process are authorities of sorts, including those liable for reinforcing and championing ableist cultural assumptions, such as literary authors. By doing so, Coetzee places himself on the receiving end of his sharp critique's sword point. Similar sentiments of authorial self-chastisement find their vent in Coetzee's second novel, *In the Heart of the Country*, where Magda's disempowerment is implicitly ascribed to various forms of authority, including the authority of the author. Still, arguably the novel's greatest strength lies in its ambiguous linking of disability with the metaphysics of writing. The question whether *In the Heart of the Country* does fictionalise mental illness is secondary to the novel's ethical thrust, which is that its formal effects partake in the questioning of the normalising discourse of reason.

Notes

1. See the Introduction for further information on the medical and social constructionist models of disability.
2. 'Normate' denotes a normal individual in a given society. According to Rosemarie Garland-Thomson, the normate position is socially constructed (1997, 8).
3. In Coetzee's works, disability is inextricably linked with ethical considerations. However, if a vast body of critical texts has addressed the complexity of Coetzee's ethics (Attridge 2004; Helgesson 2004; Leist and Singer 2010; Marais 1998) or narrative ethics and politics (Clarkson 2013; de Boever 2014; Dooley 2010; Stanton 2006; Tegla 2015; van Bever Donker 2016, Wright 2006), alongside multiple scholarly articles on the subjects, disability appears to be still under-researched in Coetzee criticism. See the Introduction for further information concerning the current scholarship on disability in Coetzee's works.
4. This line appears for the first time in the third draft of the novel (HRC 1.3). It also marks the first time when the narrator is named Eugene Dawn. In the previous drafts he is provisionally called 'X' and in the very first sketch he is only implicitly referred to by others as the husband of 'Mrs C—'. As, in the previous draft (HRC 1.2), Coetzee has already constructed a psychological profile of Dawn (including his psychotic and neurotic behaviour and hospitalisation known from the published version), it seems that an insertion of the opening formally fragmented line in this draft serves as a stylistic pointer that foreshadows the character's mental disorder.
5. This line appears for the first time in the third revised draft, 'The Vietnam Project' (HRC 1.3, 20-3-1973).

6. As in 'Lies', the second sketch for 'The Vietnam Project' (HRC 1.1).
7. He is renamed from Ewart to Harry in the next draft (see HRC 1.2) and further drafts.
8. For a discussion on metaphor as postcolonialism, see Saverese (2010).
9. For a related debate on the epistemological implications of metaphors reinforcing narratives of normalcy, see Vidali (2010).
10. See Attwell (2015, chap. 3) for detailed information about the historical figure of Jacobus Coetzee.
11. For further reference on the coupling of disability and colonial oppression in postcolonial literary works, see Barker (2018).
12. See Krentz (2022) for his in-depth analysis of disability in the novels of the Global South.
13. See Quayson (2007) and Hamel (2021) for a discussion on representations of disability in Soyinka's plays.
14. See Trotter (2008) for further information on the linking of modernist experimentalism and paranoia.
15. The following sequence of numbered entries aptly exemplifies this device:

    > 79. I stand behind my chair, gripping the back, and speak to my father.
    > 'Where is Anna? She has not been in today.' [. . .]
    > 80. *Or perhaps* as I come into the room words are already issuing from that towering black cylinder.
    > 'Anna and Jakob have gone. I have given them a holiday. You will have to get along without Anna for a while.'
    > 81. *Or perhaps* there is only the empty kitchen, and the cold stove, and the rows of gleaming copperware, and absence, two absences, three absences, four absences. (HC 40–1, italics mine)

16. This particular function of section numbering does not exhaust the possibilities of this device. Most sections are arranged sequentially rather than being alternative versions of each other. In this sense, the sequence of numbers stands for the sequentiality of their occurrence in time. However, I think that this reading of the numbering strategy partially helps account for the use of textual inconsistencies by Coetzee.
17. I elaborate further on the notion of the poetics of failure in Chapter 3.
18. In the final handwritten draft of the novel, Coetzee modifies this line: 'My ~~medium~~ theme is the endless drift of the currents of sleep and waking, not the ~~crises~~ storms of human conflict' (HRC 3.4, 15-12-1975), which survives in the published version: 'My theme is the endless drift of the currents of sleep and waking, not the storms of human conflict' (*HC* 43). The version of this line from the first draft gestures to a metafictional interpretation that is in line with Coetzee's notion of a 'reading-novel'. In the final draft and published version this line does not have the metafictional force of its prototype and reads more like Magda's comment on her relationship with other household members.

Chapter 2

Scopic Regimes, Haptic Commitments: Countering Ocularnormativism in *Waiting for the Barbarians*

In one of the scenes of J. M. Coetzee's novel *The Childhood of Jesus*, Simón takes it upon himself to teach David to read. Though a keen learner, the boy is loath to follow the rather traditional teaching methods adopted by his guardian. When Simón places the boy's forefinger on specific words, the latter 'closes his eyes' to announce his own reading strategy: 'I'm reading through my fingers' (*CJ* 191). Simón's response to the boy's unsolicited foray into the unseen is not unwelcoming: 'It doesn't matter how you read, through your eyes or through your fingers like a blind person, as long as you read' (*CJ* 192). By choosing to read beyond the default protocols of visual perception, David points his finger (figuratively speaking) at that which is too often overlooked in the present-day ocularcentric culture: namely, that reading need not be sight-centred. The fact that one is likely to think of reading as a mode that lends itself naturally to visual perception is due to our modern preoccupation with the culturally constructed modes of seeing referred to as 'scopic regimes'.[1] Although reading relies on a reconstruction of verbal codes which may or may not be deciphered through optical means, the cultural primacy of vision over the other senses means that visual reading is believed to be the dominant way of reading.[2] That is the main reason why reading is conventionally synonymous with such optical expressions, prepositional phrases or idioms as 'look' or 'glance through' 'pore over' 'scrutinise', 'run one's eye over', 'cast one's eye over' and 'scan' (*Oxford Paperback Thesaurus* 2006, 679).

However, these ocularcentric expressions tend to distract our attention from the fact that to read a text visually is just one way of approaching it. Reading is just as well informed by synonyms associated with haptic experience, such as 'flicking through', 'leafing through', 'thumbing through', to denote the materiality of reading, or being 'touched', 'struck' or 'gripped' by a text to refer to the psychosomatic affective experience of reading (*Oxford Paperback Thesaurus* 2006, 679). On top of that, the reader is likely to find herself grappling with or grasping the meaning of the text. One might as well add to the list the prepositional phrase 'swipe through' associated with haptic digital technology. Although such technologies are conceived to facilitate visual reading, they are useful reminders that reading is as much about physical as sensory perception. The same applies to the traditional codex or printed books, which rely on handwriting or print as well as the material on which it is written or printed. In this sense, haptic and olfactory experience is inextricable from (if usually secondary to) the process of reading printed books. All of these metaphors indicate that reading activates a broader spectrum of somatosensory perception than the prevalence of ocularcentric metaphors in modern culture may imply.

In the chiro- and typographic culture on which western grammatology rests, the text is an exosomatic[3] artefact in that it is believed to project outside of itself to report on the world it addresses through visual means. A text that depends on haptic hermeneutics, on the other hand, is endosomatic in that it reports on the world by probing its own devices. This is not to say, however, that such a text would be best read in Braille (although the practice of reading in Braille no doubt offers a unique experience that optical reading cannot provide).[4] What I am attempting to flag up here is a way of contemplating the text without having recourse to default visual metaphors and hermeneutic practices which, I believe, can adversely affect reading practice. Haptic reading (understood figuratively in relation to a hermeneutic method) would be thus a way of thinking about the text as an artefact that is best explored closely, where meanings unfold from the reader's encounter with the text rather than from a distance by the projecting eye. A groping hand, after all, cannot embrace the page in its entirety; it can only run across it gradually, thus reporting on the text in its minutest detail. A projecting gaze, on the other hand, scans the text holistically, synoptically, for a general meaning. Touch is metonymic of openness and close encounter with the text; seeing, of selectiveness, discrimination, distance and therefore prejudice. Consequently, a text that invites the reader to grapple with or to grope for its meanings would be one that does not lend itself too readily for interpretation. Unlike a text that yields to specular hermeneutic practices connoting distance (such as scanning, skimming or speed reading), a text that invites haptic methods of interpretation would demand from the reader a close hands-on engagement with its formal operations and meaning-making processes rather than submitting itself to the synoptic[5] forms of reading.[6]

With the above in mind, I argue in this chapter that the novels of J. M. Coetzee dramatise the crisis of seeing on several levels. Coetzee often uses blindness metaphors (such as blindness as synonymous with ignorance) or ocularcentric metaphors (seeing or light as knowledge and truth) to reflect the biases of its narrators and characters. While other metaphors of the kind act as conduits to a critique of the political oppression of social others (this includes visually impaired characters), in my reading of Coetzee's works, the crisis of seeing is most palpable in the demands that Coetzee's text makes on the reader. As persuasively argued by Jan Wilm, Coetzee's text compels the reader to 'decelerate' the process of reading – a hermeneutic practice that Wilm calls 'slow reading' – to maximise her meditation on the text (2016, 16). I find Wilm's reading to be compelling, but I am further interested in the extent to which such hermeneutic deceleration is caused by the crisis of seeing evinced in the resistance of Coetzee's text to the purely visual protocols of reading that necessitate a superficial engagement with the text, such as skimming, scanning or speed reading. The meditative mode that Coetzee's work elicits from the reader is thus more akin to haptic experiential modes of knowing and perception, such as touching, grasping, groping, grappling and gripping.

These words bring to mind (but are not limited to) the experience of those that are barred from accessing the text visually: people with visual or print disabilities. Consequently, this chapter attempts to explore how meditation on visual impairment – based on a short outline of Coetzee's fictional and semifictional works overall and a close analysis of his third novel, *Waiting for the Barbarians* – elicits the modes of reading that eschew sight-centred conventions and help examine various forms of the somatosensory experience of the text. Finally, I will attempt to chart the ways in which the 'haptic triad' of touch, feel and grope frustrates the hegemony of its 'visual counterpart' of look, stare and gaze in the works of Coetzee (Bolt 2016, 78). In *Waiting for the Barbarians*, I argue, Coetzee's use of ocularcentric textual operations is meant to elicit from the reader a critique of the literary text's perpetuation of uneven relations of power between the dominant seer and oppressed (unseeing) object of the gaze. I will also focus on the ethical effects of Coetzee's deployment of haptic narrative devices and linguistic forms.

Ocularnormative Injustices

The point that the culture of late modernity is sight-centred hardly needs belabouring. Most aspects of social functioning, such as public infrastructure and transport, education, arts and the media, depend on visual perception for their operation. This entails that the structure of modern societies is functionally tailored to the needs of the sighted. Structural ocularcentrism is thus generative of what David Bolt refers to as 'ocularnormativism', which denotes 'the mass or institutionalised endorsement of visual necessity' (2016, 5). What legitimises this privileging of the sighted is the prevailing assumption that 'the supreme means of perception is necessarily visual' (Bolt 2016, 14). Unlike the contact senses of smell, taste and touch, the distance senses of sight and hearing comprise the 'elite senses' (Kleege, as quoted in Linett 2017, 58). The implications of this hierarchisation of sensory experience is that those whose sense perception is impaired are excluded from normal functioning and that those with disabilities of the privileged senses will be more affected than those with disabilities of the culturally underprivileged senses. As western societies are structured to cater for the necessities of the sighted and hearing, people with disabilities in gustatory, tactile, or olfactory perception will be seen as less affected than those with visual and auditory impairments.[7]

Since the question about how one perceives the world is closely linked with what one knows about the world – considering that sense perception helps one learn to navigate oneself in the world for purely instrumental purposes – the ability in sensory perception correlates with cognition. In the culture dominated by scopic regimes, in which the experience of the gaze is pervasive, seeing is inextricable from knowing. However, since the sensory experience of the world is both biologically determined and socially constructed, our assumptions about what we know about seeing are rarely culturally unbiased. Bolt refers to these cultural presuppositions as 'metanarratives of blindness', meaning culturally constructed stories 'in relation to which those of us who have visual impairments often find ourselves defined' (2016, 10).

As hinted above, one of the most pervasive metanarratives around visual impairment is the linking of seeing and knowing, with the consequences being that the lack of vision naturally pairs with the lack of knowledge. The supposition that blindness is synonymous with not knowing derives from the ocularcentric premise that knowledge develops through sight. Such cultural beliefs are deeply entrenched in ordinary language, which is replete with words and expressions that are rooted in ocularcentric biases. As a result, whereas words and expressions associated with visual perception (such as 'see', 'focus on', 'illuminating', 'shine', 'insight', 'transparent', 'elucidate', 'brilliant', 'bright', 'enlightenment' or 'keep an eye for')[8] connote understanding or wisdom, phrases containing the word 'blind' (such as 'be blind to', 'turn a blind eye to', 'blind spot', 'blind drunk' and 'blind corner') are associated with not so much the inability to see as failure or unwillingness to understand. The following adjectives, which denote the lack of knowledge or intellectual disability, are conventionally synonymous with the word 'blind': 'unperceptive, [...] slow, obtuse, uncomprehending, stupid, unintelligent [...] dim, thick, dumb, dopey [...] unthinking [...] mindless' (*Oxford Paperback Thesaurus* 2006, 77). Similarly, words associated with restricted vision, such as 'dim', 'blurry', 'opaque' and 'murky', also connote limited knowledge. The fact that the pillar of modern western philosophy, the Enlightenment, takes an optical metaphor – light as knowledge – for its name entails that western epistemology is essentially sight-centred and that 'Western philosophy at its most putatively disinterested and neutral can be shown to be deeply dependent on occluded visual metaphors' (Jay 1994, 2).

The linking of knowledge with vision also entails forms of 'epistemic injustice', which term refers to a discrediting of first-hand accounts of a minority group by the culturally or politically dominant group (Fricker 2010, 1). Because the sighted depend mostly on their collective normative assumptions about what it means not to see, they tend to hold misguided and biased beliefs about the experience of vision loss or are likely to disregard the first-hand account of such experience. This variety of epistemic injustice Miranda Fricker calls 'hermeneutical injustice' (2010, 147). Another form of epistemic injustice proposed by Fricker, 'testimonial injustice', involves a reluctance of the members of the privileged group to give credibility to the personal account of the members of the minority group due to their underprivileged social status (2010, 9). The claim of the epistemic superiority of the sighted also stems from the illusion of objectivity ascribed to vision; and, by contrast, subjectivity and inwardness to blindness. Since people with visual impairments are believed to possess no means of asserting their knowledge objectively, their account does not merit credibility. The ramifications of the coupling of epistemic injustice with the assumption that vision pairs with knowledge are that the sighted might assume that they know more about the experience of being blind than blind people about being sighted. Going against the grain of such a form of hermeneutical injustice, Georgina Kleege asserts, on the basis of her own experience of restricted vision, that 'the average blind person knows more about what it means to be sighted than the average sighted person knows about what it means to be blind' (2013, 447). This is because blind people are compelled to navigate their way through the world constructed to accommodate to the needs of the sighted. Whereas, forced to inhabit the world 'designed by and for the sighted', blind people find themselves involuntarily exposed to the facilities of scopic regimes, the sighted are hardly ever forced or willing to contemplate the experience of visual impairment (Kleege 2013, 447).

Julia Miele Rodas considers this forced assimilation of people with visual impairments into the culture of the sighted as deeply embedded in and therefore reinforced by the use of common language:

> Blind and sighted are acculturated into the same symbolic order, the same language, that depends heavily on sight-connoting signs to describe non-visual experience [...] For this reason, though a blind person may exist in a culture of perception and cognition that differs radically from that of a sighted person, this sharing of language means that, on some level, blind people are necessarily members of and participants in sighted culture and experience. (2009, 16)

Because little pressure is exerted on the culture of the sighted to recalibrate its 'symbolic order' in keeping with the demands of non-visual experience, language patterns developed in such an ocularnormative cultural climate are likely to remain sightist and hostile to the needs of people with visual impairments. One of the most enduring sight-centred fallacies around vision loss has to do with sustaining a binary relation between seeing and blindness. Considering that there are multiple causes of visual impairment[9] and variations in visual acuity,[10] blindness should be more accurately conceived of as 'a spectrum of variation in visual acuity, rather than in binary opposition to sightedness' (Hall 2016, 94). The continuum of vision also includes degrees in peripheral and residual vision, colour, form and movement perception, or light and darkness distinction (Kleege 2013, 454). Rather than based on a hierarchy of visual acuity, this continuum is a testimony to the complexity of the perceptual experience of people with visual impairments.

Proper understanding of the complex nature of limited visual perception, which has the capacity to 'obscur[e] the imagined boundary between blind and sighted, confounding our abstract sense of blindness as an absolute', might help recuperate the figure of a person with vision loss from the stigma of the 'hypothetical blind man', which refers to a blind person on whose account the sighted construe their objectivising theories of what it means to be blind (Rodas 2009, 119).[11] Such forms of epistemic violence enacted on people with visual impairments are of interest in the context of the social model of disability. Since people with visual impairments 'become disabled as a result of the society's continual assumptions about visual acuity', simplistic cultural stereotypes and prejudicial metanarratives around blindness might result in garbling the cultural understanding of the experience of vision loss (Bolt 2016, 29). A recalibration of the symbolic order on which such metanarratives rest would be a starting-off point for countervailing the disabling effects of living in ocularcentric societies.

Specular Modernity

If the ocularcentric forms of epistemic injustice have manifested themselves in different ways across the history of the West, a notable shift in theorising blindness coincided with the arrival of early modernity. In pre-modern societies, blindness was attributed to divine intervention. Blindness was thought to be either a consequence of God's punishment for sins or else a test of faith. The implications of such thinking were twofold and contradictory. Blind people became either socially marked out as damned or else thought of as being endowed with some higher form of seeing. As seeing has traditionally been associated with knowing, the outward, objective and therefore worldly knowledge of a seer was counterpoised by the inward, subjective and mystical insight of a blind person. Etymologically, insight denotes 'mental vision or perception' and 'penetration by the understanding *into*' (*Oxford Dictionary of English Etymology* 1994, 477). This 'spiritual optics' later 'continued to have a powerful secular effect well after its original religious sources lost much of their legitimacy' (Jay 1994, 13). Blindness as associated with compensatory insight is well documented in the history of literature. Such fictional, mythical or historical figures as blind prophets (Tiresias), evangelists (Paul of Tarsus), poets (Homer, John Milton, Jorge Luis Borges) or musicians (Johann Sebastian Bach, Stevie Wonder, Ray Charles) have consistently reinforced the image of a blind person as possessing a psychic or mystical perception. To Maren Linett, this cultural metanarrative is fundamentally ableist: 'The attribution of extrasensory perception can also be explained by the ableist assumption that knowledge comes primarily from sight: when blind people demonstrate that they possess knowledge, sighted people conclude that they have come by it through uncanny means' (2017, 57).

The persistent pairing of seeing and knowledge is grounded in the conviction that since gaze is neurologically the most sophisticated human sense it has the capacity to feed the brain with information much more effectively than the other inferior senses. 'Having some eighteen times more nerve endings than the cochlear nerve of the ear,' as reported by Martin Jay, 'its nearest competitor, the optic nerve with its 800,000 fibers is able to transfer an astonishing amount of information to the brain, and at a rate of assimilation far greater than that of any other sense organ' (1994, 6). With the advent of optical scientific inventions, such as the microscope (late sixteenth century) and telescope (early seventeenth century), modern science became preoccupied with and dependent on the gaze. These technological advancements enabled the West to scrutinise and colonise the universe from its micro to macro scale. With the later invention of the photographic camera in the early nineteenth century, a modern human learned how to liberate the present from the shackles of passing time and to capture reality in an objective image. Finally, if with the invention of the cinema in the intervening decades modernity consolidated its scopophilic addition to the gaze, the advancement in surveillance technology of the turn of the twentieth century further reinforced the obvious link between gaze and control.

Literary authors quickly followed suit. The ambitions of the nineteenth-century novelists to portray the world realistically by following the principle of verisimilitude have roots in the same ocularcentric sentiments. However, according to Linett, this penchant for the visible nurtured by Victorian writers was frustrated by aesthetic and literary modernism. Although the invention of optical technologies (telescope, cinema and X-ray) might bespeak an obsessive preoccupation with the possibilities of the gaze, they also 'contributed to a sense of uncertainty about vision, demonstrating that what we see with the naked eye is far from the whole or true picture' (Linett 2017, 61). Since the world can be reproduced with the minutest detail with a click of a camera, the artist, with her imperfect eye, is no longer capable of competing with technology for mimetic accuracy. Because representation was hijacked by technology and its objectivising implements, art needed to turn inwards to report on existence from within through non-orthodox aesthetics. As a result, visual reconstruction of the world gave way to an exteriorisation of the inner experience of the artist. The radical disruption of mimetic representation of the world by avant-garde artists was triggered by their dedication to filter the seemingly objective reality through the inward, subjective optics of the creative mind. Similarly, the response of modernist novelists and poets to the Victorian hegemony of verisimilitude was their conscious shift from the realistic representation of outward experience to the exteriorisation of inner consciousness. Linett concludes that '[i]nstead of aiming for visual detail understood as factual, then, many modernist writers sought to depict a more subjective "shower of innumerable atoms" that fall upon the mind' (2017, 61). The 'multisensory aesthetic' of modernist writing, manifested in formal experimentalism and narrative fragmentation, helped undo 'ocularcentric epistemologies' by frustrating the 'certainties of realist equations between vision and truth' (Hall 2016, 92).

Whereas Linett regards cultural modernism as a countervailing force to the scopic regimes of modernity, thus acknowledging the hegemony of vision as a defining characteristic of the period, for W. J. T. Mitchell, the 'pictorial or visual turn' is not exclusive to the modern era (2002, 173). The prevailing assumption that modernity is dominated by vision is one of the unexamined cultural myths about modern culture, which has gathered steam in the light of the acceleration of visual media in late modernity. The image has become an easy target as a subject of cultural critique: 'The visual or pictorial turn is a recurrent trope that displaces moral and political panic onto images and so-called visual media' (ibid., 170). To Mitchell, modernity's contemplation of vision entails a meditation on a broad continuum of seeing, such as 'blindness, the invisible, the unseen, the unseeable, and the overlooked', as well as on a variation of multisensory experience of the world: 'deafness and the visible language of gesture [. . .] the tactile, the auditory, the haptic, and the phenomenon of synesthesia' (ibid., 170).

Whether the pictorial turn of modernity is hostile to the experience of visual impairment or whether it encourages a repositioning of modern ocularnormative assumptions, I venture to redirect this discussion to a contemplation of visual and non-visual aspects of the experience of reading a literary work. Given that a literary work is not a visual but linguistic medium, I discuss the extent to which the scopic regimes of modernity permeate literary form. Does a literary work serve to reconstruct pictorial imagination of modernity, or does it counter the ocularcentric preconceptions of modernity by a foregrounding of a continuum of multisensory experience of the world? To address these issues, I will now consider selected Coetzee novels in terms of their staging of the tropes and vocabularies of both visual and haptic experience in the run-up to the analysis of the haptic textual effects of *Waiting for the Barbarians*.

Between Vision and Touch in Coetzee's Fiction

Coetzee's novels show a systematic patterning of tropes or metaphors of visual impairment and haptic perception. These patterns seem to undergird the narrative structure of the ethical, psychological and (meta)textual themes, such as writing and the anxiety of authorship, responsibility towards the other, political violence, shame, grief or the crisis of logocentric reasoning. In *Dusklands*, the deployment of sightist metaphors equating blindness with ignorance partakes in Coetzee's meditation on colonial violence and the crisis of authorship. Crucially, there are two figures in *Dusklands* named Coetzee: Eugene Dawn's superior of the first part, a man 'utterly without vision', whose 'blindness' (standing for a combination of aloofness, indifference and ignorance) is scorned by Dawn, and Jacobus Coetzee, the colonial explorer of the thus far uncharted interior of South Africa (*DL* 1). The metaphors of visual impairment relating to the figure of Coetzee in 'The Vietnam Project' are deployed to aid a self-reflexive undermining of the epistemic violence of literary authors.[12]

In the second part of the novel, 'The Narrative of Jacobus Coetzee', Coetzee uses visual metaphors to make a point about the inseparability of panoptic vision from the oppressive practices of colonialism. As reported by Jacobus Coetzee: 'I am an explorer. My essence is to open what is closed, to bring to light what is dark' (*DL* 164). In this part of the novel, J. M. Coetzee uses familiar specular metaphors ironically to put into question the familiar cliché about the white explorer charting unexplored territory and 'bringing light' or enlightenment to a 'dark' and, by implication, obtuse, ignorant and uncivilised land. Elsewhere, the trope of the visual experience of reading sparks a reflection on the linking of writing and violence. As discovered by the narrator Eugene Dawn: 'Print [. . .] is sadism and properly evokes terror [. . .] Pornography is an abasement before the page [. . .] Print reading is a slave habit' (22). The linking of scopophilia, the slavish gaze addicted to the written word and the mental image it evokes, with violence inflicted through the medium of the print, which projects out of itself to enslave the seer-reader, is related to Coetzee's sustained preoccupation with writing as a necessary implement of the imperial project.

In his 1973–4 notebook for his unrealised second work, 'Burning the Books', Coetzee looks back on his first novel: 'Have you noticed that in the <u>Dusklands</u> stories one doesn't know what the heroes look like' (HRC 33.1, 24-11-1973). While his characters are typified by 'a high level of self-consciousness', they also demonstrate 'utter moral blindness. Inability to see people as other than things' (HRC 33.1, 30-11-1973). Coetzee's insights about the paucity of visual detail as well as lack of moral vision of his characters set the stage for the conceptual framework of his second novelistic endeavour. Although unfinished, the sketch of 'Burning the Books' foreshadows Coetzee's contemplation of the ocularcentric underpinnings of political violence, which the author will bring to fruition in *Waiting for the Barbarians*. 'Burning the Books' relates a story about a censor of books working for the Department of the Interior in Cape Town: 'I read, approve, and condemn books because that is my job, in this incarnation' (HRC 33.1, 27-6-1974). It is a first-person account of the narrator coming to terms with his ontological status as a fictional figure: 'You will notice that there is something unsatisfactorily schematic about all the lives I can envisage for myself' (HRC 33.1, 29-6-1974). The narrator's unreliable attempts to deny his fictional status are inextricable from the dependence of his narrative on optical forms of representation. As a 'consciousness inhabiting a tower of glass in a burning city, reading the mind of the West and amusing itself by turning a pair of binoculars of magically high power on scenes of street (violence)', the character finds himself on both ends of optical power (HRC 33.1, 28-6-1974). Working in a glass building, he is subjected to forms of surveillance at the hands of his superiors, like a 'fly in a bottle' (ibid.). On the other hand, as a book censor and a state functionary viewing the area through his binoculars, 'a reader and voyeur' (ibid.), he is complicit in the perpetuation of political violence.

But the story is not interested in what the narrator can see, but precisely what he fails to see. The scene in which he amends his own account of the acts of police brutality after readjusting his binoculars ('I am going to have to focus my binoculars again and find that I was mistaken' [HRC 33.1, 30-6-1974]) gestures towards a linking of the crisis of representation with vision-centred epistemologies, which has its roots in the longstanding assumption about the homogeneity of vision and knowledge reinforced by western metaphysics. If vision is synonymous with knowledge, the narrator's inability to recreate his world through a sight-centred narrative must result in a story that fails to satisfy the rationalistic demands of completeness, verisimilitude and clarity. So long as the philosophical certainty about the imbrication of knowledge and seeing remains intact in the narrator's worldview, his project of self-creation must end in failure and apathy. When the narrator reaches that point, there is no more story to tell – neither for the narrator nor – as the text's unfinished status would suggest – for the author.

Coetzee continues to employ metaphors of visual impairment to reflect on the metaphysics of writing in his further novels. In *In the Heart of the Country*, Magda consciously resorts to ableist metaphors (blindness as ignorance) to manifest an anxiety about writing her own story or retaining an agency over her life: 'my story is my story, even if it is a dull black blind stupid miserable story, ignorant of its meaning' (*HC* 5); 'is it I who am wilfully blind?' (140). The reference to blindness also links with questionable reliability of her account, as the conflicting versions of her story suggest.[13] Her narrative unreliability is made pronounced when she begins to hear voices: '*A blind man dancing seems not to observe his period of mourning*, said the voices. Pooh! *It is a world of words that creates a world of things.* Pah!' (146). As 'observe' means both to 'see' and 'solemnise', the figure of the dancing blind man appears to evoke the traditional sightist connotations of ignorance or indifference. That this report of Magda's phantasmagorical encounters with some extra-terrestrial beings, which is expressed through visual tropes, should be followed by an adage about the demiurgic power of words serves as a commentary on writing itself.

One of the central premises of Coetzee's second novel, which he demonstrates through the unreliable narration of Magda, appears to be that the ontology of the text does not depend on mimetic accuracy. In that way, the symbolism of limited vision connects with the text's refusal to reproduce an objectivising image of the world. Such associations of blindness with the lack of understanding and inwardness are in Coetzee's works essential components of textual production – ones that are not exhausted in sightist connotations, but by nuanced ways of manifesting the narrative immanence of the text. Coetzee's use of specular expressions that are attendant upon such narrative and textual effects as narrative unreliability (associated with limited knowledge) or hostility to mimetic verisimilitude (connoting the text's inability to see things objectively) participates in his sustained meditation on textual operations.

In Coetzee's subsequent novels, a suspicion about sight-centred epistemologies is reflected in tropes and metaphors that present multi-sensory experience in general, and haptic perception in particular, as the site of knowledge. Although these novels intermittently pander to the pervasiveness of the blindness-as-ignorance metaphor,[14] they also show a profound distrust of the epistemological superiority of seeing. In George Lakoff's typology of metaphors, 'understanding is grasping' and 'understanding is seeing' figure as categories that denote a linking of sensory perception with knowledge (2003, 27, 53). As variously shown in Coetzee's early novels, haptic perception has the capacity to counterbalance the hegemony of sight-centred assumptions about knowing. In *Waiting for the Barbarians*, the rhetoric of the intimacy of touch partakes in a dismantling of the uneven exchange of power between the oppressive seer and the oppressed unseeing object of seeing. The wilful retreat of the titular protagonist of *Life & Times of Michael K* into chthonic spaces – in which his olfactory and haptic perception sharpens at the expense of the deterioration of sight – marks his singular way of sabotaging the scopophilia of ableist urban society which consigns people with disabilities (K has a facial disfigurement) to social margins by relegating them to the category of unsightly others.[15] In *Foe*, Cruso gropes Friday's mouth to expose his mutilated tongue to Susan Barton, who, however, either fails or refuses to look. Likewise, the nameless narrator of the phantasmagorical closing part of the novel resorts to haptic experience – he gropes Friday's mouth on two occasions – in a futile attempt to counterweight the failure of sight-based perception to penetrate Friday's impermeable silence. Along these lines, the symbolism of groping doubles up as an allegory about the reader's complicity in committing hermeneutical injustice towards the other who refuses to fit in the scopocentric and phonocentric meaning-making orthodoxies.[16]

Finally, in *Age of Iron* a suspicion about ocularcentric epistemologies ('My eyes are shut in order to see' [*AI* 175]) undergirds Elizabeth Curren's seminal diatribe against the political violence of the apartheid regime, thereby bolstering the ethical core of the novel. Another ethical strand of the novel, a contemplation of the ethics of trust in the unreliable other, is brought to fruition through the linguistic ambiguity of a verb of haptic experience: 'He took me in his arms and held me with mighty force, so that the breath went out of me in a rush. From that embrace there was no warmth to be had' (*AI* 198). Typical of Coetzee's previous works, the ambiguity around the outcome of Vercueil's *embrace*[17] provokes the somehow unrelated questions around the profound complexity or impossibility of ethics and metaphysics of writing (such as narrative reliability and verisimilitude).[18]

In *The Master of Petersburg*, blindness acts in conjunction with the multifaceted ethical issues of responsibility for the other, mourning and betrayal.[19] The suspicion about vision is linked with Dostoevsky's grief and inability to connect with his deceased son through seeing. This sense of failure to get hold of that which eludes seeing translates into the narrator's meditation on blindness, groping and imagination as ways to override deceptive scopic regimes. This new optics allows Dostoevsky – in his conversation with Nechaev about the material circumstances of the working class in nineteenth-century Petersburg – to undermine the predominant ocularcentric premise about the inseparability of knowing from seeing: 'Seeing is not just a matter of the eyes, it is a matter of correct understanding' (*MP* 180). Similarly, since seeing counts for nothing when it comes to making sense of psychological and emotional complexities, Dostoevsky deploys the metaphors of blindness – thus exposing his sightist mindset – to make terms with ineffable grief, which, by way of blindness metaphors, he likens to death: 'He knows what grief is. This is not grief. This is death [. . .] It is like a dog that has taken up residence with him, a big grey dog, blind and deaf and stupid and immovable' (52). Elsewhere in the text the disabled dog acts as a metaphor of a necessity to respond to the call of the other in an attempt to redeem his dead stepson's soul.[20] That prompts him to compare himself to Orpheus leading his wife, 'with the blind, dead eyes following him' (5). Since vision fails to convey the truth about both visible and invisible reality for all its claim for objectivity, the novel contemplates the cognitive and ethical possibilities of haptic perception. The intimacy of touch, therefore, presents itself as a redeeming force, an ethical token of reconciliation: 'If my lips, tender as the fingertips of the blind, had been able to brush you just once, you would not have quit this existence bitter against me' (153). Elsewhere throughout the text, numerous references to groping and blindfolding tie in with the narrator's pursuits that seek to counterweight the impotence of vision.[21]

Also, the idea of writing as a process that lends itself to haptic rather than visual experience evokes Dostoevsky's attempt to understand the new state that overtakes him. This new condition is reminiscent of madness running through his veins: 'down to the fingertips and the pen and so to the page [. . .]: if one were to pass a finger over it, one would experience a sensation both liquid and electric. A writing that even the blind could read' (*MP* 18). Dostoevsky's inability to come to terms with both the invisible (his son) and the ineffable (the visceral feeling he is reluctant to call grief) forces him to contemplate writing beyond the regimes of visibility typically ascribed to it. So it is through writing that the last-resort attempt at a confrontation with his son comes to fruition. Dostoevsky's treacherous rewriting of his son's story marks his desperate attempt to bully God into breaking his implacable silence about Pavel: 'Now God must speak, now God dare no longer remain silent' (249). However, the provocation is also an unethical act of betrayal from which his self and soul will not emerge unscathed: 'If he were to look in a mirror now, he would not be surprised if another face were to loom up, staring back blindly at him' (250). As the face both oppressively stares out of the mirror and fails to see, the adverb 'blindly' reinforces the liminality of the image of the self which by betraying the other betrays itself. Even though the mirror should faithfully reflect his image, he sees himself beyond the surface of the visible. In this sense, the inability to see helps him draw nearer to grasping that which does not submit to the unyielding gaze, and to understand that from the act of betrayal he cannot return as his former self.

Coetzee's trilogy of fictionalised semi-autobiographical memoirs, collectively referred to as *Scenes from Provincial Life*, shows a complicity between the disruption of vision and a foreshadowing of authorial self-knowledge, as hinted at in the following passage, quoted at length:

> He visits an ophthalmologist and comes away with a pair of black horn-rimmed spectacles. In the mirror he resembles even more closely Major Arkwright's comic boffin. On the other hand, looking out through the window he is amazed to discover he can make out individual leaves on the trees. Trees have been a blur of green ever since he can remember. Should he have been wearing glasses all his life? Does this explain why he was so bad at cricket, why the ball always seemed to be coming at him out of nowhere?
>
> We end up looking like our ideal selves, says Baudelaire. The face we are born with is slowly overwhelmed by the desired face, the face of our secret dreams. Is the face in the mirror the face of his dreams, this long, lugubrious face with the soft, vulnerable mouth and now the blank eyes shielded behind glass?
>
> The first film he sees with his new glasses is Pasolini's Gospel According to St Matthew. It is an unsettling experience. After five years of Catholic schooling he had thought he was forever beyond the appeal of the Christian message. But he is not. The pale, bony Jesus of the film, shrinking back from the touch of others, striding

about barefoot issuing prophecies and fulminations, is real in a way that Jesus of the bleeding heart never was. He winces when nails are hammered through the hands of Jesus; when his tomb is revealed to be empty and the angel announces to the mourning women, 'Look not here, for he is risen,' and the Missa Luba bursts out and the common folk of the land, the halt and the maimed, the despised and rejected, come running or hobbling, their faces alight with joy, to share the good news, his own heart wants to burst; tears of an exultation he does not understand stream down his cheeks, tears that he has surreptitiously to wipe away before he can emerge into the world again. (Y 154)

This passage offers a triangulation of the trope of vision, self-knowledge and Christology. The most apparent reading that imposes itself is allegorical. John undergoes a Pauline experience of finding Christ through the interplay of vision impairment and recovery of sight. Like Paul of Tarsus, John is ready to affirm Christ following his restoration of sight. Sight, culturally coded as knowledge, symbolically salvages John from the shackles of unknowing. However, this one-to-one allegory does not deprive the epiphanic experience of its symbolic import. The reflections on vision are followed by John's contemplation of a visual idealisation of the self. John's epiphanic moment of the acceptance of Christ, if tentative, overlaps with an act of affirmation of his face (albeit delivered not without a distinctive touch of irony). The rediscovery of Christ, the Messiah, the one, becomes inseparable from the affirmation of the self.

In *Youth*, the foreshadowing of artistic self-knowledge paves the way for John's gradual affirmation of himself as a novelist, a writer in the making. This will also have a further resonance. The *Scenes from Provincial Life* trilogy can be read as a prelude to the *Jesus* novels through its foreshadowing of the character of David through John. David is both gifted and yet strangely detached and socially deficient, which is much in line with the ways in which Coetzee presents himself – in a characteristically self-deprecating manner – in the memoirs. The John of the autobiographical fictions is a poet to be, painfully aware, or else misguidedly convinced, of his weaknesses and defects as well as his uniqueness. Both *Scenes* and the *Jesus* novels are rife with mixed references to their protagonists' exceptionalism garbled by the painful awareness of their limitations.[22]

Although Coetzee's later novel *Slow Man* centres on Paul's struggle with physical impairment, tropes and metaphors associated with vision loss permeate central themes of the novel. Unlike in *The Master of Petersburg*, where blindness is used figuratively to manifest the intradiegetic narrator's ethical struggle, *Slow Man* turns to the literal representation of blindness. On the face of it, the blind Marianna appears to fulfil a prosthetic function in the text. She features in the text in two scenes. In the first one, Paul catches a glance of her in the elevator. The second time, they meet for a sexual tryst arranged by Elizabeth Costello, only for the plot to move on without her. However, one aspect frustrates a reading of the novel along the lines of Mitchell and Snyder's concept of narrative prosthesis. As I argue at length in Chapter 7, in *Slow Man* disability partakes in the suspension of realistic effects that the novel dramatises. Similarly, visual impairment is inextricable from the novel's rupturing of the seamless divide between the author and text. When Costello arranges for Paul and Marianna to meet, the possibility that the tryst is a ruse orchestrated by an author-figure of sorts haunts the novel throughout. Costello, as an established writer in the novel, acts as a sort of fictionalised author-figure who exploits the encounter between Marianna and Paul for her creative purposes. The farcical sex scene involving two unseeing characters, with Marianna being blind and Paul blindfolded, as arranged by Costello, is reminiscent of an act of stage-managing actors by a theatre director or developing fictional characters by an author. Paul notices that: '[w]e are on stage, in a certain sense, even if we are not being watched. [. . .] But in a certain sense they are being watched, he is sure of that' (*SM* 103). Paul's anxiety about being watched brings to mind a dynamic between the all-seeing author or narrator and the seen but unseeing characters. By insisting on meeting in the dark, as reported by Elizabeth, Marianna implicitly tackles the issue of uneven power relation between the dominating seer and the passive seen-unseeing object of the gaze: 'Marianna does not want you to see her' (102); 'She cannot bear being in the open, where she can be looked at [. . .] She is conscious of the gaze of others like fingers groping at her, groping and retreating' (96). This anxiety about being seen, registered through the cross-sensory metaphor of the groping gaze, which falls into Lakoff's category 'seeing is touching', reflects the oppressive logic of ocularcentric societies in which one's agency relies on their ability to dominate others through the gaze (2003, 55).

The ambiguity around Costello as either a character or authorial figure is also inseparable from the questions of visibility: 'Damn her!' – Paul remonstrates – 'All the time he thought he was his own master he has been in a cage like a rat [. . .] with the infernal woman standing over him, observing, listening, taking notes, recording his progress' (*SM* 122). It is the power of Costello to command the watching game that leads Paul to suspect that his own life might be a figment of her imagination,[23] with the implication being that whoever controls the gaze controls the story. However, the incursion of the author-figure into the text disturbs the realist order also because of the rupturing of the conventional protocols of seeing between the author and the reader. If the reader is complicit with the author by overseeing narrative events and characters, Costello's intrusion makes problematic the author's role as a detached seer-knower. By exposing the author-figure to the controlling gaze of the reader, Coetzee forces the reader to question the ontological status of the author and his authority over the text. In this manner, Coetzee brings Elizabeth into play to mount a critique of how literary authors (himself included) use characters (also with disabilities) as useful pawns in the game of storytelling. Coetzee probes, in doing so, the tactical entanglement of metafiction and ambiguity, the problem of narrative objectification and instrumentalisation of characters with disabilities.[24]

If *Slow Man* is centred around the suspension of realism materialising through the linking of the metanarratives of seeing and the relationship between text and author, the sex scene involving Marianna takes a step further the text's meditation on the coupling of the limitations of seeing and textual ontology through the possibilities of haptic perception. Unaccustomed to depending on tactile sensations, Paul is sceptical about the success of this foray into new sensory experience: 'To her he must be even more of a jumble of sense-data: the cold of his hands; the roughness of his skin; the rasp of his voice; and an odour probably unpleasing to her supersensitive nostrils. Is that enough for her to construct the image of a man from?' (*SM* 107). Forced to confront 'what one cannot see but what the fingertips report' (*SM* 104), Paul is 'placed in the condition of complete dependency', and thus forced to 'imagine another point of view' beyond and despite his culturally acquired ocularcentric habits (Hall 2012, 137). The confrontation appears to be fruitful in that Paul forces himself to reimagine abstract concepts through the metaphors of haptic perception: 'And is this what it is like, being blind: having to weigh each word in one's hand, weigh each tone, fumble for equivalents [. . .]?' (*SM* 105). In availing himself of metaphors of tactile experience to report on the process of searching for the meaning of being blind, Paul implicitly alludes to the reader's encounter with the text. Alice Hall states that Paul's detachment from visual experience resembles that of a reader who must 'formulate an image' through 'snippets of speech' (Hall 2012, 137). One could argue further that reading is an exercise in a reconstruction of the experience of blindness. The reader is confronted with a description of the world which she must construe out of a linguistic code. A mental image that emerges from this process is not inherent in visual perception. Instead, its meaning derives from a continuum of sensory experience. Like Rayment, then, the reader is obliged to weigh words in her hand, fumble for equivalents, or, to complement the tally of metaphors, grapple with complexities or grope for meaning.

Finally, the aspect of seeing beyond vision begs the question about what Paul *can* see and what eludes his gaze. Costello, for instance, repeatedly chastises Paul for his less than impressive powers of observation: 'Perhaps once upon a time you took her photograph, and it happened that all your attention was concentrated on the image you were making, not on her, the source of the image' (*SM* 97). It is possible to jump to the hasty conclusion that Paul is merely *blind to* his own emotions and others. In this way, blindness would be a metaphor for moral blindness. It could be argued that the eponymous slowness is linked with blindness as well: Paul Rayment, the slow man, *blind* and *groping* slowly for the meaning of his own life. However, the mileage of such a reading would be limited. What is more productive is Coetzee's unsettling of the modes of seeing in the novel. Paul might not be very perceptive in his relationship with others or about his own emotions, but part of this has to do with his retreat into photography: a medium of a simulation of reality. Like his new life as a disabled person, the digitalised world around him feels like a simulacrum of itself. So configured, the world has become super-visible, but somehow non-existent. Photography, which has a tactile quality to it, helps Paul offset the sense of unreality. Although Costello persuades him that it is precisely his preoccupation with the image that diverts his attention from reality, for him, it offers a way to salvage the real. Still, Coetzee does not allow the blindness–seeing binary to fall into an easy matching game with the reality–fiction or knowing–ignorance dichotomies. In so doing, for all Paul's entrenched ableism – 'Blindness is a handicap pure and simple. A man without sight is a lesser man, as a man with one leg is a lesser man, not a new man' (*SM* 113) – Coetzee counters the easy stereotypes around blindness.

Whereas *Slow Man* forces the reader to rethink what Paul is capable of seeing figuratively, *Diary of a Bad Year* creates ambiguity around what JC can see literally. With its triple simultaneous narration, the novel recounts its events from different narratorial angles. Although JC bemoans his deteriorating eyesight and motor skills,[25] Anya hints at the limited veracity of his assertions: 'El Señor's eyesight isn't that good, according to him. Nevertheless, when I make my silky moves I can feel his eyes lock onto me' (*DBY* 28). Anya's use of Lakoff's seeing-is-touching metaphor seems to fulfil the double function of confirming the common assumption about gaze as an instrument of male domination and of raising the reader's suspicion about conflicting narratorial accounts. These 'multiple voices' force the reader 'into the process of construction' of the text, says Hall (2012, 139). Through the double gesture of rendering the text visually confusing (as the triple-layered layout of the novel hampers the eye's tracing of lines across the page) and turning the vector onto the text's construction, Coetzee appears to make manifest his suspicion about sight as the ultimate arbitrator of the meaning of the text. By disrupting familiar visual modes of reading, Coetzee encourages non-sight-centred ways of approaching the text. Along these lines, reading is a process in which meanings are to be made, grappled with, grasped, groped for – with all of these metaphors connoting the immediacy of haptic experience – rather than scanned through, which signals passive receptivity and an impulse to embrace the meaning synoptically. The demands that Coetzee's text make on the reader elicit a response that suspends the receptivity of seeing and invites productive engagement with the text's meanings. These effects, as the following section proposes, derive from the haptic visuality of Coetzee's text.

The Haptic Visuality of *Waiting for the Barbarians*

Even a cursory reading of *Waiting for the Barbarians* reveals an abundance of the novel's competing tropes of visual perception and embodied existence. As will transpire from the ensuing analysis, whereas the profusion of visual tropes and metaphors is inextricably linked with questions of power and dominance, their counterparts of tactile perception highlight ethical concerns. Coetzee's suspicion of scopic regimes in favour of the ethics focused on the other translates into the hermeneutic effects his text enacts upon the reader. The haptic hermeneutics of Coetzee's novels demands from the reader an activation of affective reading processes associated with contact senses. Although 'haptic reading' might seem to entail an 'inevitably violent dissolution of the optical', the point is instead to reclaim the potentialities of non-optical forms of approaching a literary text rather than seek to depose optical strategies from their dominant position (Marinkova 2011, 38).

As rightly observed by Laura Marks, these two modalities of perception need not be hostile to each other. Haptic perception can vastly enhance visual perception, resulting in what Laura Marks refers to as 'haptic visuality' (2002, 2). Because haptic perception 'draws from other forms of sense experience, primarily touch and kinesthetics', haptic visuality implies that eyes act as 'organs of touch', and consequently 'the viewer's body is more obviously involved in the process of seeing than is the case of optical visuality' (2). Rather than being disparaging of the perceptive limitation of visual seeing, Marks argues that these forms of perception complement each other, and the disembodiment of visual experience characteristic of modernity results from the misguided rationalistic assumptions of the post-Enlightenment age (viii). Along similar lines, Hall advocates an 'embodied approach' to reading a text, which 'requires us to flesh out our metaphors, to challenge established aesthetic and sensory hierarchies, and to think through the ways in which bodily representations are mediated through text' (2016, 102). With the above concepts in mind, the 'haptic visuality' of Coetzee's text depends on a reconfiguration of 'sensory hierarchies' dominated by 'optical visuality' and reclamation of the hermeneutics of embodiment.

Much of the ethical thrust of *Waiting for the Barbarians* depends on the relationship between vision and power. As amply summarised by Richard Mosse, '[v]ision and blindness are important motifs within the book, and I feel this translates as the vision of surveillance and the entanglement of the political and the visual, especially in relation to ideas of empire: charting, surveilling, mapping, controlling' (2021, 213). The power of the seer is manifested in the novel twofold in his ability to control the object of seeing and to conceal himself from the reciprocated gaze of this object. Consequently, whereas vision is emblematic of power, visibility is a marker of vulnerability. This dynamic is well exemplified in the opening scene of the novel, in which the dark glasses of Colonel Joll perform the triple function of instruments of surveillance, concealment, domination and blindness.[26] Similarly, the makeshift sunglasses sported by one of Joll's soldiers are metonymic of moral indifference: 'They avert their eyes from the glare [of the sun], all save one, who looks sternly ahead through a strip of smoked glass glued to a stick which he holds up before his eyes in imitation of his leader' (*WB* 14). Although the sun brings about the conflicting connotations of blindness (as in 'blinded by the sun') and enlightenment, it appears that in this passage the sun glares (the connotations with anger are telling here) to avert the cruel intentions of the empire. The sunglasses of Joll and his followers betoken a wilful disrespect of ethics and obsequiousness. The glasses may also connote one's attempt to shield oneself from moral responsibility as well as protection. In one of the closing scenes, when Joll loses his power in the town and prepares to leave it, the disgraced Magistrate attempts to confront him in his carriage, where, although seen through and thus protected by the windowpane of the carriage, he is found without his glasses: 'He looks out at me, his eyes searching my face. The dark lenses are gone' (160). The loss of glasses stands here for vulnerability and powerlessness. To Dick Penner, the figurative associations with blindness in the novel signify ethical blindness. The Magistrate's curiosity about the function of the glasses, of which invention he is ignorant, together with the later atrocities committed on Joll's behalf, implies that the Colonel 'is ethically blind, as is the empire that he represents' (1986, 36). Along these lines, blindness figuratively foreshadows the violence of the empire. However, rather than rehashing the old myth equating blindness with a 'deprivation of moral sight', the novel foregrounds seeing rather than blindness as a signifier of moral deprivation (Fontanier, as quoted in Schor 1999, 78).

The power dynamic between seeing and visibility is demonstrated in the scenes of a close encounter between the Magistrate and the so-called barbarian woman. In the published version of the novel, partially blinded and crippled by the colonial soldiers, the woman is now left with partial peripheral vision[27] and a disfigured foot. The evolution of the character of the barbarian woman in Coetzee's notebooks as well as the novel's sketches and drafts throws further light on the novel's problematic relationship between blindness and power. Coetzee's notes for the novel reveal that he was toying with the idea of making the woman mute rather than visually impaired. 'A military commander', the prototype of the later Magistrate, 'begins to notice a girl hobbling about on sticks. He hears that it is the daughter of the man who died under torture. Her tongue was torn out, her ankles broken' (HRC 33.3, 28-11-1977). At this early stage, the woman resembles the woman from the published version in all but the choice of sensory impairment. A week later, Coetzee revises his initial idea: 'I have thought so far of having the girl's feet broken + her tongue pulled out. What of blindness? Can her eyes be pulled out too?' (HRC 33.3, 4-12-1977). It transpires that at this point Coetzee is still looking for a character who would occupy the position of a victim of colonial power. Eventually, the commander's 'barbarian concubine whose tongue has been cut out' turns into a 'blind crippled girl', and it should be mentioned that here the woman is completely blind rather than, as she would later become, partially blind (HRC 33.3, 10-12-1977). The fact that the prototype of the barbarian woman foreshadows the character of Friday from Coetzee's later *Foe* suggests that Coetzee did not easily give up on the idea of interrogating the link between mutism and colonial oppression. But the choice of visual impairment in *Waiting for the Barbarians* is tactical and indicative of the novel's broader theme of the empire's dependence on optical forms of domination and violence. The empire can survive so long as it is capable of retaining its panoptical position over the seen and unseeing subjects, which predicament is epitomised by the barbarian woman.

In multiple scenes, the Magistrate occupies the position of the seer as he asserts his dominance over the woman who in her inability to fully reciprocate the gaze is unable to restore the balance of power between them: 'I prowl around her, talking about our vagrancy ordinances, sick at myself [. . .] The distance between myself and her torturers, I realize, is negligible; I shudder' (WB 29). The Magistrate's own act of encircling the woman, reminiscent of the panoptical relation between the observer and the object of seeing, forces him to contemplate his role as an oppressor. That he is struck by this awareness after making a visual description of her appearance is telling and indicative of the fact that total control of the colonial subject would be impossible without the panoptical gaze of the coloniser. For all his disgust with himself as the gazing oppressor, the Magistrate interviews the girl about her condition while inspecting her body,[28] only to pander to a form of testimonial injustice towards the girl in the process of these inquiries.[29] Scenes of this sort imply that the oppressive tactics of western colonialism, such as physical and epistemic violence, depend heavily on optical regimes, such as scrutiny, surveillance, inspection and scopophilia. Most importantly, even if the seer is aware of his complicity in committing acts of scopic violence, the addiction to the inquisitive gaze appears to eclipse the voice of conscience.

However, the Magistrate's profound self-awareness about the oppressive regimes of vision makes him acutely scopophobic when he finds himself on the receiving end of the struggle for optical domination: 'Sometimes I can feel the weight of a resentful gaze resting upon me; I do not look up' (WB 136).[30] Tellingly, the Magistrate's failure to redress the balance of power connects with his awareness of being watched and the inability to reciprocate the gaze.[31] Disgusted with the public displays of torture orchestrated by Joll, the Magistrate realises that these 'spectacles of abasement' (131) depend on scopophilia for their efficacy. Commenting on the gazing spectators, he notices that what galvanises them is 'not hatred, not bloodlust, but a curiosity so intense that their bodies are drained by it and only their eyes live, organs of a new and ravening appetite' (115). However, the characters' apprehension about being seen is most forcefully conveyed in the central trope: the waiting for the barbarians. The imperial officers and inhabitants of the town do not fear the barbarians per se, in fact, the status quo of the empire is predicated on the existence of the barbarians in opposition to whom the empire defines itself. Instead, they dread the prospect of being attacked by an invisible enemy: the barbarians, after all, 'come out at night' (134), a belief that the townspeople firmly cling to despite the fact that 'no one saw them' (108); it is in the dark, then, that 'fierce barbarian faces leer through' (134).

The spectral and specular metaphors used to perpetuate the myth of the barbarians serve to expose the empire's own mythical status. If the myth of the barbarians is a figment of the empire's imagination, it is merely indicative of the more deep-seated argument that the myth of the empire is a form of optical illusion. With its optical implements of cartographic navigation (a map, compass, spyglass or sundial), the empire's status quo is predicated on sustaining visual control. The awareness of the possibility of barbarians lurking behind the fringes of the empire, no matter how misguided, puts a different spin on the ancient question: *Quis custodiet ipsos custodes?* (Who watches the watchers?). As noted by Foucault, '[d]isciplinary power [. . .] is exercised through its invisibility; at the same time it imposes on those whom it subjects a principle of compulsory visibility' (1995, 187). Following this thread, the empire will prevail as long as it is capable of retaining its status as the unseen watcher of the visible unseeing subjects. The invisibility of the barbarians strikes at the ideological foundations of the empire, whose dominant status depends on claiming the position of the seer, and, to obtain it, denigrate the other to the status of the seen. J. C. Kannemayer proposes that: 'The anticipated barbarians do not materialise because they are in truth an ideological convenience [. . .] These people can bring no "solution" because they never appear' (2011, 337). The interminable waiting frustrates the empire's yearning for the realisation of the attack of the barbarians. It is not the attack that the empire fears, but the possibility that the barbarians will not come and therefore will never be seen. The fact that the Magistrate refers to the colonial project as 'the Empire of light' gives away the empire's obsession with optical domination

(*WB* 114). By refusing to complete the optical waiting game that the empire is desperate to terminate, Coetzee produces a text in which 'naive expectations of closure are disconfirmed' (Attwell 1993, 71).

Unlike the colonial officers, the Magistrate is not apprehensive of the penetrating gaze of the barbarians, but rather of the overwhelming passive gaze of the girl. This sense of trepidation is most forcefully registered in the early version of the novel, in which the girl is completely rather than partially blinded at the hands of the officers: 'He does not shudder when his fingertips pass over her face, ~~though~~. It is only that he does not want to be looked at by that dead look' (HRC 5.1, 12-1-1978, original deletion). It is not so much her impairment that makes him 'afraid to meet her face to face' as her inability to assert her autonomy through seeing (HRC 5.1, 2-1-1978). As a reminder of colonial violence, the 'blind gaze' of the girl reinforces the Magistrate's sense of complicity in the crimes committed by the empire (HRC 5.1, 19-12-1977). As the notebooks reveal, Coetzee contemplated the idea of writing a scene in which 'He paints eyes on her eyelids' (HRC 33.3, 4-1-1978). Although this scene is not developed in later drafts, it foreshadows the Magistrate's obsession with the girl's inability to reciprocate his gaze.

Coetzee's way of countering the oppressive consequences of scopic regimes comes through an entanglement of haptic visuality with ethics, that is to say, moments in which visual perception submits to or is aided by somatic experience to report on ethical issues. The Magistrate's symbolic crossing of his moral Rubicon occurs when he 'took a lantern and went to see for' himself the plight of the prisoners (*WB* 10). He divulges: 'I ought never to have taken my lantern to see what was going on in the hut by the granary. On the other hand, there was no way, once I had picked up the lantern, for me to put it down again' (23). Consistent with the Cartesian tradition of regarding vision as a form of 'long-distance touching', the passage demonstrates the symbolic gesture of 'taking' or 'picking up' (both synonymous with grasping) the lantern to gain insight into that which eludes his physical grasp (Kleege 2010, 4; see also W. J. T. Mitchell 2002, 174). With this insight, in the vein of Levinasian ethics, the ethical encounter with the other cannot be undone: the Magistrate has been enjoined to respond to the suffering of the other, much as he might later regret or seek to revoke the gesture. 'When some men suffer unjustly,' Magistrate later ruminates, 'it is the fate of those who witness their suffering to suffer the shame of it' (*WB* 152). With its mixed connotations of 'observing' and 'attending', the verb 'witness' hints at the double function of the witness figure as a distant spectator and a close participant (*Oxford Paperback Thesaurus* 2006, 919). The shame of witnessing suffering, likewise, conventionally derives from vision (reminiscent of the biblical story about the shaming of Ham for having seen his father Noah naked) as well as physical participation: refusal to take action in the face of the event.

Participation, deriving from the combination of the words 'share' (*pars*) and 'grasp' or 'take' (*capere*), is a vital part of the haptic visuality of Coetzee's text at narrational, representational and hermeneutic levels. Both the narrator and the reader are often invited to share in events that evoke sensory and somatic responses. The ability of a scene, be it real or fictional, to elicit bodily reactions can be subsumed under the category of 'affect', which is a form of somatosensation that the witness or reader 'can feel "on the skin" or "in the pit of the stomach"' (Attridge 2015, 260). On several occasions, the Magistrate expresses a physical revulsion at witnessing or remembering an act of violence committed on innocent people, particularly when he thinks himself complicit in such acts: 'the memory leaves me sick with myself' (*WB* 25); 'I prowl around her [. . .] sick at myself' (29); 'My heart grows sick' (113). Emmanuela Tegla suggests that the Magistrate's sense of moral sickness translates into the reader's hermeneutic experience: the scenes depicting Joll's elaborate means of torture and other atrocities 'can make the reader sick' (2015, 25). Tegla argues that Coetzee's use of first-person present-tense narration 'is inseparably connected with the moral dimension of the novel, on the level of content, and expresses the fundamental ethical concern of the text as a whole' (2015, 8). Along these lines, Coetzee's narrative devices, such as autodiegetic simultaneous narration or internal focalisation, tend to underpin the reader's sense of proximity with the events described. It appears that the moral force of the novel is premised on reducing the distance between the witness/reader and the event. 'Narrative', as proclaimed by Adam Zachary Newton, is, after all, a 'participatory act', one whose 'ethical imperative' is to trigger 'participatory consciousness' (1997, 3, 30).

Since vision is culturally coded as distance and touch as proximity, scenes of ethical encounters between characters often involve a suspension of vision in favour of a foregrounding of haptic experience. Such haptic interventions in Coetzee's text involve two conflicting functions of touch: as a supplement to vision, denoting 'see[ing] by the skin', and as a corrective force for the undoing of scopic regimes (Derrida 1993, 101). A prelude to the Magistrate's departure from the optical to the haptic is the activation of meditative processes triggered by the other's inability to reciprocate the gaze. In *Memoirs of the Blind*, Jacques Derrida notes that:

> When I look at someone who sees, the living signification of their gaze dissimulates for me [. . .] this body of the eye, which, on the contrary, I can easily stare at in a blind man, and right up to the point of indecency. It follows from this that as a general rule [. . .] we are all the more blind to the eye of the other the more the other shows themselves capable of sight, the more we can exchange a look or gaze with them. (1993, 106)

While the gaze of the other conceals the seer's projecting vision, the absence of sight is generative of the seer's unimpeded meditation on seeing (even if this entails the seer's epistemic domination over the unseeing other through gaze). 'Meditation' is the operative word here in that, as in the case of Joll's sunglasses, the reflection of the Magistrate's face in the barbarian woman's partially blind eyes causes him to reflect upon his position as the oppressor:

> [. . .] I take her face between my hands and stare into the dead centres of her eyes, from which twin reflections of myself stare solemnly back. (*WB* 44)
>
> I behold the answer that has been waiting all the time offer itself to me in the image of a face masked by two black glassy insect eyes from which there comes no reciprocal gaze but only my doubled image cast back at me [. . .] It is I who am seducing myself, out of vanity, into these meanings and correspondences. (47)

Faced with the inability to arrive at the answers that he is looking for through the gaze, the Magistrate resorts to haptic perception to reach out to the woman: 'Lightly I trace the lines of her face with my fingertip [. . .] Lightly I touch her eyelids. [. . .] I shut my eyes [. . .] and concentrate wholly on seeing her through my blind fingertips' (46). The reiteration of the adverb 'lightly', connoting both vision and touch, in the process of his tactual explorations, in conjunction with the emphasis on the 'blindness' of his fingertips, bespeak the Magistrate's dawning awareness that ethical vision lies beyond sight-centred protocols of understanding. The Magistrate's reluctance to succumb to scopic regimes in his ethical pursuits of the truth about the history of the colonial outpost that he oversees is amply exemplified in this passage:

> I stare all day at the empty walls, unable to believe that the imprint of all the pain and degradation they have enclosed will not materialize under an intent enough gaze; or shut my eyes, trying to attune my

hearing to that infinitely faint level at which the cries of all who suffered here must still beat from wall to wall. (87)

The Magistrate comes to realise that the gaze is incapable of deciphering the marks of suffering. The tactual associations of the 'imprint of pain' or the 'beating of suffering', aided by the subtleties of auditory perception, are emblematic of the haptic visuality of Coetzee's ethics: one whose complexity is best conveyed by the language of a continuum of perception and somatosensation rather than conventional modalities of vision.

The scenes of haptic visuality are further reinforced in the cycle of episodes in which the Magistrate dedicates himself to the ritual of washing the barbarian girl's feet in an act indicative of self-imposed expiation of guilt. In all three scenes, the Magistrate meticulously washes the girl's feet while inspecting and interrogating her about her experience, only to fall asleep in the process of the ritual.[32] Falling asleep, with its connotations of darkness and leisure, carries the double signification of a suspension of consciousness and conscience. A ceremonial cleansing of the feet, a form of lowliest service symbolising humility before the other, together with the purgative properties of water,[33] is for the Magistrate a form of voluntary penance. Some passages from the early draft of the novel (which was at this point tentatively titled 'Disposal of the Dead' and narrated in the third person) reinforce the Magistrate's commitment to the self-imposed rituals of expiation of guilt through a relinquishment of visual perception: 'He experiments with a world of blindness. When the girl comes to his room in the evenings he blows out the lamp. The ritual of the oil is carried out in the dark' (HRC 5.1, 9-1-1978). If the empire exercises its dominance over its subjects by claiming the position of 'lateral invisibility', thus reducing the other to the role of unseeing objects of seeing, the Magistrate must now perform a ritual of renunciation of sight to both connect with the girl on a sensory level and renounce the oppressive optical practices of the empire (Foucault 1995, 200). Although the girl's body does not yield to any conclusive interpretation, be it through haptic or visual means, the Magistrate intuits that unless 'the marks on this girl's body are deciphered and understood' (*WB* 33) he will be forever barred from its meanings and history. When feeling 'a phantom crisscross of ridges under the skin' of his fingers 'running over her buttocks', he resignedly concludes that '[n]othing is worse than what we can imagine' (34). If there is a truth, it must be arrived at through a close, first-hand encounter with the other; one that stimulates an inner vision of imagination as opposed to a synoptic projection of the eye.[34]

Conclusions

As a person with a severe visual impairment, Georgina Kleege describes her daily reading routines this way:

> I always read close. I always read every word, every syllable, every letter. So the literary practice, to read every word, to dwell on them, to contemplate not only their meanings but connotations, resonances, and history, came very naturally to me. Close reading presupposes that the text is worth taking time over. Close reading is a task of discovery, recovery, uncovering, detection, dissection – struggle. Sometimes close reading is even painful. Since all print is fine print to me, I must always read it closely. Fine print is not only the part that gives you headaches but also the part that only the truly patient, diligent, and discerning reader can decipher. I felt physically well-suited, if not predestined, to be a close reader. (1999, 197–8)

For Kleege, as a person who relies on peripheral vision, close reading is not a metaphor. Her limited vision, which forces her to read the text up close, results in her adopting the reading habits of a quintessential close reader, also in the theoretical sense of the word. If in literary theory 'close reading' denotes '[d]etailed, balanced and rigorous examination of a text to discover its meanings and to assess its effects', Kleege, with her routines of careful and painstaking scrutiny of textual minutiae, fits the bill perfectly (Cuddon 1999, 142). Her personal experience entails that physical or sensory exigencies of the body can affect the reader's reception and response to the text. However, does the reverse hold as well? Is the text capable of reproducing some sensory hermeneutic effects?

Jan Wilm proposes that 'various narrative techniques' of Coetzee's text 'continually slow down a quick and inattentive reading and instead call for stillness, meditativeness, and reflection' (2016, 14). Coetzee's novels produce narrative effects that elicit from the reader a deceleration of her reading habits, which, in turn, result in a more engaged and meditative approach to the text. Along similar lines, Derek Attridge claims that the narrative effects of Coetzee's text, which rely on formal estrangement and eschewal of narrative closure, make exacting ethical demands on the reader (2004, 11). Drawing on these concepts, I have sought to propose that both the hermeneutic deceleration and ethical demands that result from reading a Coetzee novel are inextricable from his dismantling of ocularcentric reading practices. The implications of this approach are twofold. Firstly, Coetzee renders vision secondary to the sensory experience associated with contact senses: a practice to which I refer above, following Laura Marks, as haptic visuality. Secondly, the ethical thrust of Coetzee's text relies on the formal effects that compel the reader to imagine herself reading the text tactually, thus suspending her visual reading protocols and ocularcentric assumptions.

The eye of the sighted reader 'does not track along the line but moves in short jumps, or saccades, fixating briefly on small groups of characters before jumping to a new location' (Kleege 1999, 198). The impatient eye of the regularly sighted person enables the reader to develop selective methods of reading, such as skimming, scanning, speed reading, chunking or meta guiding, which are calculated to maximise the reader's comprehension of the general meaning and short-circuit her engagement with the text. This is consistent with the tendency of the eye to register multiple words at a single glance.[35] In *Waiting for the Barbarians*, sloppy reading has significant moral repercussions. When the Magistrate puts a seal on the investigative report 'after skimming over it with an incurious eye', he pronounces himself complicit in the series of tortures on the captured barbarians that ensue as a result of his negligence (*WB* 9). The reductive reading method of skimming is thus symbolic of moral cowardice. Such selective reading practices are antithetical to the experience of readers with visual impairments. Both the 'close readers' with limited or peripheral vision and 'touch readers' of Braille depend on reading practices that limit discriminatory methods and involve close engagement with the text. Both reading close up and haptically – approaches often involving reading deceleration and meticulous attention to textual details – appear to parallel the hermeneutic experience of reading a Coetzee text.

The hermeneutic responses that Coetzee's writing elicits from the reader are closely tied with the narrative themes he undertakes. That Coetzee's text does evoke haptic reading effects is perhaps best epitomised in Regina Janes's description of Coetzee's fiction as '[o]ily smooth, prickly, repellent, the prose [that] presses, probes, and lets drop the conditions it touches' (1997, 103). If the reader is invited to read the text carefully or imagine herself reading it haptically, it is due to Coetzee's elaborate staging of tropes and vocabularies of somatic experience, which further translates into hermeneutic effects. Kleege goes so far as to claim that Coetzee's subtle description of the barbarian girl's peripheral vision has helped her better comprehend the nature of her own optical condition (1999, 82). In much the same fashion, some descriptions of the character's somatic or sensory experience can elicit similar affective or sympathetic responses. Following the passages in which the Magistrate performs his ritual ablution on the girl, traces with his fingers along the cryptic meanders of her scars, contemplates the spurious logic of the colonial project while 'groping [his] way out to the ruins' (*WB* 146), then 'grop[ing] [his] way back to dry land' (147); or when during his purposeless escape from his cell he 'creeps towards [. . .] the window [. . .] feeling with [his] hand before [him]' (99); or, when tortured, he 'tr[ies] to grope towards' his torturer 'and grapple' (117), the reader is lured into sharing the experience of the protagonist through forms of affective engagement. The combination of a decelerated pace of narration and the foregrounding of bodily experience compels us to align our reading methods with the ethical demands the text makes on us. Wilm asserts that the 'slowness of the body may ultimately require the mind to engage in thinking', thereby activating the reader's reflexive hermeneutic processes (Wilm 2016, 105). Likewise, the Magistrate's hand, a metonymy for a quest for meaning, slowly groping for clues that elude optical certainties (be they about the meaning of barbarians, poplar slips, or marks on the girl's body) prompts the reader to delve into the meaning-making processes of the text through a repositioning of conventional orders of sensory perception.

The deployment of the trope of the suffering body as a conduit for ethical or metafictional themes might strike one as morally questionable. As an object of colonial violence and a metonymy of a text on which the colonial oppressors write their violent history or from which they read the signs of history,[36] the barbarian woman might be read as a figure of 'narrative prosthesis', that is, to remind, 'a crutch upon which literary narratives lean for their representational power, disruptive potentiality, and analytical insight' (Mitchell and Synder 2000, 224). Kleege also argues along these lines that 'a blind character becomes a useful device through which' literary authors 'meditate on the relationship between the reader and the text' (2010, 14). Coetzee's text might not be entirely innocent of instrumentalising blind characters or having them 'hold up a mirror in which the reader' and other sighted characters 'can see' themselves (Kleege 2010, 14). However, as I argue above, and in Chapter 1 at length, some of these prosthetic effects have to do with Coetzee's self-reflexive critique of literary authors' oppressive tactics enacted on their characters, including his own complicity in this process. Rather than pandering to unexamined ableism characteristic of many literary texts, Coetzee 'is willing to bare his own back to his own rod, to declare himself at once part of suffering humanity and of that which makes it suffer' (Kannemeyer 2012, 343).

In my view, Coetzee's deployment of haptic metaphors and tropes also partakes in this self-reflexive undoing of ableist, specifically ocularcentric, narrative conventions that limit the meaning-making possibilities of the text. When Magda, in *In the Heart of the Country*, announces: 'Reading the brown folk I grope, as they grope reading me' (*HC* 8), Coetzee explores through her 'the inadequacy of colonial language to communicate with "the brown folk"' (Kossew 1993). Implicitly, however, the use of expressions connoting tactual perception in Coetzee's work performs the double function of tacitly hinting at the longing for restoring the severed intimacy between characters and appealing to the reader to engage hands-on with the text's open significances. It follows from this that recuperation of ethics heavily depends on the reader's close engagement with the text. The reader might not have physical access to the characters, but neither do the characters – being figments of the author's imagination – themselves. The reader's haptic commitments, therefore, rely on the activation of imaginative processes that – through the text's deployment of linguistic and narrative effects, aimed at undermining the culturally prevalent protocols of observation – compel the reader to reconfigure her assumptions about the sensory perception of the world and text. Perhaps it is JC, from *Diary of a Bad Year*, who most aptly summarises Coetzee's suspicion of ocularcentric literary evocations of reality: 'The truth is, I have never taken much pleasure in the visible world, don't feel with much conviction the urge to recreate it in words' (*DBY* 192). If the reader's haptic commitments rely heavily on her imaginative engagement with the text, Coetzee's earlier novels seem to foreshadow what comes to fruition explicitly in the passage from *The Childhood of Jesus* quoted at the beginning of this chapter. Perhaps the reader would be well advised to take a leaf from David's book, close her eyes, and read through her fingers.

Notes

1. Film critic Christian Metz coins the term 'scopic regime' to distinguish cinematic practices from earlier visual forms, specifically the theatre. To Metz, the voyeuristic strategies on which the cinema depends for its effects (unlike the theatre) are founded on 'the absence

of the object seen' (1982, 61). Martin Jay borrows the term from Metz to discuss the prevalence of sight-centred practices in western modernity (see Jay 1988, 1994). Since then, 'the concept has been used in visual studies to account for how practices of seeing, representing, and subject positioning are linked to systems of knowledge and power that shape what can be understood as true' (Grayson and Mawdsley 2018, 2).
2. Even such common reading alternatives to printed text as audiobooks are considered by many as second-rate substitutes for print books or a necessary facility for people with visual or print disabilities. Though vastly popular of late, audiobooks seem to enjoy a lower cultural status than printed books. Also, although haptic digital technologies such as e-books may rely on tactile as well as visual means for their operation (fittingly, the Latin word *digitus* means 'finger') they serve to facilitate or speed up the visual reading of texts. Finally, such haptic forms of reading as Braille are in popular conception conceived to be reserved only to visually impaired people rather than being an alternative form of reading for all readers.
3. On the exosomatic quality of vision, see Innis (1984, 67) and Jay (1994, 3).
4. However, not being a Braille reader myself, I can only report on it vicariously.
5. Etymologically, synoptic denotes 'a general view', literally 'a seeing all at once' (*Online Etymology Dictionary* 2019).
6. Unlike sight and hearing, which are classified as 'distance senses', smell, taste and touch, as 'contact senses', are characteristic of ethical encounters between people (Bolt 2016, 72-73).
7. It follows from this argument that the predominantly audio-visual character of modern western societies entails their phonocentric and ocularcentric underpinnings. In this chapter, I focus on the latter aspect alone. For the argument about the ramifications of the privileging of phonocentrism, see Chapter 4.
8. See Lakoff (2003, 53) for a list of metaphors linking understanding with seeing.
9. Among them 'uncorrected refractive errors, cataract, age-related macular degeneration, glaucoma, diabetic retinopathy, corneal opacity, trachoma' (World Health Organisation 2018).
10. The 20/20 visual acuity is registered as normal vision, whereas 20/200 or less as legal blindness (Hall 2016, 94). Furthermore, there is a spectrum of variation in distance vision, ranging from hyperopia (farsightedness), presbyopia (loss of focusing ability), to myopia (nearsightedness) (American Optometric Association 2018).
11. Further on the cultural construct of the so-called hypothetical blind man, see Hall (2016, 97–8) and Kleege (2013).
12. See Chapter 1 for an argument on the use of disability metaphors and tropes as a way to question authorial authority in *Dusklands*.

13. Compare, for instance, Magda's contradictory accounts of the death of her father in sections 26, 116 and 262 of the novel.
14. Consider the following examples of metaphors of blindness as ignorance or limitation (my italics): 'The girl [...] *blindly* follows her leader' (*WB* 64); 'What kind of being is she, so serenely *blind to* the evidence of her senses?' (*F* 76); 'We must cultivate, all of us, *a certain ignorance, a certain blindness*' (*F* 106); 'I come back to the mark (which is a sign to myself of my *blindness and incapacity*)' (*F* 136); 'The soul, neophyte, wet, *blind, ignorant*' (*AI* 186).
15. For more information on the anti-ocularnormative force of the multisensory perception in *Life & Times of Michael K*, see Chapter 3.
16. See Chapter 4 for an extended discussion about the role of groping in conveying the epistemic injustice of the narrators and characters meted out to Friday.
17. Is Elizabeth reporting on her own death posthumously or on her experience of a momentary loss of breath? The expression 'breath went out of me' allows for both possibilities. Is, therefore, the *embrace* to be understood literally, as a synonym of a hug, or as a euphemism for death by suffocation?
18. I elaborate on the ethical import of the closing lines of *Age of Iron* at greater length in Chapter 5.
19. For an extended discussion about specular tropes and expressions in *The Master of Petersburg*, see Chapter 6.
20. 'Don't you become like someone called in from the street, a beggar, for instance, offered fifty kopeks to dispose of an old, blind dog [...]?' (*MP* 98–9); 'Is this what I will be doing for the rest of my days, he wonders: peering into the eyes of dogs and beggars?' (81); '[B]et on everyone, every beggar, every mangy dog' (84).
21. 'The corridor is in pitch darkness. Stretching out his arms like a blind man, he gropes his way to the head of the stairs and, holding to the banister, taking one step at a time, begins to descend' (*MP* 68); 'He can pretend he is blind and I am leading him' (161).
22. I elaborate further on the link between exceptionalism and disability in the *Jesus* trilogy in Chapter 9.
23. 'Please be serious for once. Please answer me: Am I alive or am I dead? Did something happen to me on Magill Road that I have failed to grasp?' (*SM* 233).
24. For a related argument in *Dusklands*, see Chapter 1.
25. 'My eyesight is going, and everything else too, but principally my eyesight' (*BDY* 42); '[M]y handwriting is deteriorating. I am losing motor control. That is part of my condition. That is part of what is happening to me. There are days when I squint at what I have just written, barely able to decipher it myself' (31).
26. On seeing Joll's glasses, the Magistrate wonders: 'Is he blind?' (*WB* 1).
27. 'I can see out of the sides of my eyes' (*WB* 31).

28. '"Show me your feet [...] Show me what they have done to your feet [...] Let me see," I say [...] I watch her eat' (*WB* 29–31); 'Let me look' (33); 'I watch her as she undresses' (36); 'What did they do?' (31).
29. 'I don't believe you can see, I say' (*WB* 31); 'I look into the eye. Am I to believe that gazing back at me she sees nothing [...]?' (33).
30. Another example of the Magistrate's scopophobia is revealed in his description of the quartermaster's wife: 'Her eyes glitter, avid though cautious [...] I ramble on; she listens to these half-truths, nodding, watching me like a hawk' (*WB* 139).
31. Elsewhere, he expresses his relief at the privilege of being unseen: 'How fortunate that no one sees me' (*WB* 18); 'from my window I stare down, invisible behind the glass' (21); 'under her blind gaze [...] I can undress without embarrassment' (33). Similarly, contemplating his nakedness in front of his cat in the essay 'The Animal That Therefore I Am', Jacques Derrida interrogates the sense of anxiety attendant on being seen by the other (2002, 373).
32. The feet-washing scene 1: 'I wash slowly, working up a lather, gripping her firm-fleshed calves, manipulating the bones and tendons of her feet, running my fingers between her toes [...] My eyes close. It becomes an intense pleasure to keep them closed, to savour the blissful giddiness. [...] In an instant I am asleep' (*WB* 30); scene 2: 'I begin to wash her. She raises her feet for me in turn. I knead and massage the lax toes through the soft milky soap. Soon my eyes close, my head droops' (31); scene 3: 'I wash her feet, as before, her legs, her buttocks' (32), 'My arm folds around her, my lips are at the hollow of her ear, I struggle to speak; then blackness falls' (34).
33. Elsewhere in the text the Magistrate muses about Joll washing his hands in an act of cleansing of his sins ('Does he wash his hands very carefully [...]?' [*WB* 13]) and asks Mandel directly whether he gives himself to ceremonial ablutions to wash away the blood of those he has tortured: 'How do you find it possible to eat afterwards, after you have been... working with people? [...] I have imagined that one would want to wash one's hands. But no ordinary washing would be enough, one would require priestly intervention, a ceremonial of cleansing, don't you think? Some kind of purging of one's soul too – that is how I have imagined it' (138).
34. The image of the Magistrate 'scan[ning] the world from horizon to horizon for signs of the barbarians' (*WB* 16) evokes the ways in which the synoptic projection of the eye links with the totalising control over the colonised territory.
35. While a normally sighted person can see a dozen words at a time, a person with no central vision can see up to three words (Kleege 1999, 199).
36. For further information on the symbolism of the barbarian woman's body, see Jolly (1996, 128) and Nashef (2010, 24–5).

Chapter 3

Eco-Ability and Narrative Violence in *Life & Times of Michael K*

J. M. Coetzee's fourth novel, *Life & Times of Michael K*, has opened long vistas of inquiry for literary scholars. It has been read as a semi-allegorical indictment of apartheid South Africa,[1] and a rewriting of Kafka's novels and short stories,[2] typical of Coetzee's multiple intertextual allusions to the works of his precursors, including Daniel Defoe, Fyodor Dostoevsky and Samuel Beckett. It also lends itself as a metafictional novel centred on the inability of the author to graft his characters onto the fictional canvas, or else a reworking of the *plaasroman* genre.[3] But how does disability perspective complement this picture? *Life & Times of Michael K* tells a story about a character with facial disfigurement struggling with the debilitating effects of oppressive political regime and social exclusion. The novel offers a denunciation of isolationist policies towards people with disabilities in South Africa, such as segregated education, forced hospitalisation and labour, or deplorable healthcare conditions. Read along these lines, it is an allegory about how modern societies produce disabilities by failing to cater for the needs of people who do not match the accepted standards of physical or mental normalcy, and in doing so consign people with disabilities to social fringes, with K's self-imposed exile figuring as a reaction to ableist social norms and lack of adequate facilities to accommodate diversely bodied people.

Although legitimate and important for the present purposes, this reading does not exhaust the novel's potential for disability representation. Attridge observes that, rather than 'an allegorical indicator of the handicaps suffered by certain sectors of the South African population', disability in the novel figures as 'an important part of the causal chain that has produced the particular individual he is revealed to be during the events of the novel' (2004, 59). Attridge is correct in pointing to the links between disability and K's ontological position. What complicates K's status as a disabled person is the ways in which his interactions with the natural environment help him reconfigure his sensory and physical abilities. This transitional and liminal state, in my reading of it, can be seen as a call for reflecting on alternative forms of embodiment that resist both biomedical categories and social stereotypes around physical and sensory normalcy.

Taking account of these perspectives, I begin my discussion by contemplating the ways in which Michael K's disabilities and disabling states, such as facial disfigurement and body emaciation, as well as the metaphors by which these states are conveyed, collude with ecological themes and terms to account for the protagonist's notoriously elusive ontological status. I will focus on the ways in which Michael K's (dis)abilities are a product of socio-ecological factors. The interlocking of ecological and disability vocabularies takes the analysis deeper into the narrative construction of the novel. Here I look at K as an object of 'testimonial injustice' of other characters or narrators and his agency in countering the acts of narrative violence (Fricker 2010, 135). I also examine Coetzee's term of the 'poetics of failure' (*DP* 87) to take account of the crisis of narrativisation in the novel, both on the part of the author-narrators and focalisers, as well as study the implications of the use of this term in relation to disability.

Cripped Environmentalism

As befits the 'life and times' genre, Coetzee's fourth novel tells a linear and narratively unambiguous story about a socially alienated 'coloured' South African man with a facial disfigurement and arguably learning difficulties, who is victimised by the oppressive political regime steeped in civil war. Because of his impairment, Michael is forced into segregated education at Huis Horenius, an institution that prepares its 'handicapped' pupils for basic, unskilled jobs. Traumatised by his early schooling experience, Michael associates Huis Horenius with oppressive institutionalisation. Later in life, Michael works as a gardener in Cape Town, but quits his job to escort his sick mother, Anna, to a farmhouse nearby Prince Albert, an alleged place of her upbringing, on a makeshift wheelbarrow of his own making, where they are meant to continue to live together. Having contracted dropsy, Anna becomes hospitalised in Stellenbosch as her health deteriorates. Partly due to inadequate hospital healthcare conditions, Anna soon dies. Determined to bury his mother's ashes in the farm of her childhood, K resumes the journey to finally arrive in Prince Albert, even though it remains unclear whether the farm he arrives in is the one intended by his mother. While at the farm, K begins to cultivate the adjacent patch of land until intruded upon by the grandson of the Visagies (the landowners), an army deserter seeking refuge in his family farmhouse. His dream of rural solitude being thwarted, K leaves the farm, soon falling into the clutches of state institutions: first hospitalised, then forced into a labour camp for the unemployed at Jakkalsdrif. Michael escapes the camp and returns to Prince Albert, where he now begins to cultivate pumpkins and melons. Here, again, his sojourn is interrupted first by the arrival of rebels and later soldiers, who detain K for his alleged collaboration with the rebels. At this point, the first part of the novel narrated by the third-person heterodiegetic narrator ends.

Part two, told by the first-person homodiegetic narrator, a nameless medical officer, begins with K being interned at the Kenilworth camp. While there, dismayed at the forced labour and hospitalisation he is subjected to, K refuses to accept hospital food. He becomes the object of the medical officer's obsessive endeavours to comprehend the reasons for his wilful fasting and unresponsiveness. Although extremely emaciated, K escapes again. In the last section, in which the third-person narration resumes, K is roaming the streets of Cape Town, soon to become an involuntary object of the misguided charity of a local pimp and his sex workers. The novel ends with K fantasising about a simple life with an imaginary companion based on minimal dietary sustenance.

In terms of disability representation, whereas K's cleft lip is announced directly in the novel's opening lines, the protagonist's intellectual status remains controversial. Some scholars, such as Christopher Krentz, refer to K as a 'cognitively disabled' person (2022, 3). However, although Michael is presented as having learning difficulties at school, it is unclear whether these difficulties match the medical description of intellectual disability. It is possible that K has specific learning disabilities, such as dyscalculia: 'He did not know what to do with the numbers [. . .] I will die, he thought, still not knowing what the quotient is' (*MK* 110). But for all the possibility of his having a form of intellectual disability, social ostracism figures as a major factor in relocating K from a mainstream school to a special school as a child:

> Because of his disfigurement and because his mind was not quick, Michael was taken out of school after a short trial and committed to the protection of Huis Norenius in Faure, where at the expense of

the state he spent the rest of his childhood in the company of other variously afflicted and unfortunate children learning the elements of reading, writing, counting, sweeping, scrubbing, bedmaking, dishwashing, basketweaving, woodwork and digging. (4)

Crucially, the disfigurement is mentioned as the first reason for his consignment to a segregated school. Given that K has not been diagnosed with cleft palate,[4] which is a more severe form of the cleft lip, often resulting in serious developmental problems (De Sousa et al. 2009), there seems to have been no specific reason for sending K to a school with segregated education. According to Tom Shakespeare, due to pervasive discrimination or lack of proper understanding of the needs of people with disabilities, people with minor physical disabilities are systematically lumped together with people with learning disabilities in special schools, irrespective of the different educational support that they might require. As he explains:

> Segregation, it is argued, breeds segregation. While there may be a rationale for a very small number of children to receive targeted support, the existence of alternative provision becomes a rationale for segregating far more children where there is no practical or pedagogical need to do so. For example, not only children with learning difficulties, but also children with physical or sensory impairments might end up being segregated. (Shakespeare 2018, 112)

The fact that K feels 'the old hopeless stupidity invading him' (*MK* 60) the moment he has met the Visagie grandson (which is also the reason he flees the farm for the first time) may be an indication of social anxiety rather than an intellectual disability. Some scholars also suggest a possibility of K being on the spectrum of autism.[5] However, K's symptoms that may be associated with intellectual disability or autism, such as unresponsiveness, may be symptoms of severe undernourishment rather than a congenital mental disorder. While the novel invites all of these biomedical interpretations, it also consciously holds them off in order to, as I will argue later, question normative notions of physical embodiment and sensory as well as intellectual ability.

One of the central issues the novel tackles is the social stigmatisation of Michael K. In his seminal work on stigma, Erving Goffman lists three types of socially stigmatising conditions: physical deformity, blemishes of character and tribal stigma (1963, 4). As a socially withdrawn Coloured South African man with a facial disfigurement, K roughly falls within most of Goffman's categories. Liliana Sikorska observes that '[t]he hare lip as well as his "simplicity" become the symbols of "otherness" visible and repeatedly stressed in his communication with others' (2006, 94). Similarly, Engelhard Weigl argues that K's cleft lip is more socially stigmatising than his class, ethnic background and social status (2011, 79).[6] Living under a regime based on racial segregation, where 'treatment of disability was based on the medical and deficit-oriented understanding', 'coloured' and 'black' people with disabilities were doubly discriminated against in apartheid South Africa (Bertmann 2018, 94). Consequently, 'the struggle of disabled people had to be both a struggle against apartheid and against how people understood and responded to disability' (Howell 2006, 49).

But K's social marginalisation is also a factor in the shaping of his ecological sensitivity. The bare bones of the plot and narrative structure show an intersectional character of the novel in terms of an imbrication of environmental and disability-related issues. Michael's recurrent escapes from various forms of dependence or places exerting institutional control into natural spaces suggests that for him natural environments have the capacity for offsetting the disabling effects of social and political existence. Some of these intersections operate in conjunction with K's rather unambiguously oedipal relationship with his parents: 'My mother was the one whose ashes I brought back, he thought, and my father was Huis Horenius. My father was the list of rules on the door of the dormitory' (*MK* 104–5). Brought up fatherless, socially estranged, K shows excessive attachment to his mother. In the absence of his father, it is the formative institutions of the state, such as Huis Horenius, that fill in this role in K's life. Crucially, after acquiring basic qualifications at the special school for the 'handicapped', K embarks on his first job as a municipal gardener at fifteen. At this point, however, he submits to his duties reluctantly, happy to walk out at the drop of a hat. This is because his job is at the service of paternalistic injunctions of productivity characteristic of modern nation-states; an extension of the 'list of rules' at Huis Horenius. It is not the gardening that he resists at this point, but its entrenchment in the organised structures of state apparatus; a factor that contradicts the rudimentary organic nature of gardening, as K will realise in the novel's enigmatic ending.

The farm near Prince Albert, on the other hand, as the place of his mother's upbringing and endpoint of the thwarted pilgrimage of Anna and her son, is where K reinvents himself as a gardener. Crucially, K's personal epiphany, 'the beginning of his life as a cultivator' (59), takes place immediately after 'return[ing] his mother to the earth' (58). Anna's buried ashes act here as a symbolic fertiliser for her son's inner growth. For K, the farm is a maternal space of organic nature, untainted by the rigours of the politicised life of the war-stricken municipal areas. To reclaim gardening from the paternal social order and return it to the maternal domain of nature, Michael will now recurrently resort to escaping various forms of compulsory confinement to which he has been committed. Michael's dedication to his mother – an impulse that is both deontological and teleological: 'he had been brought into the world to look after his mother' (*MK* 7) – germinates in his frustration at the inability to connect with her at infancy, partially because of his physical condition: 'But from the first Anna K did not like the mouth that would not close and the living pink flesh it bared to her. She shivered to think of what had been growing in her all these months. The child could not suck from the breast and cried with hunger' (3). K's affliction has two important implications: a disruption of dietary sustenance, and a severing of the filial bond with the mother, a predicament that leaves Michael in a state of perpetual longing for her attentions, which he comes to realise soon after her death: 'But he did not miss her, he found, except insofar as he had missed her all his life' (34).

If K's impairment is an unconscious catalyst for his dedication to the care of his mother, which later translates into a penchant for the cultivation of the land – as a symbolic surrogate of the mother figure after Anna's untimely decease – his other affliction, the self-inflicted bodily emaciation, offers another point of intersection of the natural and the maternal. Unable to obtain food from his mother's breast as a child, later in his life Michael seems to associate food abstinence with the perpetual desire to reconnect with his mother. As a result, K's rejection of hospital food at Kenilworth marks a re-enactment, both symbolic and actual, of the disruption of his alimentary routine at infancy. Fasting is thus a platform for the reconstruction of the yearning for the living mother: one that dissipates after her death. But K's neglect of nourishment is also a symptom of resistance against the father principle:

> As a child K had been hungry, like all the children of Huis Norenius. Hunger had turned them into animals who stole from one another's plates and climbed the kitchen enclosure to rifle the garbage cans for bones and peelings. Then he had grown older and stopped wanting. Whatever the nature of the beast that had howled inside him, it was starved into stillness. (*MK* 68)

As noted above, K's school acts a metonymy of a paternal society which trains individuals to adopt the competitive, masculine, individualistic mindset nurtured since the prehistoric hunter-gatherer model of society up until the present-day neoliberal economy. At the basic level, the struggle for food is the most fundamental principle of both the animal world and human societies. K's refusal to suppress this basic instinct marks a gesture of resistance to the progressive logic of paternalistic injunctions and animal drives, in favour of the ontological passivity of the organic.

Bodily desiccation as a symptom of oedipal tensions crystallises in Michael's withdrawal to chthonic spaces. Roman Silvani proposes that K's retreat into his makeshift burrow marks a fulfilment of his desire to return to the mother's womb, which also figuratively doubles up as a tomb in that the earth is now the repository of his mother's ashes and customary burial site for humans (2012, 67). K's undernourished and emaciated body manifests itself as a way of reducing the body to the prenatal state to make it fit into the protective womb of Mother Earth: 'let the earth swallow me up and protect me' (*MK* 107). But the burrow is also a burial place that claims the body, reducing it to the state of desiccation and decomposition: 'It is no longer the green and the brown that I want but the yellow and the red; not the wet but the dry [. . .] I am becoming smaller and harder and drier every day' (67). K's is therefore a liminal body, one that symbolically inhabits both the uterine and organic milieu. Enfeebled by undernutrition,[7] K's body gradually descends into the phthisic, vegetative state, thus refusing to yield to the laws of vitalistic dualism, which assumes an ontological separation between living organisms and inanimate matter. In this sense, K embodies the assumptions of 'the ecosomatic paradigm', which 'foregrounds the inseparability of ecological context and somatic experience' (Cella 2013, 585). K not only adapts to the natural environment, but also physically merges with the soil and its produce as his body humbles itself to follow the organic pattern of its new abode at the expense of corporeal needs:

> He had become so much a creature of twilight and night that daylight hurt his eyes. He no longer needed to keep to paths in his movements around the dam. A sense less of sight than of touch, the pressure of presences upon his eyeballs and the skin of his face, warned him of any obstacle. His eyes remained unfocussed for hours on end like those of a blind person. He had learned to rely on smell too. He breathed into his lungs the clear sweet smell of water brought up from inside the earth. It intoxicated him, he could not have enough of it. Though he knew no names he could tell one bush from another by the smell of their leaves. He could smell rain-weather in the air. (*MK* 115)

Significant here is K's recalibration of his abilities in keeping with the pressures of the immediate environment. Although his sight is gradually deteriorating, his sense of smell has become hypersensitive. The transition from the scopic to the osmatic existence is a product of K's interaction with the environment. This sensory displacement marks not only a shift from the human to non-human, but also, most of all, on the symbolic level, from political to politically neutral. As argued in Chapter 2, sight is culturally coded as an implement of western suppression of the other, as well as being a metaphor for knowledge (seeing as understanding). The power dynamic between the seer and seen is that the former projects her gaze onto the object of seeing to claim control over the latter. Being the implement of knowledge and control, sight is therefore complicit in institutionalised oppression, the domain that K adamantly shuns.

While sight is a sense of distance, smell is a contact sense. Smell facilitates the subject's symbiotic comingling with the environment, rather than its violent appropriation. K's acquired hyper-ability to 'tell one bush from another by the smell of their leaves' marks a notable shift in his somatic experience towards organic actuality. Crucially, however, this ability operates beyond the parameters of the logos ('he knew no names'), which colludes with the scopophilia of modern science in establishing the categories that serve to justify political violence towards disenfranchised groups, such as ethnic hierarchies, medical notions of (dis)ability and social standards of normalcy. K is therefore a figure of 'eco-ability', which term 'combines the concepts of interdependency, inclusion, and respect for difference within a community; and this includes all life, sentient and nonsentient' (Nocella 2017, 141). Far from an ontological turn towards the animalistic, the embracing of the sense of smell figures as an ethical gesture that resists the instrumentalising and political impulses of modernity. In his opening up to new sensory, ecosomatic experience, K epitomises a form of 'cripped environmentalism', a concept that assumes 'that the experience of illness and disability presents alternative ways of understanding ourselves in relation to the environment' (Kafer 2017, 204).

This new way of understanding himself in relation to the new surroundings is exemplified upon K's first retreat to the farm. While on his way there, he is accosted by a soldier, who intimidates K and mocks his speech impediment (*MK* 37). When on the farm, K reinvents his relationship with speech and voice: 'Though his throat hurt, he made the sound again. It was the first time he had heard his own voice since Prince Albert. He thought: Here I can make any sound

I like' (56). Reading K's experience along the lines of biomedical categories, it could be argued that his occasional refusal to speak in his encounters with others is a symptom of 'selective mutism'. Defined by *DSM-5* as 'an anxiety disorder that is characterized by a lack of speech in one or more contexts or settings', selective mutism may 'develop in children with a speech disorder because of embarrassment about their impairments', who otherwise 'exhibit normal speech in "safe" settings' (*Diagnostic and Statistical Manual of Mental Disorders* 2013, 45). This would suggest that some of K's disabilities are produced by the socially estranging effects of his physical impairment. Disabled by society, K learns to suppress his voice, which figures as a marker of social stigma. The rehearsal of his voice in the farm prompts him to reconsider his vocal abilities beyond the medical notions of impairment and their biometric systems of measurement. The new environment, K's 'safe setting', serves the function of annulling the socially constructed category of speech disorder and – considering his triumphalist use of the modal verb of ability 'can' – reclaiming speech as a marker of ability.

Overpowered by social institutions (school, hospital, camp), K choses an environment in which his reputed disabilities annul themselves. Although, as Shakespeare claims, extreme natural environments (such as mountains, cliffs, deep waters), far from being places of 'barrier-free utopia', can pose insurmountable challenges to people with physical impairments, K's case is a reminder that nature is a space of invalidating the disabling effects of social and political injunctions (2006, 45). K's adaptive tactics resulting in a rethinking of his relationship with nature leads him to resist the norms of social functioning:

> But most of all, as summer slanted to an end, he was learning to love idleness, idleness no longer as stretches of freedom reclaimed by stealth here and there from involuntary labour, surreptitious thefts to be enjoyed sitting on his heels before a flowerbed with the fork dangling from his fingers, but as a yielding up of himself to time, to a time flowing slowly like oil from horizon to horizon over the face of the world, washing over his body, circulating in his armpits and his groin, stirring his eyelids. He was neither pleased nor displeased when there was work to do; it was all the same. He could lie all afternoon with his eyes open, staring at the corrugations in the roof-iron and the tracings of rust; his mind would not wander, he would see nothing but the iron, the lines would not transform themselves into pattern or fantasy; he was himself, lying in his own house, the rust was merely rust, all that was moving was time, bearing him onward in its flow. (*MK* 115)

The operative principle of capitalistic societies is 'time is money'. An individual is expected to work against the clock and think fast to maximise her productivity levels in the present-day 'culture of speed' (Murray 2018, 96).[8] This injunction might result in barring people with disabilities, who often fail to keep up with the impossible demands of efficiency and flexibility, from contributing to the market economy or disparaging them for their limited productivity. According to Beata Borowska-Beszta, people with intellectual disabilities (a category which K may or may not fall into) have a limited sense of time pressure, which counts as a severe handicap in societies predicated on rapid development and accelerated productivity (2012, 74). K's embracing of idleness is antithetical to the demands of the culture of speed: his disregard for the passing of time, his nominal working regime, as well as the deterioration of his capacity for ratiocination and imaginative thinking (symptoms which, again, may be precipitated by malnutrition), run counter to the intransigent work ethic of the post-war liberal economies. Inaction and slow thinking are considered as vices in individualistic industrial societies and are often negatively ascribed to those relegated to the economic fringes, such as the unemployed, people on benefits, the sick and disabled.

The natural environment, on the other hand, is a space in which the failure to demonstrate adaptability to social demands is not considered as deficient or dysfunctional. Nature is a milieu of 'ecological indifference', namely, 'a literal, material ecology that is irreducibly present, that is simply there, irrespective of its recognition – or, rather, the lack thereof – by the imperial forces that confront it' (Bradstreet 2017, 4–5). In *Life & Times of Michael K*, the natural environment is an apolitical space in which social and political laws are suspended. The environment, however, is not a host to political resistance, as, in so doing, it would put itself in a relation (albeit oppositional) with politics, which is itself a political act. Instead, it is a milieu of the annulment of the political and an activation of impulses, abilities and sensory experiences operating beyond the dialectical pressures of history and politics. On the word of Mike Marais, when K first arrives in the farm, he plays the role of a coloniser who seeks to appropriate the land and the farmhouse (2009, 39). These colonising ambitions gradually dissipate upon his second visit, when he reconstructs his relationship with the land by inhabiting rather than exploiting it. This reconstructed relationship with the land marks a shift from the anthropomorphic and colonial mindset to a form of empathetic ecological imagination.

As observed by K: 'The pineapples don't know there is a war on' (*MK* 16). Nature is not antithetical to war, nor is it a symbolic remedy to the political violence of apartheid South Africa. Ecology in *Life & Times of Michael K* is rather staged to demonstrate a singular ontological and ethical relationship of an individual with nature. It is a space of teleological indifference, which eludes generalising impulses of dogmatic prescriptivism. Derek Attridge, while cautioning against reading the novel as a display of Coetzee's 'ecological sensitivity', admits that it conveys 'the intensity which the bond between human and plant life can acquire' (2004, 53). Ultimately, *Life & Times of Michael K* is neither a story about an everyman's encounter with nature as an idyllic counterpoint to socialised existence, nor one about a disabled man's experience of organic existence away from the ableist politics of the state. The most profound effects that the novel produces take place when it reconstructs a unique bond between a socially disabled man and nature, which serves to countervail the ableist and anthropomorphic discourses. Dominic Head argues that K fulfils his pastoral ideal without imposing on the land a grand anthropomorphic narrative (1997, 101). K's withdrawal to the farm is an implicit call that his physical state be considered beyond the social narratives of disablement. Natural spaces, therefore, serve to annul both anthropocentric and normative forms of appropriation.

As I have argued so far, *Life & Times of Michael K* foregrounds the ways in which K's turn to organic existence subverts the normative narratives of embodiment to which disabled people are often keyed. In doing so, the novel can be said to anticipate the assumptions of 'neomaterialism', which involves a deep reflection on 'materiality's agential capacities without continuing to consign disability to a reductively pathologized and thus wholly human discursive fate' (Mitchell, Antebi and Snyder 2019, 4). Coetzee's neomaterialist position serves both to unsettle the biomedical stance about the disabled body as deficient and complement the social constructionist position, which in its excessive focus on the social underpinnings of disability perpetuates a 'disembodied notion of disability' (Hughes and Paterson 1997, 330). While K's exile and resistance to forms of institutionalisation exemplify a critique of social exclusionism, his complex embodiment refuses to contain itself within the medical perimeters of ability.

Narrative Violence

While Coetzee brings his narratives to bear on social and biomedical underpinnings of ableism, he also retains his focus on the oppressive capacities of the narrative form itself. K is forced to negotiate his autonomy not only against the social and political context, but also against immaterial textual and narrative forces that, much like physical environments, can have disabling effects on the protagonist. To spell out Coetzee's investment with the ways in which disabled characters are involved in the novel's oppressive textualism, I will first refer to a term coined by Coetzee in *Doubling the Point* as a starting point for my discussion around narrative violence. In discussing the fictions of Samuel Beckett, Vladimir Nabokov and John Barth, Coetzee mentions 'a poetics of failure', which he defines as 'a program for constructing artifacts out of an endlessly recessive, etiolated self-consciousness lost in the labyrinth of language and endlessly failing to erect itself into autonomy' (*DP* 87). In Coetzee's reading of it, the characters that fall within the remit of the poetics of failure are unable to navigate their autonomous ontological position amid the contradictions engendered by the self-reflexive text they inhabit. Coetzee's *Slow Man*, for instance, is a useful reminder that a disruption of the diegetic world by metatextual devices comes at the cost of the protagonist's personal autonomy. Michael K's position is also precarious. Although one should read K along the lines of a poetics of failure with caution (after all, the materialistic reading of the novel in the previous section has helped me situate K in a more affirmative position than the one allowed by postmodern formal and ethical relativism), what invites scrutiny is his ambiguous ontological status. Is he an engineer of his personal *Bildung* or a function of the repressive textual strategies of the author-narrator(s)? And, on the hermeneutic plane, to what extent does the character–narrator dynamic in the novel serve as an implicit indictment of the ways in which prevailing discourses of normalcy suppress the voice of people with disabilities?

Nadine Gordimer, in her review of *Life & Times of Michael K*, dismisses the novel's identity representation as 'yet another evocation of human misery' (1998, 141). She goes on to ask: 'Does the man have to be harelipped, etc., on top of everything else?' (ibid.). Although Gordimer overlooks the multifaceted and intersectional role of disability in Coetzee's works, she also implicitly highlights a wider problem of the negative symbolisation and instrumentalisation of disability prevalent in literary fiction. Her question could therefore for the present purposes be rephrased as: what is the place and function of disability in the novel's narrative structure? Wladimir Propp's morphology of the folk tale demonstrates that such elements of plot complication as misfortune and its resolution are indispensable aspects of narrative construction (Propp 2003, as quoted in Thomas 2016, 17–18). Likewise, Todorov's analysis of five basic stages of narrative shows that a recognition and reparation of disruption is necessary to restore the state of equilibrium of the narrative (Todorov 1971). Narratively framed as figures of narrative disruption, lack or failure, disabled characters in literature (much like people with disabilities in modern societies) occupy a precarious position of victims of the structures they inhabit. This pattern of structural or narrative violence translates in turn into the hermeneutic plane. Confronted with the defamiliarising effects of the encounter with disabled characters, the reader is likely to respond in accordance with the cultural biases she has absorbed. Such attitudinal prejudice may manifest itself as 'testimonial injustice', which 'occurs when prejudice causes a hearer to give a deflated level of credibility to a speaker's word', or, from the literary hermeneutic perspective, when the reader's acquired cultural biases hinder their interpretation of the first-hand account of disabled characters' experience (Fricker 2010, 1).

In their theory of 'narrative prosthesis', David T. Mitchell and Sharon L. Snyder famously claimed that an instrumentalisation of people with disabilities in works of literature has served to reinforce traditional narrative structures (2000). Epitomising lack or failure, disabled characters have often acted as antagonists or else foils to able-bodied characters in traditional literary works. The lack embodied by disabled characters has conventionally legitimised the wholeness of the non-disabled body, just as the marginality of the former has secured the centrality of the latter. Simply, disability often figures as a disruption that both unsettles and underpins the structural coherence of the whole. Such instrumentalising tactics are embedded in the narrative structure of the novel. *Life & Times of Michael K* is an interesting case in point of a novel that both demonstrates and resists the effects of narrative prosthesis. Mitchell and Snyder propose that a removal of disability or a character with disability from the plot, or, as they put it, 'the extermination of the deviant as a purification of the social body', works as a catalyst for narrative development or resolution (2000, 54). In his 1979–82 notebook, Coetzee is candid about the concessions he feels he needs to make to keep the plot of his novel in progress going: 'There is no feeling between Michael and his mother, and I can't induce it. The longer she is around, the duller + heavier the narrative. Kill her off in Stellenbosch' (HRC 33.5, 26-5-1981).[9] Although undecided about Anna's relation to the titular character or his prototypes – as she is variously shown as his sister, wife, mother and grandmother in the different versions of early drafts of the novel[10] – Coetzee is consistent in all versions about the type of her impairment. Physically incapacitated by dropsy in the legs, Anna K is a heavy burden on both K, who takes it on himself to transport her out of the town on a makeshift cart, and on the narrative, as Coetzee's statement above implies. Having fulfilled the prosthetic narrative role of setting K on the path of his personal journey, she can now be conveniently removed from plot to allow the narrative to centre on the titular character. In the figurative sense, Anna's disability is an obstacle, a complication to be overcome for the narrative to develop and eventually obtain closure.

Similarly, the history of iterations of K's bodily and mental states reveals a correlation between disability representation and pressures of storytelling. In the early stages of the novel's progress Coetzee did not intend his protagonist to be a person with physical or intellectual disabilities. Albert, K's earliest prototype, is a young poet.[11] In the later drafts, the protagonist, now named Michael K, turns into a refuse collector, and later into a gardener (HRC 7.1). Until this point, however, although semi-illiterate, K does not show signs of any recognisable disabilities. However, as Coetzee divulges in his notebook, there is something about the protagonist's character construction that stalls the novel's progress: 'It isn't working. This young man just isn't interesting enough – interesting above all to me' (HRC 33.5, 15-1-1981). It soon dawns on Coetzee that to remedy this predicament he must '[m]ake him much more abject' (HRC 33.5, 10-4-1981). From this moment, Coetzee contemplates a host of figures – such as a 'holy fool' (HRC 33.5, 10-4-1981), 'idiot' (31-10-1981), 'epileptic' (26-4-1981), 'albino' (1-8-1981), 'hermaphrodite' (3-7-1981) – or conditions – 'a facial disfigurement (no nose?)' (1-8-1981) – before he settles on the cleft-lipped character with (arguably) learning difficulties of the published version. This combination of stock character types links various forms of non-normative embodiment and neurodiversity with the literary tradition. Some of these figures bring to mind stereotypical literary characters, such as a fool or a village idiot; others hint at the novel's intertextual influences (such as Dostoevsky's Myshkin, the eponymous 'idiot' and epileptic). It is therefore by rendering K disabled that Coetzee turns his character into a literary character par excellence. It should also be pointed out that the iterations of Michael K claim a long literary pedigree. Elsewhere in his notebooks, Coetzee intends to model K, in the various stages of the character's development, on a host of literary characters, ranging from the little boy from Chaucer's 'The Prioress's Tale', Don Quixote, Robinson Crusoe, Heinrich von Kleist's Michael Kohlhaas and Günter Grass's the tin drum boy, through the heroes of American nineteenth-century adventure novels, such as James Fenimore Cooper's Natty Bumppo and Mark Twain's Huckleberry Finn, to the unnamed protagonists of Knut Hamsun's *Hunger* and Kafka's 'A Hunger Artist'[12] (HRC 33.5, 28-2-1982). This mixture of influences reflects, as Coetzee explains, K's 'struggle to exist between the Scylla of Representativeness (the Historical Novel) and the Charybdis of Individuality (the Modern Novel)' (HRC 33.5, 18-11-1981).

Seemingly, K is a classic case of narrative prosthesis as a character whose disability figures 'as a stock feature of characterization' (Mitchell and Snyder 47, 2000). But the possibility of K's position as a narrative prosthesis in the narrative is derailed by K's sustained refutation of his literary status. When Coetzee finally finds a form and voice for his protagonist, he begins to develop the latter's agency to question the textual reality he has been forced into: 'You would prefer it if I was some kind of interesting madman' (HRC 33.5, 5-7-1981). And the accusation appears to be aimed at the author figure. K's contemplation of his textuality and his marginalisation is embroiled in the author's self-deprecating sense of complicity in narrative oppression. In another version of the story, Coetzee writes this about K: 'He addresses the "angel" who rescues him when he is hungry [...] "You are only keeping me alive for the entertainment of my story. But you keep me poor + miserable because that is the only kind of story you like"' (HRC 33.5, 28-8-1981). Although the fragmentary nature of this passage does not make it clear whether this scene is intended as an oneiric vision or otherwise, Coetzee seems to develop in K a voice of resistance to narrative forms of violence. In his more experimental moment in the notebook and drafts, Coetzee is toying with the idea of removing K from the plot and letting his voice be narrated in the first person as a 'voiceover': 'K moves away from the plot, and seems to be thinking of quoting it.'[13] Although the experimental form of the novel's draft would eventually be traded for literary realism, Coetzee's preoccupation with the author's complicity in sustaining a discourse of violence vis-à-vis his characters remained as the chief theme of the final version of the novel. In one of the most self-searching passages in the notebook, Coetzee confesses:

> I am outraged by tyranny, but only because I am identified with the tyrants, not because I love (or 'am with') their victims. I am incorrigibly an elitist (if not worse); and in the present conflict the material interests of the intellectual elite and oppressors are the same. There is a fundamental flaw in my novels: I am unable to move from the side of the oppressors to the side of the oppressed. (HRC 33.5, 16-6-1980)

Coetzee's narrative forms of resistance voiced or represented by oppressed characters are staged to dramatise the author's sense of inability to do justice to the other due to his affiliation with the oppressors. For all his alleged inability to identify with the oppressed, Coetzee takes the imaginative plunge in *Life & Times of Michael K*. The gradual progression of the titular protagonist and his prototypes from a poet to a person with disabilities marks the moment in which Coetzee refuses to tell the story from the narrative position of privilege. Nevertheless, mindful of the impossibility of repudiating his claim for superiority, Coetzee creates a literary form that manifests its own futile attempts at rescinding its effects of narrative violence. If disability in *Life & Times of Michael K* is a prosthetic narrative device, the novel self-reflexively recognises its failure to counter its complicity in sustaining ableist narratives. Through its self-reflexive strategies Coetzee's fiction counterbalances the forms of injustice it purports to produce.

Coetzee's interrogation of the oppressive status of the literary narrative is further explored in the second section of *Life & Times of Michael K*. A turn from the heterodiegetic narrator of part one to the homodiegetic narrator of part two – a medical officer at Kenilworth hospital in which K is interned – suggests that the position of the narrator is inextricably linked with power. As observed by Carrol Clarkson, the style of narration in the first and third part of the novel – far from being a traditional 'first-person interior monologue', 'external third-person perspective' or a 'dominating authorial voice speaking on behalf of the characters' – 'seems to vibrate *between* a narrating and narrated consciousness' (2013, 30). Although the prevalence of the third-person narrator in the novel does not stand up to scrutiny, I agree with Clarkson that the style of narration in the first and last part is a venue for a vacillation of narrative consciousnesses, which allows K a degree of discursive autonomy. Part two, on the other hand, offers no such variety. Narration here is dominated by the voice of the nameless medical officer, who embodies a Foucauldian figure of authority in a double sense. As an anonymous medical officer (with his anonymity indicating his functionalism within the structures he represents) he wields the panoptic power of continual surveillance over his patient (Foucault 2011), and as the narrator who by usurping the subject position dominates discourse and in so doing controls the voice of the character he narrates (Foucault 2010).

Although the officer appears to have all the best intentions in his unrelenting attempts to persuade K to yield to the dietary prescriptions and other medical protocols against his will, the language and style of discourse he uses contains all ingredients of structural ableism typical of medicalised discourses about disability. In pandering to these discursive patterns, the officer becomes an envoy of the prevailing power structures rather than a voice of sympathetic imagination towards the singular other. The narrator's acts of testimonial injustice make themselves felt in his face-to-face encounters with K. To remind, testimonial injustice indicates a situation in which a non-disabled person refuses to acknowledge the account provided by a disabled person, especially when this account does not agree with the former's normative assumptions about the world (Fricker 2010, 1). Although K corrects the officer as to his real name ('He says his name is not Michaels but Michael', *MK* 131), the latter continues to refer to K by the name he has retrieved from the hospital register, which suggests that, for all the officer's unsolicited sympathy with his patient, Michael's version of his name is given less credibility than the one foisted on him for identification purposes by hospital authorities. Similarly, when the medical officer offers to arrange for the operation on K's mouth and K responds, 'I am what I am. I was never a great one for girls' (130), the officer narrates: 'I felt like telling him that, never mind the girls, he would find it easier to get along if he could talk like everyone else; but said nothing, not wanting to hurt him' (131). Both K and the officer subscribe to different forms of epistemic ableism. The officer dismisses K's response as an instance of the 'happy slave' concept, which implies that the main reason that people with disabilities fail to aspire to the standards of normalcy is because they accept their fate; that is, they do not know that it would be better for them not to be disabled (Shakespeare 2018, 47). Such conclusions are in line with the 'normatively laden distinctions', predicated on the recognition of a person with disabilities qua disabled, rather than qua person, and the subsequent pronouncement of prejudicial non-sequiturs based on the person's impairment (for example, disabled therefore unhappy or inept) (Barnes 2016, 173). K, on his part, is a figure of internalised ableism: he accepts the position of marginalisation by internalising social standards of normative embodiment.

On multiple occasions, the medical officer continues to refuse to challenge his own presuppositions. When K confides in him about what has befallen his mother – 'They burned her [. . .] Her hair was burning round her head like a halo' (*MK* 130) – the officer's response is typical of the culture of suspicion prevalent in the exchanges between institutional authorities and their patients: 'He makes a statement like that as impassively as if talking about the weather. I am not sure he is wholly of our world' (130). The officer's comment on K's use of language is indicative of the ways in which one assumes the position of power by claiming authority over discourse. The patient's refusal to respond in keeping with the protocols of standard speech prompts the authority to apply all sorts of corrective measures to counteract the testimonial insubordination of the patient. Such is the case when the officer's prescriptions meet K's resistance on two occasions: when the latter refuses to accept hospital diet and when he is unwilling to account for his apparent collusion with political dissenters. Although these oppressive measures are presumably intended by the officer to protect K from the effects of malnutrition (and in so doing he only duly follows his job description) and further persecution by state authorities, he mostly reduces the singularity of K's testimony, or lack thereof, to prescriptive patters of interpretation: '[Y]out won't eat! Why? Is this a protest fast? [. . .] what are you protesting against?' (145). An inability of a western mind, trained on the principles of logical reasoning, to accommodate silence within recognisable epistemic structures is a function of what Ato Quayson refers to as 'hermeneutical impasse', by which he means a failure of a normative mind to cope with the lack of closure caused by the defamiliarising effects of one's encounter with the other (be the otherness grounded in ethnicity, ability, sexual preference or otherwise) (2007, 49). Seen via such optics, K is a figure that resonates with the Kafkaesque hunger artist, whose public display of prolonged fasting galvanises public fascination – a response that typifies a moment in which the self is called upon by the alterity of the other. And the officer is prepared to admit that K's pleas for respecting his personal autonomy – 'Why fuss over me, why am I so important?' *MK* 135 – are not wholly ungrounded: 'Nevertheless, he is right: I do indeed pay too much attention to him. Who is he, after all?' (136).

Confronted with a failure to accommodate the other within familiar structures of cognition, one is likely to impose an interpretive framework that helps them to ameliorate the sense of estrangement triggered by the encounter. When the other is a person with disabilities, this attitude might result in reinforcing simplistic or prejudicial metaphors, speech patterns or forms of address that devalue the complexity of disability experience. Perhaps the most conspicuous example of such linguistic reductionism in *Life & Times of Michael K* is the medical officer's use of figurative language. Throughout the novel, and predominantly in part two, K is variously described with a volley of environmental and animal metaphors and similes. Socially detached, he is presented as 'holding his face up to the sun like a lizard basking' (*MK* 132); 'he is like a stone' due to his reduced mobility caused by undernourishment (135); an outcast: 'a mouse who quit an overcrowded, foundering ship' (136); as a troublesome patient, K is a burden: an 'albatross around [the officer's] neck' (146); his disfigured smile is 'sharklike' (147), his harelip like 'a snail's foot' (3); his emaciated body resembles that of a 'stick insect' (149); finally, by K's own admission, he is much 'like an earthworm' (182). If unchecked, the use of animal metaphors in reference to people with disabilities can have harmful consequences. Elizabeth A. Wheeler would go as far as to argue that '[t]hey have justified the subjugation, murder, and incarceration of people with disabilities, ethnic minorities, and colonized populations' (2017, 599). Along these lines, a linking of disability and animality might lead to a denigration of people with disabilities to a symbolic status of the sub-human; an argument that was advocated by early eugenicists to justify oppressive practices and atrocities enacted on people with disabilities. Although the medical officer attempts to do the opposite – he appears genuinely concerned about the fate of his internee – the proliferation of animal similes in reference to K in his narration is striking. All the more so because most of these expressions are correlated with – implicitly or explicitly – K's impairments. Seen in this light, animal metaphors may be seen as products of discursive violence.

On the other hand, Jarad Zimbler proposes to read these figurative mappings as an inherent part of 'narrative consciousness' of the novel (2014, 128). In his reading of it, the regressive animal metaphors are part and parcel of Coetzee's 'poetics of reduction' calculated to blur the boundaries between different forms of being (150). While I find this reading compelling, as there is a degree to which Coetzee's linking of disability and environmental themes displays affirmative ethical interventions, many animal or ecological metaphors are also narratively staged to make the point about various forms of narrative ableism. At such moments, Coetzee's text turns into a self-conscious commentary about the ways in which such narrative staging is linked with the appropriation of the text by the author or narrator – appropriation that also involves an oppressive tactics against disabled characters. K is therefore not only disabled by his physical impairment, but also by the narrative structures that fail to accommodate non-normatively embodied characters within traditional literary conventions. Unlike some of Coetzee's earlier and later novels, *Life & Times of Michael K* is structurally conventional and realistic. Because traditional novelistic forms have perpetually served to reinforce ableist assumptions (Davis 1995, 41), the choice of the non-experimental form of the novel is central for Coetzee to reconstruct a structure of oppression with an eye to demonstrating various mechanisms of social injustice, ableist prejudices included.

This takes my argument back to the question about the position of the character within this narrative system of oppression and the place that the novel occupies on the continuum between a poetics of failure (which refuses to sustain itself within familiar ethical and epistemological structures) and narratives of affirmation. David Attwell cautions against reading *Life & Times of Michael K* as a novel about 'a metafictional preempting of interpretation', such as is typical of postmodern rhetoric of exhaustion (*DP* 204). Such radical descent into recessive textualism is countered in the novel by 'the resistance implied by the open-endedness of writing' – an act that is 'symbolically valuable in itself' (205). In doing so, the novel fosters an economy of resistance to its own metatextual practices which renders unsustainable its recessive operations. And Coetzee deploys these failures and resistances on the representational, narrational and metafictional level of the novel. Along these lines, K's acts of insubordination (protracted silences, rejection of hospital food and refusal to testify) represent the literary character's resistance to the instrumentalising discourses and injunctions of the author. Since literary authors have been consistently complicit in reinforcing normative discourses, Coetzee self-consciously puts himself forward as an oppressive author-figure while endowing his disabled characters with instruments of resistance operating beyond the discursive injunctions of the logos.

The epistolary closing of the second part of the novel most vehemently communicates the narrator's coercive impulse to foist an interpretive framework on K:

> Your stay in the camp was merely an allegory, if you know that word. It was an allegory – speaking at the highest level – of how scandalously, how outrageously a meaning can take up residence in a system without becoming a term in it. Did you notice how, whenever I tried to pin you down, you slipped away? I noticed. (*MK* 166)

This fragment is characteristic of the dynamic between the officer and Michael, which on the metafictional level translates into the character and author/narrator relationship. Attwell refers to such narrative tactics as 'the poetics of reciprocity', which 'involve questions of authorship, the tensions between readers, storytellers, and the subjects or characters of stories' (*DP* 58). In the metafictional reading of the passage, the narrator launches into a self-conscious meditation on the impossible task of the author-narrator to foist a closure on the ever-proliferating textual signifiers or to reduce a character to a set of predetermined characteristics. If K is an allegory, which denotes a story with a closed system of references, he allegorises that which does not succumb to the semantic closure of allegory. These metafictional clues are employed in the novel to shore up the assumption that writing is appropriation and that writing the other into the text comes at the price of reducing her singularity. When the narrator attempts to coerce K to tell his story – 'We brought you here to talk, Michaels [...] You've got a story to tell and we want to hear it' (*MK* 140) – he essentially puts on the mantle of the author forcing his characters to play specific roles in the narrative, thus instrumentalising them. Coetzee is aware that writing is an instrument of appropriation. Unable to write beyond the normative discourse of power, he proposes various tactics of undoing the prejudices he unwillingly stages. K's elective silence, exile and yearning for organic existence are meant to offset the effects of narrative violence and mark the ways in which the character can evade the pressure exerted upon him by the author.

Finally, the ending of *Life & Times of Michael K* continues to contemplate the novel's own narrative devices. Having ultimately settled on the farm and committed himself to the cadences of organic life, K wonders: 'Is that the moral of it all, he thought, the moral of the whole story: that there is enough time for everything?' (*MK* 183). Not unlike allegory, moral is a conventional narrative device used in literary works to enforce a unifying didactic framework on the reader. The text's self-conscious meditation on its moral meaning at this point in the novel serves to introduce a disjunction between the character's ultimate reclamation of his personal autonomy (in contravention of the laws of the poetics of failure) and the novel's reassertion of its conventions. This ultimate reminder of the novel's textual operations entails that the novel does not offer redemption because K's claims for autonomy are frustrated by the text's and its author's violent tactics. But to read K as a figure of the postmodernist poetics of failure, on the other hand, would be to disregard the novel's structure of ambiguity, reflected in both K's elusive acts and embodiment as well as in the novel's capacity for undoing its own exclusionary strategies through its poetics of reciprocity. I address this tension between Coetzee's poetics of failure and reciprocity in the ensuing closing section.

Failing Better? Concluding Remarks

There is a general consensus among Disability Studies scholars that expressions connoting lack to describe people with disabilities are for the most part inappropriate. These metaphors have been introduced and reinforced by medical discourses which, in turn, have adversely shaped cultural assumptions about disability. An unexamined use of such metaphors serves to perpetuate harmful stereotypes, such as disability as a site of incompleteness, deficiency, dysfunction or failure. As these stereotypes have contributed to fostering a negative image of people with disabilities, the task of disability scholars has been to unite in countering and undoing them and the social effects they have caused. If to associate disability with a lack is ableist, most scholars have become suspicious of speech patterns that tend to shore up negative cultural symbolisation of disability – a gesture that is much in line with a wider task of identity politics activists, which is to attempt to subvert unexamined language used to denigrate the position of social minorities.

Few doubt that insensitive and obsolete expressions (for example 'cripple', 'lunatic', 'idiot' or 'feeble-minded') should be countered in popular parlance and cultural discourses. Nevertheless, the injunctions of positivity in the debates around disability can be just as harmful, or impractical at best. While the 'supercrip' theory, for example, may appear as liberating in its portrayal of a disabled person's extraordinary abilities, it only reinforces the negative assumption of 'disability as adversity to be overcome' (Barton 201, 185). Also, not many people with disabilities welcome such apparently positive euphemistic labels as 'vertically challenged' or 'differently abled'. On the other hand, the seemingly negative metaphors can demonstrate positively subversive agency that does justice to the complexity of disability experience, and which helps reorient social perceptions of disability. For these reasons many disability commentators have sought to reclaim the word 'crip', which is now associated with disability pride movements and is no longer considered insensitive or offensive (although the word 'cripple', from which this word stems, still is). This subversive currency lies in the fact that the existence of disability and possibility of one's becoming disabled forces the able-bodied to rethink the wholeness of their own body. For example, disability critics use the term 'TAB', which stands for 'temporarily able-bodied', as a reminder that able-bodiedness is often transitory and that everyone, if one lives long enough, may become impaired in some way (Hall 2016, 168). Along similar lines, Tom Shakespeare states that '[h]uman perfection does not exist. Everyone is limited in some way, whether it's a minor blemish or an allergy or something more serious' (2018, 5). Therefore, rather than claiming that a disabled body is complete and therefore normal (as maintained by some neoliberal inclusionist narratives), it could be more productive to propose that every body is incomplete and therefore in a certain sense disabled.[14] On the strength of the premise that 'the body is never a single physical thing so much as a series of attitudes toward it', the ability to see deficiencies in one's own body helps develop a sympathetic imagination towards people who are variously embodied (Davis 2002, 22). To propose the reverse, that is, to claim that every body – impaired or not – meets the standards of normalcy, would only serve to buttress the homogenising norms that have been liable for side-lining those who have not satisfied the conventional measures of embodiment. If embracing a lack as an inherent condition of every human being helps redress negative associations about disability, a literary text that partakes in an undoing of normative discourses would be one which resists realist pretensions to completeness and challenges the reader to rethink their normative assumptions or ableist biases.[15]

These considerations are of import in discussing Coetzee's novels. As argued above, Coetzee refuses to pander to either triumphalist or reductionist frameworks of character representation. Simply, K is neither a supercrip (as a disabled escape artist), nor wholly a postmodernist figure of 'etiolated self-consciousness [...] endlessly failing to erect itself into autonomy' (*DP* 87). Instead, K is the subversive object of narrative violence and testimonial injustice: victimised on the diegetic level by the narrator, and extradiegetic level by the author-narrator function. Let us revisit Gordimer's provocative question: 'Does the man have to be harelipped, etc., on top of everything else?' (1998, 141), or in other words, did Coetzee, like some sort of ableist demiurge, need to make K into a disabled victim of political violence and social prejudice? It seems that Coetzee's impulses are, however, less gratuitous than Gordimer is willing to accept. Coetzee demonstrates how narratives must fail; how writers (such as himself) are liable to perpetuate repressive practices against socially disadvantaged people by toeing the line of prevailing powers or reinforcing normative discourses. It is in the self-reflexive acknowledgement of these problems as well as the staging of ontological resistances and ecological indifference that Coetzee's fourth novel puts itself in line with the poetics of failure, while opposing its wholly regressive effects and in so doing reconstructing some forms of singular ethics. This is the novel's way of dramatising a form of affirmative poetics of failure, which is Coetzee's way to make his characters, to reiterate Beckett's formulation, '[f]ail better' (2009, 81).

Notes

1. See Attwell (1993, chap. 4) for an extensive study of *MK* in the light of the politics of South Africa.
2. See Daniel L. Medin for traces of 'Kafka's literary paternity' in Coetzee's works (2010, 7).
3. Coetzee's vivid interest in the *plaasroman*, or farm novel, genre is documented by the author himself in his article 'Farm Novel and "Plaasroman" in South Africa' (1986). In this work Coetzee points to differences between the English farm novels of Olive Schreiner and Pauline Smith and the Afrikaner *plaasroman* novels that romanticise rural life on the farm, as represented by Daniël Francois Malherbe, Jochem van Bruggen, Johannes van Meile, Christiaan Maurits van den Heever, Christoffel Hermanus Kühn and Abraham Jonk. Partially set in a farm, *Life & Times of Michael K* shows certain affinities with this genre, while eluding its sentimental impulses. For more information about the *plaasroman* influences in Coetzee's 'South African' fiction, see Koch and Zajas (2006) and Białas (2022).
4. As indicated by the narrator of the first part, who tells us that his mother 'prodded open the tiny bud of a mouth and was thankful to find the palate whole' (*MK* 3), and by the medical officer's report in the second: 'A simple incomplete cleft, with some displacement in the septum. The palate intact' (130, 116–26).
5. See, for example, Quayson 2007, chap. 6.
6. See Wojtas (2021b) for further references on the implications of social and political disablement in the early fictions of J. M. Coetzee.
7. 'His legs were weak, his head hammered, every time he looked downward he grew dizzy and had to grip the earth till the whirling stopped' (*MK* 69).
8. See also Chapter 7 below.
9. See Russell Samolsky's reading of Coetzee's resolve to remove Anna from the plot as a manifestation of 'the paradox of poetic sovereignty' (2021, 200–2).

10. The first version of early drafts of the novel is narrated by Annie K, who writes a letter to her brother Albert (see HRC 7.1). In the second version, narrated in the third person, Annie K is the mother of Michael K (see ibid.). In version 3 she is, again, Michael K's mother, but the story is narrated by her grandson, Michael's eleven-year-old son (see ibid.). In version 4, she is Michael K's grandmother (see ibid.). In version 5, Anna is K's common-law wife (see HRC 7.2). In later drafts and the published novel, Anna K is invariably K's mother (see versions 6, 7, 9, HRC 7.3-5 and 8.1-3). In all versions, Annie or Anna suffers from incapacitating effects of dropsy in the legs.
11. See version 1 of the early drafts of the novel (HRC 7.1).
12. *Life & Times of Michael K* offers more points of triangulation of intertextual references to Kafka's works, disability and environmental themes. Coetzee's fourth novel echoes Kafka's short story 'The Burrow', a story of the mole-like non-human creature narrating in first person the process of construction of a burrow, which links with K's penchant for the chthonic (K builds his own cave or burrow to live in) and disregard for the social existence. The novel carries also a distant echo of Kafka's famous story of bodily transformation 'The Metamorphosis'.
13. See the notebook (HRC 33.5) and version 6 of the drafts (HRC 7.3).
14. See Chapter 7 to read more about Lennard J. Davis's discussion about disability as a universal human condition.
15. In Chapter 7 I discuss the ways in which the metaphors of lack align themselves with the defamiliarising effects of formal fragmentation, thus being representative of the subversive tactics of modernist aesthetics.

Chapter 4

Mute Letters: Against Phonocentrism in *Foe*

In one of the scenes of *Summertime*, the third instalment of Coetzee's fictionalised memoirs, *Scenes from Provincial Life*, Margot asks her cousin John about his reasons for learning an extinct language thus:

'And Xhosa? Do you speak Xhosa?'
He shakes his head. 'I am interested in the things we have lost, not the things we have kept. Why should I speak Xhosa? There are millions of people who can do that already. They don't need me.'
'I thought languages exist so that we can communicate with each other,' she says. 'What is the point of speaking Hottentot if no one else does?' [...] 'Once you have learned Hottentot out of your old grammar books, who can you speak to?' [...]
'The dead. You can speak with the dead. Who otherwise are cast out into everlasting silence.' (*ST* 103–4)

This is a curious and telling scene, but also one that connects with one of the most persistent themes of Coetzee's fiction: one's refusal or inability to adopt the language of power. Margot takes a pragmatic approach to language learning. She appears to have internalised the logic of western globalisation which depends on interlingual communication for its dominance. In such a climate, the centripetal force of the linguistic hegemony of colonial masters absorbs local languages that become rendered unsustainable and doomed to nonexistence. For Margot, language is a tool of communication. If language loses its capacity to sustain communication between its users, its inevitable fate is to fall into disuse. But John has a point. Who will speak with those that can be spoken to or heard no longer? Who will reach out to them to hear what they have to say, in the language of their choosing and ability? How to speak to connect (pace E. M. Forster), rather than to claim a subject position, and thus power (pace Michel Foucault)?[1] Or perhaps the deeper question is this: how to communicate with those who will not respond in a common language? This, of course, baffles linguistically trained minds, Coetzee's included: 'Why should one want to think outside language?' asks Coetzee. 'Would there be anything worth thinking there?' (*DP* 198–9).

This chapter attempts to interrogate Coetzee's forays into the other of speech: silence and muteness. I will first discuss the various ways of representing silence in Coetzee's novels as a prelude to probing the metaphysics and materiality of muteness in *Foe*. I will also investigate the ways in which writing pairs with muteness to examine the complex ways of giving voice to those that refuse or are unable to operate within accepted linguistic protocols, or those to whom the access to dominant language and forms of writing has been denied. I argue that Coetzee's interlinking of the metaphysics of writing and materiality of the disabled body has the capacity to unsettle prosthetic forms of allegorising disability typical of traditional literary representations. Nor does disability in Coetzee's works serve only as a conduit for contemplating postcolonial concerns, such as the 'silencing' of the subaltern subject by the colonisers. Therefore, a starting-off point for the above considerations will be to interrogate the divide between speech and writing vis-à-vis the modalities of silence and muteness.

Mute Speech, Mute Letters

In a video interview, Wim Kayzer asks J. M. Coetzee about issues concerning beauty and consolation. Characteristically, Coetzee addresses the questions in a measured and restrained manner, up to the point when he guardedly, though politely, admits:

> The questions you've posed to me are, many of them, difficult questions, and it's my habit of mind to reflect and revise and try to attain a certain completion and perfection in my responses, and that is incompatible with the interview medium. That's why I've been so extremely uncomfortable [. . .] These are really things that one needs to write about, not to improvise on. (Coetzee and Kayzer 2000)

Coetzee makes it clear that these heavyweight philosophical matters are better responded to in writing rather than speech. Whereas writing affords one to revise, edit and amend the material discussed, speech, which relies on the spontaneity of expression, allows for minimal editorial alterations. Writing offers a refuge of sorts; it permits the writer to relinquish the pressure of space and time as well as the repressive gaze of the stranger. In his interview with

David Atwell, when asked directly about his dislike of the interview form, Coetzee complains that the interviewer tends to usurp control over the interview, while retaining an illusion of spontaneity in the exchange. What appears to be 'a flow of speech' becomes 'take[n] away, edit[ed] and censor[ed]' in keeping with some 'monolithic ideal' of the interviewer, which only manages to obliterate a true dialogue (*DP* 65). This dialogic exchange, Coetzee proposes, can be obtained in writing: 'There is a true sense in which writing is dialogic: a matter of awakening the countervoices in oneself and embarking upon speech with them' (ibid.). It is as if speech was able to claim its spontaneity not from itself but from its encounter with writing, which becomes the organising principle of its production. The voiceless site of writing is thus generative of the voices and countervoices that make possible the production of speech in its turn. Free from the tyranny of speed and immediacy, writing helps one regain control over the vicissitudes of language and thought. If the 'living' and audible speech is the domain of constraint and limitation, the 'mute', 'absent' or 'dead' writing (in line with the phonocentric logic) is by contrast a venue of the recuperation of personal autonomy.

Some of the characters of Coetzee's novels understand this liberating quality of writing as a way to restore the severed bonds with the other or reclaim power over them. When David Lurie's verbal persuasions, which are intended to bend his daughter Lucy to his will, fail, he unexpectedly resorts to writing a letter to her (although at this point in the novel they continue to live under the same roof) in which he warns her of the error of her ways. J. C. of *Diary of a Bad Year* sends a letter to Anya (although she lives several floors above) to persuade her to resume her position as his amanuensis. Likewise, the medical officer in *Life & Times of Michael K*, desperate to break K's silence about his collusion with the rebels, writes his ultimate plea for the latter's complicity in an epistolary form.[2] And these examples do not exhaust the tally of similar epistolary efforts of Coetzee's characters. It is as if the only way to make the recipient 'hear' or 'see' the message is to submit them to the authority of the 'mute' letter, and it is the perlocutionary effects of these mute letters, including the ways in which writing links with subjective agency and power, that become central to Coetzee's ethical concerns. If Claude Lévi-Strauss is correct by stating that writing is an implement of subjugation that 'facilitates slavery', Coetzee is rather interested in ceding this instrument of control to those consigned to the receiving end of power exchange (1976, 299). In other words, how does the mute speech of writing help the other reclaim his or her 'voice' and (per)locutionary agency?

In his seminal work, *Mute Speech*, a study of a history of aesthetics and literature, Jacques Rancière considers writing as a site of two competing forms of muteness: 'the mute speech that romantic poetics grants to all things' and 'the mute letter of overly talkative writing' (2011, 100). 'Mute speech', whose birth Rancière dates to the emergence of Romantic poetry in the nineteenth century, is attributed to forms of writing that give voice to silent things. The voice that materialises from this form of muteness is one of embodied meaning, of materiality arising from the symbolic potency of that which does not speak. The 'mute letter' of 'nomadic' writing, on the other hand, is excessively 'loquacious', and its verbal prolixity obscures the symbolic and semantic energy of the word. The mute letter is thus a form of disembodied speech, one that produces forms that have lost the ability to voice the things they are summoned to express.

These insights are valuable in that Rancière rigorously questions the metaphysics of speech. Since language is a disembodied form with no capacity to reconstruct an embodied world of being, muteness overrides the inability of language to hide its own constructedness, which distances the reader from the materiality of the things it describes. As argued by David T. Mitchell, in his reading of Rancière's work, 'mute speech operates as a value in literature in that Rancière uses it to serve as the desirable struggle to communicate the sentient life of objects into imperfect "non-embodied" language' (2015, 370). He further claims that:

> Muteness performs significant work in Rancière's argument in that the silence that literature invokes in order to gesture toward its own insufficiency of articulation proves as valuable as the process of coming to voice. Muteness could be said to be the way in which literature self-reflexively contemplates its own founding ineffectuality of communication. (ibid., 370)

According to Mitchell, it is therefore muteness rather than speech, voice or language that becomes a basis for literature's capacity for self-reflection. However, muteness should not be understood as a metaphor for literature's internal operations. Literature is mute in the literal sense of being written rather than spoken. Etymologically, literature stands for writings (Ong 2000, 10). Although different forms of storytelling might have their roots in speech rather than writing (epic, with *epos* standing for voice, or *rhapsode* standing for songs), Ong argues that the statement that a literature is 'oral' or 'preliterate' is a form of back-projection and only reveals the chiro/typographic biases of modern scholars. Calling literature oral, Ong continues, is as anachronistic as calling a horse 'an automobile without wheels' (ibid., 13). At its best, literature can be said to belong to the order of 'secondary orality': that is, the orality of modern technologies, which, however, 'depends on writing and print for its existence' (ibid., 3).

This grammatocentric view, which implies that literacy is absorptive of its oral forerunners, stands in a stark contrast to the phonocentric approach championed by many leading linguists, such as Ferdinand de Saussure, Edward Sapir or Leonard Bloomfield, who argue that writing is a visual representation of speech. But the question of the cultural primacy of speech or writing, particularly in relation to the privileging of voice, entails serious political and ethical considerations. H-Dirksen Bauman claims that Jacques Derrida's critique of phonocentrism proves instrumental for the undoing of audist assumptions that privilege oral and phonic over pictorial or ideographic models of communication on which Deaf communities depend (2008). The hegemony of phonocentrism, enforced through cultural production and institutional education, sets in motion forms of structural audism which have led to an exclusion of sign-language-based communities lacking sufficient facilities to excel to the extent comparable to oral communities. The grammatological turn thus serves to offset the privileging of these phonologic practices based on the non-pictorial and linear structure of oral speech, which is incompatible with the forms of communication used by Deaf people. Naturally, the phonocentric-grammatological shift does not provide a universal solution to the problem of communicational ableism. If the phonocentric approach has proved detrimental to people with hearing and speech disorders, the dominance of pictorial and sign-based forms of communication has been instrumental in social and cultural side-lining of people with visual impairments. This discussion entails further considerations about the extent to which the current proliferation of multimodal forms of communication, facilitated by the development of postmodern digital cultures – combining haptic, oral and audio-visual technologies – has succeeded in solving the problems caused by privileging either phonocentric or ocularcentric models of communication.

In the interview quoted above, Coetzee goes on to say that a spoken 'exchange' between the interviewer and interviewee is uneven and involves a relation of power.[3] The interviewer assumes the role of an interrogator or a priest 'drawing out this truth-speech' (*DP* 65).

For Coetzee, on the other hand, 'truth is related to silence, to reflection, to the practice of writing. Speech is not a fount of truth but a pale and provisional version of writing' (ibid., 65–6). The implications of Coetzee's statement are twofold. Firstly, speech comes second to writing in terms of communicating the 'truth'. Secondly, truth originates from a very specific quality of writing – silence – which marks an absence or refusal of speech or voice. What Coetzee means by truth is, however, left unexplained in any further depth. It could be supposed that for Coetzee truth is an effect of countervoices unfolding in writing and contingent on its internal pressures and contradictions rather than a preconceived idea conveyed spontaneously by speech. Behind its smokescreen of immediacy, speech only manages to conceal the fact that its loquaciousness obscures the truth rather than revealing it. The silence of writing, on the other hand, is productive of a sustained meditation and countervoices – ones that are contradictory, polysemic, non-linear, open-ended and resistant to a semantic closure – involved in this process. Counterintuitively, the truth of the mute speech of silence develops from a contemplation of its own inability to provide a single authoritative truth, and this is what silence shares with writing and literature.

Coetzee's Silences

Coetzee has variously explored the complexities of silence in his fictions. One of the most pervasive tropes of his early novels are the violent forms of silencing the other. Ethnic minorities, disabled people, women and animals often figure as those whose 'voice' is either ignored or suppressed. Silence, as 'the fact of abstaining or forbearing from speech or utterance' and 'the state or condition resulting from this', is a marker of the agency of the user or speaker to withhold speech (*Oxford English Dictionary* 2022). But the word derives its meanings from the activity of 'hushing or commanding silence by a hiss', which effect is caused by the sibilant quality of the word (as in the Gothic [*silan*], Latin [*sileo*] and Greek [*σιγή*] varieties) (Hensleigh 1872, 588). This reveals an oppressive dynamic of power in which the speaker subjugates the interlocutor into the state of voicelessness by verbally commanding silence. The suppression of voice is synonymous with the withdrawal of one's personal agency to counter the voice of the suppressor, and thus to redress the balance of power. Following from this is a double symbolism of silence as a marker of defiance and subjection of the oppressed.

Characteristically attentive to the connotational and denotational ambiguities of words, Coetzee is committed to interrogating this double meaning of silence. However, although some characters occupy defined places in the hierarchy of power, Coetzee is interested in the ways in which their silences elude either end of the binary of defiance and subjugation.

The novel that forcefully demonstrates the traffic between agency and submission, registered in the silences of its characters, is *Disgrace*. The novel's silences are most acutely felt in: the refusal of David Lurie to speak in his defence during the interrogation by the university committee after the exposure of his illicit liaison with one of his students; the tacit persistence of Lucy to remain in Cape after her brutal rape by the locals and marry a man related to her perpetrators (a commitment that her father finds incomprehensible); Lurie's resolution to accept the job of putting down homeless dogs; and the silence of the dogs that quietly await their turn of being put down. At the heart of the story lies the idea that since language is the implement of those who occupy the position of power, there is no other way to reclaim this position after falling into 'disgrace' than through language. When David's ex-wife, Rosalind, confronts him about his refusal to speak for himself to the university committee – 'What was the principle you were standing up for?' – David retorts: 'Freedom of speech. Freedom to remain silent' (*DG* 188). Crucial here is the linking of the notions of agency and language. The freedom of speech, that is, the freedom to speak uninhibitedly, should, according to Lurie, include the freedom to refrain from speaking. This wish, however, cannot be respected by the custodians of the order that formulates its legal and ethical protocols in language, thereby allowing no leeway to those who seek to exempt themselves from the limiting injunctions of the logos.

But David's commitment to his own proposition loses credibility the moment when he presses his daughter to justify her intention to stay in Cape in the aftermath of her rape, marry Petrus and refuse to undergo abortion (after being impregnated by one of the perpetrators). To his persistent pleas to account for her choices, Lucy responds: 'I know I am not being clear. I wish I could explain. But I can't' (*DG* 155). Elsewhere, Lucy is reluctant to employ reason and language to defend herself, as if in a desperate act of defiance against the basic implement of male violence. In her curious tirade against David, which echoes his committee speech, she exclaims: 'and if there is one right I have, it is the right not to [. . .] have to justify myself' (133). If the wilful silences of Lucy and David serve as the acts of defiance of those who feel oppressed by political institutions or social norms, the silence of the dogs dramatises the plight of those that cannot negotiate their condition in a language. Therefore, attendant on the silence of David who commits himself to the ungrateful task of putting dogs to sleep in the clinic is the absolute silence of dogs that not only lack the capacity to speak for themselves, but also to produce the silences that stand for the political acts of defiance (like David and Lucy). Carrol Clarkson writes that 'Lurie tries to make sense of his mourning of the deaths of creatures who themselves are oblivious to the concept of mourning' (2013, 119). While dogs occupy the unambiguous position of the oppressed other, their voicelessness escapes the illocutionary force of the human elective silence. The difference lies in the modality: the inability to produce a response in keeping with conceptual modes of thinking renders one unable to produce a countervoice. This is, however, not to claim that the silence of the dogs has no capacity to speak beyond language. Their silence occupies the place of mute speech that signifies without speaking. It therefore seems that elective silence still has the capacity to operate within the framework of discourse, whereas the silence of the negative modality, or incapacity, becomes the marker of bare life that is unable to reinscribe itself back onto the political space of power, but which retains its symbolic energy.

If, as argued, Lucy and David use elective silence as a form of resistance to political power, the silence of the titular protagonist of *Life & Times of Michael K* eludes such straightforward ascriptions. K's refusal to speak for himself has been widely read as a conscious effort on the part of the protagonist to sabotage the oppressive political tactics he has been forced into. Roman Silvani, among others, claims that 'Michael's silence and starving, then, constitute withdrawal and resistance at the same time – withdrawal from history and the body politic and resistance to history and the body politic' (2012, 72). While K's silence may be read as a refusal to comply with oppressive structures of power, they are also a function of K's retreat from social to organic existence. Seen in this light, rather than a political statement, Michael's refusal to speak marks a turn towards non-anthropocentric protocols of being and self-expression. His inability or reluctance to account for his actions has also been associated by some as a symptom of autism. Ato Quayson claims that 'it is Michael's K's endemic silence that provides the most significant clues to the ways in which he might be taken as an illustration of autistic spectrum' (2007, 164). But, as I argue in Chapter 3, such medical readings of K's intellectual status undermine the more nuanced possibilities of K's elusive ontological status.

Waiting for the Barbarians, in turn, dramatises a variety of silence that is reflected in the mute symbolism of the suffering body. The barbarian girl occupies an interstitial space on the symbolic plane of the novel: she speaks, but she fails to offer answers; her 'alien' body evokes desire and revulsion alternately; she can see, but not completely; her 'secret body', full of scars and disfigurations, is one of the most forceful reminders of colonial and patriarchal violence (*WB* 46). It seems that for all this liminal semiotics of female embodied presence, it is what escapes language – or, pace Rancière, the loquacity of the mute letter – that speaks most meaningfully. But silence in the novel is also a sign of the submission of the other to the colonial or patriarchal power. When on the way back to the place of her upbringing the girl begins to menstruate, she becomes sequestered by the Magistrate's male crew and marked as unclean. By accepting her fate – 'she does not question her exclusion' (*WB* 76) – the woman becomes a figure of internalised sexism, trained not to question patriarchal norms. Similarly, silence as a sign of powerlessness is emphatically conveyed in the fragment in which a raped girl, deeply disturbed and unable to comprehend what has been done to her, refuses or cannot speak about her experience: 'Nothing would induce her to tell her story' (134). If speechlessness is meant to represent the experience of the subjugated other, it is also a forceful evocation of the inability of language to communicate the complexity of the suffering body.

Another iteration of silence that is typical of Coetzee's novels emerges from the moments of ambiguity or complex meaning-making operations. These moments, which, according to Sławomir Masłoń, mark 'an enigma that the narrative will try to unravel but by which it will be ultimately defeated', are signifiers of the text's reluctance to lay bare its meanings to the reader (2018, 9). Many readers have been mystified by why David Lurie, for instance, chooses not to take the dog he has befriended, why Mrs Curren of *Age of Iron* entrusts the undependable Vercueil with posting the letter to her daughter, why Dostoevsky of *The Master of Petersburg* betrays the memory of his son by deceitfully rewriting the latter's diary, why Paul Rayment of *Slow Man* refuses the prosthesis prescribed to him by the hospital doctors, among other examples. These baffling but thought-provoking moments appear to reproduce the paradox of ethics itself: the doubling of the inevitability of ethical encounters with others and the unethical consequences of one's efforts to act ethically. By raising these questions and leaving them unanswered, Coetzee shifts the centre of gravity from politics to philosophical ethics. But it seems that in the *Jesus* novels the textual sites of indeterminacy are structured around ideational patterns rather than being the effects of the self-reflexive mechanisms of the text, or of an interrogation of the boundary between fiction, autobiography and authorship, or else of a socio-political allegory.[4] All of the instalments of the *Jesus* novels are replete with cryptic silences. How does Simón know that Inés is David's mother? What is the content of the lost letter? What role do the non-linguistic patterns and symbols, such as the abstract numerical configurations of dance, play in filling in these textual blind-spots? What is the *message* David is supposed to have left behind before his untimely death? Finally, why does David's story fail to exhaust itself in the biblical allegory it advertises in the title? If in Platonic terms *idea* denotes a pure transcendental pattern, Coetzee's constellations of ideas contain blind-spots that cannot be easily untangled by following a fixed philosophical paradigm. Coetzee's mute speech of ideas speaks in order to conceal.

Muteness, Writing and (Dis)empowerment

Silence in Coetzee's fictions also chimes with the questions of ability and embodiment. The novel that contemplates silence not only in terms of its figurative meanings but also as an effect of embodied experience of muteness is *Foe*. Published in 1986, Coetzee's fifth novel is a retelling of the familiar story of Robinson Crusoe. However, if Daniel Defoe's original story is centred around the adventures of the eponymous protagonist, Coetzee tells a story of an Englishwoman named Susan Barton who shares her lot with Cruso and his slave Friday as a castaway on an uninhabited island. The first section of the novel comprises a memoir of Susan Barton in which she recounts her life on the island with the ageing Cruso – whose account of his life on the island is inconsequential, due either to his wilful obscurantism or memory loss – and his mute slave, Friday. Although Cruso claims that Friday was probably violently mutilated by his former slavers, it is hinted that the former himself may be behind the act of mutilation. Another possibility is, as will be discussed below, that Friday is wilfully silent rather than mute. The first part ends with the three of them being rescued by a ship and taken to England. Cruso, who is rather forcefully taken from the island, dies en route.

Part two of the novel focuses on Susan's efforts to persuade Mr Foe to ghost-write the story of her life on the island. This, she hopes, will help her get back on her feet financially and help Friday return to Africa (an attempt that will prove unsuccessful). While Susan is writing her memoir for Mr Foe, the latter flees in hiding from his debtors without notice. As she illicitly lodges with Friday in Foe's abandoned house – a time which Susan spends on writing and eliciting from Friday, unsuccessfully, his own story – she is visited by a girl. The girl claims to be Susan's daughter who has mysteriously gone missing in Bahia. Susan suspects the girl must have been sent by none other than the fugitive Foe himself. Part three revolves around the events after Foe's sudden return, which include Barton's adamant denial of any maternal filiation with the girl and the joint endeavours of Barton and Foe to make sense of Friday's silence as well as translate his silence into writing of Friday's own making. The section ends with Friday, dressed in Foe's wig and robe, scribbling on Foe's papers. The final, and the most cryptic, part of the novel, offers two alternative endings to the story narrated by a nameless narrator. In the first part, the narrator visits the house of the writer 'Daniel Defoe', as advertised on the door plaque, and finds the bodies of a woman and a girl lying in bed. Venturing further, the narrator finds the body of Friday, checks his pulsing throat, and presses the ear closely to Friday's mouth and hears 'the roar of the waves' and 'the call of a voice' (*F* 154). In the second ending, apart from the already familiar scene of the narrator entering the house and finding the bodies, albeit in a different configuration, the narrator plunges into the depths of the sea to spot a shipwreck containing the bodies of Susan, the captain and Friday. Approaching Friday, the narrator notices a stream issuing from his mouth.

Foe is a story of a complex intertwining of the metaphysics of silence, writing and colonial power, as well as the ways in which this power dynamic is inflected by the disablement of the mute body. In medical terms, the word 'mute' denotes 'unwilling or unable to speak' (Collin 2005, 254). Whereas 'mute' can be paired with 'silence', in that both denote one's refusal to speak, 'muteness' as the medical category of 'mutism', that is, the condition of being unable to speak, departs from the definition of silence, which is not characterised by one's capability or lack thereof. However, the separation of silence and muteness produces a binary relation that seems to undermine the complexity of either position. The fallacy of this binary is represented in *Foe* by Susan Barton, who self-consciously distinguishes two kinds of silence between herself and Friday thus:

> No matter what he is to himself (is he anything to himself? – how can he tell us?), what he is to the world is what I make of him. Therefore the silence of Friday is a helpless silence. He is the child of his silence, a child unborn, a child waiting to be born that cannot be born. Whereas the silence I keep regarding Bahia and other matters is chosen and purposeful: it is my own silence. (F 122)

While her 'purposeful' silence manifests itself in her reluctance to discuss things she chooses to remain silent about, Friday's is a 'helpless silence' of a mute person who is consigned to the world of silence by his sensory or intellectual disability. Susan's distinction is not only ableist – the elective silence of the non-disabled as a sign of agency as opposed to the helpless silence of the disabled as indicative of absence – but also simplistic in her inability to recognise a subversive ambiguity of both kinds of silence she distinguishes. Although Susan Barton appears to occupy the position of the other – as a woman whose account is doomed to oblivion in the world controlled by men – her persistent attempts to force Friday to tell his story put her in the position of a person who fails to comprehend the other outside of the comfortable domain of the dominant discourse she relies on. According to Derek Attridge, a dominant discourse occupies the position of silence itself:

> All canons rest on exclusion: the voice they give to some can be heard only by virtue of the silence they impose on others. But it is not just a silencing by exclusion, it is a silencing by inclusion as well: any voice we can hear is by that fact purged of its uniqueness and alterity. (2004, 82)

It could be argued that the homogenising tactics of a dominant or canonical discourse lead to a silencing of that which it attempts to privilege. The dominant voice or canon is doomed to the impotent silence of the mute letter, whereas the silenced, excluded, mute speech of the other retains its heterogeneity, and thus capacity for significations that are unconstrained by the exclusive rules of the prevailing power discourses.

But if Susan fails to recognise the subversive agency of muteness, it is because she has internalised the triumphalist notions of power as well as the means by which power asserts itself. Throughout the novel Susan laments her inability to tell or control her own story as well as to remain an agent in the story of her life on the island. As the reader knows well, there is indeed no Susan Barton in Defoe's account of the adventures of the celebrated castaway. Her inability to sustain her presence in the story is signalled in the fact that, when she is cast adrift, Cruso and Friday have already inhabited the island for nearly two decades. This moment is telling in that the island becomes a microcosm of the western world which sustains the Judaeo-Christian narrative of the chronological precedence of man over woman, thereby legitimising male authority over all creation. Susan's urgency to tell the unadulterated account of her life on the island ('If I cannot come forward, as author, and swear to the truth of my tale, what will be the worth of it?' [F 40]) does not come from her commitment to an abstract notion of truth, but her reluctance to yield to men's story. If femininity has traditionally been relegated to the domain of domesticity, silence, inaction and fragility, masculinity has appropriated the privileged opposites on the spectrum: mobility, voice, action and power. Having absorbed the male-supremacist logic of the world, Susan realises she needs to claim the position she has been excluded from by default.

If Susan has indeed imbibed normative assumptions, it is hardly surprising that she refuses to acknowledge Friday's silence as a form of autonomous countervoice: 'The true story will not be heard till by art we have found a means of giving voice to Friday' (F 117–18). In one of the early drafts of the novel Susan expresses her preoccupation with Friday in these words: 'To In my simple narrative Friday is dumb; it is for you, Mr Foe, to give him words, if that is possible, by what means I do not know.'[5] Susan is adamant that the only way to sanction Friday's presence is by conveying it in language. Again, by assuming that art must speak, Susan commits the fallacy of the mute letter. She fails to identify the currency of the unsaid to assert the presence and agency of these that refuse to claim a position within the normative structures through speech. If Friday refuses to speak, he will find himself on the receiving end of the illocutionary speech acts, that is, his story will be chosen for him by those that command the power of discourse, herself included: 'Friday has no command of words and therefore no defence against being re-shaped day by day in conformity with the desires of others. I say he is a cannibal and he becomes a cannibal' (F 121).

For Barton, Friday does not represent the phallic power that threatens to destabilise her centrality in the story. Instead, he is her partner in exclusion. As the mirror image of Susan's own consignment to silence, Friday's muteness represents a gap that must be filled. Only that way will Susan be able to reclaim the power of self-articulation: 'In every story there is a silence, some sight concealed, some word unspoken, I believe. Till we have spoken the unspoken we have not come to the heart of the story' (F 141). In her account, silence is intended to destabilise the centre, the 'heart', of the story; it is a Derridean supplement that threatens to displace speech from its authoritative position. Aware of the subversive agency of silence, Susan is obsessed with taming it. She recognises that the potency of her story lies not only in controlling discourse by claiming the subject position within it, but fundamentally to command the unsaid. Apprehensive of the phallogocentric power of Foe's authority as the author of her 'story', she remonstrates: 'I am not a story, Mr Foe' (131). She vows that there is much more to her life story than what she is willing to reveal in writing: 'I choose not to tell it because to no one, not even to you, do I owe proof that I am a substantial being with a substantial history in the world' (131). Like David Lurie, Susan recognises that the freedom to speak, to tell and to authorise her life story, is predicated on the freedom to refrain from speaking. This is because the control over one's own elective silence is a pre-emptive measure against those who threaten to foist their story on the other.

It appears that Friday's means by which to safeguard himself from such harmful ascriptions are limited. Michael Bérubé proposes that 'Friday's story [. . .] is not properly story at all [. . .] Friday is not even capable of attempting narrative self-representation, and is therefore assigned the role of puzzle or hole' (*F* 152). Friday's story risks being subsumed under the narratives of those that dominate the discourse. Unable to claim his own narrative, his indomitable silence becomes a palimpsest for others on which to write their own stories. Friday's muteness, as opposed to the elective silence of those who have the capacity to translate the unsaid into power, is therefore metonymic of powerlessness par excellence. But this surmise should not be accepted at face value. A diagnostic reading of Friday's silence – in both textual and medical terms – yields more questions than answers. The early drafts of the novel show that in his earlier iterations, Friday, much like Defoe's counterpart, is articulate in his unspecified mother tongue. There is, however, a caveat. 'But though he has learned in his three years ~~on~~ with Crusoe to understand perfectly his master's commands,' complains Susan, 'he has barely learned more words ~~than~~ to speak than <u>Yes</u> and <u>No</u>.'[6] This detail, however, is soon to undergo necessary alterations due to Coetzee's reluctance to write another postcolonial moral tale with an oppressed colonial subject at its centre. As Coetzee writes in his 1982–5 unpublished notebook: 'Be careful not to turn Friday into the white man's stereotype: opaque, threatening, belonging to a world of darkness, magic' (HRC 33.6, 11-1-1985). For Coetzee this novelistic territory has already been well traversed and its creative currency exhausted. From these sentiments emerges the idea, which is developed in version 3 and later versions of the early drafts, that Friday's tongue has been cut out. As Coetzee further writes in a marginal note of one of the novel's early drafts:

> Friday is at the center of this story; but I am incapable of conceiving for him any role in this story. How much interest do I really have in Friday? By robbing him of his tongue (and hinting that it is Cruso, not I, who cut it out) I deny him a chance to speak for himself: because I cannot imagine how anything that Friday might say would have a place in my text. Defoe's text is full of Friday's Yes; now it is impossible to fantasize that Yes; all the ways in which Friday can say No are not only stereotyped [. . .] but so destructive (murder, rape, bloodthirsty tyranny). (HRC 10.2, 1-12-1983)

Recognising his own complicity in depriving Friday of his voice, Coetzee conceives muteness as a necessary counternarrative to reductionist cultural depictions of the subaltern. According to Attwell, Friday's mutism offers a middle way between two forms of representational reductionism: Friday as Defoe's yes-man or a colonial dissident typical of a postcolonial novel (2015, 157). Located between the extremes of the consensual 'Yes' and the declinatory 'No', his mutism serves to unsettle colonial relations of power.

As Gabriel Rockhill reminds us, '[t]he privileged spectators within the representative framework are men and women of action, and more specifically those who act through speech' (2011, 12). Those figures, such as orators or generals, are trained to perform their oratorical skills as a means to impose a form of authority on others, which can be obtained by way of uttering directive illocutionary acts such as commanding or instructing. Since the mute Friday eludes ascriptions to either end of the power dynamics necessitated by speech acts (he is neither one that commands nor one that responds to the command), his mutism is meant to not only counter simplistic (post)colonial binarisms but also to undo the phonocentric protocols of the literary text. This includes a turn towards interrogating the possibilities of the mute speech of the written word and the questioning of the author's command over the text. As regards the latter, Bill Ashcroft proposes that '[t]he weight of Coetzee's novels comes [. . .] from the novelist's exhausting need to relinquish authority' (2011, 141). Along similar lines, Attwell states that Friday is a conduit via which the author seeks to 'confront his own limitations' (2015, 154).

Although both in the passage quoted above and in his interview with Attwell, Coetzee confirms rather unequivocally that 'Friday is mute' (*DP* 248), his notebooks reveal a more nuanced reading of Friday's status. In his early 1983 notes on the novel, Coetzee thinks of having Friday mutilated but tells himself to 'leave in abeyance the question of whether this is true' (HRC 33.6, 12-8-1983). Two years later Coetzee refines this idea by leaving the ambiguity around Friday's mutilation to be resolved by the text rather than, as earlier on, his intention: 'Has she ever looked in Friday's mouth? Perhaps the story of the missing tongue was made by Cruso and it suits Friday to maintain it. A vow of silence?' (HRC 33.6, 30-9-1985). The scene that registers this ambiguity, in which Cruso invites Susan to see for herself that Friday has no tongue, shows interesting alterations from early drafts of the novel to its published version:

> For answer Crusoe motioned Friday closer and motioned to him to open his mouth. ~~Friday gaped~~ Friday opened his mouth. 'Look,' said Crusoe to me: 'look in there.' But I could see nothing save a black hole and some very white teeth. '<u>La-la-la,</u>' said Crusoe – 'Go on, Friday, say <u>la-la-la</u>.' '<u>Ha-ha-ha</u>' said Friday from the back of his throat. 'Do you see now?' said Crusoe to me. – 'He has no tongue.' And gripping Friday by his woolly hair he pushed his face forward and held his jaw open. 'Say <u>la-la-la</u>,' he said. '<u>Ha-ha-ha</u>' gasped Friday. 'Take him away.' I said to Crusoe. Crusoe released the black man. 'They cut out his tongue,' he said to me. 'That is why he ~~cannot~~ can no longer utter the words of his heart.' (HRC 10.1, 19-8-1983)

> Cruso motioned Friday nearer. 'Open your mouth,' he told him, and opened his own. Friday opened his mouth. 'Look,' said Cruso. I looked, but saw nothing in the dark save the glint of teeth white as ivory. 'La-la-la,' said Cruso, and motioned to Friday to repeat. 'Ha-ha-ha,' said Friday from the back of his throat. 'He has no tongue,' said Cruso. Gripping Friday by the hair, he brought his face close to mine. 'Do you see?' he said. 'It is too dark,' said I. 'La-la-la,' said Cruso. 'Ha-ha-ha,' said Friday. I drew away, and Cruso released Friday's hair. 'He has no tongue,' he said. 'That is why he does not speak. They cut out his tongue.' (*F* 22–3)

While in both versions Susan claims not to have seen anything but Friday's open mouth and teeth after Crusoe's/Cruso's first attempt to show her Friday's stump of tongue, it is only in the later and published versions that Susan claims it is too dark to see after the second attempt, thus confirming her original assertion. In the early drafts, on the other hand, this line is missing, which implies she may or may not have seen the missing tongue the second time. What Coetzee achieves in the later and published versions of the novel, therefore, is to reinforce the possibility that 'the story of the missing tongue was made by Cruso' (HRC 33.6, 30-9-1985).

Some critics are in favour of this interpretation. In his reading of this scene, Lewis MacLeod concludes that there is no solid textual evidence that Friday has no tongue and the fact that the reader chooses to see him as tongueless is merely a demonstration of how 'discursive supposition becomes incontrovertible fact' (2006, 7). The process that MacLeod refers to operates both on the narrative and hermeneutic level: both Susan and the reader fall into the trap of taking Friday's tonguelessness, and therefore mutism too, at face value. Having missed her opportunity to look into Friday's mouth, Susan (and it seems readers by extension) no longer enquires into *whether* Friday is mute, but *who* has mutilated him. But doubts continue to haunt her. When Friday performs his trance-like dance, attired only in the robe belonging to Mr Foe, Susan discovers that Friday may have been castrated: 'What had been hidden from me was revealed' (*F* 119). This is the point in which the ambiguity around Friday's castration complements the previous supposition about his mutism. As Coetzee's private papers and drafts of *Foe* demonstrate, Friday's physical state undergoes gradual alterations from the earliest drafts to the published novel. While, in the earliest versions, Friday is shown as both capable of speech and sexually active,[7] his tongue is later cut out, but he is not castrated.[8] Another variation on this theme is that Friday is mute and his penis is mutilated but not excised.[9] Finally, in the late drafts as in the published version, he is assumed by Susan to be both mute and castrated. In a private note Coetzee has Susan contemplate Friday's physical impairments: 'she says to herself: he has no tongue, very likely they castrated him too' (HRC 33.6, 10-9-1983). These alterations appear to demonstrate that, by finally turning Friday into an ambiguous figure, Coetzee tests Susan's capacity to suspend her cultural biases. As the question of Friday's oral or genital mutilation remains undecided in the text, Susan's (and possibly the reader's) hints at these possibilities may rise from her inability to question the normative stereotypes that reduce Friday to a stereotypical other of the phono-phallogocentric discourse of power. Unable or unwilling to claim the command of the *logos* (both speech through mutism and writing through intellectual disability[10]) and *phallus* (through castration), Friday is unfit to satisfy the basic prerequisite of western logic: to claim and exercise male power through language.

However, the comment that Susan makes after her discovery turns into an auto-irony of her investigative pursuits: 'I saw and believed I had seen, though afterwards I remembered Thomas, who also saw, but could not be brought to believe till he had put his hand in the wound' (*F* 119–20). This biblical reference does not confine itself to Susan's own uncertainties (what tangible proof is there that Friday is truly mute and castrated?) but extends to the reader's hermeneutic exploits too. Although Friday's muteness may cause 'aesthetic nervousness', understood as the defamiliarising effects that a character with disabilities has on the reader in the process of reading, his muteness also offers a form of closure (Quayson 2007, 19). When Friday is identified as disabled, he ceases to be unknowable. The defamiliarising effects of disability which challenge normative assumptions become thus re-accommodated to offset the nervousness they produce. Therefore, the ambiguity that symbolically ties in with incompleteness (associated with disability) must be resolved through narrative closure. The unexamined 'discursive suppositions' that MacLeod refers to – the unchallenged, though haunting, assumption on the part of Susan and the reader that Friday is mute – stems from the logic of narrative prosthesis that is predicated on the containment of disability within the familiar protocols of representation and interpretation. The biblical hand-in-the-wound allegory also serves to expose a certain hermeneutic fallacy of the reader: a disabled character in a literary text is often there to be looked at, probed, interpreted. Such simplistic modes of interpretation turn the character into her own disability, thereby depriving her of complexity that might otherwise evince itself outside reductive identity-based ascriptions. Unable to push herself to look, touch and therefore to substantiate her conjectures, Susan seems to respect Friday's singular ontological status. But there is a flipside to this acknowledgement. Susan falls victim to her own unexamined biases, on the strength of which she feels authorised to claim the position of power over Friday by endeavouring to teach him to express himself – 'to educate him out of darkness and silence' – and thus to speak, through chiro/pictographic modes of articulation (*F* 60). In doing so, she exercises the power of the archetypal coloniser who is on the mission to civilise the barbaric other. Although Susan is capable of seeing through her own biases – 'There are times when benevolence deserts me and I use words only as the shortest way to subject him to my will' (ibid.) – she appears unable to act against them.

Maria Lopez puts forward a milder reading of Friday's muteness than MacLeod does. She states that there is no way of asserting whether Friday has his tongue cut out, because 'the text, through a dialectic of blindness and vision', fails to furnish the reader with the definitive answer (2011, 197). She further claims that the affirmative suppositions of the readers derive from common misreadings of the text's ambiguities: '*Foe* constantly obliges us, interpreters, to question the authoritarian assumptions upon which our critical categories are built and to recognise our own deafness and blindness' (ibid., 202). Ultimately, the novel is a commentary on the failure of the reader to think beyond his or her normative hermeneutic practices. In recognising that the 'muteness' of Friday is often a function of the 'deafness and blindness' of the reader, Lopez points at the complex interdependence of various forms of disability symbolisation.

Along the same lines, '[t]he idea central to European modernity', avers Ashcroft, 'is that to speak and thus to understand, is to see. Silence is therefore threatening to the civilizing mission because it is the equivalent of darkness' (2011, 152). As we already know, Susan admits that her efforts to teach Friday to write serve 'to educate him out of darkness and silence'. If sight is culturally coded to connote light and reason (as in *seeing* as *understanding*) and voice is synonymous with articulation and truth (as in the word of God), blindness and muteness represent darkness and silence (which are associated with the lack of understanding and agency, or intellectual disability). As the metaphors of sensory functions translate into those of intellectual ability, they serve the purposes of asserting reason as the measure of normativity. The reductive dialectic doubling of these metaphors is due to a symbolic hierarchisation of sensory abilities that is ingrained in the structure of the logos. If, after Ashcroft, speech and sight are the major implements of reason – which in its turn is an instrument of western civilisation – what about their paradigmatic counterparts extended on the continuum of articulation and reasoning? With sight as the ultimate epitome of reason, other components of the sensorium, such as audition, olfaction and somatosensation, are subsumed under the regimes of vision – just as writing (as the secondary form of orality) and silence (or muteness) come second to speech. It is therefore tactical that Coetzee uses these culturally underprivileged abilities and instruments as sites of subversion. Ashcroft, echoing Lévi-Strauss, is right that '[t]he absence of writing would mean the impossibility of empire' (2011, 149). But this is not because writing has superseded speech from the dominant position of power, but rather that it is an instrument of asserting the power of speech. Much like a silenced slave who reinforces the power of the master by affirming his superiority, writing is a silent instrument of speech and language which sustains the power of logos. The opposites of speech (silence and writing) and sight (blindness and unreason), like a mutinous slave towards his master, have the capacity to subvert dominant power structures. But while writing inscribes itself on the same paradigmatic continuum as speech (writing is subordinate to speech, but is part of the paradigm of logos), muteness and blindness act as paradigmatic opposites to their privileged counterparts: of speech, sight and reason. Writing is therefore a positive implement of speech or reason, and muteness or silence is a negative ontological opposite thereof: muteness, unlike writing, is not a medium via which the prevailing power asserts itself, but rather a site to which power puts itself in opposition to claim its superiority.

Coetzee, however, implicitly asks an important question: what does it mean for the other who suffers various forms of debilitation at the hands of normative power to be unable to access, or be at the mercy of, the instruments of power? Writing is, for Coetzee, a double-edged sword of privilege and oppression. The characters of *Foe* demonstrate various ways of comprehending writing and its functions. Cruso seems a champion of the most debased form of phonocentrism. Not only does he refuse to write at all, but when, in his incredibly rare moments, he speaks to Friday, he uses single-word commands to subject Friday to his will. Susan is unable or unwilling to summon up her writing powers,[11] but recognises the power of writing, its ability to record, preserve and archive memories which otherwise might risk being consigned to oblivion. Mr Foe's position, in turn, is strongly grammatological:

> Speech is but a means through which the word may be uttered, it is not the word itself. Friday has no speech, but he has fingers, and those fingers shall be his means. Even if he had no fingers, even if the slavers had lopped them all off, he can hold a stick of charcoal between his toes, or between his teeth, like the beggars on the Strand. The waterskater, that is an insect and dumb, traces the name of God on the surfaces of ponds, or so the Arabians say. None is so deprived that he cannot write. (F 143–4)

If Foe may not be innocent of practising oppressive or manipulative forms of writing,[12] his definition of writing appears to be nuanced. For him, speech is not a direct conduit of thought, and writing itself need not be answerable to the chiro- or typographic technologies of the word. He thereby affirms the agency of Friday's body (language) to convey his own story. Along these lines, is Friday's act of throwing petals of flowers upon the surface of water, which is a source of Susan's fascination on the island, a form of body writing that they must be alert to if they are to comprehend his story? Is this to mean that the author-figure drops a hint to the character (and reader) that the possibility of diminishing the limiting effects of silence is not in the linear modes of storytelling produced by speech but in the formal qualities of writing? It is possible that in so doing Coetzee attempts to invite ethics through form – form as a kind of subversive muteness that offsets normative discourses. Importantly also, it is not muteness (as a disability) but silence itself, the end result of being silenced, that has these limiting effects. Writing as a form of evocative muteness, or mute speech, has the ability to reverse the oppressive tactics of the author-figure that reduce the marginalised characters to silence. Muteness itself does not deprive Friday of expression; his cryptic mute forms of self-articulation, as suggested by Ashcroft, may be 'the most damaging "writing back" performed by any post-colonial text' (2011, 155–6).

Conclusions: Endings

Let us return to one of the most pressing questions asked throughout this chapter: to what extent is it possible to accept that Friday is mute if there is hardly any textual evidence to confirm this supposition? The ambiguity itself seems to be much in sync with the ending of the novel, or strictly two endings, which is indicative of the open-endedness of any interpretive efforts to settle the burning questions around Friday's silence. It seems that the ambiguity around Friday's muteness or else elective silence is secondary to the question of who claims the authority to decide whether Friday is mute or wilfully silent. This links with the uncertainty around who the two first-person narrators of the fourth section of the novel are (or is it the same person at different times?) and why they provide contradictory accounts of what seems to be the same scene. Either way, they prove to be more searching than Susan Barton in their attempts to understand Friday's silence: narrator 1 – 'I raise a hand to his face. His teeth part. I press closer, and with an ear to his mouth lie waiting' (*F* 154); narrator 2 – 'I pass a fingernail across his teeth, trying to find a way in' (157). Although they bring Susan's pursuit to the logical conclusion through the tactile inspection of Friday's mouth, they provide no answers to our question. This may be because the question that the novel addresses has nothing to do with Friday's ability, but rather with the ontological status of the body that either cannot or is unwilling to speak. The novel is thus 'a place where bodies are their own signs' (157). It seems that the only way the reader can make terms with the enigma of his silence is by reading, by decoding the mute speech of the body that says nothing. And yet, the ontology of its own textual presence is paradoxically productive of releasing the limitless forces of expressivity, the unbound possibilities of meaning, which includes the possibility of it meaning nothing; that it only is there.

If Friday is not mute or otherwise disabled, his silence may represent an indifference to history, progress, power and so on, or else a resistance to authority. If he is mute, his disability means nothing but itself. It is not a metaphor, and again, if it is read as such, it is because of the reader's impulse to break the hermeneutical impasse of Friday's silence. Ultimately, thus, *Foe* is a story about the inability of the reader to override the familiar hermeneutic habits and prejudices shaped by their cultural assumptions. It is a novel about the failure of the reader to come to terms with that which does not meet the familiar linguistic and interpretive protocols. The moment the nameless narrator is overcome with the stream flowing from Friday's mouth upon his or her face, the question is not what it all means but on whose authority she or he has put the ear and hand to Friday's mouth in the first place. The narrator is the envoy of the reader or writer delegated to plunge into the text to feel, if seeing has failed, the mute/mutilated body of Friday in order to overcome the aesthetic nervousness on our behalf. After all, what is the difference between Cruso's violent inspection and the nameless narrator's unsolicited interrogation of Friday's unspeaking mouth? But the narrator emerges from this encounter none the wiser; the only thing that we learn from the ending is that Friday has a body, one extended between the forces of expressivity of the mute speech and the resistance of its mute embodiment to familiar modes of interpretation. Rather than reproducing simplistic dialogic relations, typical of the phonocentric rules of exchange, between able-bodied and disabled characters, Coetzee refuses to provide guidelines via which to interrogate the silence of an unspeaking character. Instead, he creates a space in which the locutionary force of silence, predicated on the inability or reluctance of the author to provide familiar narrative frameworks of interpretation, has the capacity to undercut his own authority over the text. Or perhaps the ambiguity around the novel's cryptic silences is best summarised by one of Coetzee's later fictional avatars of Robinson Crusoe in 'He and His Man': 'It seemed to him, [Robin Crusoe], coming from his island, where until Friday arrived he lived a silent life, that there was too much speech in the world' (*HHM* 54).

Notes

1. According to Foucault, the speaker claims and asserts power over the interlocutor by usurping and dominating the position of the grammatical subject (Foucault 2010).
2. However, it remains unclear how the medical officer intends to have K read or hear the letter he has composed. If indeed this text is intended as a letter to be dispatched to the recipient or whether this is merely a kind of epistolary internal monologue of the narrator.
3. The likely fate of any interview is that it is a kind of usurped exchange, 'and exchange with a complete stranger, yet a stranger permitted by the conventions of the genre to cross the boundaries of what is proper in conversation between strangers' (*DP* 64–5). As good as his word, Coetzee has proven committed to the practice of written exchange which eludes the power dynamics typical of the interviewer–interviewee relation, as he sees it. The fruit of this commitment has been, apart from the mentioned collected essays and interviews *Doubling the Point* edited by Attwell, the published series of letters between Coetzee and Paul Auster, *Here and Now* (2013), which was initiated by Coetzee, and the joint book publication of Coetzee and Arabella Kurtz, *The Good Story: The Exchanges on Truth, Fiction and Psychotherapy* (2015) – with the 'exchanges' of the subtitle being the operative word bespeaking Coetzee's fondness for the idea of unconstrained exchange of opinions and dislike of appropriating such practices for political purposes.
4. In a curious moment in *Diary of a Bad Year*, when asked by Anya why he would not write a novel in place of the essay of opinions he is currently working on, J. C. responds: 'A novel. No. I don't have the endurance anymore. To write a novel you have to be like Atlas, holding up a whole world on your shoulders and supporting it there for months and years while its affairs work themselves out' (*DBY* 54). Of course, one should not believe this to be Coetzee's authorial confession. After all, both Coetzee's early and late fictions rest on his ability to stage ethical and philosophical questions by pushing the limits of fiction and form. But this self-diagnosis has some currency too. The Australian period of Coetzee's fictional output is replete with works in which fictional construction appears to come second to the ideas it delivers (*Elizabeth Costello, Diary of a Bad Year, The Childhood of Jesus, The Schooldays of Jesus*). Also, the prolific bulk of Coetzee's non-fictional works of the late period could also substantiate the hypothesis about Coetzee's turn from fictional concerns to ideas.

5. See version 3 of the novel's early drafts in HRC 10.1.
6. See version 2 of early drafts of *Foe* in HRC 10.1.
7. In version 2 of the novel's first drafts, Susan witnesses Friday's ritual of masturbation in front of an idol figurine. In version 3, Friday is seen masturbating by the shore (see HRC 33.6, 10.1). Furthermore, while in the published version Friday is not sexually attracted to Susan, in the earlier drafts he makes sexual advances to her: 'Friday wished to possess me [. . .] He tried to touch me; I forbade him; that was enough' (HRC 10.1, 23-6-1983).
8. Coetzee's note reads: 'S does not sleep with F; the climax comes when she puts her tongue in his mouth and feels the stub of tongue' (HRC 33.6, 25-8-1983).
9. In a note dated 13 March 1985 Coetzee writes: 'When she sees Friday's penis, she is stunned: it is scarred/decorated/mutilated. In some sense it makes up for the tongue' (HRC 33.6).
10. Susan concludes that Friday is intellectually disabled: 'Is Friday an imbecile incapable of speech? I asked. Is that what you mean to tell me? (For I repeat, I found Friday in all matters a dull fellow)' (*F* 22).
11. '[W]hat little I know of book-writing tells me its charm will quite vanish when it is set down baldly in print. A liveliness is lost in the writing down which must be supplied by art, and I have no art' (*F* 40).
12. Does he use the girl who poses as Susan's daughter as an actress who is to inspire his own story? Will he eventually write the story of Susan Barton or will he write her into his own story? These and other textual silences must remain unresolved.

Chapter 5

Impossible Modalities, Ailing Selves: Illness, Metaphor and Selfhood in *Age of Iron*

In *Summertime*, Coetzee's third fictionalised memoir, John Coetzee's cousin Margot relates an episode from her cousin's childhood days in which John pulls out a locust's leg to watch its slow and painful end. When asked by Margot whether he has any recollection of this moment, John, now in his thirties, responds, humbled and humiliated: 'I remember it every day of my life' [. . .] 'Every day I ask the poor thing's forgiveness. I was just a child, I say to it, just an ignorant child who did not know better' (*ST* 96). At the heart of this episode lies an imbrication of the themes of violence, a suffering body, guilt and critical self-reflection or self-abnegation that permeate most of Coetzee's works in various combinations. Coetzee's ethical considerations are rarely unmediated by the exigencies of embodied experience. The John Coetzee that emerges from the violent encounter with the insect is no Kantian deontologist structuring his morality around universal imperatives, but a subjective thinker who has learned his lessons in morality from one-to-one confrontations with the other in pain.

This chapter attempts to chart the formation of a narrative self whose experience of the ailing body translates into ethical encounters with others. The novel that typifies the overlapping strands of introspection, ethics and embodiment is Coetzee's *Age of Iron*. Symptomatic of Coetzee's works, ethical concerns are heavily contingent on textual operations. Mrs Curren's grappling with cancer operates as a metaphor for her subjective experience (her self-abnegation), ethics (sickness as a retribution for sins of the past) and as a historical diagnosis (South Africa as a site of moral decomposition of the body politic). Although illness metaphors permeate the narrative, they are complicated by the constructions of narratorial subjectivity and ethical responses which elude allegorical interpretations.[1] Tested in equal measure by the competing pressures of bodily experience and a historical sense of guilt, further inflected by the encounter with the incomprehensible other, a portrait emerges of a self incapable of constituting itself in familiar ethical structures – a conflicted self subjected to the constraints and paradoxes of embodied existence. I read *Age of Iron* in tandem with Søren Kierkegaard's concepts of despair and sickness unto death to account for the ethical implications of the representations of the ailing body in Coetzee's fiction.[2]

Cancer and Metaphor

Disability scholars are suspicious of metaphors. Many consider these rhetorical devices detrimental to the cultural representations of disability and illness, and thus to be avoided completely. Even those who make a case for the affirmative use of illness and disability metaphors tread their figurative grounds carefully, mindful that metaphors are elusive. Where there is a metaphor, there is also a risk of appropriating, simplifying or denigrating the experience of illness or disability. Charged with received meanings, metaphors are often carriers of cultural biases, which, if left unexamined, may serve to reinforce hegemonic narratives of normalcy that are hostile to fostering nuanced views of disability and illness in cultural discourses. One of the earliest and most vocal opponents of referring to illness as a metaphor is Susan Sontag, who states in no uncertain terms that 'illness is *not* a metaphor' and that 'the most truthful way of regarding illness [. . .] is [. . .] resistant to metaphoric thinking' (1978, 3). Along similar lines, Penson et al. conclude that metaphor is a 'two-edged sword', because, 'while metaphors are fundamental to individual and collective expression, they are also capable of creating negative forces, such as confusion, stereotype, and stigma, within society' (Penson et al. 2004, 712). On the other hand, Clare Barker, although aware of the problematic nature of metaphors, takes the view that metaphors can do justice to the complexities of embodiment in nurturing 'empathetic connections between characters, communities and readers' (2011, 20).

Illness is a pervasive theme in *Age of Iron*, and metaphor is part of Coetzee's figurative arsenal deployed to convey it. The novel relates the story of Mrs Curren, a retired classics professor, who is having to face the prospect of her impending death from cancer. Her struggle with terminal illness is further complicated by two other events: the ongoing atrocities and injustices of the apartheid regime raging in South Africa, and an unsolicited visit from a vagrant stranger, Vercueil. At this juncture, the vocabularies of cancer and illness are employed to depict the narrator's deteriorating health, the dehumanising politics of South Africa and the ethical encounter with the unknowable other alike (Silvani 2012, 97). *Age of Iron* does not mark Coetzee's very first foray into fictionalising cancer, but it is the first novel in which Coetzee brings this theme to fruition. In a discarded sketch of 'Burning the Books', an unfinished second novel about censorship, Coetzee was planning to make cancer a part of the protagonist's life: 'In the bath he discovers a tumor. It grows and grows' (HRC 33.3, 31-5-1974). But it is not until he begins to write his sixth novel that he finds his way into exploring the consciousness of a person in illness through Elizabeth Curren.

As Coetzee proposes in his private papers, cancer not only serves to typify abject forms of human experience but also defines life itself. If life is a process involving a temporal functional activity followed by gradual decline and eventual cessation of biological functions, it could be argued that 'we all have cancer. In all of us the body is consuming itself' (HRC 33.6, 19-10-1988). In *Age of Iron*, the epistolary narrator, Mrs Curren, deploys numerous types of illness metaphors which vary depending on whether she refers to her own mental state or whether they are intended as a form of socio-political commentary. One of the most common cancer metaphors in use in medical discourse is the military metaphor, one that is invoked as an 'imperative for patients to have a fighting spirit' (Penson et al. 2004, 708). And yet, there is the obvious flipside to this seemingly uplifting role of militaristic imagery. To what extent is it possible to 'reconcile that instinct to fight, and our words of coaching and encouragement, with expressions of healing and acceptance?' (ibid., 709). This is a pertinent question, and one that, considering that illness metaphors in *Age of Iron* often eschew militaristic connotations, Coetzee might have pondered himself. Mrs Curren admits that '[t]he news' of contracting breast cancer 'was not good, but it was mine, for me, mine only, not to be refused. It was for me to take in my arms and fold to my chest and take home, without headshaking, without tears' (*AI* 4). Rather than describing her relationship with illness as a scene of battle through such typical cancer-related collocations as 'victim', 'to be mobilised to battle', 'fight' or 'struggle against',[3] she adopts vocabulary associated with childcare: counterintuitively, one to be welcomed, embraced and nursed, rather than fought against and annihilated.

Nor is Coetzee's disarmament of illness metaphors intended to foster a wholly positive illness imagery that is often advocated in disability and oncological discourse. Although vocabularies of childcare or pregnancy pervade Mrs Curren's descriptions of her illness, she often refers to her state in more traditional terms. It is an age-old tradition to associate cancer with pregnancy. St Jerome, for instance, is reputed to have referred to a man who was presumably suffering from abdominal cancer as 'pregnant with his own death' (Sontag 1978, 14). In much the same vein, Mrs Curren speaks of her illness in terms of tokophobic metaphors associated with cannibalism, monstrosity and parasitism when she claims '[t]o have fallen pregnant with these growths, these cold, obscene swellings [...] children inside me eating more every day, not growing but bloating, toothed, clawed, forever cold and ravenous' (*AI* 64). These 'children' are '[m]onstrous growths, misbirths' (65). She further laments, 'I have a child inside that I cannot give birth to' (82).

Cancer imagery in *Age of Iron* extends beyond metaphorical expressions to accommodate a broader spectrum of political allegory and autobiographical allusions. Few commentators have failed to notice the allegorical potential of the novel, pointing to the various ways in which cancer typifies the 'ills' as well as moral 'decomposition' of the 'decaying' body politic of South Africa.[4] The period of the novel's composition – 1986–9, as specified by the author under the closing lines of the novel – coincided with the years of the States of Emergency which marked the moments of extreme political turbulence in South Africa. Under emergency laws, the relationship between the people and the state was heated, and the police had the mandate to inflict violence on the rebels for insubordination. In response to these state-induced constraints, the young generation of militants took the hard line, prepared to sacrifice the lives of the youngest supporters of the insurrectionary cause (Attwell 1993, 120). Under such strained political circumstances, the cancer metaphor represents South Africa as a host that is gradually being devoured by the corrupting forces inside its body politic. Examples to this effect abound throughout the novel. South Africa is being consumed under the 'reign of locust' – the 'truth' that Mrs Curren finds sickening (*AI* 29). The new generation of South Africans, with 'contagions and infections in their blood' (5), contract the shameful heritage of apartheid like an infectious disease. Curren goes as far as to ironically, if desperately, deliteralise her health status: 'I have cancer of the heart' (155), thus attributing the root of her sickness to the hereditary disgrace of her generation: 'I have cancer from the accumulation of shame I have endured in my life' (145). Similarly, the protagonist of the early drafts of *Age of Iron* describes the politics of South Africa as 'a provocation to which his body [...] responded with its retchings of despair. I am dying at a distance, he thought; they are killing me with their rays; this is how one gets cancer' (HRC 14.1, 8-7-1987). If politics is contagious, it is not only the mind that gets infected by its corrupting agency, but the body too. Somatic metaphors also populate the published version of the novel: South Africa is now a 'barren' (*AI* 25), 'dry' land (196); the land of desolation, mindless violence – '[a] country prodigal of blood' (63). Mrs Curren likens her estrangement from this land to the condition of a man who has been 'castrated in maturity' (121). It is also telling that, in the initial stages of the novel's progress, Coetzee intended to 'base her', the future Elizabeth Curren, 'on Nadine Gordimer', one of the seminal anti-apartheid South African writers, who 'has cancer' (see HRC 33.6, 23-10-1988). In this way, from the book's earliest sketches, Coetzee seems to have intended to strengthen the tie between the representation of illness and its political connotations.

The early drafts of the novel, in which the narrator looks after his paralysed mother in her dying days, demonstrate another iteration of the conceptual metaphor of South African politics as illness. Here, the son presents an unsympathetic view of his mother's generation. While Elizabeth Curren is an unwilling host of the cancer in the literal and figurative sense of the word, as she vehemently contests oppressive state politics, her prototype, the narrator's mother from the drafts, is shown as a product of her generation of 'not farmers but predators' and the discriminatory politics it stands for (HRC 14.1, 19-9-1987). He is a voice of the angry young generation accusing the elders of cynically benefitting from the system of oppression and bestowing on their heirs the shameful legacy of social discrimination and economic decline: 'you and your white generation will sink into your last sleep with no more anguish than ~~you sank~~ on any other night', 'leaving only ~~an~~ the echo of your laughter hanging in the air' (ibid.). But the death of the old does not entail the demise of the bigoted mindset they represent. What is dying is the country consumed by the parasite of bigotry and violence. It could be therefore argued that the alteration announced in Coetzee's notebook that gave birth to Elizabeth Curren as we know her – 'Paralysis no good. Give her cancer' (HRC 33.6, 11-9-1987) – lends itself as a way to explore the parasitical agency of apartheid, thus provoking a question about the extent to which cancer serves as a political metaphor or allegory in the novel.

Although the novel's allegorical potentialities strongly inform its political preoccupations, Chielozona Eze proposes that *Age of Iron* does not yield as easily to allegorical interpretations as Coetzee's earlier novels. Eze traces the moment of Coetzee's departure from allegory to a specific historical event within the years of the States of Emergency, namely apartheid's genocide on children of 1986, which 'must have alerted Coetzee to the limits of allegory in the face of human suffering' (2011, 20). Ethics and history do cross-fertilise in the novel, but the political context overlapping with the timeframe of the novel's composition, which both invites and complicates any allegorical reading of it, fails to fully inform the rationale behind the choice of the cancer theme and metaphors. Cancer haunts the 1986–9 years for not only political but also deeply personal reasons associated with the author's life. This is the moment in which illness moves from political allegory towards autobiography.

Embodied Selves

'Everyone seems to see bleakness and despair in my books,' remarks Coetzee in an interview, 'I don't read them that way. I see myself as writing comic books, books about ordinary people trying to live ordinary, dull, happy lives while the world is falling to pieces around them' (Kannemeyer 2012, 428). Coetzee has remained true to this principle of characterisation in many of his further novels since the publication of this interview in 1983. Many characters of Coetzee's works experience various forms of physical debilitation, illness, or death of those close to them. Among notable examples are K's mother's death, Mrs Curren's cancer, Dostoevsky's stepson's death and Paul Rayment's physical impairment. Some of these characters or their experiences may have been inspired by actual events in Coetzee's life. The dedication note of *Age of Iron* reads as follows:

V.H.MC. (1904–1985)
Z.C. (1912–1988)
N.G.C. (1966–1989)

The novel is dedicated to Coetzee's mother Vera, father Zacharias and son Nicolas, respectively, all of whom died within the four years that roughly overlapped with the period of drafting and completion of *Age of Iron*. The visual aspect of the dedication, which brings to mind an image of a gravestone inscription, may be taken as a tacit invitation to the reader to consider the novel's fictional events in the light of the author's life experiences. Coetzee's biographer, J. C. Kannemeyer, supports this line of thinking by proposing that, while a dedication might conventionally be little else than the author's expression of respect to the dedicatees, it may also serve as 'an integral part of the text, pointing towards the raw material or motifs to be developed in the text' (2012, 443).

The spectre of illness and its disabling effects, as well as death, were haunting the progress and completion of the novel. Among the events in Coetzee's life that took place around that time were Vera's visual impairment and death after a heart attack, Zacharias's death by larynx cancer, Nicolas's tragic and untimely death from falling off the balcony of his flat as well as Coetzee's ex-wife Phillipa's breast cancer and consequent death two months prior to the novel's publication.[5] Coetzee, on his part, does not seem to have been tested by illnesses or impairments in his life at that time. With his commitment to a healthy and active lifestyle, vegetarian diet, and sports such as running, cycling or cricket, Coetzee enjoyed good health for years to come (Kannemeyer 2012, 423–6). From this it follows that he drew the inspirations for the accounts of illness and disability experience at second hand,[6] presumably from the experience of others, among whom members of his own family figure most prominently, but also from his research into facts about cancer treatment carried out to complete the novel. One of Coetzee's personal letters shows his commitment to the factual veracity of his fictional accounts related to cancer. The archive of Coetzee's private papers at The Harry Ransom Center contains evidence that Coetzee sought information about palliative treatment for cancer from a Cape Town oncologist, Dr Christine Dare – a founder of St Luke's Hospice in 1980 in Cape Town (Gwyther et al. 2016, 49) – but received no reply. That it was part of Coetzee's research for *Age of Iron* is evident from the letter itself, in which Coetzee makes it explicit that he is writing a novel about a woman with cancer, as well as from the heading dated 6 July 1989, when *Age of Iron* was still in progress (HRC 17.2). Coetzee's research materials for *Age of Iron* also show that he read a number of medical textbooks relating to cancer treatment, care of the cancer patient and clinical oncology when completing the novel (ibid.).

What Coetzee's private notebooks and drafts of *Age of Iron* also reveal is the extent to which the text pivots on Coetzee's relationship with his mother. In a note preceding the drafting of the early versions of the novel Coetzee makes a telling resolution that will set the tone for his novel's plot: 'Write the story of my life for Gisela, and the story of my mother's life'[7] (HRC 33.6, 24-11-1986). Implied in this line is a complex triangulation of family relationships – namely those of the mother, son and daughter – which Coetzee will laboriously seek to disentangle in the dozen or so drafts of the novel. Written one year after Vera Coetzee's death, one of Coetzee's earliest notes for the novel mentions an idea for a story about an 'Old woman, blind (nearly blind)', titled 'Night', which calls to mind Coetzee's mother's visual impairment (HRC 33.6, 23-6-1986). Later plot sketches and novel drafts highlight the relationship between the son and the mother. In one of these developments, the focaliser attends to his paralysed and invalid mother addressing her in the second person.[8] Themes of the care of the dying and taking stock of one's past prevail in these versions. When the progress of the early drafts is drawing to a halt, Coetzee announces a turning point in his notebooks: 'give her back her voice' (HRC 33.6, 11-9-1987). Coetzee inverts the narrative perspective, rendering the dying mother the first-person narrator and author of the confessional letter addressed to her child, but this time the son is replaced by a daughter.[9] The formal, characterological and narrative transformations of the plot demonstrate Coetzee's gradual distancing from his life experiences, which now put on more and more elaborate formal and narrative guises.[10] The rationale behind these changes seems to be that, to understand the suffering other, Coetzee has to make an imaginative leap, which doubles up as a narrational leap. To grant a narrative voice to a son ruminating over his dying mother would be tantamount to doing a testimonial injustice to a suffering self. To complete the leap Coetzee must therefore resort to refracting the narrative position to have the mother reclaim her voice.

But how is one to give voice to a self that is different from one's self? And what does the experience of pain, illness or disability do to one's subjective sense of selfhood? Kathlyn Conway persuasively argues that, when the body is damaged or dysfunctional, the self refuses to recognise the body as part of itself (2013). Consequently, the body 'disowned' by the self turns into a form of 'disembodied self' (ibid.). The experience of physical dysfunctions, which may unsettle the balance between the body and self, can cause 'proprioception', denoting a sense in which the self recognises the body as its property. If the stability of the body entails the stability of the self, it follows that a sense of incompleteness of the body may translate into one's sense of inability to recognise one's self as complete and unchanging. The damaged body is therefore disowned by the self to safeguard itself from disintegration. But Conway argues that this sense of disavowal of the defective body by the self is not inherent in human experience of illness or disability. It is rather a function of objectification of impairment in cultural and medical discourses. Bullied into the state of renunciation of its own body, the ailing self must confront not as much the 'presence' of the disease as the 'absence' of the self's sense of itself.

Mrs Curren expresses similar anxieties about a separation of her sense of self from the ailing body:

> What do I care for this body that has betrayed me? I look at my hand and see only a tool, a hook, a thing for gripping other things. And these legs, these clumsy, ugly stilts: why should I have to carry them with me everywhere? Why should I take them to bed with me night after night and pack them in under the sheets, and pack the arms in too, higher up near the face, and lie there sleepless amid the clutter? The abdomen too, with its dead gurglings, and the heart beating, beating: why? What have they to do with me? (*AI* 12–13)

Objectification of illness is common in medical and cultural discourses. The patient often internalises the stereotype about illness as abject and the body as a host liable for housing this undesirable entity. In an act of metonymic displacement, the body is symbolically transmuted into the parasite it hosts, thus becoming foreign to itself. In this act of the self's disavowal of the body, the body becomes a separate object rather than an extension of the self. Disowned, the body can at best perform prosthetic and mechanical functions necessary for its maintenance: the hands are tools, the legs perform motoric functions, and the abdomen is a receptacle for digesting food. But the renunciation of the body goes a step further, culminating in a sense of wilful detachment, when Mrs Curren complains about the sad burden of having to carry this abject body with her, as if the self was better off without the cumbersome weight of the body.

But the self's renunciation of its body is an act of apostasy for which the rejected repays in kind: 'But now, during these spasms of coughing, I cannot keep any distance from myself. There is no mind, there is no body, there is just I, a creature thrashing about, struggling for air, drowning. Terror, and the ignominy of terror!' (*AI* 132). The body is quick to reclaim its rightful place by reminding the self that its embodiment is the only existence it has access to; that its metaphysical claims yield to the irreducible gravity of embodied being. Fragments like these exemplify the profundity of Coetzee's embodied understanding. They are powerful reminders that no considerations of selfhood are legitimate except when mediated by the experience of the body and its demands. The suffering body in Coetzee's fiction is an ultimate testing ground of the self's claims for self-assertion, and

Mrs Curren is a character whose experience of illness is a platform for revising her own notions of selfhood in ethical encounters with others. To consider the complexities of the self in sickness, let us now turn to the thinker who committed his life and works to traversing an interlinking of subjectivity and suffering, Søren Kierkegaard.

The Sickness unto Death

'Slight, thin, and weak, denied in almost every respect the physical basis for being reckoned as a whole person, comparable with others', writes Kierkegaard about himself, 'melancholic, sick at heart, in many ways profoundly and internally devastated' (Garff 2005, 431). As can be gathered from his self-description, Kierkegaard was a man of frail physical health – or at least posed as one in his writings – easily given to bouts of depression and melancholy. Yet his view of disability can hardly be viewed as uplifting. His avowal seems to reinforce ableist language relegating disability to the state of incompleteness and deficiency. Nor is he wholly self-deprecating; he goes on: 'I was granted one thing: brilliant intelligence, presumably so that I would not be completely defenseless' (ibid.). The imbalance between his physical weakness and intellectual acuity, the compensatory advantage of reflective intellect over the disabling limitations of the frail body, may have been a factor in fortifying Kierkegaard's both existentialist and theological thinking, which could be sketchily summarised thus: because human embodied existence is paradoxical, a human being is a self in despair; therefore, in order to rise above the paradox, one must become oneself, or choose to become oneself in God, and in so doing overcome the despairing self. In my view, if Kierkegaard is of interest to Disability Studies at all, it is not for his views on disability, although some scholars, such as Christopher Brittain (2012) and Kevin McCabe (2017), have made convincing cases for the valuable contribution of Kierkegaard's thought to disability theory. Kierkegaard is an intriguing case in point here because his complex philosophy of existence, theological thought, ethical theory and ferociously prolific writing productivity appear to develop from this tension between the consciousness of bodily limitations and performative possibilities of the willing self – a tension that helps spell out paradoxes of embodied understanding in Coetzee's *Age of Iron*.

In his *The Sickness unto Death*, Kierkegaard argues that 'the sickness unto death' is 'despair', which, understood in theological terms, marks an inability of the self to embrace itself and by doing so to reach fulfilment in God (2004, 48). Both literal and spiritual readings of this biblical phrase seem uncontroversial: sickness must be a sort of recessive process leading the body or self to its demise. And yet both Coetzee and Kierkegaard complicate such an unequivocal reading of sickness. If, for Kierkegaard, the self can only achieve a fulfilment by becoming itself, rather than by being itself a priori, it follows that the self's overcoming of despair and becoming itself can only be fulfilled through its progression through sickness (Hannay 2004, 5). In *Age of Iron*, illness partakes in the process of a repudiation of the self in a double sense. Conway suggests that sickness causes a separation of the body and self as a result of which the self no longer recognises itself in sickness, or does not acknowledge its own body in sickness, thus developing its sense of self away from the damaged body (2013). Mrs Curren's desperate, half-ironic proclamations that she suffers from a 'cancer of the heart' (*AI* 155), or 'cancer from the accumulation of shame' (145) strongly suggest that the ailing body is not as much a source of self-abnegation as a figure of self-devouring guilt. Mrs Curren's resignation and despair are most forcefully conveyed in her desire to take her own life by self-immolation ('An old woman sets herself on fire, for instance. Why? Because she has been driven mad? Because she is in despair?' [114]), which is precipitated by the anguish of witnessing the mindless violence of the apartheid regime in South Africa, rather than her own illness: 'What set me off was not my own condition, my sickness, but something quite different. [. . .] I saw the body [. . .] I was shaken' (123–4). But her tenacity to end her despair by resorting to suicide is conflicted. When the opportunity presents itself, as Vercueil a little too keenly offers himself to aid her in her suicide attempt, she keeps him at bay, expressing her double thoughts thus:

> I meant to go through with it: is that the truth? Yes. No. Yes-no. There is such a word, but it has never been allowed into the dictionaries. Yes-no: every woman knows what it means as it defeats every man. 'Are you going to do it?' asked Vercueil, his man-eyes gleaming. 'Yes-no,' I should have answered. (*AI* 116)

The desire to end her life cannot reach its logical conclusion: she is determined and yet unable to get it done. Although such indecision may strike one as familiar – the will to live often ultimately trumps the death drive – the paradoxical grammar of Mrs Curren's hesitation is indicative of Kierkegaard's notion of the 'impotent self-consumption' of the despairing self. For Kierkegaard:

> despair is exactly a consumption of the self, but an impotent self-consumption not capable of doing what it wants. But what it wants is to consume itself, which it cannot do, and this impotence is a new form of self-consumption, but in which despair is once again incapable of doing what it wants, to consume itself. (2004, 48)

This marks a double bind of self that wills to annihilate itself but is unable to annihilate itself completely, and this inability of the self to bring the process of self-annihilation to an end is in itself self-annihilating, yet incompletely so, and so the cycle turns ad infinitum. Mrs Curren suggests that this refusal of the self to annihilate itself develops outside of will and reason:

> But how hard it is to kill oneself! One clings so tight to life! It seems to me that something other than the will must come into play at the last instant, something foreign, something thoughtless, to sweep you over the brink. You have to become someone other than yourself. But who? (*AI* 119)

If the self *wills* to annihilate itself, what is it that stops it in its tracks? Kierkegaard proposes that the self 'want[s] in despair to be oneself' and yet 'the self which, in his despair, he wants to be is a self he is not' (2004, 50). Caught up in the irresolvable yearning to annihilate itself by virtue of being incapable of being oneself, and yet being unable to do so because the self continues to want to be the self that it cannot be, means that the will to annihilate the self will always be offset by the very force that attempts to preserve it. For that reason, it is not the will that needs to be overcome, but the self that reins it in. So, Mrs Curren suggests a way out. To override the unruly self by the guiding will, the self must become other than itself.

To Kierkegaard, this act of repudiation of self, 'wanting in despair to be someone else, wanting a new self', is the lowest form of despair (2004, 83). To overcome despair the self must acknowledge itself as itself, to choose itself, as opposed to claim a new self. What complicates this self-acknowledgement of self is that it is not a given entity, but rather it comes into existence in the 'process of becoming': 'In so far, then, as the self does not become itself, it is not itself; but not to be oneself is exactly despair' (ibid., 60). The existence of self in Kierkegaard's terms is paradoxical. If to be oneself one must become oneself, it is to imply that in the act of becoming itself the self is perpetually in flux, or, in other words, always other to its former selves developing in this formative process of becoming. And yet the self that desires to be other than itself is in despair, which precludes its possibility to become itself. Therefore, the becoming of self is predicated on the principle it excludes. But Kierkegaard does not yield to self-contradiction easily. He acknowledges that becoming oneself involves a degree of self-annihilation, which he reinforces by claiming that 'self-annihilation [is] the essential form of the God-relationship' (2009, 386). Kierkegaard's solution is ultimately theological. The self can assume its fullest form only in God. As the 'synthesis of infinitude and finitude', the self's goal is to relate to itself in becoming itself, 'which can only be done in relationship to God' (2004, 59). But coming into this idealised self demands a form of annihilation of a self within oneself.

As a figurative expression, 'self-annihilation' therefore puts itself in line with illness or parasitic metaphors, such as 'sickness unto death' or 'self-consumption', to refer to the process of a becoming of self fulfilled through a complex interlacing of self-affirmation and self-abnegation. Coincidentally, it is not only Kierkegaard who employs the term 'sickness unto death' to theorise his notions of subjectivity. Also, Mrs Curren avails herself of some iterations of this phrase in moments of anxiety, despair or when she pushes her body to the extremes: 'I am sick to death of feeding you!' (*AI* 12); 'Don't you understand? I wanted to say: I am tired, tired unto death' (183). Similar vocabularies are deployed to stage Mrs Curren's internal strife. Alongside expressions connoting illness and parasitism, there are metaphors of emptiness and burning as manifestations of Mrs Curren's self-destructive sense of historical guilt. Bheki's death at the hands of the police is followed by Mrs Curren's inspection of a family photograph coupled with her fantasy of having been replaced by a doll in infancy: 'a child was taken and a doll left in its place to be nursed and reared, and that doll is what I call I' (109). Photographs are heterotopic places which, through an act of imaginative disjunction of the real from its representation, reinforce our belief that the real inhabits the here and now of the continuous present vis-à-vis the non-presence, and thus non-existence, of the image that merely imitates the real. But Mrs Curren is suspicious; for her, it is the obverse that holds true: 'I, in my doll's way, know that it [the camera] will see what the eye cannot: that I am not there?' (111). If the picture is a locus of absence it is because the original, the living self, is not there in the first place; that the self has never been the self it has proclaimed itself to be; that the self's idea of itself has always been an act of usurpation.

Mrs Curren's sense of emptiness, demarcating a self with a false history, chimes in with her identity as a white South African woman, a member of the race of invaders who claim for themselves what is not rightfully theirs. The awareness of her illicit, parasitic existence in South Africa drives her to despair, a process of an emptying of self, which figures as an iteration of Kierkegaard's concept of self-consumption:

> Grief past weeping. I am hollow, I am a shell. To each of us fate sends the right disease. Mine a disease that eats me out from inside. Were I to be opened up they would find me hollow as a doll, a doll with a crab sitting inside licking its lips, dazed by the flood of light. (*AI* 112)

The feeling of despair at the irrevocability of the self-consuming political forces is a marker of Mrs Curren's internalisation of collective historical guilt as she claims as her own the condition of self-consuming body politic. The allusions to dryness ('past weeping'), similes of emptiness ('shell', 'doll') and illness imagery (manifested in the etymological doubling of cancer as both 'crab' and 'tumour') act in tandem as hallmarks of a recessive subjectivity incapable of reaffirming itself amid the chaos of violence. Curren's prototype of the novel's early sketches prefigures some of these self-cancelling sentiments: 'She has a burning sense, not that she has not lived, but that the course of history is in the process of rendering the life she has lived [...] invalid and of no worth' (HRC, 33.7, 15-5-1987). Occupying the position of privilege in apartheid South Africa, Curren does not need to suffer the debilitating effects of political oppression. What suffers, however, is not the body, but the self that refuses to claim the position consigned to it by history. Is it possible, therefore, asks Coetzee in his notebooks, that 'this inability to conceive of a possible future, this inability to project the self, is a reflection of a white experience of South African reality?' (HRC 33.7, 6-5-1987). For Coetzee, the failure of his character to validate her ontological status in the confusion of historical reality must end in an impasse that stalls any possibility to claim or imagine a future for herself; future foreclosed by both cancer of the body and 'cancer of the heart', a marker of her complicity with crimes committed by the social class she is associated with (*AI* 155).

Further metaphors of consumption and annihilation abound in the novel to complete the image of the self's inability to relate to itself, and the crucible of self-consumption is a trial by fire:

> The country smolders [...] I too am burning! (*AI* 39)

> To walk into the fire, [...] to burn and be gone, to be rid of, to leave, the world clean. [...] This country too: time for fire, time for an end [...] (65)

Do you want to know why I set my mind on burning myself? Because I thought I would burn well. / Whereas these people will not burn [. . .] (124)

'Fire' is used in the novel in a threefold way: as an eschatological metaphor signifying an end, exhaustion and destruction; as a sickness metaphor – a byword for the narrator's devastating tumour; and as a narrative figure denoting an act of political defiance. It is curious that the fire metaphors often travel in tandem as a form of political commentary and as the narrator's self-diagnosis, as if Mrs Curren is unable to employ the metaphor to admonish the devastations of apartheid politics without simultaneously applying the metaphor to herself, and the other way around. Flames of destruction spread fast, and Mrs Curren's body – and presumably her self by association – is by her own account a highly inflammable material. For her, fire is a form of cleansing. And yet, what kind of cleansing is it exactly? What good does it do to respond to fire with fire? Mrs Curren has her doubts about it: 'If dying in bed over weeks and months, in a purgatory of pain and shame, will not save my soul, why should I be saved by dying in two minutes in a pillar of flames? Will the lies stop because a sick old woman kills herself?' (*AI* 141). If her despair is a form of self-consumption, it is an impotent self-consumption: impotent in the ability to restore the severed ethico-political balance in the country as a conduit for reconstructing her damaged self. And the unconscious may prove her correct in these suspicions. In her dream Mrs Curren sees herself putting on a public show of self-immolation, burning with a blue flame (178). While traditionally a red flame brings to mind infernal imagery of desolation, blue flame, as its opposite, is a celestial flame connoting highest forms of spiritual intensity: not a flame of self-consumption, but perpetual spiritual nourishment. The dream appears to buttress Mrs Curren's reluctance to yield to easy forms of moral prescriptivism. An act of self-immolation is not a manifestation of the reflective self, but rather a convention on which the despairing self hinges when confronted with the inability to relate to itself. In Kierkegaard's terms, the public show of self-immolation marks a regressive impulse of the self that wants to adopt a new self, which precludes a possibility of the self to become truly itself. Mrs Curren realises that this act of retributive self-consumption must fail to restore ethical equilibrium in South Africa.

Inextricably linked with the rhetoric of self-destruction of *Age of Iron* is the novel's contemplation of the juncture between despair and madness. In a sketch prefiguring the early drafts of the novel, Coetzee questions himself about the premise of the novel he is writing: 'And does this book not become a mere cover to allow me to do a little ranting and raving?' (HRC 33.7, 5-5-1987). The raving and ranting Coetzee indulges himself in is meted out to the oppressive politics of the state. Some ironic manifestations of these sentiments are palpable when Curren's early counterpart covers her television set in excrement in an act of disgust with politics, but has it cleaned before long, 'frightened that she may be going crazy' (ibid.). Briefly contemplating such tentative titles for what would eventually become *Age of Iron* as 'Madness' (HRC 33.6, 15-3-1988) or 'The Reign of Madness' (17-3-1988), Coetzee continues to develop the concepts of madness as a manifestation of the annihilation of self: 'Whom the gods wish to destroy they first strike mad' (13-3-1988). Obsessed with the possibility of her mental derangement, she harbours the wish 'not to die mad. Because the mad are undying' (HRC 33.6, 15-3-1988). Echoing these anxieties, Elizabeth Curren later reveals to Vercueil that she longs to 'redeem myself' but is 'full of confusion, about how to do it. That, if you like, is the craziness that has got into me. [. . .] You know this country. There is madness in the air here' (*AI* 117). Like cancer, madness is a symptom of the self's failure to reclaim its agency and autonomy in the social climate permeated by the politics of violence. It is a reminder that certain forms of collectivism are fundamentally hostile to human ethical relations. Drawing on Kierkegaard's ethical concepts, the closing section of this chapter will focus on the ways in which Coetzee's programme for the reconstruction of ethical relations eludes traditional forms of moral prescriptivism.

Body, Ethics and Impossible Modalities

'Above all do not forget your duty to love yourself; do not permit the fact [. . .] that you are superfluous in the obtuse eyes of a busy world, busy with wasting life and losing itself,' writes Kierkegaard in a letter to his cousin with hemiplegia, Hans Peter Kierkegaard (Kierkegaard 1978, 83, as quoted in Brittain 2012, 301). Echoing this guidance is another letter to his sister-in-law, Sophie Henriette, bedridden for most of her life as a result of a severe illness and depression: 'I consider it *my duty to say to every sufferer* with whom I come into contact: *See to it that you love yourself*' (Kierkegaard 1978, 425–7, as quoted in Brittain 2012, 303). Kierkegaard's vivid interest in his own impairments, as well as those of his kin, links with his preoccupation with subjectivity and ethics. For Kierkegaard, the life of becoming is inextricable from suffering, and an essential part of a nurturing of inwardness. It is in experiencing or contemplating 'useless suffering' that *'one comes to know unmistakably what the highest is'* (Kierkegaard 1948, 160, as quoted in Brittain 2012, 312; original italics). In the above letters he not only implores his relatives to endure the effects of illness and disability, but also upbraids 'Christendom' for sustaining ableist discourses calculated to relegate the 'sufferers' to the position of social others.[11] Kierkegaard considers such forms of marginalisation of disability as a failure of the collective imagination to recognise one's individual purpose beyond common norms. Failing to meet these norms, an individual may be considered as incomplete. Since individuality needs no such standards, as an individual is a standard only to herself, Kierkegaard's emphasis on subjectivity counteracts the hegemonic notions of normalcy and in doing so foreshadows some premises of the social constructionist model of disability.

Although suffering is central to the foundations of Christian ethics, Christian societies are 'primarily concerned with providing comfort to the comfortable and lauding the most productive and busiest members of society with praise' (McCabe 2017, 46). But the modern injunctions of positivity are for Kierkegaard fundamentally irreconcilable with the commitment to nurturing inwardness in God. For him to love God directly is an impossibility (for how is one, who is a body, to love and be loved by an immaterial, thus bodily nonexistent, entity?), and thus every such attempt must be mediated by suffering or unhappiness to outweigh the paradox. As he writes in '*Faedrelandet* Articles': '[W]hat does it mean to love God? It is to be willing to become, humanly speaking, unhappy in this life, yet blessedly expecting an eternal happiness – a person cannot love God, who is spirit, in another way' (2000, 437). To love God, the immaterial spirit, by an embodied subjectivity is absurd, and therefore the self, in order to restore the severed link with God, must speak in its own language that cannot supersede the burden of embodiment and suffering attendant upon it: 'only inwardness in sufferings gains the eternal' (Kierkegaard 1993, 235).[12]

Kierkegaard's concerns are overtly theological, with self-interrogation as a conduit for reconstructing the bond with God, but inextricable in his thought is the centrality of existence and suffering for a development of human subjectivity. Being essentially anti-Cartesian, like Coetzee, Kierkegaard gives ontological priority to subjective suffering and ethics over thinking. It is only when the thought enters into a relation with the ethical that the self is exempted from the necessity to demonstrate its existence. Subjectivity is not grounded in one's capacity to think oneself as a self, or else to think oneself into existence, but to become oneself through ethics: 'The actual subjectivity is not the knowing subjectivity [...]; it is the ethically existing subjectivity' (Kierkegaard 2009, 265). According to John J. Davenport:

> Kierkegaard's writings depict human selves as essentially *dialogical* or inextricably related to others – first of all to God, but through God to human neighbours. The capacity for love, which is the shared mark of personhood in all of us and the origin of each individual will is oriented outwards [...] though it also enables reflexively proper self-love. (2013, 232)

The dialogical dynamic between self-love and a concern for the other results in a singular ethics of inwardness directed outwards, or 'ethical subjectivity', developing independent of objective or collective ethical ideals (Kierkegaard 2009, 252). Inwardness is a response to the objective ethical standards that cannot be applied to a singular subjectivity by virtue of their being objective. As a synthesis of the *finite* and *infinite*, the self can aspire to be the latter by becoming an individual self rather than subscribing to superficial externalities as templates for a universal ethical conduct.

Age of Iron in its own way dramatises a failure of universal ethics, which in the novel is, however, culturally specific rather than universal. Mrs Curren's ethical choices arise from her refusal to conform to public morality which she sees as mangled by the violent tactics of oppressive apartheid politics. And this failure of the community to develop a working ethical code to live by results from an absence of what Coetzee chooses to call 'transcendental imperative' (*DP* 340), which, as elucidated by Attwell, does not denote a specific 'ethical code, but whether the society in question has a culturally embedded code of ethics to which most of its members have shared access' (1998, 176). Attwell goes on to argue that the novel's 'ethical consciousness' arises from the necessity to fill the void left by an absence of an ethical baseline for collective conduct (ibid., 176). To further illuminate this juncture, Derek Attridge considers *Age of Iron* as a demonstration of competing pressures of the ethical and political, with neither being unmixed (2004). Although a line between these terms can be drawn tentatively, with ethics marking a commitment to a singular other and the political representing prescriptive programmes pertaining to a shared moral code, Attridge points to the mutual imbrication of these notions. He argues that:

> in the political arena we often think we are engaging with the concrete when we are imposing generalities, and that the generalities on which philosophical ethics has usually rested are evasions of the genuinely ethical, which can only be thought through in relation to the singular and the contingent. (2004, 105)

It does not follow from this that politics and ethics are fundamentally antithetical to each other, or that the former necessarily displaces or usurps the latter. The point here is about society's or an individual's failure to recognise politics when it is disguised as ethics. Kierkegaard's fierce diatribes against Christendom (as opposed to Christianity) are driven by the same awareness of usurpation of singular ethics by the forms of objective prescriptivism. Christendom, preoccupied by a forced institutionalisation of ethical doctrines, has long disengaged itself from Christianity, understood as the singular ethics of love to the other.

Mrs Curren's stance on the ethical-political plane is conflicted. Although it is partly the case that she confuses the ethical with the political in her attempt to restore an ethical balance in South Africa, what merits attention is her endeavour to recuperate the ethical notions of care, trust and truth in relation to the other. But Mrs Curren's attempt to reclaim ethics refuses to yield to the logic of language. She realises that in order to be 'saved', she must accomplish the impossible: 'I must love, first of all, the unlovable' (*AI* 136). But when she is given this opportunity, meditating on her duty to the boy who has narrowly escaped a police attack, she confesses: 'He is part of my salvation. I must love him. But I do not love him. Nor do I want to love him enough to love him despite myself' (136). Salvation of self is here predicated on the love of the other. Nor should the love to the other diminish if the other's relation to the giver of love is parasitical, which marks a love which 'we have no alternative to feel toward those to whom we give ourselves to devour or discard' (9). The parasites plaguing Mrs Curren's body figuratively metastasise onto the ethical relations with the other. Vercueil has often been read as a parasitic visitor, and Mrs Curren a victimised host that is taken hostage by the ungrateful guest who outstays his welcome. However, I agree with Maria Lopez that one should be suspicious of such easy ascriptions. She states that the novel offers:

> the possibility of moving beyond parasitism and contestation. If Vercueil is the emissary of the punitive plague that is going to

> devastate South Africa, he could also be seen as a friendly visitor and benign guest, and the relationship between him and Mrs Curren may be one that suspends, interrupts or departs from the host/parasite relationship [...] Vercueil's menacing potential, however, does not recede completely; there is only one certainty in the novel: one *must* love, one *must* give. (Lopez 2011, 157)

Although the parasitic agency of Vercueil is signalled throughout the text, Lopez argues that this question comes second to the ethical considerations that the novel provokes. The injunctions to love, trust and open oneself to the other serve to offset these metaphorical allusions.

But it is precisely the possibility that Vercueil is ultimately a parasitical figure that opens up a venue for a staging of ethics in the novel. This is because the ethical potential of the novel does not rest on prearranged codes of ethical behaviour, but on the overcoming of the limits of conventional ethics. A person with a disability himself (his hand is permanently impaired after a sea accident[13]), alcoholic, homeless, foul-smelling, Vercueil is up to a point a stock character: a social pariah and thus a perfect object of Christian pity and charity. A response to such an other, albeit ethical, fails to progress beyond the typical middle-class condescension that merely serves to appease the guilty conscience of the privileged and reinforce their misguided sense of superiority over the object of charity. But Vercueil is a demanding other. He will not return the favour of being helped. If he does, the favour is dubious: '"If you want me to help you, I'll help you," he said. He leaned over and took me by the throat, his thumbs resting lightly on my larynx, the three bad fingers bunched under my ear' (*AI* 184–5). By repaying love with death, Vercueil transgresses the terms of the ethical contract. If Vercueil offers a 'help' to end the meaningless existence of the body plagued by a tumour, his remedial ministry is symbolically performed with hands, reminiscent of the healing hands of the biblical miracle healers. But these maimed hands are made to bring death, not life; they are calculated to consume rather than bring nourishment: 'Yet he is as far from being a nurse, a *nourrice*, a nourisher as I can imagine' (196). Such a guest demands an ethics that operates beyond a transactional exchange between self and the other. By choosing Vercueil, by throwing herself at his mercy for care, by choosing to depend on the undependable, she chooses an impasse that refuses to yield to language. The only language left is one that defies the logic of linguistic modality: '[b]ecause I cannot trust Vercueil I must trust him [...] I love him because I do not love him' (130, 131). Curren's paradoxical necessity resonates with Kierkegaard's famous formulation: 'If I can grasp God objectively, then I do not have faith, but just because I cannot do this, I must have faith' (Kierkegaard 2009, 172). Both Curren and Kierkegaard assume that a response to the other or the Other requires taking a leap of faith or trust to overcome the anxiety created by the subjective uncertainty of ethical choices and objective uncertainty of reason. But the impossible modality of Curren's pronouncements also echoes Samuel Beckett's sustained exploration of human alienation through verbal and grammatical impasse, as registered in the closing words of *The Unnameable*: 'you must go on, I can't go on, I'll go on' (2015, 476).

But the final ambiguity appears in the closing lines of the novel, where Vercueil lends his helping hand anew: 'He took me in his arms and held me with mighty force, so that the breath went out of me in a rush. From that embrace there was no warmth to be had' (*AI* 198). To save herself, become herself, she must first offer herself up to the other, to leave herself at his mercy. A possible consequence of the trust in the other is that the self may not return to itself from the parasitic embrace of the other. The notion of the deadly embrace of the other was nurtured from the earliest conceptions of the novel. In his private papers, Coetzee considers an ending in which Elizabeth's earlier counterpart wakes up from a dream in which she has overdosed pills. Unsure whether she has dreamed it or not, she embraces the sleeping Pratt (Vercueil's prototype) and can feel that he returns the embrace but is shocked to find him bony and reeking of death: 'Holding his back she feels more bones than there ought to be. "Am I still writing this? No"' (HRC 33.6, 29-4-1989). Although Gothic imagery permeates the abandoned ending, Coetzee holds in abeyance the prospect of the protagonist's death. Similarly, symptomatic of Coetzeean linguistic ambiguity, the phrase 'the breath went out of me' from the ending of the published novel may imply Mrs Curren's death, which would entail a suspension of the epistolary convention predicated on the survival of the speaking narrator, or else her momentary loss of breath. After all, the cold embrace may as well be a metaphor of the loss of faith in the untrustworthy other, thus hinting at the impossibility of breaking the cycle of the Kierkegaardian impotent self-consumption. However, what ultimately emerges from the ambiguity of these endings is that ethics, like the laws of fiction, does not trade in certainties; that a welcoming of the other involves risks that neither preclude nor warrant the survival of self after the encounter with the other. The self that responds to the impossibility of ethics and complexity of subjective embodied existence can only speak in the language of impossible modality: it must, because it cannot; it cannot, therefore it must; will it? 'Yes-no.'

Notes

1. See Eze (2011) for further information concerning the limits of allegory in referring to human suffering in *Age of Iron*.
2. There is a strong tendency among Coetzee scholars to read Coetzee's fictional staging of ethics towards the other in his works, and in *Age of Iron* in particular, along the lines of the ethical philosophy of Jacques Derrida and Emmanuel Levinas. Notable works in this terrain would be Attridge (2004), Clarkson (2013) or Jordaan (2005), among others. Although such considerations would no doubt enrich my reading of *Age of Iron*, I feel that this territory has been sufficiently charted by the above scholars. But most importantly, in my view, Kierkegaard's philosophy is better suited to illuminating what I see as a central concern of the novel, that is an inextricability of ethics from the notions of a suffering self – preoccupations that are most pronounced in Kierkegaard's writing.
3. See *Oxford Collocations Dictionary* for collocations of the word 'cancer'.
4. For further reference, see Attwell 1993, 120; Eze 2011, 20; Kannemeyer 2012, 445; Lopez 2011, 148; Nashef 2009, 122, 124–5; Probyn 1998, 215; Silvani 2012, 94–5; Worthington 2011, 116, 120, among others.
5. See Kannemeyer 2012, 440–3, 455–6.
6. With the notable exception of a biking accident that left Coetzee hospitalised. This experience too was soon translated into a creative effort and inspired the plotline of *Slow Man* (see Attwell 2015, 242).
7. Born 1968, Gisela is Coetzee's daughter.
8. See HRC 14.1, drafts 0-2.
9. This shift in narrative perspective persists in later drafts. See HRC 14.2, drafts 3–5.
10. See Attwell 2015, chap. 9, for a detailed elaboration of autobiographical influences in *Age of Iron*. Studying early drafts of *Age of Iron*, Attwell points to the ways in which Coetzee's relationship with his mother inspires the plot and characterization of the novel. Attwell charts the structural and narrative transformations the novel underwent from its early versions in which these autobiographical parallels were much more pronounced than in the published version.
11. 'If Christianity has any special affinity for anyone [...] then it is for those who suffer, the poor, the sick, the lepers, the mentally ill, and similar people, sinners, criminals. And look at what Christendom has done to them, see how they have been removed from life so as not to

create a disturbance [...] Christ did not divide people in this manner; it was precisely for these people that he was pastor [...] What has happened to Christianity in Christendom is like what happens when you give something to a sick child – and then a couple of stronger children come along and grab it' (Kierkegaard, as quoted in Brittain 2012, 316–17).
12. In *Doubling the Point* Coetzee spells out this Kierkegaardian paradox of existence thus: 'The presence of God is an absence [...] because, if we follow Kierkegaard, God remains always "incognito" and the relation of the eternal of God to the existent of man a "paradox" that never loses its irrationality' (*DP* 74).
13. Like Mrs Curren's cancer, Vercueil's impaired hand may also have been inspired by Coetzee's own life experience. *Boyhood*, Coetzee's fictional memoir, includes an episode in which John, still a child, persuades his brother to put his hand into the mealie-grinding machine which results in the amputation of half of his finger (119). Similarly, Vercueil's hand 'was caught in the pulley and crushed' (*AI* 186).

Chapter 6

Disability Ethics and Gothic Form in *The Master of Petersburg*

In Coetzee's 1994 novel, *The Master of Petersburg*, optical metaphors and expressions abound. While some of them relate to vision loss, others connote spectral appearance. The conflation of these specular and spectral metaphors raise questions about the extent to which Coetzee's novel engages with disability representation and Gothic themes. Although *The Master of Petersburg* fails to satisfy the requirements of a traditional Gothic novel, nor does it deal explicitly with representations of sensory disabilities, Gothic and disability signifiers inform the ethical and formal constructions of the novel. As I will show in the opening part of this chapter, there are risks incurred in reading literary representations of disability or illness in terms of Gothic metaphors. And yet it is also worth considering some more productive ways in which both fields either cross-fertilise or overlap. Following this thread, in the chapter to follow I probe the extent to which this imbrication of disability and illness vocabularies and Gothic form in *The Master of Petersburg* informs the ethical commitments of Coetzee's fiction. I begin with observations on intersections between disability and Gothic forms of representation. I further examine the ways in which the interlacing of Gothic and illness tropes (such as haunting and falling) partakes in the novel's refusal to acknowledge the limits between fictional representation and factual accuracy. The next part studies ethical implications of Coetzee's staging of optical and spectral metaphors alongside Derrida's concepts of spectre and hauntology. In the closing section of this chapter, discussing the problem of the instrumentalisation of disability in *The Master of Petersburg* and, by comparison, *Disgrace*, I propose that Coetzee's fiction's resistance to affirmative modes of disability representation challenges normative notions of morality.

Gothic Disability

The Gothic and disability share a history which dates back to the advent of the European Enlightenment. The Cartesian body–mind dualism led to a radical rethinking of the relationship between the body and mind. However, Georg Wilhelm Hegel offered an important insight about the logic of dualistic reasoning. Rather than coexisting, the opposites in the dialectic relation compete for dominance until one of the opposites overcomes the other one. Thus, the dominant entity 'must proceed to supersede the other independent being in order thereby to become certain of itself as the essential being' (Hegel 1998, 111). Hegel's insights help account for the mechanisms of social exclusion and normalisation that have been prevalent since (and are characteristic of) the Enlightenment. As Michel Foucault observes, man was now defined, in keeping with the privileged ends of social dichotomies, as white, male, heterosexual, upper-class, rational, mentally stable and able-bodied.[1] Individuals or groups that failed to meet the standards of the new model of social normativity were subjected to various forms of marginalisation, subjugation and institutionalisation: ranging from a domestication of women, ownership of colonial subjects, hospitalisation of people with intellectual and physical disabilities, or the incarceration of homosexuals.

The relegation of certain groups to social margins has been assisted by a promotion of cultural narratives that serve to denigrate the authentic experience of the cultural other. This is how 'the non-normative human, excluded from the category of the human, becomes the human Other, as mysterious and unknowable, as inhuman, as any ghost or monster lurking in the darkness' (Anolik 2010, 2). Threatening to question the narratives of normalcy, the other is not allowed to exist as a neutral non-entity; it must be branded as subversive, deviant or monstrous. In other words, the discourse of normalcy depends on Gothic tropes ('mystery', 'darkness', 'ghost', 'monster', 'inhuman') for a legitimation of its superiority. This is what Ruth Anolik refers to as a 'repressive aspect' of the Gothic: one 'figuring human difference as monstrosity' (2010, 2). In its more 'progressive' forms, however, the Gothic responds sympathetically to the humanity of the demonised other. And the latter aspect gestures towards the ways in which Gothic themes participate in undoing, rather than safeguarding, exclusionary discourses of power sanctified by the Enlightenment. In its adherence to reason, order, realism and normativity, the Enlightenment man harbours repressed desires that 'rationality is now powerless to control' (Botting 1996, 8). If these desires come back with a vengeance, they find their vent in the Gothic, with its penchant for excess, passion, the supernatural and deviation. The transgressive agency of Gothic tropes has the capacity to overthrow modern paradigms of normalcy championed since the Enlightenment, particularly in respect of the Gothic's celebration of the non-normative body.

Along with the recognition of non-normative bodies and minds at the dawn of the Enlightenment came a forced institutionalisation of those that had hitherto been pushed to social fringes – a procedure referred to by Foucault as 'The Great Confinement' (2006, 38). Rather than being merely socially marginalised, people with disabilities are now subjected to the corrective practices of state medical institutions: the 'minority body' is now in need of a cure (Barnes 2016, 6). This renders modernity a prosthetic project. Commonly understood as a medical category, disability is negatively branded in cultural discourses and therefore believed to be in need of institutional treatment. This biomedical view of disability is opposed by the social constructionist model which proposes that disability is an effect of social barriers and prejudices rather than an impairment of the body.[2] The early modern shift towards normalisation has reinforced cultural narratives founded on 'epistemic injustice' (Fricker 2010, 1), a term denoting the ways in which the normate appropriates knowledge so as to denigrate the credibility of first-hand accounts of people with disabilities. Similarly, Merri Lisa Johnson and Robert McRuer's term 'cripistemology' opposes normative epistemologies by 'challenging subjects who confidently "know" about "disability" as though it could be a thoroughly comprehended object of knowledge' (2014, 130). Both of these approaches counter the prevailing conception of disability as a state that fundamentally reduces the quality of life of an individual as well as other normative cultural narratives that devalue disability experience.

So understood, both Gothic and Disability Studies emerge as cultural projects aimed at offsetting the normative injunctions of early and late modernity which have legitimated forms of social exclusion and epistemic injustice. And yet, the common stakes of the Gothic and disability extend beyond the parameters of identity politics. Other points of intersection include cultural and literary tropes prevalent in debates about disability and Gothic representation, such as trauma, insanity, deformity, illness, suffering, pain and forced confinement, to list a notable few. But there are some risks involved in conflating the Gothic and illness or disability tropes, and Sara Wasson warns us against such dangers: 'Images of illness as exile, of people rendered ghostly by affliction, and mourning for a pre-illness self, can imply that illness or disability are unnatural interruptions to the story of a "normal" body' (2020, 72). When used to describe disability experience, Gothic metaphors or rhetoric may activate forms of epistemic injustice. An unexamined linking of these framing metaphors sanctions rehabilitative practices endorsed by pre-modern religious concepts – such as that disability is God's way of punishing sinners or their kin – as well as modern biomedical models and cultural stereotypes about disability, thus serving to uphold prejudicial ideas about people with disabilities as demons to be exorcised, mad patients to be cured, or monsters to be tamed. But dismissing all negative associations as objectionable risks oversimplifying figurative potentialities of Gothic rhetoric and, by implication, privileging positive forms of representation and discourse. Wasson usefully reminds us that positivity can be a dangerous injunction which reinforces the negative metaphors that it seeks to displace. 'In the illness and disability narratives that have received the most celebratory critical attention,' she argues, 'negative emotions are either transmuted (for example, into wisdom, growth, serenity) or come to be seen as "generative" (productive of valuable states or modes of being)' (2017). In pointing to the limitations of such restorative narratives, in which illness or disability are sublimated into some higher forms of affirmative experience, Wasson calls for resisting simplistic injunctions of positivity championed by both medical models and cultural discourses of normalcy.

Gothic Fiction and Disability

Gothic fiction has traditionally relied on disability representation to reinforce its effects of terror. Many early Gothic novels tend to perpetuate the normative desire to brand the atypical other as abnormal to reassert the reader's identification with normativity. The physical deformity of Frankenstein's monster in Mary Shelley's *Frankenstein*, the titular villain of Robert Louis Stevenson's *Strange Case of Dr Jekyll and Mr Hyde*, the titular protagonist in Oscar Wilde's *The Picture of Dorian Gray*, the facial disfigurement of Erik in *The Phantom of the Opera* by Gaston Leroux, and the mental disorders of such female characters as Bertha Mason in Charlotte Brontë's *Jane Eyre*, are often meant to inspire the reader's dread in order to reinforce the normative notions of embodiment and intellectual ability as well as serve the non-disabled characters' personal growth. The character's impairment, often intended as a foil to the socially desired notions of normativity, is thus both a marker of the character's physical monstrosity and a symptom of their moral flaw, usually sexual deviance or psychopathy. Mr Rochester's description – which is strongly imbued with Gothic rhetoric and imagery – of his wife as a 'monster' (Brontë 1999, 273) with 'pigmy intellect' and 'giant propensities' (270), and Henry Jekyll's description of the body of Mr Hyde as one on which '[e]vil [...] had left [...] an imprint of deformity and decay' (Stevenson 2003, 58) exemplify this reductive equation of physical deformity or intellectual atypicality with moral depravity.

While reinforcing deleterious cultural narratives about disability, early Gothic novels also offer a less stigmatising account of disability experience 'by construct[ing] a clear relationship between monstrosity and humanity' (Wheatley 2018, 19) – Frankenstein's monster and Erik lend themselves as examples of this trope – or by introducing the elements of 'stigmaphilia', a position that is based on 'finding a commonality with those who suffer from stigma, and in this alternative realm to value the very things that the rest of the world despises' (Warner 1999, 43). Frankenstein's monster's yearning for a female companion 'with whom I can live in the interchange of those sympathies necessary for my being' (Shelley [1818] 2018, 136), shows aspects of his stigmaphilic longing for a person who shares the character's marginalised position: 'It is true, we shall be monsters, cut off from all the world; but on that account we shall be more attached to one another' (ibid., 137). Other classic Gothic fictions present disability as an effect of physical or psychological violence, thus mounting a critique of the hegemonic power liable for committing this violence. The psychological disturbances of Wilkie Collins's Anne Catherick in *A Woman in White* and the unnamed narrator of 'The Yellow Wallpaper' by Charlotte Perkins Gilman are an effect of domestic or institutional captivity they have been involuntary exposed to. Although in these works disability is a source of the narrative's Gothic effects, the real sense of dread does not so much come from the demonisation of mental illness as from the psychological terrors of the characters succumbing to the debilitating force of patriarchal injunctions, an aspect Coetzee explores (albeit in a manner departing from the Gothic form) in *In the Heart of the Country*.[3] Along similar lines, Jean Rhys's rewriting of *Jane Eyre* in her *Wide Sargasso Sea* is an attempt to retrace the history of Bertha's mental breakdown by interrogating the patriarchal and colonial pressures that have precipitated these symptoms.

Contemporary Gothic fiction in many ways perpetuates reductive depictions of characters defined by their disabilities. Some novelists, such as Stephen King in *Misery*, Thomas Harris in *Hannibal*, Joyce Carol Oates in *The Doll-Master and Other Tales of Terror* and Joe Hill in *Horns*, continue to exploit the trope of the physically impaired or neuroatypical villain, thus 'reinforcing a link between disability and criminality or evil' (Cheyne 2019, 31). In Graham Masterton's *Unspeakable* and Dean Koontz's *77 Shadow Street*, on the other hand, the authors position their disabled characters as defenceless victims whose vulnerability renders them either dependent on the able-bodied characters' help, or else, as in the case of Zelda in King's *Pet Sematary*, a trigger of the guilt complex of other characters. Although the Gothic fiction has generally failed to recuperate itself from the reductive patterns of disability representation, it bears mentioning certain ways in which a mediation on the limitations of normative bodily, sensory and intellectual experience can inform Gothic tropes and themes or vice versa. The section to follow introduces Coetzee's *The Master of Petersburg*, a novel that, in my further reading of it, challenges the normative notions of visibility and seeing through a nuanced staging of Gothic imagery.

Haunted (Hi)stories

Set in 1869, *The Master of Petersburg* is a fictionalised account of the life of the writer Fyodor Dostoevsky, who leaves Dresden for St Petersburg to inquire into his stepson Pavel's mysterious death and collect the latter's belongings. As it is revealed that Pavel was affiliated with an underground anarchist-nihilist organisation masterminded by Sergey Nechaev, Dostoevsky's stay in Petersburg is monitored by the local police. While awaiting access to the papers which Pavel has left behind, Dostoevsky is lodged in the flat rented by Pavel prior to his death, which is owned by Anna Sergeyevna Kolenkina, a widow, and Matryona, her eleven-year-old daughter. Dostoevsky's sojourn is interrupted by Nechaev himself, who informs Dostoevsky that Pavel has been assassinated by the police and takes pains to inveigle Dostoevsky into writing a pamphlet about his stepson's murder by the police. Instead, Dostoevsky dictates a pamphlet in which he accuses Nechaev of the murder, soon realising he has been tricked, as such an acrimonious testimony made by an accomplished writer is exactly what Nechaev needs to precipitate a social, anti-establishment upheaval. Surrounded by Pavel's writings, which he has retrieved from the police, Dostoevsky gets down to writing his own provocative account of Pavel's life.

As any reader acquainted with Dostoevsky's life will notice, Coetzee takes considerable liberties with historical facts. His most notable transgression is to have Pavel killed in the novel. The historical Pavel outlived his stepfather, eking out a living as a clerk until his death in 1900. Instead, it was Dostoevsky's own son, Alyosha, who died of epilepsy in 1878 (Kossew 1996, 82). But according to David Attwell this alteration is justified 'because it enables [Coetzee] to focus the events of the novel entirely on the relationship between the stepfather and stepson and on the fictional Dostoevsky's grief' (2015, 189). If *The Master of Petersburg*'s chief preoccupation is to dramatise its protagonist's sense of grief, Pavel's fictional death serves as a platform on which to stage the ethics of mourning, characteristic of Coetzee's novels of ideas. Coetzee scholars and biographers have pointed out that the trope of fatherly grief in the novel is inspired by the tragic death of Coetzee's own son Nicolas at the age of 23. Attwell speculates that an entry from an early draft of the novel in which Dostoevsky is determined to 'write his son into immortality' (HRC 19.1, 3-6-1991) may be an indication that Pavel serves as a fictional avatar for Nicolas Coetzee, which would substantiate the choice of grief as the novel's leitmotif (Attwell 2015, 191).

As well as modifying historical facts, Coetzee complicates intertextual references to Dostoevsky's work in his seventh novel. *The Master of Petersburg* is essentially a 'fictional account of the period in Dostoevsky's life when he was working on *The Devils*' (Leatherbarrow 1999, 158). Although never mentioned in the text explicitly, *The Devils* features some characters that either inspire those from *The Master of Petersburg* (the character of Nechaev refers to a real-life Russian revolutionary, but in Coetzee's novel he is visibly modelled on Pyotr Verkhovensky, a conspirator in *The Devils*) or are borrowed directly (like the mentally and physically disabled Marya Lebyadkina, or Matryosha, who is a character in the chapter 'At Tikhon', censored out of the original version of *The Devils*). Furthermore, the unexpected title of the closing chapter of *The Master of Petersburg*, 'Stavrogin' (unexpected, given that no character in the novel bears that name), is a strong indication that Coetzee models Pavel on Nikolai Stavrogin, the antagonist of *The Devils*. Also, the fact that Stavrogin is also Coetzee's own son's namesake suggests that Coetzee's novel offers a complex imbrication of intertextual and (auto)biographical references.

The novel's tropology is instrumental in informing the fact–fiction binary. Critical here is the meaning of the title of Dostoevsky's novel. The original Russian title, *Bésy*, stands for 'demons' or 'devils', and English translators have rendered the title variously as *The Possessed*, *The Devils* and *The Demons*. Historical Dostoevsky's 'devil' is Stavrogin, a young man 'possessed' by the 'demons' of western revolutionary nihilism that threatens the social and cultural integrity of Russia's future. Coetzee's Dostoevsky, on the other hand, is haunted by the ghosts of his guilty conscience for allowing his son to die prematurely. These are ghosts of the past – ones that, unlike those of the future, cannot be averted. Dealing with such irrevocable entities requires drastic measures. Therefore, Dostoevsky vows 'He would write his son into immortality' even if this entails betraying his son's memory in the process of writing (HRC 19.1, 3-6-1991). Although Pavel is the implied object of haunting in the novel – he is possessed by the demons of the revolutionary zeal that will precipitate his death – he is also, in a sense, the agent of the possession of his father. Coetzee's annotations to an early draft of the novel spell out this dynamic thus: 'D is working all the time on *The Possessed*. Private reference: to him, he is the possessed, and he is possessed by Pavel. In fact, he is getting to write under possession [. . .]' (HRC 19.1, 5-9-1991).

Although Coetzee confounds *The Master of Petersburg*'s easy ascription to Gothic fiction, the novel bears some important hallmarks of the genre. It does not tell a ghost story explicitly, but rather the story of the deferral of the ghost's arrival, of the impossibility of summoning up the ghost of the loved one in grief. If the novel is a tale of terror, it is a tale of the psychological terror of the aggrieved father, and in doing so it taps into the psychoanalytical underpinnings of the contemporary Gothic genre. 'What makes the contemporary Gothic contemporary', suggests Steven Bruhm, 'is that the Freudian machinery is more than a tool for discussing narrative; it is in large part the subject matter of the narrative itself' (2002, 262). In centring on Pavel as a lost object of Dostoevsky's fatherly desires, Coetzee studies the interior dread of the self consumed by the trauma of grief. Dostoevsky's yearning to reconnect with his dead stepson marks a psychological pursuit that is set to unify the fractured subjectivity of the traumatised self. In *The Master of Petersburg*, as in such novels as Cormac McCarthy's *Outer Dark* and Toni Morrison's *Beloved*, psychological horrors materialising in spectral images or hallucinations emanate from a mediation on the parent's sense of guilt for losing their children. As reminded by

Cathy Caruth, 'the survival of trauma is not the fortunate passage beyond a violent event [...] but rather the endless *inherent necessity* of repetition, which ultimately may lead to destruction' (1996, 62–3). Dostoevsky's perverse attempts to defile the memory of his son – through the treacherous retelling of his life or by putting on his white suit (which doubles up as a form of desecration and symbolic possession of the son by the father) – mark an enactment of a self-destructive iteration of the Freudian repetition-compulsion principle. But the possession of the son entails the father's drive for death: 'I am the one who is dead, he thinks; or rather, I died but my death failed to arrive' (*MP* 19). This sentiment is reinforced in Coetzee's early drafts of the novel. Dostoevsky realises that, although he apparently abandons himself to the pursuit of truth of his son's death, in fact, 'it is my own death I am chasing after' (HRC 19.1, 8-5-1991). As a result, 'His heart's desire is to return to those black waters where his son floats and to stay there forever, among the speechless drowned' (HRC 19.1, 22-10-1991).

Dostoevsky's displacement of the psychological subject position through an appropriation of his son also hints at another Freudian schema that is widely in use in contemporary Gothic fiction, in which one's 'craving for power' represented by the tyrannical father causes them to admire and 'identify themselves with him' (Freud 2004, 166). In Joyce Carol Oates's *The Doll-Master and Other Tales of Terror*, for instance, the protagonist of the titular story turns into a collector of the bodies of little girls he has killed after his father's refusal to allow him to keep the doll of his tragically deceased childhood friend. The father's prohibition acts as a catalyst for the boy's transformation into the self-proclaimed doll-master, thus enabling him to usurp the controlling agency of the father after he replaces him in the household. As in Oates's story, Coetzee's use of the 'master' metaphor in the title of his seventh novel hints at the controlling function associated with the father figure. Although Dostoevsky holds himself accountable for failing to protect his stepson from death, he does not take all the blame. God, the ultimate father, who had it in his power to save Pavel from death, refused to interfere: 'He [Pavel] asked God a question – Will you save me? – and God gave him an answer. God said: No. God said: Die' (*MP* 75). Dostoevsky's appropriation of his stepson through writing carries within it the double ambition to assume the life-giving power of the father, which he, as a stepfather to Pavel, could never claim, as well as the life-restoring power of God the Father: 'In the blood of this young man, this version of Pavel, is a sense of triumph. [. . .] He is, in some sense, beyond the human, beyond man. There is nothing he is not capable of' (*MP* 242).

Complementing this picture is the common Gothic theme of the tyrannical father threatening the safety of the family or the psychological well-being of its members.[4] In a certain sense, Coetzee's Dostoevsky represents a destructive paternal force that is not unlike the one epitomised by another fictional struggling writer, Jack Torrance in Stephen King's *The Shining*. Along similar lines, the transformation of the (apparently) benign Pavel into the diabolical Stavrogin, at the hands of Dostoevsky, carries a distant echo of Victor Frankenstein's monstrous creation. Writing in *The Master of Petersburg*, like modern science in Mary Shelley's classic Gothic novel, typifies a foreboding of an uncontainable evil force, the consequences of which lie beyond the creator's control. But while classic Gothic fictions serve as cautionary tales that aim to restore the lost equilibrium caused by the social dangers and fears they warn against, the contemporary Gothic offers no such comfortable sense of narrative closure. This tendency can be attributed to the postmodern subject's lost hope for the possibility of historical progress, which is often dramatised in contemporary Gothic fiction through an impossibility of resolving 'its characters' psychological complications' (Bruhm 2002, 267). Such post-war novels as Shirley Jackson's *The Haunting of Hill House*, Ira Levin's *Rosemary's Baby* or Cormac McCarthy's *Blood Meridian*, which rely on the characters' psychological terrors and anticipatory dread rather than conventionally frightening experiences and events, refuse to restore order to its fictional worlds, and, as will be explained in further sections, the ending of *The Master of Petersburg* follows suit in its foretelling of the arrival of a sinister force.

Finally, the Gothic lends itself as a platform for a recapitulation of socially accepted ethical standards. Fred Botting claims that the Gothic's transgressive quality has the capacity to reposition accepted limits of collective morality. In an attachment to aesthetic excess and violation of social inhibitions Gothic narratives act as cautionary tales 'warning of dangers of social and moral transgression by presenting them in their darkest and most threatening form', thus helping 'reassert the values of society, virtue and propriety' (Botting 1996, 5). In its weaker forms, however, the Gothic's transgressivity occasions a mediation on the unexamined standards of orthodox morality. Coetzee's characters often resort to moral transgression as a way to call into question rather than reaffirm social and ethical norms. In *Master of Petersburg*, the threat of moral decline is heralded by the ambiguities of the act of falling.

The Falling Sickness

The fall is one of the master tropes of *The Master of Petersburg*, so much so that Coetzee initially contemplated giving his novel the title 'Falling' (Attwell 2015, 203). The theme of falling, which calls to mind the biblical Fall of Man, is epitomised by Dostoevsky's epilepsy (which in turn intersects with metaphors of insanity, demonic possession and writing), Pavel's descent into moral nihilism (as implied in Dostoevsky's controversial rewriting of his stepson's life) and Pavel's death from being pushed from the shot tower. Another thread extends to Coetzee's own son's, Nicolas's, death from falling from the balcony of his flat in Johannesburg.[5] By re-enacting Nicolas's death through Pavel's, Coetzee makes an 'empathic leap', via which he possibly 'imagin[es] his own grief as Dostoevsky's' (Attwell 2015, 194). Furthermore, the triangulation of Nicolas Coetzee (Stavrogin's near-namesake), Nikolai Stavrogin (a model for Pavel) and Pavel (his reincarnation as Stavrogin and possibly a fictional model for Nicolas) positions the metaphor of the fall at the problematic crossroads of fictional representation and historical referentiality, inflected by both to varying degrees. In one of further asides in an early draft of the novel, Coetzee reveals that 'Pavel comes to embody' a number of characters, such as 'Pyotr V., Kirillov and Stavrogin (the revolutionary background, the suicide, the crime against the girl)' (HRC 19.1, 4-9-1991). Although Coetzee limits the list to the figures associated with the historical Dostoevsky's novel, elsewhere in the draft he also drops hints about his family situation inspiring the novel's preoccupations: 'My own family – Nicolas, Gisela, myself – so ephemeral, so ghostly' (HRC 19.1, 16-10-1991).

Falling also mingles with representations of illness – a theme inspired by Dostoevsky's life experience. Epilepsy affected the historical Dostoevsky and his family, causing his young son's Alyosha's untimely death – an episode that has its imprint in Coetzee's novel.[6] 'Fortunate for Pavel [. . .] that he did not have to suffer the falling sickness, fortunate he was not born of me!' ponders Dostoevsky, '[t]hen the irony of his words bursts in upon him and he gnashes his teeth' (*MP* 70). Although Coetzee refuses to grant Alyosha a place in his novel by distorting the historical fact, the metaphor of falling helps restore the historical integrity of the novel, while refusing to yield to the pressures of factual accuracy. Sue Kossew suggests that this fragment evokes the real Dostoevsky's sense of guilt for passing onto his son a genetic disorder (1996, 82), an idea which Coetzee, as his notes reveal, chose not to abandon even after he had finally settled on replacing Dostoevsky's son with a stepson:[7]

> Pavel is not his biological son, therefore he should not suffer from epilepsy, but D wonders (a) whether in the process of abstract paternity – and in the process of becoming his father in order to supplant him – he has not picked it up; (b) whether epilepsy is not the appropriate spiritual sickness for the age; in falling to his death, Pavel may be an emblem, pushing the falling sickness as far as it can go. (HRC 19.1, 14-10-1991)

For Dostoevsky, his predicament transcends its biomedical parameters – it is an affliction that gets into its prey insidiously, like a form of haunting. Nor do the political implications of the falling metaphor escape Coetzee. Epilepsy is an allegory of Russia's gradual descent into nihilism which historical Dostoevsky so despised as to write a heated diatribe against it – the novel *The Possessed*.[8]

Furthermore, the falling sickness is also a symptom of Dostoevsky's sense of grief and despair. For Kierkegaard, the torment of despair is one's inability to die: 'despair is veritably a self-consuming, but an impotent self-consuming that cannot do what it wants to do' (1983, 18). Kierkegaard's notion of despair as 'the sickness of the self' that annihilates the self through the self's own inability to annihilate itself completely is evocative of fictional Dostoevsky's complex experience of grief: 'He knows what grief is. This is not grief. This is death, death coming before its time, come not to overwhelm him and devour him but simply to be with him. It is like a dog that has taken up residence with him, a big grey dog, blind and deaf and stupid and immovable' (*MP* 52). Dostoevsky's denial of his stepson's death defers conventional protocols of mourning, resulting in a sense of impasse of the self. Interestingly, to grasp the complexity of this deadlock, Gothic ('grief', 'death', 'devour') and disability ('blind and deaf and stupid and immovable') signifiers underpin the narratorial account of Dostoevsky's coming to terms with the news of Pavel's murder or suicide. Rather than wholly self-consumed, the self inhabited by the disabled dog communicates the epistemological crisis of human reason confronted with the experience of the death of the other. But the phantasmagorical disabled dog is also a figure of haunting: 'When he sleeps, the dog sleeps, when he wakes, the dog wakes; when he leaves the house, the dog shambles behind him' (*MP* 52). Grief materialises as a presence which supplants that which cannot be present but returns in haunting to encumber either reassertion or annihilation of self. The dog is thus a figure of Kierkegaardian 'impotent self-consuming' or 'sickness of the self' in despair.[9]

Like grief, which 'complicates any presumption of the self as autonomous' (Wasson 2010, 158), epileptic fits are markers of Dostoevsky's suspension of self:

> He lets himself out. The corridor is in pitch darkness. Stretching out his arms like a blind man, he [...] begins to descend. On the second-floor landing a wave of terror overtakes him, terror without object [...] Let it come, he thinks in despair; I have done all I can [...] These attacks are the burden he carries with him through the world [...] Why am I accursed? [...] They are not visitations. Far from it: they are nothing – mouthfuls of his life sucked out of him as if by a whirlwind that leaves behind not even a memory of darkness. (*MP* 68–9)

Again, disability and Gothic metaphors underlie the verbal architecture of the novel to mirror the condition of the despairing self. 'Blind', 'terror'-stricken, 'accursed', awaiting the impending fit, Dostoevsky surrenders himself to the coming of 'nothing': nothing that, however, has the ability to 'suck out his life out of him'. Although the narrator asserts that Dostoevsky's attacks 'are not visitations', it is because Dostoevsky expects a 'visitation' to materialise in presence. This is how he yearns to reclaim his son – in a state of active self-presence of the ghost: 'his ghost, entering me' (4). It is only when he accepts that '[i]f he expects his son to speak in the voice of the unexpected, he will never hear him' and consequently 'must answer to what he does not expect' (80) that he comes to grips with the impossible presence of the haunting. At this point epilepsy – that self-consuming 'nothing' – doubles as a metaphor of haunting: the coming of 'nothing' is also the coming of that which does not come, that annuls its coming in its 'nothingness'. And yet the 'nothing' that haunts (as seizure or ghost) refuses to dissolve in negativity, in absolute absence: it has the agency to consume and annul the self and life,[10] rather than itself being annulled. Its existence is predicated on what Derrida calls 'a dislocation in being' which 'come[s] to presence in disjunction' (1994, 31–2). In this sense, both an epileptic fit and haunting depend on this impossible (non)presence, or a coming in and out of presence of self as a dislocated being.

The realisation of an interlacing of epileptic seizure and haunting suddenly dawns on Dostoevsky himself, who:

> must wonder whether *seizure* is any longer the right word, whether the word has not all along been *possession* – whether everything that for the past twenty years has gone under the name of seizure has not

been a mere presentiment of what is now happening, the quaking and dancing of the body a long-drawn-out prelude to a quaking of the soul. (*MP* 213)

What is captivating here is Dostoevsky's effort to find the 'right word' for his experience, as if a verbal label, a marker of reason, were to restore the sense of control lost in epileptic fits. For Dostoevsky this must also be a moment that marks a recovery from the epistemological crisis reinforced by both his disability and obsession with his son's awaited visitation. Along these lines, Derek Attridge proposes that the act of renaming 'seizure' for 'possession' foreshadows Dostoevsky's yet unwritten novel which 'lies ahead in his career as a novelist' – with *The Master of Petersburg* being thus a hypothetical prequel to *The Possessed* (2004, 125). This act also implies that it is only through writing that he can conjure up the spirit of Pavel – writing that surrenders itself to, rather than defies, the gravity of the fall. This is how he 'become[s] a body [. . .] which contains its own falling and its own darkness' (*MP* 234). Symptomatically, his last resort to writing is aided by familiar metaphors intimating Gothic tropes or experience of disability. At this point, writing triangulates with epilepsy (also as falling) and possession as a platform for staging the impossibility of affirmative ethics.

The linking of writing and illness (and its incapacitating symptoms) echoes facts from historical Dostoevsky's life. Elizabeth Barnes mentions that Dostoevsky's epilepsy 'had profoundly positive effects on his creative activity' as a writer (2016, 109). She quotes Dostoevsky commenting on his own experience of epilepsy:

> For several instants I experience a happiness that is impossible in an ordinary state, and of which other people have no conception. I feel full harmony in myself and in the whole world, and the feeling is so strong and sweet that for a few seconds of such bliss one could give up ten years of life, perhaps all of life. / I felt that heaven descended to earth and swallowed me. I really attained God and was imbued with him. All of you healthy people don't even suspect what happiness is, that happiness that we epileptics experience for a second before an attack. (Ibid. 91)

Rather than merely a disabling condition, an epileptic fit is related as a nearly transcendental experience that has a transformative effect on the creative process. In *The Master of Petersburg*, too, Dostoevsky is aware of the productive intersection of falling and writing: 'Not to emerge from the fall unscathed, but to achieve what his son did not: to wrestle with the whistling darkness, to absorb it, to make it his medium; to turn the falling into a flying' (*MP* 235). If there is resurrection and closure, it is to be subversively granted by a 'falling' that is also 'flying'. He must now (re)write his son into existence to recoil from the consuming 'darkness' of grief and oblivion. But resurrection is not redemption, and there are ethical costs incurred in defying the gravity of the fall. According to Attwell, a 'descent into obscenity and an ethical malaise [. . .] is represented as epileptic fitting, falling, flying and madness' (2015, 203). And the activity that epitomises both madness and moral decay is writing: 'But the writing, he fears, would be that of a madman – vileness, obscenity, page after page of it, untameable' (*MP* 18). Rather than helping Dostoevsky recover from the debilitating state of grief, writing colludes with insanity, leading him straight into a downward spiral of moral decline. And this descent is modulated by the exigencies of the body: 'He thinks of the madness as running through the artery of his right arm down to the fingertips and the pen and so to the page' (18). The visceral Gothic image of the vascular flow of 'madness' down the limbs culminating in the act of writing, as a sort of transubstantiation of poisoned blood into ink, implies that writing 'becomes a thing, as opposed to a representation', a material agent that is instrumental in the ultimate undoing of culturally sanctified ethical paradigms (Kelly 2011, 134). Writing, as the paradoxical flying by falling, inflected by madness and obscenity, must part ways with traditional ethics, marking the moment when Pavel must become Stavrogin. Where Coetzee ends, Dostoevsky will begin.

Ghost Writing

If, as stated above, *The Master of Petersburg* is a kind of biographical prequel to *The Possessed*, Coetzee in a certain sense ghost-writes Dostoevsky's story (in a manner that is reminiscent of Philip Roth's rewriting of the story of Anne Frank in *The Ghost Writer*) just as Coetzee's Dostoevsky ghost-writes the story of his son's life – a story which is also partly ghost-written (in the sense of being written by a ghost) by the deceased Pavel himself if, to recall, Dostoevsky 'is possessed by Pavel [. . .] getting to write under possession' (HRC 19.1, 5-9-1991). But 'writing his son into immortality' is harder than he thinks: 'The death of his son looms over him as something that must be written and something he cannot write' (HRC 19.1, 27-7-1991). He must first coax the silent and invisible ones, those who would not speak or materialise (and who are they? Pavel's ghost, muse, God?)

into submission. And the only means available for him to ensure that 'God dare no longer remain silent' is to betray his son in the writing by presenting him as a depraved villain and a moral nihilist with little or no factual evidence to support his account (*MP* 249).

Nor is this necessary task itself something that the aggrieved father takes kindly to do: 'It has never been a joy, this writing, not for an instant, not ever. Always a punishment, a spell on the treadmill. When I find joy, you will be free. Till then, the chasing of a ghost' (HRC 19.1, 7-5-1991). For the Dostoevsky of the early drafts, therefore, writing doubles up as a final course of action required to reconnect with his son and a form of self-inflicted penance. This sentiment echoes Coetzee's own reflections about his experience of writing, which he reveals in no uncertain terms in one of his notebooks, written over a decade earlier: 'Every morning since 1 Jan 1970 I have sat down to write. I HATE it' (HRC 33.3, 30-5-78).

Another reason why the Dostoevsky of the early drafts and notes is convinced that his son's resurrection must be achieved through writing is because he thinks he has had his hand in his son's untimely death: 'He thinks the letters' – those in which he admonishes Pavel and lectures him on morality – 'as having been absorbed, eaten: Pavel has "lived on" and "died of" the letters. (Hence the new book is to bring him back to life?)' (HRC 19.1, 5-9-1991). Having literally died of writing, Pavel must now be brought back to life by the same means, and Dostoevsky is aware of his part and its consequences in this process:

> He is aware that he is a writer [...] that he will not forget this moment, that it is not impossible it will be written into a book. He is far from despising himself for that. If anything is betrayed by this appetite that devours life and reconstitutes it as stories, it is not the lives he appropriates but his own integrity. That is what the vocation of writer is to him: a continual betrayal of his human integrity in the service of a production. (HRC 19.1, 2-6-1991)

The writer's integrity is a necessary price to pay for committing the other to writing, a process involving the 'appropriation' of the lives of these written about. Writing thus marks an act of a double betrayal: of both the author and his subject of writing. As Coetzee shows in his personal notes and published works to be constantly aware of the appropriating agency of writing as well as the inextricability of writing from the writer's experience,[11] it is not unlikely that these words, written only two years after Coetzee's son's tragic death, and in large part not included in the published version of the novel, carry within them Coetzee's self-admonishment for alluding to his son's death through Pavel's.

But if writing marks an act of betrayal, can it also offer redemption? Coetzee's reflections on the novel's plot development suggest it can: '(4) Creation of Stavrogin: betrayal of his son. (5) Liberation into love that follows betrayal'; 'The story can't be utterly negative. Forgiveness. That is its final focus' (HRC 19.1, 1-6-1991). The betrayal is thus a ploy that must bring the plot to its logical conclusion and offer a closure – a form of cleansing that paves the way for the liberating forces of love and forgiveness. However, the reader of the published version of the novel knows this initial promise has been broken. When Dostoevsky 'begins to taste' the fruits of his treachery, it only 'tastes like gall' (*MP* 250). Fittingly, by failing to fulfil his promises, Coetzee, like Dostoevsky, 'has betrayed everyone' (ibid.) – the reader and himself alike. But what Coetzee is faithful to in his act of betrayal is his own philosophy of writing, which he articulated around the time of writing his first drafts of *The Master of Petersburg* in an interview with David Attwell (published in *Doubling the Point*). Coetzee states there that what writing 'reveals (or asserts) may be quite different from what you thought (or half-thought) you wanted to say in the first place. That is the sense in which one can say that writing writes us' (*DP* 18). Writing, therefore, is a process that constantly sabotages the author's intentions. Along these lines, writing, as a force operating outside of the writer's designs, like a form of haunting, or ghost-writing (a ghost writing through and for the writer), is betrayal par excellence.

Spectral and Specular Commitments

As argued so far, the interlacing of the signifiers of writing, illness and haunting informs *The Master of Petersburg*'s problematic ethics of grief as well as entanglements of fact and fiction in relation to the lives of Dostoevsky and Coetzee. Correspondingly, the metaphors and tropes of visual perception and spectral presence further animate the novel's preoccupation with the ethical complexities of mourning. Considering that Coetzee's early drafts of the novel include parenthetical reflections on the scopic underpinnings of western culture means that the choice of optical metaphors in the novel was premeditated.[12] Another book committed to probing the affinities between spectrality and visibility is Jacques Derrida's *Specters of Marx*. Both Derrida and Coetzee deploy these metaphors as points of departure for considerations of ethical issues rooted in the notions of waiting and hospitality.

Derrida's attention to linguistic morphology in his writings elicits questions relevant to disability theory. Prefixes, these 'seemingly innocent morphemes [...] denoting liminality', observes Paweł Jędrzejko, 'have the power of collapsing binary oppositions upon which Western metanarratives so heavily depend' (2011, 13). The prefix's resistance to binary oppositions mentioned by Jędrzejko manifests itself in its ability to alter the meanings of the word's stem (both at its denotational and connotational level), and thus to frustrate the word's ambitions for semantic closure. These disruptive modalities of prefixes are key to grasping Derrida's concept of haunting and hauntology. For Derrida the 'specter' is a being that comes in a 'temporal disjoining':

> in a dis-located time of the present, at the joining of a radically disjointed time, without certain conjunction. Not a time whose joinings are [...] dysfunctional, disadjusted, according to a dys- of negative opposition and dialectical disjunction, but a time without certain joining or determinable conjunction [...] time is disarticulated, dislocated, dislodged, [...] deranged, both out of order and mad [...] disadjusted. (1994, 20)

In his deconstruction of spatio-temporal presence, Derrida points to two qualities of the prefix 'dis-' or 'dys-': one that has a negative, oppositional, dialectical agency, and one that has the ability to unsettle the metaphysics of presence. If spectre is that which is 'neither living nor dead, present nor absent' (63), its coming into presence in disjunction signifies a liminal state in which it can neither assert its presence nor annul its absence. Curiously, reflections on the liminal temporality of the spectre prompt Derrida to think of time as 'deranged' and 'mad'. The use of these framing disability metaphors is telling because disability is also defined by the prefix 'dis-'. Rather than only signifying the lack of ability, the prefix also announces a subversive agency in the meaning of dis- as anti-, which denotes a different ability, or the other of ability, as opposed to the lack thereof. In doing so, in embracing its liminal (both negative and oppositional) semantic status, disability has the capacity to subvert comfortable notions of normalcy claimed by the stem of ability.

But metaphors of disability in Derrida's work do not exhaust themselves in the liminal temporality of the coming of a ghost, but also provoke questions about its materiality. Derrida goes on to argue that a ghost does not appear as a spirit, but as a body: 'For there is no ghost, there is never any becoming-specter of the spirit without at least an appearance of flesh' (1994, 157). This body, however, is not wholly material either. It announces its (non)presence in 'visible invisibility', in a 'dis-appearing', which is both an absence of appearing and the other of appearing – its antithesis, rather than an annulment. Such a body is not a 'living body' but a 'prosthetic body' (158), continues Derrida. Again, the use of a metaphor of disability is telling. The liminal ontology of the non/present, in/visible, dis/appearing spectre approximates the state of a prosthetic body: a body that is not itself, a body dis/embodied, or embodied by being supplemented by the body of the other of itself.

Unlike Derrida, Jean Baudrillard does not see spectre as a liminal being; instead he points to the double meaning of the term. It is not the ontology but etymology of spectre that positions it in a problematic relation with itself. Baudrillard points to two meanings of the word 'spectral': 'ghostly spectrality (phantoms and ghosts) and a prismatic spectrality, the refraction of different colors from light or the different facets found in an "individual"' (Baudrillard and Guillaume 2008, 40). Whereas ghostly spectrality 'relates to a disconnection', thus occupying the place of a 'singular Other', a being that doubles itself in the haunting of the spectre, prismatic spectrality marks an individual as a diffracted being of 'multiple connections' (ibid., 41). Baudrillard argues that these two meanings cannot be reconciled, in that the 'disconnection' of ghostly spectrality asserts the alterity of a being in its duality, while spectral 'diffraction' or 'dispersion' annuls the alterity of a being in its multiplicity: 'No longer a ghost, the individual is in this case a being with protrusions in every direction' (ibid.). Baudrillard's spectre is thus a twofold being: either an eidolic figure of alterity, or one of prismatic multimodality. And that the multimodal condition of a spectre derives from its optical qualities is revealing for coming to terms with the ambiguity of the haunting in Coetzee's *The Master of Petersburg*.

To be precise, there are no ghosts in Coetzee's seventh novel as such. Not in the sense that traditional Gothic literary conventions would allow it. And yet, the novel is replete with ghosts that inhabit its metaphors, language and imagery, acting as figures of fatherly grief rather than diegetic presences. And this indeterminate presence of the spectre departs from Baudrillard's understanding of ghostly spectrality which is defined by the symmetrical relation of the dead appearing as a spectre vis-à-vis the living. Coetzee's ghosts announce, while evading, their unequivocal self-presence. And optical symbolism and vocabularies undergird the uncertainty of the act of haunting. Dostoevsky intuits that in order to connect with Pavel he must suspend his attachment with the existing world. Upon visiting Pavel's grave, 'he has begun to cry. *Why now?* [. . .] Yet the tears are welcome in their way, a soft veil of blindness between himself and the world' (*MP* 8). A deferral of sensory experience of reality, a paradoxical suspension of seeing in order to see that which cannot be seen, marks an involuntary coping mechanism of the body that partakes in Dostoevsky's summoning of his stepson's ghost. If he abandons his commitment to invoke Pavel, 'the memories of him' will be 'caught by the wind and borne up into the blinding heavens' (14). To accomplish his goal, he will stop at nothing: he will write, if he must, to conjure up his son, but even this fails him. His writing is impotent, treacherous, mad, perverse, tactile, a 'writing even the blind could read' (18). Writing has him question his own existence ('Am I dead already?') and selfhood ('He recognises nothing of himself. If he were to look in a mirror now, he would not be surprised if another face were to loom up, staring back blindly at him' [245]).

He will visit the shot tower, where Pavel has met his end, but it soon dawns on him that it is to no avail either: 'I should never have agreed to come. Now for the rest of my life I will have this before my eyes like ghost-vision' (*MP* 118). His defiance generates nothing but aporia: '*I should not be here therefore I should be here. I will see nothing else therefore I will see all*. What sickness is this, what sickness of reasoning?' (118). Dostoevsky senses that to experience a ghostly visitation involves a paradox. 'The specter is', says Derrida, 'the frequency of [. . .] the visibility of the invisible [. . .] And visibility, by its essence [. . .] is not seen [. . .]. The spectre is also [. . .] what one thinks one sees and which one projects – on an imaginary screen where there is nothing to see' (1994, 125). If to see the spectre is to experience the impossible condition of seeing the invisible, Coetzee's optical metaphor helps dispel the paradox. Vision impairment is characterised by a perception of reality unaided by visual apparatus. But vision loss is not antithetical to seeing by default. Although the etymology of the word 'image' points invariably to visual experience ('representation', 'likeness', 'picture', '(optical) counterpart' [*Oxford Dictionary of English Etymology* 1994, 462]), it does not follow from this that every mental image must imply a visual image. People with congenital blindness can imagine or construct mental images, even if these images may not be visual. To come across an image, therefore, is to see that which may operate outside of the visual framework. Coetzee's Dostoevsky intuits that it is only by annulling the ability to see that he will be able to recuperate what he fails to see visually; he will see nothing and therefore he will see all. Interestingly, the double meaning of the Latin *imaginem* as both a 'copy, imitation, likeness; statue, picture, [...] idea, appearance' and a 'phantom, ghost, apparition' (*Online Etymology Dictionary* 2017) is in keeping with this problematic visibility of the image – as if the visibility of the image is always-already summoned up by its own spectrality.

In *The Master of Petersburg* Gothic imagery often arises out of an indeterminacy between what is seen and what is imagined. In the following versions of the same scene, adopted from Coetzee's early drafts and the published version of the novel respectively, Dostoevsky watches Anna Sergeyevna and her daughter Matryona in their sleep:

> They are asleep, the widow on her face, the child on her back, in the same bed. Impression of unity. The same thing the next night. This time he can swear the girl has her eyes open. She looks to him like a bat (effects of eyebrows), a vampire in possession of the (drugged) woman. (HRC 19.1, 12-8-1991)

> Anna lies turned away from him, Matryona on her back facing toward him. Again he is convinced she is watching him, though he knows it cannot be so. He bends over closer to reassure himself. From a few inches away he stares into her open eyes. He says to himself: they are painted eyes, like the eyes painted on the eyeballs of statues or the eyes on the back of certain moths. But he is wrong: in the slow time of exhaustion, he understands that the child has lain there all the time staring at him. She is asleep with her eyes open, he thinks; but that too is not true. / He thinks: she is like a bat with a wing folded over its victim. Under his stare, the corners of her mouth seem to curve faintly upward in a triumphant bestial animal grin. (HRC 19.1, 14-8-1991)

> The two women have not stirred. Again he has the uncanny feeling that Matryona is watching him. He bends closer. / He is not mistaken: he is staring into open, unblinking eyes. A chill runs through him. She sleeps with her eyes open, he tells himself. But it is not true. She is awake and has been awake all the time; thumb in mouth, she has been watching his every motion with unremitting vigilance. As he peers, holding his breath, the corners of her mouth seem to curve faintly upward in a victorious, bat-like grin. And the arm too, extended loosely over her mother, is like a wing. (*MP* 57–8)

Bearing in mind that the process of imagination begins when what is seen is withdrawn from sight – since what is immediately seen does not need to be imagined – Coetzee creates the effects of the uncanny when the characters cannot see (or see completely) the object of seeing. The gruesome images that animate Dostoevsky's imagination are fuelled by a combination of his fatherly grief and that which is barred from vision (due to the dim light in the room). Limited vision unleashes Dostoevsky's paedophobic anxieties, as he pictures Matryosha as a vampire, a bat, a moth or a statue. It should be noted that paedophobia is a prominent trope in Gothic fiction. The theme of Gothic children, including spectral, homicidal, possessed or vampiric children, has been variously explored in such novels of the genre as *Beloved* by Toni Morrison, *The Fifth Child* by Doris Lessing, *The Boy Who Followed Ripley* by Patricia Highsmith, *Crooked House* by Agatha Christie, *The Exorcist* by William Peter Blatty, *The Omen* by David Seltzer and *Salem's Lot* by Stephen King, to list a few. In Dostoevsky's vision Matryosha matches the description of a Gothic child that 'threaten[s] the role of the parent by consuming or incorporating that parent's power' (Bruhm 2002, 267). These optical and affective impressions evoke further paedophobic delusions and spectral images: 'The house of possession. The demon-girl. Later he wonders whether the mother too is an agent of possession, a succubus [. . .]' (HRC 19.1, 5-9-1991). Although the Gothic imagery is palpably more pronounced in the drafts than in the published novel, both versions of the text convey a strong sense of a crisis of visibility and its impact on the protagonist's tortured psyche.

The crisis of visibility is a recurrent theme variously articulated throughout the novel. It is a marker of betrayal of Dostoevsky's stepson: 'He thinks of Orpheus walking backwards step by step [. . .] of the wife in graveclothes with the blind, dead eyes following him' (*MP 5*). Dostoevsky is haunted by his failure to protect his son. Pavel departs from the world betrayed by his stepfather, like Eurydice by her lover's gaze. It is therefore in the touch that Dostoevsky seeks his final chance of assuaging his guilt: 'I came too late to raise the coffin-lid [. . .] If my lips, tender as the fingertips of the blind, had been able to brush you just once, you would not have quit this existence bitter against me' (153). Again, a disability metaphor, 'fingertips of the blind', denotes seeing outside vision. Unable to conjure up his son ('How long can he go on waiting for a ghost?' [154]) Dostoevsky is seeking alternative forms of sensory experience to offset the limitations of sight which bar him from the image he yearns for. 'He tries to summon up Pavel's face' (49), but since the face that appears instead is not Pavel's, he is determined to expel it: '"Go away!" he says, trying to dismiss the image' (49). Not that the image fails to arrive completely (Pavel continues to return in multiple visions, dreams and phantasms), but, when it does arrive, it is a laughable palliative: 'What does the vision mean?' (143). He continuously learns the hard way that 'visions' in fact mean nothing, as they only offer empty visual images, whereas what he is after is an essence that transcends the functional limitations of vision.

Perhaps Pavel will appear, Dostoevsky ponders, in the form of the other in need. But he soon accepts that the waiting for the coming of the spectre must operate beyond traditional ethics: 'If he expects his son to come as a thief in the night [. . .] he will never see him [. . .] As long as he expects what he does not expect, what he does not expect will not come. Therefore [. . .] he must answer to what he does not expect' (*MP* 80). Dostoevsky's epiphany of the impossible dynamics of waiting for the unexpected has the hallmarks of Derrida's concept of the *arrivant* – one that arrives or the arriving. For Derrida this impossible waiting, 'awaiting without horizon of the wait, awaiting what one does not expect yet or any longer', is a condition of unconditional hospitality – 'hospitality without reserve' – to the *arrivant* 'from whom or from which one will not ask anything in return' (1994, 81). The other that arrives, or the event of the arriving of the other itself, necessitates a 'messianic opening to what is coming, that is, to the event that cannot be awaited as such [. . .] and this is the very place of spectrality' (82). Coetzee's Dostoevsky and Derrida, therefore, see the spectre as a figure that demands unconditional hospitality. However, it is not the spectre as such that makes these impossible demands, but the event of its arrival. One must respond to the *arrivant* as the radical other as well as to the *arriving* of the other, none of which or whom can be awaited or anticipated. Rather than a prosthetic Gothic allegory, haunting approximates the condition of ethics itself. It is 'not the horror ridden and clichéd affair that is played upon in popular culture', asserts Matt Foley, but 'the necessary zero point of building a hauntological ethics of living' (2011, 23).

Crip Ex Machina

If Gothic and disability metaphors act in tandem in *The Master of Petersburg* to resist traditional notions of ethics of hospitality, fictional representations of such themes bring sharply into focus complex ethical issues as well. One such instance is dramatised in the chapter 'The White Suit'. The episode features Maria Lebyadkina, a person with physical and intellectual disabilities, who is secretly in love with Pavel. On hearing of her infatuation, Pavel acts as Maria's suitor by paying her visits in his smart white suit to please her. In relating this episode to Matryosha, Dostoevsky puts Pavel's feigned courtship down to his kind-heartedness: 'Pavel has a kind heart, that was one of the nicest things about him, wasn't it?' (*MP* 74). However, that this episode has its counterpart in *The Possessed* is revealing in that the historical Dostoevsky provides a very different suitor. Rather than a paragon of virtue and charity, Stavrogin courts and marries Marya to win a bet, paying little heed to the fact that, heartbroken, the girl takes her life as a consequence of his ruthless scheming. The striking discord between these two accounts, and the ethical implications thereof, will play a pivotal role in the fictional Dostoevsky's seditious rewriting of his stepson's diary, in which the father is setting the scene for his son's debauchment of Matryona as a harbinger of the birth of Stavrogin. It also merits mentioning that the theme of psychosexual abuse of children, as an epitome of the corruption of innocence, belongs to the staple repertoire of Gothic tropes, exemplified variously in Henry James's *The Turn of the Screw*, Stephen King's *The Shining* or Joyce Carol Oates's *First Love: A Gothic Tale*, among others. So in Coetzee's as in these works, which riff on the double meaning of possession, the power that adults wield over children, seen as the lawful possessions of their parents, often rhymes with or prompts mediation on demonic possession. Parents or adults in such tales are possessed by the demons of obsessive love or driven by the masochistic fantasies of lust and devourment towards children.

Although Coetzee departs from Dostoevsky's account of the episode featuring Maria on its first appearance in the novel, the description of the woman remains unchanged. And this detail is telling. The sparse description of Maria leaves little doubt as to the attributes that define her: 'She was a cripple. She was also weak in the head. A good soul, but not capable of taking care of herself' (*MP* 72). So configured, the disabled Maria is a classic case of 'crip ex machina', understood as a narrative device which 'provide[s] the able-bodied viewer', or reader for that matter, with 'a measure of compassion for the victim while permitting an identification with the able-bodied hero who survives' (Davidson 2008, 15). Her role in both iterations of the episode is tangential, calculated as a gauge of the characters' moral fibre: Stavrogin's depravity and Pavel's benevolence. But Coetzee makes problematic Pavel's seemingly morally unequivocal treatment of Maria. As proposed above,

Dostoevsky's eventual rewriting of Pavel's papers figures as his perverse form of conjuring up his deceased stepson: 'He is writing for the dead' (245). For this purpose, Dostoevsky puts on Pavel's white suit and by so doing reverses the logic of the haunting. If the son refuses to haunt the father, it is the father who will now possess the son: 'A ghost, as every father is the ghost of his son; ~~but~~ now a ghost of a ghost' (HRC 19.1, 25-6-1991). In both early drafts and in the published version, Dostoevsky stresses the interpenetration of himself and his son: 'We are the same person, he thinks; he is in me or I am in him' (HRC 19.1, 29-6-1991); 'Because I am he. Because he is I' (*MP* 53). To bring the reversal to its logical conclusion, the writing Dostoevsky embarks on must succumb to the pressures of subversion in its turn, and ethics, including Pavel's treatment of Maria, follows suit. The Pavel that emerges from the rewriting derides Maria, refers to her as 'a kind of witch' and courts her 'for a joke' (249).

Seemingly, such a reframing of the story does little to recuperate Maria from the role of 'crip ex machina' foisted upon her. Structurally, she is a figure of 'narrative prosthesis', tactically positioned, according to Mitchell and Snyder, as a narrative ploy to sustain discourses of social normativity (2001, 6). Also, the fact that Coetzee borrows the character of Maria from the real Dostoevsky's work serves as an implicit commentary on the complicity of the literary canon in exploiting and side-lining the characters with disabilities.[13] But if Coetzee instrumentalises Maria, he does not do it to bring the narrative to a satisfactory closure, as would befit more traditional literary accounts, but to stage his ethics of resurrection without redemption.

Another Coetzee novel that uses a disabled character to challenge the reader's reading expectations is *Disgrace*. When David Lurie befriends a dog 'with a withered left hindquarter which it drags behind it' (*DG* 215) and is offered a chance to save him from being put down, the scene is set for a double salvation: of the life of the dog, and the dignity of his failed saviour. Before this expectation is frustrated by Lurie's final resolve – 'Yes, I am giving him up' (220) – it is heightened by a poignant depiction of the relationship between Lurie and the dog: 'The dog wags its crippled rear, sniffs his face, licks his cheeks, his lips, his ears. He does nothing to stop it' (ibid.). Characteristically, the nameless dog's physical impairment is tactically foregrounded to arouse the reader's sympathy with his plight, thus reinforcing the 'myth' of disabled characters 'as evoking pity and charity' (Dolmage 2018, 215). While Coetzee's characters with disabilities are often presented as objects of pity, Coetzee refuses to use disability as a catalyst for the protagonist's moral growth. Just as Dostoevsky completes his scheme of defiling the memory of his son by imagining him mocking the physically and intellectually disabled Maria in his writings, so too Lurie needs a 'crippled' dog to assert his refusal to accept cosmic forgiveness for his former transgressions.

Intriguingly, as Coetzee's preparatory notes for *Disgrace* reveal, Lurie very nearly ended up as a figure of 'crip ex machina' himself. While in the published novel he sustains minor injuries in the head after a violent assault on him and his daughter, the notes show a very different outcome of the scene:

> He is beaten up, incurs brain damage that results in some ugly, ungainly defect: drooling? hobbling? blindness? He continues to work with the animals, which don't find him ugly. Slowly he degenerates. He establishes a point beyond which he won't go. His daughter agrees. Eventually she helps him to kill himself. (HRC 35.2, 16-04-1996)

What is notable is that Lurie's disability is set as a predicament on which the novel's resolution (the protagonist's assisted suicide) rests in this unrealised plot outline. But Coetzee quickly abandons this scheme, offering 'a displacement that leaves its trace' in the final version of the novel (Samolsky 2021, 207). Lurie will be spared severe incapacitation and euthanasia; instead, this fate will befall the nameless dog. This narrative shift allows Coetzee to stall a resolution that would allow Lurie to atone for his disgrace through suicide and thereby offer narrative closure.[14]

Disability representation is instrumental (if also instrumentalised) in staging Coetzee's complex ethics that eschews easy notions of morality predicated on redemption through charity. Coetzee's resistance to ableist biases lies not in the affirmative modes of disability representation, but in the ways in which these depictions disrupt the reader's identification with normative assumptions and morality (usually epitomised by non-disabled characters). When Coetzee summons spectral images and Gothic signifiers to disrupt the familiar modes of seeing or knowing that facilitate epistemic injustice, or when he refuses to offer disabled characters as conduits for narrative closure or the moral growth of characters and readers alike, normative discourses are constantly under threat in his fiction.

Notes

1. Foucault explores the history of normalisation in *Discipline and Punish* ([1975] 1995) and *The History of Sexuality* ([1976] 1998).
2. On the medical and social constructionist model of disability, see Hall (2016, 166–8).
3. See Chapter 1 for an extended discussion on this point.
4. In Coetzee's fiction the destructive agency of the father is a cause of the possible psychological disturbance of Magda in *In the Heart of the Country* and social reclusiveness of Michael K in *Life & Times of Michael K*.
5. See Attwell 2015, 187–210.
6. In his essay 'Dostoevsky: The Miraculous Years' (2001) Coetzee discusses the historical Dostoevsky's epilepsy and its effects on his relationship with his wife, Anna.
7. In the early drafts, completed in 1991, Nikolai Fyodorovich Stavrogin is Dostoevsky's biological son. In the entry for 20 August 1991, this character is replaced by Pavel Aleksandrovich Isaev, Dostoevsky's stepson (HRC 19.1-2).
8. For further reference on Dostoevsky's anti-nihilistic sympathies, see Attwell 2015, chap. 11.
9. See Chapter 5 for an extended discussion about links between Coetzee's illness and disability ethics and Kierkegaard's philosophy of subjectivity and despair.
10. From early on in Coetzee's drafts Dostoevsky resigns himself to the destructive force of his illness: 'Who would take care of him if he had a fit in his lodgings? Perhaps the answer is: No one – this is a time in his life when, if he dies, he dies' (HRC 19.1).
11. Coetzee famously stated that 'All autobiography is storytelling, all writing is autobiography' (*DP* 391).
12. In one of these notes, Coetzee discusses an idea which he attributes to Emmanuel Levinas thus: 'Emmanuel Levinas: The Greek tradition is scopic. In the Hebrew tradition, to have regard for someone is not to look at him/her with the gaze of desire' (HRC 19.1, 8-8-1991).
13. I discuss the problem of instrumentalisation of characters with disabilities by literary authors in Chapters 1–4.
14. The possibilities of speculating over an unfulfilled plot sketch are, needless to say, limited. It is also possible to argue that Lurie's suicide in the quoted outline was intended to be precipitated by his incapacitation rather than a need to make up for his moral transgressions. However, considering that the trope of Lurie's fall from grace was developed consistently from the earliest drafts, it is likely that his unrealised suicide would be somehow linked to this theme.

Chapter 7

Dismodernism and Forms of Dependency in *Slow Man*

In the closing chapter of Joseph Conrad's *The Secret Agent*, Ossipon and the Professor are engaged in a debate about the forces that are likely to shape the world order to come:

> You can't heal weakness [. . .] In two hundred years doctors will rule the world. Science reigns already. It reigns in the shade maybe – but it reigns. And all science must culminate at least in the science of healing – not the weak, but the strong. Mankind wants to live – to live. (2016, 279)

The Professor sneers at Michaelis's benevolent vision of the world 'planned out like an immense and nice hospital [. . .] in which the strong are to devote themselves to the nursing of the weak', militantly advocating as an alternative the world where 'the weak would be taken in hand for utter extermination' (277). In this short exchange, Conrad intuits the advent of two major political systems that would come to dominate the twentieth-century political landscape in the West not long after the publication of his 1907 novel: the rise of welfare state envisioned by Michaelis, and fascism championed by the megalomaniacal Professor.

Extended between the radical ends of the left–right political divide, modernity at large turns into a venue of normalisation and the perfectibility of the body politic. Lennard J. Davis argues that 'Marxist thought encourages us toward an enforcing of normalcy in the sense that the deviations in society, in terms of the distribution of wealth, must be minimised' (1995, 29). For Davis, Marxism proved to be much in line with the larger project of modern industrial societies, which via the means of modern statistics, eugenics[1] and forced institutionalisation[2] sought to curtail the incidence of bodily and mental degeneracy, thus maximising the average levels of socially constructed normalcy. If welfare states aiming at reducing economic disparities between social groups became the instruments of normalisation of the collective body, fascist states championed a model of racial and corporeal purity obtained through a total deracination of defective bodies. These idealised standards of the New Aryan Man modelled on the 'Greek ideals of masculinity' were rigorously pursued with an eye to obtaining an 'ideal human form' in the 'healthy nation' (Jackson 2006, 466). The extermination and sterilisation of hundreds of thousands of people with disabilities was part of Nazi Germany's eugenics programme (Evans 2004, 18). Whether a normal body of welfare states or ideal body of fascist regimes, the modern body submits to corrective practices calculated to eliminate corporeal dysfunction. And it appears that post-war neoliberal states have drawn on the dual legacy of normalisation and perfectibility of the body in different ways. If western neoliberal democracies, absorbing to varying degrees both the welfare and free market economy, continue to provide healthcare for disenfranchised groups through social policies, and in so doing make possible an implementation of medical practices aimed at a normalisation of the body, the privileged find new ways of enhancing the statistically healthy body. Expensive cosmetic and reconstructive surgeries and other prosthetic means are thus at the service of repositioning the perimeters of bodily perfectibility that relegate the disabled body to further depths of social undesirability.

Rosemarie Garland-Thomson considers these normalising procedures an assault on the ontological autonomy of the non-standard body. Modern societies 'enact often virulent measures to deny, avoid, and eliminate disability and other forms of human variation' that depart from the commonly accepted models of corporeal normalcy (2005, 524). On the other hand, if the dysfunctional body is subjected to the curative regimes of normalisation, and the normal body yields to the pressures of cosmetic and surgical enhancement, it transpires that postmodernity marks a culture of universal dependency of every body on various methods of correction and provision offered by modern medicine and technology. In such a culture dependency occupies a paradoxical position of being both a marker of exclusion and a universal condition of the postmodern human. The late modern culture of dependency is thus, according to Lennard J. Davis, 'dismodernist', with the term denoting a late modern subjectivity predicated on dependence and difference as its operative condition (2002, 26). This chapter attempts to show how Coetzee's fiction demonstrates affinities with Davis's notion of dismodernism in terms of disability representation and ethics of care. I will also focus on how this term can be revised in the terms facilitated by Coetzee's late modernist style. In the opening section I examine the extent to which modernism as a cultural practice responds to the biopolitical coercions of late modernity.

Disability and Modernism

Davis maintains that the novel in general, and the nineteenth- and twentieth-century novel in particular, has facilitated the social regimes of normalcy (1995, 49). In its adherence to hegemonic forms of representation – such as character construction, the normalisation and structuration of plot, the side-lining or elimination of disabled characters, and narrative closure – the nineteenth-century realist novel turned into a vehicle for a negative symbolisation of disability. These normalising narrative tactics worked in tandem with patriarchal notions of bourgeois morality predicated on the domesticating and rehabilitative measures of handling social otherness. Modernism, in its wilful disengagement from the realist form and traditional morality, undertook to undo some of these standardising modes of literary representation.

And yet the rectification of literary realism's perpetuation of traditional morality through the modernist notions of higher ethics, a belief that human nature can be transformed by art (Oser 2009, 1), seemed to offer little in terms of overturning normative structures. In fact, as observed by Michael Davidson, the modernists exploited disability metaphors for the purposes of pursuing their own aesthetic and political agendas: 'these metaphors are produced within a modernity dedicated to the perfectible body and improved mind. Modernist literature in its attack on bourgeois domesticity, positivist science and mass culture drew on disabled figures as examples of deracinated body politic' (Davidson 2018, 86). Disability figures here as a symbol of the cultural demise and moral backwardness of the bourgeoisie, to which high modernism lends itself as a necessary corrective. In this sense, not only did modernism fail to undo ableist discourses and forms, but it managed to reinforce them. As argued by Deborah Susan McLeod (2014), in modernist literature disability is no longer symptomatic of individual characters, as it used to be in the preceding period, but extends to a new cultural logic. In the new age of uncertainty and fragmentation precipitated by the Industrial Revolution, Darwinist theistic scepticism, the emergence of psychoanalysis, the crisis of Cartesian rationalism, the outbreak of World War I, and so forth, it is now the whole generation 'that exhibits signs of physical and psychological damage' (ibid., 3).

While taking account of the ableist legacy of modernism, such as the eugenic views and rhetoric of high-brow modernists, Maren Tova Milett argues that the anti-traditionalistic impulses of modernist writers helped them develop formal tactics of interrogating and contesting 'normative understandings of embodiment' (2017, 2). The modernist commitment to 'the process of de-forming the novel' was a driving force of literary experimentalism that sought to liberate the novel from the constraints of narrative linearity, linguistic conventionalism and structural coherence, just as sensory disability helped cater for a new optics of subjective inwardness instrumental in disproving the objectivising claims of the nineteenth-century novel (ibid., 17). Although describing bodily disfigurement or sensory disability through metaphors risks being yet another form of appropriation of disability representation, such figurative depictions may prove productive in terms of countervailing the ableist sentiments of modernism. In its frontal assault on the instrumentalising forces of modernity,[3] which often saw disability as standing in the way of progress, modernist aesthetics drew heavily on disability rhetoric. It is largely in its deconstruction of normative embodiment, objectivising optics and a penchant for fragmentation that modernism extricates itself from a eugenic 'biofuturity' – as Davidson would call it – intrinsic to the modernist project (2018, 77).

Along similar lines, Siebers commends modern art for its 'embrace of disability as a distinct version of the beautiful' – an approach that allowed disability to play a key role in the shaping of modernist aesthetics (2010, 27). For Derek Attridge, modernism – though resistant to categorisation – is a cultural practice that in the foregrounding and self-reflexive interrogation of its own textual strategies opens up the space for an apprehension of otherness (2004, 4). It is the textual defamiliarisation, which the reader confronts when reading a modernist text, that elicits her response to the text as the other, and this by extension is commensurate with an ethical response to the human other. In this sense, the formal qualities of a modernist text, and the hermeneutic resistance they mount, activate the reader's 'moral imagination' (Nussbaum 1990, 148). If modernism is defined by its defamiliarising aesthetics, and part of these formal effects it owes to the ways it rethinks normative embodiment, modernist form, in the figuring of itself as incomplete, fragmentary and inward, champions a new aesthetics that is hostile to the oppressive regimes of modernity predicated on the containment of the other.

But to accept unconditionally modernism's resistance to modernity is to ignore the extent to which modernism welcomed the totalising progressivism and oppressive biopolitics of the brave new world. Whether modernism reinforces ableist discourses by appropriating disability metaphors or helps undo normative symbolisation of disability is subject of many heated critical debates. The section that follows probes Coetzee's own indebtedness to modernist aesthetics and his response to the political pressures of modernisation: a point of departure, as will be argued, for theorising Coetzee's dismodernist ethics.

Coetzee's Modernisms

Much has been written about the question of periodising Coetzee's works. A mixture of formal experimentalism and realism undergirded by political and ethical engagements of his fiction has invited critics and scholars to position Coetzee's works on the problematic threshold between modernism and postmodernism. Coetzee has experimented robustly with formal devices practised by modernists (narrative unreliability, multimodal narrative perspective, formal fragmentation, disruption of narrative linearity, generic self-reflexiveness) and postmodernists (intertextuality, metafiction, suspension of realism, lack of definite ethical guidance). While some critics took more definitive sides, others were careful not to consign Coetzee to any end of this historical and aesthetic divide, proposing instead alternative periodic points of reference. Linda Hutcheon suggests that Coetzee intuits a distinctly postmodern aesthetics which she links with his use of irony and a propensity for questioning meaning-making processes through self-reflexive literary strategies (2010, 78). Likewise, Anton Leist concludes that Coetzee occupies the position of an 'experimental' or 'pragmatic postmodernist' due to his profound distrust of traditional rationality and western imperial legacy as well as reluctance to follow the staple postmodernist diet of 'arbitrary playfulness' (2010, 217, 219).

While other scholars – Annamaria Carusi (1990), Teresa Dovey (1989) and Kenneth Parker (1996) – are among numerous other commentators reading Coetzee alongside postmodernist rubrics, Coetzee has more often been credited by later critics with practising a form of modernism in its various iterations. David Attwell's position on the question of periodisation is that Coetzee occupies a middle ground between modernism and postmodernism. While he affirms

Coetzee's indebtedness to modernists, he points to the problematic anachronism of the term in reference to Coetzee's works. Similarly, although Coetzee does practise some postmodernist techniques, the form of postmodernism that some of his works typify is offset by ethical and political engagements nurtured in the postcolonial context (Attwell 1993, 21). Instead, in his interview with Coetzee in *Doubling the Point*, Attwell proposes 'late modernism' as a plausible label under which Coetzee's fiction could be couched, which Coetzee neither approves nor repudiates (*DP* 198). Correspondingly, Emanuela Tegla says that Coetzee's works should not be considered along the lines of postmodernism. Rather, she agrees with Attridge that Coetzee's fiction could be labelled as late or neo modernist (2015, 239). Stephen Watson, in his turn, locates Coetzee's modernism in his ethical response to the pressures of modernity, in 'the attempt to restore to the world a quality of being emptied out of it by modern political and technological developments' (1986, 385). Following a similar thread, Attridge affirms that Coetzee's modernism depends on a deployment of the formal modes of questioning its own conventions as a means of resistance to the repressive impulses of the prevailing discourses of power (2004, 17). It is therefore in an imbrication of ethics and formal literary strategies, or ways in which these strategies open venues for questioning epistemic and political injustices of modernity, rather than a regurgitation of familiar modes of modernist aesthetics, that a claim about a form of rebranded modernism in Coetzee's works can be vindicated.

Such potentialities of Coetzee's fictions invite considerations about the extent to which Coetzee's experimental aesthetic partakes in countering discourses of normative embodiment. As suggested above, modernism depends on disability for its reframing of formal operations. As a result, '[m]uch Modernist writing, including [D. H] Lawrence's', proposes Alice Hall, 'is marked by a multisensory aesthetic, an attempt to write from and about the body in new ways' (2016, 92). In this sense, Lawrence's fictions resonate with the works of such modernist or late modernist writers as William Faulkner or Samuel Beckett, who in different ways test the limits of form to contain the complexity of disability. Whereas Faulkner employs radical temporal and formal disruptions to reproduce the intellectually disabled Benjy's first-person perspective in *The Sound and the Fury*, Beckett's infinitely recessive language holds up a mirror to his character's mental anxieties or intellectual symptoms of senescence, as in *Molly*, *Malone Dies* and *The Unnameable*. Counting among Coetzee's major influences, these modernist writers foreshadow the formal and structural underpinnings of Coetzee's disability representations, ones that derive from his reformulation of modernist aesthetics. In its reliance on modernist form and disability representation, Coetzee practises a form of disability modernism – a term that intends to call to mind Davis's term dismodernism. In the section that follows I study ethical and social implications of Davis's dismodernism as well as suggest alternative ways in which this term reflects Coetzee's engagement with form in his later disability fictions.

Dismodernism and the Culture of Dependency

Davis's notion of dismodernism emerges from his contestation of postmodernist identity formation. Instrumental in challenging the neoclassical notions of normative embodiment, the central postmodernist assumptions of social constructionism and performativity of the body have helped pave the way for the emergence of disability as an identity category. However, Davis argues that for all its commitment to undoing the injunctions of completeness, the postmodern subject itself remains 'whole, independent, unified, self-making, and capable' (2002, 26). The failure to topple corporal essentialism has to do with the fact the postmodernism has seriously undermined the materiality of the body through the claims of social constructedness. As an alternative, '[t]he dismodern era ushers in the concept that difference is what all of us have in common. That identity is not fixed but malleable [. . .] That dependence, not individual independence, is the rule' (ibid., 26). Dismodernism proposes a corrective to the ideological biases of its predecessors. Like the Enlightenment, dismodernism assumes a universal human condition, but rejects the neoclassical assumptions of wholeness as a model for universal embodiment; like postmodernism, dismodernism rejects the notions of the stability of the subject, but contests the postmodern 'localization of identity' (ibid., 27).

So configured, the dismodernist subject is one that in self-consciously positioning itself as incomplete manifests its condition as reliant on various forms of dependency. In the light of the above, Davis insists on a new dismodernist ethics of the body based on three aspects of dependency: 'care of' the body, which relates to the reliance of the contemporary body on the 'means of consumption'; 'care for' the body, involving a dependence of the body on the health-care industry; and 'care about' the body, interrogating the ways the disabled body operates in social structures, focusing on people with disabilities as an identity group (2002, 27–8). Since in present-day late-capitalist societies everyone depends to varying degrees on various forms of medication and other prosthetic modes of bodily enhancement, it is impairment, rather than normalcy, that is the rule (ibid., 31). Therefore, the limitations of the body define the universal experience of a dismodern subject (ibid., 32). This new dismodern subject rejects the normative illusion that her body is independent and complete. She cares about the body as it is, accepting all forms of embodiment. There are no normal bodies; there are only bodies with varying needs of adaptation to living space. The dismodern subjectivity rejects the neoliberal pressures of care for the body that forces it to conform to the standards of productivity of modern states and care of the body, designed to maintain newly emerging normative standards of embodiment. If, therefore, dismodernism presumes an ethic, it is one that dedicates itself to countering these normative aspects of postmodernity.

Considering the devastating effects of eugenics programmes as products of technological modernity, one could argue that there is a strong sense in which modernism, which embraces alienation, disruption, incompletion, fragmentation, deviation as its operative modes, lends itself as more conducive to dismodernism than the relativistic tactics of postmodernism. Jessica Berman avers that 'literary modernism knits together aesthetics and the ethicopolitical experience of modernity so that the world becomes the problematic to be addressed, transformed, configured, and reconfigured, rather than refused' (2012, 26). Although Berman refuses to subscribe to Attridge's argument that formal disruption is calculated to generate an ethical response, she recognises that modernist form offers implements for responding affirmatively to the ethical and political predicaments of modernity. In postmodernism this ethical impulse has been thwarted by a simulacrum culture that is unable to reconfigure itself around the 'grand narrative' of affirmative ethics. If dismodernism prefigures a culture of dependency and care in which the subject self-reflexively comes to terms with the awareness of herself as incomplete, and in so doing repudiates the oppressive narratives of normalcy nurtured by modern neoliberal states, modernism, in like manner, deploys formal strategies that in highlighting its modes of disruption engage ethically with the totalising forces shaping the modern world.

And yet, Coetzee refuses to conform to prescriptive models of ethics. Rarely do his novels demonstrate plot resolutions that are in line with traditional or affirmative ethics, which often poses an insurmountable hermeneutic obstacle to the reader. As argued by

David Davies, whereas readers are generally willing to suspend their disbelief in the representation of fictional worlds, no matter how unrealistic, they 'seem resistant to the invitation to imagine worlds in which moral truths obtain that are strikingly incompatible with our actual moral beliefs' (2007, 179–80). David Lurie's refusal to save a dog he has befriended, or Dostoevsky's heretical rewriting of his deceased stepson's diary, count among conspicuous examples of characters' choices that confound the reader's ethical expectations. Nor does Coetzee acknowledge that his fictional staging of ethical encounters progresses from a 'negative position', thus 'making the ethical as the pole with the lack' (*DP* 200). Herein lies the thrust of Coetzee's liminal ethics, one committed to overriding both wholly affirmative and negativistic impulses of orthodox ethical paradigms. In doing so, Coetzee manages to circumvent traditional notions of morality symptomatic of realist fiction, modernist ethicopolitical revisionism, or postmodern moral relativism alike.

Likewise, although, as argued above, there are productive points of intersection between dismodernism and modernism, the former offers points of resistance to modernist ethics. And the resistance is embedded in the etymological ambiguity of 'dis-', which figures as a morpheme in the portmanteau consisting of the words 'disability' and 'modernism' (in this sense dismodernism is short for disabled modernism), and a prefix that 'expresses the reverse or lack' or 'the negative or opposite' (*Oxford Dictionary of English Etymology* 1994, 271). Correspondingly, dismodernism makes the double gesture of positioning itself in 'opposition' to, or else marking an 'absence' of modernism, while deploying its self-reflexive formal devices. Coetzee is not a model modernist. In fact, much of his fiction is defined by a wilful departure from modernism. Coetzee's detour from modernism is also palpable in his staging of complex ethics as well as in the partial absorption of postmodern formal operations in his writings.[4]

This close attention to etymology invites a tripartite understanding of the term 'dismodernism'. Davis's original proposition presumes dismodernism as an alternative to the culture of normalcy prevalent in neoliberal nation-states, or a revisionist reflection on the condition of disability in modernity. For my present purposes, I also refer to other potentialities of the term: dismodernism as a tactical response or opposition to the aesthetics and politics of modernism (and postmodernism in turn) as well as modernism's dependence on disability metaphors for its operation. In the latter sense modernism self-reflexively absorbs the metaphors of non-normative embodiment (disruption, fragmentation, inwardness) as its ontological basis. So configured, modernism is modelled on what Davis proposes for a catchphrase of dismodernism: 'Form follows dysfunction' (2002, 27). Coetzee's practising of dismodernist sensibilities lies in the ways he takes account of embodied ethics by deploying literary devices that both embrace and resist modernist assumptions as well as in the ways in which his fictions elicit from the reader a sustained meditation on its own structural incompleteness and insufficiency. The Coetzee novel that forcefully exemplifies the ethics of dependency underpinned by forms of narrative disruption is *Slow Man* (2005), which is the subject of the following discussion.

Against Prosthetic Postmodernity

The plot of *Slow Man* centres around the life of middle-aged Paul Rayment who loses his leg in a cycling accident.[5] When incapacitated, Rayment's social life is restricted to the regular ministrations of his dependence-care nurses. Paul's infatuation with one of them, Marijana, marks a pivotal moment in his life: one of promise and complication. To remedy the latter, the renowned Australian novelist, Elizabeth Costello, enters the scene, but the remedy is no guarantee of redemption. From this point on, a linear tale about existential anxieties of a physically impaired man and his dependence on the neoliberal healthcare facilities, veers precariously between realist verisimilitude and metafictional commentary on the interdependence between characters and their author.

From its beginning, the novel stages Paul's uneasy relationship with healthcare services on which he depends. He caustically mocks the instrumentalising practices of institutional care. When instructed by his doctor about 'the care of [his] leg', Rayment muses angrily: '*Care of my leg?* [. . .] *You anaesthetised me and hacked off my leg and dropped it in the refuse for someone to collect and toss into the fire*' (SM 10, original italics). The use of euphemisms to cover the embarrassment of the abject body speaks to a general tendency to remove disability from public view. This renders common parlance an implement of the marginalising practices and discourses of normalcy prevailing in modern states. But Rayment's irony fails to offset his self-defeatism. For him, his present state is little else than 'a rehearsal for losing everything' (15). His suicidal thoughts – 'I am resolved not to be any trouble' (13) – seem a consequence of his own conviction about the futility of a return to social existence.

His refusal of a prosthesis ('I don't want a prosthesis' *SM* 10) marks the moment of a wilful self-consignment to seclusion as an act of surrender to the pressures of 'the culture of speed' (Murray 2018, 96). Stuart Murray argues that the neoliberal climate of immediacy is bound to exclude those that fail to conform to its regimes of multitasking and productivity (ibid.). An internalisation of this cultural logic by people with disabilities means that they accept their position as socially deficient and are willing to retreat into the private domain: 'In his own vision of the long term [. . .] his crippled self (stark word, but why equivocate?) will somehow, with the aid of a crutch or some other support, get by in the world, more slowly than before, perhaps, but what do slow and fast matter any more?' (*SM* 16–17). Although a prosthesis would offer him a reclamation of access to the social sphere, Paul seems to have ingested the consciousness of a disabled selfhood that fails to chime with the tyranny of the culture of speed (which contrasts with Paul's dedication to active life prior to the accident). His choice of 'restoring his body to functionality', as noted by Coetzee in the early draft fragments of the novel, generates a tension between a disabled person's acceptance of themselves and the injunctions of the modern state to submit the dysfunctional body to corrective and rehabilitative regimens (HRC 39.2, 2).

Prosthesis is a token of compulsory dependence of the body on technical modernity. Tim Mehigan considers prosthesis as an extension of Hegelian progressivism: 'a new forward movement of the dialectic' (2011b, 195). By refusing the prosthesis Paul resists the injunctions of modern political consciousness. But Rayment is no radical neo-Luddite: he does not resist all the bounty of technological modernity. A retired darkroom technician, he is no stranger to modern devices and the regimes of mechanical reproducibility (pace Walter Benjamin) that cushion them. But he remonstrates when technology goes beyond its basic function of facilitating nature and begins to supersede it. Photography holds its appeal as long as it connects to the material: 'as veins of darkness on the paper began to knit together and grown visible, he would sometimes experience a little shiver of ecstasy, as though he were present at the day of creation' (*SM* 65). But he loses his interest in the technology of the image the moment the spectre of digital photography, 'a *techne* of images without substance' (65), begins to supplant its analogue predecessor. To Rayment, to use Benjamin's terms, analogue photography retains 'the here and now of the work of art – its unique existence', whereas digital technology eludes the authenticity and materiality of a singular artwork in its infinite reproducibility and proliferation

(2010, 1053). Likewise, Rayment appears at peace with the obsolete technology of crutches, which 'are at least honest' (*SM* 58). The crutches are 'honest' because they complement the organic; a prosthesis, on the other hand, supplants it. The word 'prosthesis', etymologically signifying placing something in addition to something else,[6] turns into a Derridean supplement, which 'adds only to replace' (1998, 145).

Rayment's apprehensions seem to suggest that he does not as much defy the impositions of modernity as postmodernity. He displays symptoms of anthropomorphobia in relation to the prosthetic body, which may be linked to the fear of technological singularity of the simulacrum age that marks the postmodern anxiety about a self-sufficiency of the technological and the resultant redundancy of the human. Although, as stated by Jean-François Lyotard, modernity is defined by a necessity 'to break with tradition and new way of thinking', the very opposition to tradition puts modernity in a firm relation with its predecessors (2010, 1466). And it is through the oppositional tactics that modernists were able to engage with the challenges of modernity. The postmodern simulacrum age, in Baudrillard's terms, 'bears no relation to any reality whatever' and in so doing it cuts all references with nature and history (1988, 173). If a prosthesis affirms an organic referent (the missing limb), it discloses the lack rather than existence of the referent it professes to represent, thus merely 'mask[ing] the absence of a basic reality' (ibid.). A prosthesis is a marker of *care for* the body. It attempts to restore the body to normalcy by means of medical technology. By rejecting it, Rayment resists the injunctions of the prosthetic age to correct or enhance the body by means of the biotechnological simulacra of postmodernity which aim to restore the body to the rigours of the culture of speed. But Rayment's act of defiance marks also the moment in which dismodernist ethics counters the oppressive demands of neoliberalism.

Although, after Murray, the neoliberal culture of speed foists upon the disabled person notions of selfhood predicated on lack and absence, it is not the impairment itself that forces Rayment to reconfigure his new identity around the notions of lack, but the moment in which hospital authorities insist on prescribing the prosthesis and other rehabilitative measures. The missing leg asserts its absence only at the moment when a prosthesis threatens to plant itself in its place. Following Baudrillard's logic of simulacrum, the leg ceases to exist the moment its simulacrum appropriates the space of the non-existing referent, thus exposing its absence. The pressurising tactics of dependence-care industry push Rayment to what Mitchell refers to as 'a life of oppressive idiosyncrasy' (2000, 313), which he attempts to counterbalance by reclaiming his subjective autonomy: 'If you don't want a prosthesis, what would you prefer?' / 'I would prefer to take care of myself' (*SM* 10). Therefore, Rayment's militant denial of prosthesis marks an ontological assertion of 'his crippled self' (17) configured in opposition to the forms of biopolitical appropriation of the body, symptomatic of the age of prosthetic postmodernity.

(Dis)modernism and Embodied Textuality

Alice Hall observes that in Coetzee's works 'textual concerns are inseparable from an embodied physical perspective' (2012b, 136). Seen from this vantage point, *Slow Man* typifies an attempt to position the body at the forefront of considerations about textual ontology. The novel demonstrates an extent to which textual strategies approximate the complexities of embodiment. For this purpose, Coetzee employs a wide range of stylistic and narrative devices, ranging from realist to experimental. In defining 'illusionism', by which he means realism, and 'anti-illusionism', denoting postmodernist self-reflexive strategies of text, Coetzee points to the limitations of the latter term: 'But in the end there is only so much mileage to be got out of the ploy' (*DP* 27).[7] Crucially, the narrative construction of *Slow Man* is extended between both of these styles, and yet the ways in which Coetzee navigates between realism and metafiction is heavily inflected by the experience of the body. To Hall, the novel exemplifies a sort of 'realism of the body', that is, 'a fictional account that is deeply concerned with the physical' (2016, 67).

Coetzee's realism is also attuned to the pressing social and political issues of the worlds his characters inhabit. Attwell notes that Coetzee's later fiction shows earmarks of 'limited realism': 'Instead of the "simple urge to represent," Coetzee says that what engages him more is the "second order" questions. Examples would be, "What am I doing when I represent? What is the difference between living in the real world and living in a world of representation?"' (2015, 236–7). It transpires from this that Coetzee's wilful reduction of realism in his late fiction in favour of incorporating metafictional strategies marks the moment in which the evacuated pressures of commitment to realism become rerouted to a fictionalisation of social issues relevant to his immediate surrounding: an approach that helps Coetzee assume the position of a semi-detached social commentator. This position, according to Elleke Boehmer, was achieved by Coetzee's status as a naturalised Australian citizen (2011, 5). It could be argued that *Slow Man*'s depiction of the experience of an ageing middle-class naturalised Australian, filtered through metafictional tactics, derives from this combination of autobiographical references.[8]

But *Slow Man* is a novel that puts to test Coetzee's forays into realism. The realist veneer is first shaken when, upon her unsolicited visit to Rayment's flat, Elizabeth Costello begins to recite the opening lines of *Slow Man* almost in verbatim. This act of assertion of authorial control over Rayment's life is immediately recognised by him as an encroachment on his personal autonomy. From this moment on, Costello is consistently addressed as an intruder by Rayment, to which she responds repeatedly with her enigmatic mantra: 'You came to me' (*SM* 85), thus confirming the possibility that the text may now operate on the extradiegetic level, beyond the generic confines of realist representation. Attridge says that Coetzee's tactical disruption of realist modes of fictional representation partakes in his questioning of prevailing discourses of power and conventional morality (2004, 13). Whether a guardian angel or a Mephistophelean figure, Costello bullies Rayment into self-reflection: 'I return to my first question. Who are you, Paul Rayment, and what is so special about your amorous inclinations? [. . .] Two a penny, Mr Rayment, stories like that are two a penny. You will have to make a stronger case for yourself' (*SM* 82). That Costello appears immediately after Rayment has professed love to Marijana is telling. Not only does she attempt to save Paul from falling into an over-romanticised, inexorably hopeless, conventional love, but she also attempts to prevent the text from lapsing into a cheap romance. Therefore, Costello's assault on conventionality inscribes itself at the heart of textual operations and ethical themes alike.

Attwell traces a possible rationale for the (meta)fictional arrival of Elizabeth to an actual moment of Coetzee's crisis of writing: 'In this period, when Coetzee reached what had become a familiar moment of doubt with *Slow Man*, when he reached that typical point of crisis at which the metafictional impulse asserts itself, on this occasion he opened the door and let Elizabeth Costello in' (2015, 243). This point at which the novel skims its realist surface is followed by a summoning of an author-figure so as to reconstruct the shattered edifice of realist verisimilitude. For that reason, Elizabeth offers her own substitute of Marijana by introducing him to her blind near-namesake Marianna and stage-managing their sexual intercourse. But the all-too-convenient coincidence of names together with the farcical theatricality of the act ('Does [Elizabeth] intend, do you think, that you and I should become a couple? For entertainment perhaps? The halt leading the blind?' [*SM* 110–11]) implies that metafictional staginess continues to compromise any attempts at the novel's realist reassertion. But tables are about to turn. If Costello endeavours to save the novel from the constraints of realism, her further attempts to control Paul threaten to restore the totalising traditionalism she takes pains to counter.

Assuming that 'storytelling' is 'an attempt to control discomforting bodies', conventional literary narratives are complicit in perpetuating the narrow definitions of non-standard embodiment (Hall 2012b, 126). Clare Barker claims that, when novelists apply narrative or formal devices resulting in reducing the complexity of disability experience or removing disability or disabled characters from the text altogether, 'a kind of narrative eugenics is at work' (2018, 145). Costello's persistent attempts to write Rayment into narratives of her own making, culminating in her unsuccessful proposal to have Paul live with her, are redolent of the familiar moment in which a narrative closure is employed to satisfy the hermeneutic expectations of the readers. On such occasions, to counterbalance the reader's 'hermeneutical impasse' (Quayson 2007, 49) – resulting from the reader's inability to accommodate otherness within her reading expectations – a conventional plot resolution or narrative closure serves the purposes of refamiliarising the story in keeping with normative or traditional narrative laws. That such techniques often result in a reduction of a complex life experience of the non-normatively embodied characters means that literary narratives can act as biopolitical instruments designed to curb the ontological autonomy of the disabled body. Paul's refusal of such a neat narrative closure provides a counternarrative to reductive disability discourses that offer simplistic, sentimental or tragic plot resolutions to otherwise complex life experiences of embodied beings.

And Coetzee takes the matter of doing justice to embodied ethics seriously. The body is often an active narrative agent endowed with distinct ontological autonomy:

> In his sessions with the physiotherapist he was warned about the tendency of the severed thigh muscles to retract, pulling the hip and pelvis backward [...] If he were to give in and accept a prosthesis there would be a stronger reason for exercising the stump. As it is, the stump is of no use to him at all. All he can do with it is carry it around like an unwanted child. No wonder it wants to shirk, retract, withdraw. (*SM* 58)

This passage demonstrates Coetzee's empathetic imagination towards the body. Rather than a site of abjection, as Rayment no doubt believes it to be, the amputated leg is presented by the narrator as an agential self-reflexive being capable of human responses. The stump is doubly injured: physically – as a result of the amputation; and emotionally – disclaimed by its owner. Rayment's proud refusal of prosthesis, resulting in his self-induced idiosyncrasy, is intuited by the stump, which retreats into itself likewise. But the anthropomorphic agency operates not only at the allegorical but also metanarrative level, and in doing so it is indicative of wider formal preoccupations of the novel. Paul's reluctance to accept the prosthesis doubles as a refusal of the narrative to exhaust itself in the linear form. The point at which the text turns on itself through metafictional interventions resonates with the shock of the mutilated body: the retraction of the severed muscles paralleling metafictional implosion of the narrative and resultant subversion of the generic laws of the genre, marking the novel's inability to restore itself to realist fictional modes.[9] If traditional narrative devices lend themselves as conduits for ventriloquising political biases meted out to those that fail to conform to socially sanctified standards of embodiment, disruptive formal effects open up new potentialities for embodied ethics. The moment the storyline meanders away from the diegetic, disability resonates beyond the fictionalised physical state. The truncation of Paul's 'complete' body prefigures the mechanisms of narrative fragmentation that follow through metafictional disruption. Similarly, the character's awareness of his body as a site of dependency translates into modes of textual self-reflexivity: text as a venue for a dramatisation of the character's awareness of his dependence on authorial intention and generic conventions.

Slow Man is preoccupied with the issues of dependency at the representational, contextual and metatextual narrative levels. The characters are entangled in a set of relations involving mutual dependence and care. Indeed, the word 'care' appears in all manner of semantic iterations and modalities. Rayment depends on the professionalised care delivered by Marijana Jokic, 'who has no studio and promises to cure, just care' (*SM* 63). But the dynamic of their relationship takes an unexpected turn the moment Paul offers to pay for her son's exorbitant tuition fees: '*You have taken care of me; now I [. . .] offer to take care of you [. . .] I offer to do so because in my heart, in my core, I care for you*' (165). This marks a familiar moment in which Coetzee's use of linguistic ambiguity reflects the character's intentions: the phrase *to care for* means 'to do the necessary things for someone who needs help or protection', and 'to love someone', thus revealing Paul's engagement as both emotional and protective (*Macmillan Dictionary* 2022). An awareness of emotional detachment in professional care is conveyed forcefully when Marijana admonishes Paul for having called on her to visit him after his shower accident, although in her view no professional intervention was required. But Paul's assertive response to the reprimand reveals much about his own notions of the ethics of professional care: 'I always thought [. . .] that nursing was a vocation. I thought that was what set it apart, what justified the long hours and the poor pay and the ingratitude and the indignities too [. . .]: that you were following a calling [. . .] when a nurse is called, a proper nurse, she doesn't ask questions, she comes' (*SM* 213). Utilitarian consequentialism represented by Marijana is here offset by Paul's deontological ethics of care, an unconditional duty to respond to the call of the other, which no longer seems to have much currency in neoliberal states, where a condition of an individual is quantifiable, and responded to accordingly with appropriate measures.

The connotations of Marijana's name, which in the earlier drafts is spelled consistently as 'Marjana',[10] are in line with Paul's idea about her role as a carer. 'Marijana of the Balkans, the giver of care' (*SM* 165) brings to mind Mariana of Quito, the patron saint of the sick and bodily ills (Quintana 2014, 234). Following this line of association, the other woman, Marianna, acts as a carer of another sort. The scene of sexual intercourse arranged by Costello involving Marianna and Rayment is reminiscent of an episode from 'The Humanities in Africa', in which Elizabeth Costello voluntarily offers sexual favours to a terminally ill cancer patient in an act of charity. The early drafts of *Slow Man* further explore the link between care and sex. Although in the published version of the novel Paul and Marjana's relationship remains unconsummated, in the previous stages of the work in progress their intercourse is more explicitly carnal. In these early scenes, Marjana offers Rayment intimate services: 'Without asking Marjana masturbates him', including sexual intercourse, during which she 'plunge[s] into the act with so much bodily passion' (HRC 39.2, 17). In these scenes, Rayment goes so far towards moving their relationship onto 'quite another footing' as to make a desperate promise to accept the prosthesis in exchange for her erotic favours: 'If you will have me I will change my mind about the prosthesis' (ibid.). But Coetzee abandons these ideas in later drafts. This narrative volta allows Coetzee to challenge the neoliberal culture of desirability of the normal body through Rayment's refusal of a prosthesis and to explore the ethical consequences of the entanglement of platonic love and care by removing from the plot the erotic liaison between the protagonists.

Paul's own grappling with the meanings of care further plays on the complexities of embodied existence:

> But her question echoes in his mind. *Who is going to take care of you?* The more he stares at the words *take care of*, the more inscrutable they seem. He remembers a dog they had when he was a child in Lourdes, lying in its basket in the last stages of canine distemper, whimpering without cease, its muzzle hot and dry, its limbs jerking. '*Bon, je m'en occupe,*' his father said at a certain point, and picked the dog up, basket and all, and walked out of the house. Five minutes later, from the woods, he heard the flat report of a shotgun, and that was that, he never saw the dog again. *Je m'en occupe*: I'll take charge of it; I'll take care of it [...] That kind of caring, with a shotgun, was certainly not what Marijana had in mind. Nevertheless, it lay englobed in the phrase, waiting to leak out. If so, what of his reply: *I'll take care of myself?* What did his words mean, objectively? (SM 43–4)

The double meaning of the phrase 'take care of' connects with Paul's own experience as a solitary amputee, ranging from his avowal of self-sufficiency to his suicidal thoughts. His persistent attempts to grasp the meaning of the words 'objectively' denotes a failure of reason to resolve the aporia of embodied being intuited by linguistic ambiguity. But the semantic doubling of significations of care also gestures towards larger issues that extend beyond the novel's fictional framework. The entanglement of responsibility and violence inscribed into the metaphysics of care evokes the sense of forced privacy that people with impairments are consigned to as a result of part paternalistic, part repressive regimes of containment and exclusion towards the non-normatively embodied. In doing so, Coetzee tacitly takes to task the modern notions of dependency, be they based on welfare politics or neoliberal economy. Rayment is apprehensive of the biopolitical powers of dependence-care authorities embodied by Mrs Putts: 'Welfare means caring for people who cannot care for themselves. If, somewhere down the line, Mrs Putts were to decide that he is incapable of caring for himself, that he needs to be protected from his own incompetence, what recourse would he have? He has no allies to do battle on his behalf' (SM 22). Rayment's anxiety is born from the recognition of the biopolitical power of the state and of himself as a Foucauldian 'modern man' – 'an animal whose politics calls his existence as a living being into question' (Foucault 1998, 143). Paul is trapped in the biopolitical strategies of the state, 'which assumes and integrates the care of the natural life of individuals into [the] very center' of its political mechanisms (Agamben 1998, 5). Dialectical structures of dependency and power between the state and its subjects involve complex relations in which care becomes indistinguishable from control. The enmeshment of dependency and power means not only that the individual that claims social care is subjected to forms of organised control, but also that the state has the power to subjugate the body into a state of dependency, by which the political state claims a mandate to submit the body to all manner of rehabilitative or carceral procedures.

Davis proposes that dependency is 'a state of exception in one sense of being a state outside the norm. But in another sense, it is a state well within the norm' (2007, 4). A disabled body plays a double role in modern societies: one of an *exception*, a cultural other against whom the able-bodied construct notions of themselves as normal and authoritative; and one of a *rule* – the dependence of every body on 'vast networks of assistance and provision that make modern life possible' (ibid., 4). This double function need not be seen as a paradox, but a political logic of modernity. According to Giorgio Agamben, '[t]he exception does not subtract itself from the rule; rather, the rule suspending itself, gives rise to the exception and, maintaining itself in relation to the exception, first constitutes itself as the rule' (1998, 18). The exception does not confirm the rule; it becomes the rule. Drawing on Agamben's terms, dependency as a state of exception operates in two ways. The individual – the disabled or in other ways disenfranchised person claiming different forms of special institutional or legal assistance – held in the state of dependency is reduced to a 'bare life' (*zoê*) over which the power claims ultimate control. This foists upon the dependent person a sense of themselves as occupying the state of exception to the general principle of independency and self-sufficiency fostered by modern individualised capitalist societies. Marked by a state of exception, a bare life has no claims for a social and political life (*bios*) characteristic of a regular, 'normal' citizen. But the state does not stop at socio-political marginalisation of those relegated to the state of exception; rather, every individual must in a sense occupy this state in order to be available for state control. In other words, the state reinforces its power and order through the narrative of every individual's dependence on state provision and protection. Unless an individual is reduced to a bare life, the state has no mandate to wield total control. But Rayment's fear of being reduced to a bare life is reflected not only in the questioning of welfarist paternalism, but also the opposite end of the political spectrum:

> It is possible, of course, that he overestimates Mrs Put's concern. When it comes to welfare, when it comes to care and the caring professions, he is almost certainly out of date. In the brave new world into which both he and Mrs Putts have been reborn, whose watchword is *Laissez faire!*, perhaps Mrs Putts regards herself as neither his keeper nor [...] anyone else's. If in this new world the crippled and the infirm or the indigent or the homeless wish to eat from rubbish bins and spread their bedroll in the nearest entranceway, let them to this: let them huddle tight, and if they wake up alive next morning, good on them. (SM 22–3)

In neoliberal economies with minimum state intervention and limited power of state over the citizens, where an individual's social worth is gauged by her market value and economic independence, an individual that fails to participate in the competitive logic of the marketplace becomes banished to the outside of socioeconomic existence, or relegated to its margins through forced institutionalisation, kept in a state of perpetual dependency. But this does not absolve the economically able as well as able-bodied of the injunctions of dependency either. Liberated, if partly, from the reliance on national healthcare, the individual becomes inveigled by the system into a participation in commercial rituals calculated to fine-tune the body to the new idealised canons of embodiment. And Coetzee's *Slow Man* is a voice of socio-political conscience that is suspicious of modern political mechanisms that attempt to ensnare an individual in the culture of dependency. With neither welfarist care 'for' nor neoliberal care 'of' the body being capable of breaking the cycle of repression and exclusion.

The dismodernist sensibilities of *Slow Man* manifest themselves in the novel's contemplation of the non-normative body's aesthetic status in neoliberal societies. Coetzee's meditation on the able-bodied person's sense of 'aesthetic nervousness'[11] in their confrontation with representations of disability is amply registered in the narrator's account of the statue of the *Venus of Milo*, a scene which had its prototype in the early drafts of the novel:

> A leg can be an aesthetic object but half a leg cannot. Why? The answer has something to do with the break. The Venus of Milo is still beautiful because there is poignancy in the roughness of the break. Whereas the careful suturing of his stump is merely a comic effort to pretend that the limb naturally ends there. (HRC 39.6, 167)

> Despite having no arms the Venus of Milo is held up as an ideal of feminine beauty. Once she had arms, the story goes, then her arms were broken off; their loss only makes her beauty more poignant. Yet if it were discovered tomorrow that the Venus was in fact modelled on an amputee, she would be removed at once to a basement store. Why? Why can the fragmentary image of a woman be admired but not the image of a fragmentary woman, no matter how neatly sewn up the stumps? (*SM* 59)

The reflections on the celebrated statue in the draft calls into question the internalised ableism of people with disabilities precipitated by their exposure to the culture of negativity around the disabled body. Rayment perceives his incomplete body as a piece of flawed art, a pathetic attempt on the part of the surgeon to imitate the complete or ideal form. The loss of Venus' arms, on the other hand, is tragic rather than pathetic precisely because no attempt to restore this otherwise perfect body has been made, and therefore the aesthetic order has not been unsettled. But in the published novel Coetzee pushes this discussion further by challenging the reader to imagine the viewer's response, and the aesthetic nervousness attendant upon it, to an artist's attempt to reproduce an incomplete body. The thrust of Coetzee's considerations lies in his implicit critique not so much of the accepted norms of embodiment but of the contingency of the aesthetic criteria that reinforce the privileging of these norms. It is a reminder that the body's status as either preferred or undesirable does not depend on its immanent qualities but on the prejudicial assumptions of the viewers. The event that echoes Coetzee's remarks is the unveiling of the statue *Alison Lapper Pregnant* by Marc Quinn on the fourth plinth of the Trafalgar Square in the year of the publication of *Slow Man*. Portraying a naked pregnant woman with phocomelia, a congenital disorder characterised by the absence or malformation of the limbs, the sculpture was greeted with much outrage and criticism in the media on the grounds of its 'subject matter' rather than 'the craftsmanship of the sculpture' (Hall 2012, 1). In this sense, like Coetzee's hypothetical disabled Venus, Lapper proved in the eyes of many commentators to be an unfit subject of aesthetic representation, thus acting as an example of the power of the aesthetic nervousness of the viewer to overshadow their appreciation of the intrinsic value of the work of art.[12]

The logic of dismodernist ethics materialises in *Slow Man* in two ways. Firstly, the novel demonstrates how fictional representations of disability anticipate the text's self-conscious foregrounding of its fictional devices. If a disabled body is defined by its embodiment, the text that ingests the logic of disability brings centre-stage the awareness of its own formal strategies. Secondly, if dismodernism, as a response to the normalising and idealising pressures of modern societies, marks a culture of universal dependency and a recognition of corporeal difference, *Slow Man* embraces and critiques the logic of dependence at several levels: fictional – the interdependence of characters and empathetic imagination towards bodily impairment; and, metafictional/metatextual – the co-dependence of the author and characters, as well as the dependence of the text on both conventional strategies and subversive formal effects for addressing the notions of embodied ethics in an attempt to respond to the repressive aspects of (dis)modernity. If Coetzee's novel is dismodernist, it is in the ways in which form is responsive to the ethics of embodied being and hostile to the normative injunctions of prevailing power discourses, including those of traditional ethics of affirmation, as well as in the active reworking of post/modernist aesthetics.

Notes

1. See Davis 1995, 23–39.
2. See Foucault 2006, 38–64.
3. For further discussion on Coetzee's modernism as an ethical response to the issues of modernity, see Attridge 2004, 1–31.
4. In *Doubling the Point*, Coetzee speaks of 'a poetics of failure' in reference to the works of Beckett, Nabokov and Barth, which he defines as 'a program for constructing artifacts out of an endlessly recessive, etiolated self-consciousness lost in the labyrinth of language and endlessly failing to erect itself into autonomy' (*DP* 87). Therefore, the poetics of failure denotes a form of existential and ethical inertia of literary characters symptomatic of postmodern fiction. Although, again, Coetzee appears to propose a less regressive ethical constitution of his characters, I reckon that Coetzee's ethics is partially inflected by the poetics of failure in his wilful resistance to affirmative ethics. I argue that it is to this limited extent that it is possible to read Coetzee's ethical interventions as postmodern.
5. Coincidentally, Nadine Gordimer's 2005 novel *Get a Life*, published in the same year as *Slow Man*, tells a similar story about Paul Bannerman, a thyroid cancer patient and his experience of isolation and care. These correspondences may be indicative of the fact that in the fictions of their later period, both writers turned away from the familiar themes of (post-)apartheid violence and focused on the vulnerability of the body – a theme that was likely inspired by both authors' experience of ageing.

6. Deriving from *prostithenai*, made up of *pros* 'in addition' + *tithenai* 'to place' (*Oxford English Dictionary* 2018).
7. See Pawlicki (2013) for an extended discussion on the self-reflexivity of Coetzee's works, particularly in respect of the concepts of illusionism and anti-illusionism.
8. Equally, in Coetzee's other late novels formal experimentation makes room for social commentary: for example, *Elizabeth Costello* contains lectures on humanitarian issues and animal rights, while *Diary of a Bad Year* provides an account of semi-autobiographical opinions on a variety of social issues. Coetzee's fictionalised diaries of this period (put together as *Scenes from Provincial Life*) appear to chart the same territory of a literary experiment negotiating the problematic space between fact and fiction.
9. Considerations about the ethics of the body provoke questions about a hermeneutic response to such self-reflexively embodied texts. Such a response may be termed 'somaesthetic': one that invites reflections about bodily reactions to the experience of literary text (Attridge 2015, 106).
10. See HRC 39.2-6 for reference.
11. See my discussion on Quayson's concept of 'aesthetic nervousness' in Chapter 1 above.
12. See Alice Hall (2012), chap. 1, for her extended analysis of the critical and popular reception of the statue of Alison Lapper.

Chapter 8

What is the World Coming to? Senility, Illness and Irony in the *Costello* fictions and *Diary of a Bad Year*

Coetzee's banquet speech, marking his reception of the Nobel Prize in Literature in 2003, must have caught off guard those who had expected something more in line with his characteristically detached, unsentimental and austere writing style. Nor were such expectations unjustified considering Coetzee's obscure and complex Nobel lecture delivered a few days earlier, which 'had done little to mend a reputation for reserve and severity' (Attwell 2015, 162). In his banquet speech, however, Coetzee chose not to prevaricate this time:

> Your Majesties, Your Royal Highnesses, Ladies and Gentlemen; Distinguished Guests, Friends
>
> The other day, suddenly, out of the blue, while we were talking about something completely different, my partner Dorothy burst out as follows: 'On the other hand,' she said, 'on the other hand, how proud your mother would have been! What a pity she isn't still alive! And your father too! How proud they would have been of you!'
>
> 'Even prouder than of my son the doctor?' I said. 'Even prouder than of my son the professor?'
>
> 'Even prouder.'
>
> 'If my mother were still alive,' I said, 'she would be ninety-nine and a half. She would probably have senile dementia. She would not know what was going on around her.'
>
> But of course I missed the point. Dorothy was right. My mother would have been bursting with pride. My son the Nobel Prize winner. And for whom, anyway, do we do the things that lead to Nobel Prizes if not for our mothers?
>
> 'Mommy, Mommy, I won a prize!'
>
> 'That's wonderful, my dear. Now eat your carrots before they get cold.'

> Why must our mothers be ninety-nine and long in the grave before we can come running home with the prize that will make up for all the trouble we have been to them?
>
> To Alfred Nobel, 107 years in the grave, and to the Foundation that so faithfully administers his will and that has created this magnificent evening for us, my heartfelt gratitude. To my parents, how sorry I am that you cannot be here.
>
> Thank you. (Coetzee 2003)

Coetzee's response to his partner prefigures two aspects that would continue to permeate his later fictions following the reception of the Nobel Prize: that is, irony and senility, or rather their mutual imbrication. Coetzee claims to have 'missed the point' by taking the meaning of Dorothy's hypothetical question literally. But his admission is ironic. Rather than mistaking the hypothetical for the literal, Coetzee practises a form of Socratic irony based on feigned ignorance and employed to 'undermine the interlocutor's case' or else to put forward a case overlooked by the interlocutor (Cuddon 1999, 427). Seen in this light, the banquet speech echoes some rhetorical effects typical of the most Socratic of Coetzee's characters, Elizabeth Costello, who, having entered the scene back in 1997 in the fictionalised speech 'What is Realism?', has appeared in several novels and shorter fictions of Coetzee's Australian period, such as *Elizabeth Costello*, 'As a Woman Grows Older', *Slow Man*, 'The Old Woman and the Cats' and 'Lies'.

Nor is the reference to Coetzee's mother's imagined senile dementia in the Nobel banquet speech inconsequential. As it is not uncommon for many literary authors, the protagonists of Coetzee's later works age with their author. Although such works of the South African period as *Age of Iron* (1990), *Disgrace* (1999) and 'A House in Spain' (2000)[1] foreshadow the themes of ageing or/and illness, it is after Coetzee had settled in Australia in his early sixties that he began to rigorously interrogate the theme of senility in his fictional and semiautobiographical works. *Elizabeth Costello*, *Diary of a Bad Year* (2007) and *Summertime* (2009) count among those works in which ethical issues associated with the infirmity of old age are counterbalanced by the characters' or narrators' ironic distance, which feeds into the effects of indeterminacy characteristic of Coetzee's works broadly. If Coetzee is a novelist of ideas, the distancing effects of irony make problematic an easy ascription of the ideas at hand to the characters and narrators that voice them, or, by extension, to the author himself.

In this chapter I discuss ways in which irony in Coetzee's fiction informs the ethical considerations of old age and physical decline.

The opening section that follows offers a theoretical introduction into the aspects of the ethics of (senile) irony. In the second section, I close-read the novels and shorter fictions that include Elizabeth Costello as a character to chart the intersection of what I refer to as ironic dialogism of Coetzee's Australian fiction and the ethical aspects of senility. In the final section of this chapter, I attempt to close-read *Diary of a Bad Year* to examine the ways in which two forms of irony, formal and overt irony, aid Coetzee in mounting a critique of neoliberal biopolitics and prejudicial discourses around senescence. Coetzee uses overt forms of irony in the novel when an interrogation of senescence is reinforced by the characters' awareness and explication of the irony of the situation. Formal irony involves the ways in which the novel's textual operations create specific ironic effects that reinforce the above critique while acting as a corrective to overt forms of irony, thus being committed to the principle of ironic dialogism.

Senility and Irony

While old age and irony need not have much in common by definition, they both, if in different ways, relate to distance. One of the functions of irony is to help the ironist distance herself from an issue, judgement or situation to which she is exposed. When used to question unexamined cultural assumptions, ironic distance helps the ironist nurture an autonomous position of critical self-reflection. Søren Kierkegaard advocates a similar conception of irony when he claims that: 'Irony as a controlled element manifests itself in its truth precisely by teaching how to actualise actuality, by placing the appropriate emphasis on actuality' (1989, 328). For Kierkegaard, irony is a 'seducer', a force better to steer clear of; however, if adequately 'controlled', it is a 'guide' that challenges one to take a liberating distance from the objectivising claims of science and other totalising cultural narratives that inhibit one from nurturing one's subjectivity (ibid., 327). Along similar lines, Linda Hutcheon considers the distancing function of irony to be positive in that it marks 'a refusal of the tyranny of explicit judgments at a time when such judgments might not be appropriate or desirable' (1992, 223). This distancing function is for Richard Rorty a defining characteristic of an ironist, who commits herself to the unending 'redescription' of her 'final vocabulary', which term denotes a set of collective and private assumptions that one deems more true or authoritative than others (1993, 73–80).

This understanding of irony also resonates with Michael Lambek's belief that irony is serious, as opposed to cynical,[2] by virtue of its 'inner recognition about the contingency of truth' (2003, 3). As observed by Johan Geertsema, irony is commonly too readily taken as unethical due to its refusal to rely on discrimination as the basis of understanding. Irony, he argues, 'subverts ideas of right and wrong by [. . .] allowing for the possibility that neither – and both – possibilities might, indeed, be valid. Quite self-evidently, such a conception might easily lead to charges of a sceptical irresponsibility, as it might be taken to celebrate undecidability and aporia' (1997, 91). However, the critical function of irony, which depends on 'ambiguity, perspective, plurality, contradiction, and uncertainty', strengthens rather than contradicts the ironist's ethical engagement with others or with a cause that calls for a responsible, ethical response (Lambek 2003, 3). Therefore, the irony of the distancing function of irony is that it distances in order to bring closer. If the act of distancing is consciously aimed at oppressive master scripts, the ironist's dismantling of received truths results in a form of ethical engagement that connotes closeness and moral responsibility.

Senescence also involves various forms of distance. The vantage point of an older age unsettles the essentialist notions of the self. The self that has acquired a temporal distance from itself understands that its identity is subject to the unending process of becoming rather than being fixed and unchanging. This self-distancing mechanism is further reinforced by one's relationship with their ageing body and mind. The declining physical and mental faculties that are common for ageing people may lead to self-estrangement that materialises when an older person identifies with her younger body and mind and disowns the present, ageing version of the self. The distance is not only self-referential but also social. The ever-widening generational gap between the old and the young causes the former to feel alienated in the world that seems to be moving on without them. This sense of alienation evinces itself in what the ageing Elizabeth Costello of Coetzee's short story 'As a Woman Grows Older' refers to as the '*what-is-the-world-coming-to* things', which indicates a complaint (which is stereotypically ascribed to older people) about all that is wrong with the world (*WGO*). Characteristically, Costello's grievance is counterbalanced by her ironic distance from this age-old platitude that reinforces the reputation of older people as irritable. Finally, the older person's confrontation with her physical and mental decline leads to her diminished sense of the 'categorical desire to go on living' (Small 2007, 214). This state of mind may help her acquire a liberating distance from the inevitability of dying as well as excessive attachment to a future self.

If these assumptions about old age are correct, the status of an older person is much akin to that of an ironist. Both are confronted with the awareness that old certainties, such as collective judgements, or assumptions about one's identity, are no longer tenable or dependable. Since for both an ironist and an older person nothing is taken for granted, they are suspicious of newly received assumptions and judgements (although they can remain entrenched in the longstanding ideas and ways they have nurtured throughout their lives). This imbrication of the distancing effects of senility and irony is epitomised by many characters of Coetzee's fictions. Coetzee's ageing characters often use irony as a conduit for questioning political oppression, discourses of power and prejudicial attitudes or narratives. Lawrence Cohen also explores this potential of irony by proposing that 'a form of listening we might term ironic may allow for less depersonalization of those we hear to be senile' (2003, 122). An ironic approach to understanding senility would be, along these lines, to think about the ageing process beyond the limiting or degrading stereotypes about older people. To listen to, or read, senility ironically is to lend an ear to it, to pay it due heed, to embrace the complexity of the ageing body and mind, while keeping a critical distance from the matter at hand. This process also involves reading the discourses of senescence critically, without pandering to ageistic metanarratives that heavily draw on the biomedical notions of the ageing body. A vital counterpoint to the biomedical and stereotypical discourses about ageing is put forward by age theorists who insist that rather than being limited by their ageing or ailing bodies, 'people are aged by culture and that decline is the narrative about aging-past-youth systematically taught to us from on high' (Gullette 2017, viii).

Nevertheless, to read senility ironically is not only to eschew normative notions of ageing but also those that offer simplistic affirmative or triumphalist narratives about old age. In fact, narratives of positive discrimination only manage to reinforce the attitude that Small refers to as 'the coercive idealization of the old', which relegates the elderly to the romantic image of wise role models, or paragons of virtue and stoicism (2007, 11). To read senility ironically is therefore to unsettle the paradoxes of the commonplace representations of older people which rely on contradictory extremes, such as asexual–lecherous,[3] wise–demented, composed–irritable, benign–hostile, and so on. The tally of popular misconceptions might be complemented by the 'well-derly' versus 'ill-derly' dichotomy, which consigns older people to either the leisured and well-to-do or ailing and impoverished group (Gullette 2017, xvi). To read senility ironically is to put into question the culture of ageism (both exclusionary and positivistic), which normalises and legitimates both ends of these reductive binaries, leaving little in between. By positioning his characters in situations that resist such facile ascriptions, Coetzee brings senility and irony to bear on normalising metanarratives (such as ageism or ableism) and expose the fallacies of political regimes, liberal and authoritarian alike.

In Coetzee's fiction the critique of simplistic binaries around old age is mediated by moments of contemplation on the suffering of the ailing body. In *Life & Times of Michael K*, Coetzee contemplates the vulnerability of the disabled, ill or ageing body of the marginalised other. Unable to obtain professional care when hospitalised in time of a (fictional) South African civil war, Anna K – dropsy-stricken and unable to walk by herself – dies en route to Prince Albert in the Karoo, wheeled on a makeshift barrow by her son.[4] Alternatively, the ill or ageing body is often tactically positioned to expose the fragility of oppressors as well as the power they represent. In *Foe*, senile and repeatedly plagued by a series tropical fever bouts, Cruso dies on his return journey to England, with his death paving the way for Susan Barton to live to tell the tale and put a different spin on the famous adventure story.[5] The staging of the vulnerability of the ageing male body is participatory of the critique of the exclusionary politics of the literary canon, which for centuries has been complicit in barring socially marginalised groups from contributing to literary production, an issue that *Foe* appears to foreground most pointedly. In this sense, the symbolic authority of the coloniser and the empire is ironically deflated by the exigencies of embodiment.

In a similar fashion, the colonial expedition to the South African interior headed by Jacobus Coetzee, *Dusklands*'s second narrator, is compromised by his recurrent bouts of fever and swelling caused by an anal abscess.[6] The temporary infirmity of the white, male coloniser aids Coetzee in debunking the myth of the completeness and immutability of the empire that Cruso and Jacobus Coetzee stand for. Coetzee's early fiction is thus a forceful reminder that the idea of the empire, with its claims for completeness, power and robustness, is fated to be tested by irony which exposes the coloniser's totalising claims as fallacious. This is not, however, to imply that Coetzee uses the ageing or ailing body as a facile metaphor of the demise of the empire. In fact, Coetzee's colonisers are rarely disabled by age or physical impairments, thus reinforcing the myth of the white, able-bodied, invariably male coloniser. Instead, Coetzee is alert to the complexity of embodied existence, which produces effects that can be deemed ironic in that they thwart the oppressor's claims for power.

According to Geertsema, the subversive effects of Coetzee's fiction generate ethico-political tension between 'the transcendental imperative of an ethical community' and 'the contingent demands of a localized politics', which is 'irreducible and that it could therefore best be understood in ironic terms' (1997, 90). Coetzee is attentive to situations that generate tensions and contingencies. He interrogates these sites of contestation while refusing to take an affirmative stance on either position; and in so doing eschewing 'incorporative formalism as premised upon the conservative conception of irony', that is, irony serving the purposes of exposing one ideology while promoting another (Geertsema 1997, 92). Coetzee is careful not to allow his fiction to lapse into overt condemnation or a diatribe against one or another ethico-political standpoint. To occupy the middle ground between these ends, Coetzee uses irony, which aids him in distancing himself from affirmative modes of articulation, while retaining the capacity for putting into question prescriptive forms of ethics and politics.

Elsewhere, the themes of the declining body mesh with Coetzee's distancing formal effects. In *In the Heart of the Country*, Magda's authoritarian father, who is reported to have been killed by his daughter twice in the early versions of her unreliable account, turns into a benign older man and unmistakeably alive, albeit in an advanced stage of senile decline,[7] in the closing sections of the story. Magda's conflicting accounts of the life and death of her father are part of the novel's strategy of resistance to narrative and hermeneutic closure. That towards the end of the novel Magda refers to herself as both 'mad' and 'old' (*HC* 136) is indicative of the fact that the ironic distancing of the meaning-making process as well as the subversion of the linearity of the events is recurrently linked with old age in the novel.[8] Although one should be suspicious of reading the novel's formal operations as reflecting the medical symptoms of its protagonist's psychological states, the use of temporal and formal disruptions marks the novel's capacity for responding to complex forms of embodiment and enmindment, including those attendant on the process of ageing, which are often overlooked in realist narratorial accounts.

The pathos of the ailing body in Coetzee's novels is often offset by the liberating ironic distance that characters assume to disengage themselves from the oppressive circumstances they have been put into by the forces beyond their control. In those instances, situational irony, which takes place when the outcome of an event is different than intended,[9] yields to verbal irony, which depends on the agency of the ironist rather than the vicissitudes of fate and occurs when the ironist utters something that is in stark contrast with what she means. In *Age of Iron*, Elizabeth Curren resorts to various forms of verbal irony as a way to countervail acts of cosmic or political injustice. Her paradoxical position of vulnerability (as an elderly woman suffering from cancer) and privilege (as a white, retired classics professor living during the apartheid period) entails that her contemplation of the inevitability of death meshes with a burden of guilt for complicity in the atrocities committed by the apartheid state. When Elizabeth laments: 'I have cancer from the accumulation of shame' (*AI* 145) or 'I have cancer of the heart' (155), she ironically uses her precarious physical state as a metaphor for the destructive consequences of political oppression of the apartheid. The fact that Elizabeth is fully aware of the effects which her rhetorical games have on her interlocutors ('What did it matter if they thought me dotty?' [156]) implies that she practises a form of verbal irony in which the metaphor serves to divert the interlocutors' (and readers') attention from the literal meaning (the cancer of the body) as a way to foreground ethical concerns.

Another ageing character of Coetzee's fictions (although, since in his early fifties, middle-aged rather than elderly) who is acutely aware of the mercurial powers of irony is David Lurie of *Disgrace*. When pressed by the university committee to make a formal statement in relation to his sexual misconduct, Lurie, sensing an ulterior motive in the demand,[10] that is to humiliate himself in public rather than simply admit his guilt, refuses to follow the circuitous guidelines of the committee members. As an English teacher, Lurie is not ignorant of the allusive illocutionary agency of speech and uses this awareness to control the irony that has befallen him. However, Small argues that 'irony isn't solely in Lurie's control: for much of the novel it is his weapon against internalising disgrace, but it is also a constant element in the reader's awareness of the gaps between his self-analysis and the reality' (2007, 223). Lurie may see through the duplicity of the committee and its narrow notions of morality, but in doing so, he is not exempt from the pressures of irony. He also fails to grasp the limitations of his own part naturalistic, part romantic justification for his misconduct: 'My case rests on the rights of desire,' he makes his case, 'On the god who makes even the small birds quiver'

(*DG* 89). Nor is he in control of situational irony when his own daughter falls victim to rape, which event echoes his own questionably consensual sexual liaison with his student, Melanie. The double irony of the situation is that by putting down his transgression to the call of desire, Lurie proleptically vindicates the crime of his daughter's oppressors (the rape scene takes place, tellingly, shortly after he utters the line quoted above). Irony in *Disgrace* is also linked with Lurie's sense of his own ageing as well as with the gradual estrangement from his professional and private life. For this reason, for Small, *Disgrace* is a novel about 'how far ageing and decline may be psychological rather than primarily physical' (2007, 215). Social alienation causes Lurie to nurture a critical and ironic distance to the reality that is no longer familiar – a distance that culminates in Lurie's disavowal of the collective moral injunctions foisted upon him and his retreat from his cosseted existence in Cape Town. This retreat may also be symptomatic of the failure of an ageing person to recognise and assert her self in the ageing processes – a theme to which *Disgrace* is only a prelude and which is brought to its logical conclusion in the later Australian period of Coetzee's fiction. The section that follows discusses Coetzee's later fiction focusing on the extent to which the neoliberal notions of ethics and care as well as the biopolitics of disability and senility chime with Coetzee's rhetoric of suspicion.

Ethical Ironies

'For some years,' says Coetzee before delivering his speech 'The Humanities in Africa' at Stanford Humanities Center, 'I have preferred to compose, instead of the lecture, something more like a philosophical dialogue, in which I have devoted considerable energy to fleshing out the narrative, so that the piece doesn't simply emerge as an argument between disembodied voices' (Attwell 2015, 213). Coetzee's career as a university professor at the University of Cape Town has left an imprint on his writing as much as his fiction writing has influenced his public lectures. The fictional character that amalgamates both of these worlds is the ageing Australian writer Elizabeth Costello. Rather than giving conventional lectures, Coetzee has been often seen to prefer to read out fictionalised accounts of his ideas. However, the reverse also holds true. As the fictional substitutes for public lectures were later published as short stories or incorporated into Coetzee's novels,[11] Elizabeth Costello turned into a character whose fictional status was compromised by her role of Coetzee's spokesperson of sorts during his public speeches. Similarly, the protagonist of *Diary of a Bad Year*, JC, who shares with his author more than only the initials, recalls his critics comment on his mixed loyalties of a professor of literature and literary writer thus: 'At heart he is not a novelist after all, they say, but a pedant who dabbles in fiction' (*DBY* 191). Like Coetzee himself, forever entangled in his dual professional loyalties – by his own admission, he lectures like a writer and writes like a scholar – Elizabeth Costello, in her various incarnations, is a character whose unremitting penchant for philosophising, dialogue and questioning the nature of reality, rarely allows the reader to suspend disbelief definitively. Is she a fictional character or a metafictional device of her creator conceived to ventriloquise his ideas? Is her fictionality simply an alibi that pre-empts the imputations of her creator's subscription to these ideas? Or does her protean onto-fictional status render her an ironic character – an instrument of the situational irony staged by her creator?

In the *Costello* fictions, ironic situations often emerge from the pressures of the declining body. As a sexagenarian and, in her later appearances, septuagenarian,[12] Costello is often forced to confront the physical, mental and emotional effects of ageing. *Elizabeth Costello* and *Slow Man* recurrently put the reader on the alert for the exigencies of the ageing body, 'As a Woman Grows Older' focuses on the reclamation of personal agency and autonomy in old age, 'The Old Woman and the Cats' addresses the link between old age and eccentricity, and 'Lies' takes as its focus the difficulty of telling the truth to the dying about their condition and the ethical consequences thereof. The thrust of these works is that, while many philosophical dialogues that the characters engage in veer towards abstract ruminations about the matters related to ethics and morality, the idealism of these conversations is intermittently refracted by the realism of embodiment. By suggesting that the symptoms of Costello's 'exceptional bodiliness', such as 'exhaustion' and 'sickness', 'inflec[t] her ways of knowing and speaking', A. Marie Houser stresses the link between the pressures of the body and ideas in *Elizabeth Costello* (2020, 236). Although palpable in all parts of the Costello series to varying degrees, the demands of the senile body are depicted most intensely in 'Lies', in which Costello (albeit not referred to in the story by name) suffers incapacitating consequences of senescence: 'Her condition is as bad as I had feared, and worse' – laments Costello's son, John, in a letter to his wife, Norma – 'She cannot walk without her stick, and even then she is very slow.

She has not been able to climb the stairs since returning from the hospital' (*L*). This conflict between abstract theorising and the demands of embodiment together with the impossibilities of applied ethics often entails effects that can be called ironic. By Coetzee's own admission quoted above, the impulse behind the construction of the Costello lecture-stories was dialogic in the literal sense of the term. They were conceived as a dialogue between two characters rather than as a lecture delivered ex-cathedra in the form of disembodied ideas. However, behind the conceptual smokescreen of the Socratic dialogue of the Costello lecture-stories, a dialogue of a different ilk is brewing – one of the mutual undercutting of irony and the ailing body. If irony announces a distance, the irreducible reality of the ailing body upsets these distancing effects as much as irony undercuts the otherwise sentimental or defeatist accounts of the body in pain which literary narratives often reproduce.

Coetzee's own experience of the challenges of embodiment at first and second hand during the first decade of the new millennium – a period that overlapped with a series of reappearances of Elizabeth Costello – might have inspired concerns about the ailing or ageing body that figure prominently in the Costello stories (and other novels of the period). So much so that Alice Hall proposes to subsume Coetzee's late fiction under the term 'disability autobiography' (2012a, 57). The tally of possible biographical blueprints for these fictional scenes centring on the suffering body, as related in J. C. Kannemeyer's ambitious biography of Coetzee, is long. These include Coetzee's fracturing of his collarbone during a bicycle accident in November 2002, ending in an extended period of convalescence,[13] as well as being diagnosed with and treated for prostate cancer in 2007, which marks and possibly alludes to the titular 'bad year' of *Diary of a Bad Year* (Kannemeyer 2012, 603–4). Health problems also weighed heavily on Coetzee's close family in that period. Numerous health issues of Coetzee's daughter Gisela, including the rare combination of epilepsy, cirrhosis of the liver and osteoporosis (a disease that usually afflicts older people rather than people in their thirties) which needed extended hospitalisation and rehabilitation (ibid., 601–2) and the untimely death of Coetzee's brother David from mesothelioma (a malignant tumour attacking the pleura) in 2010, might have sharpened Coetzee's alertness to the fragility of the ageing and ailing body.

The impulse of addressing the issue of ailing embodiment remained persistent in Coetzee's fiction of the period, which Katherine Hallemeier calls 'the literature of hospice' (2016).

Among the ailing or declining characters are JC of *Diary of a Bad Year* (Parkinson's disease), John's father in *Summertime*, Mr Philips in *Elizabeth Costello* (both suffering from the disabling symptoms of laryngectomy), the ageing leg amputee Paul Rayment of *Slow Man*, and the elderly and arthritic Joseph of *Elizabeth Costello*. Elizabeth Costello, similarly, is often described in terms of her declining physical capacities as well as mental and emotional states that are stereotypically ascribed to older people. She, 'the novelist of failing powers' (*EC* 11), looks '[o]ld and tired' (*EC* 3). Her first arrival at the doorstep of Paul Rayment's flat is marked by a reference to her physical frailty: she is panting and complains about 'bad heart' (*SM* 80). Her son, John, plays up her age to justify her erratic behaviour to his wife: 'She is old, she's my mother. Please!' (*EC* 81). She can be emotionally unstable ('She turns on him [her son] a tearful face' *EC* 115), 'obstinate, [...] stubborn, [...] self-willed' (*WGO*), irritable ('I deplore what the world is coming to' *WGO*), moody and absentminded ('the mood does not leave her: the smile on her lips, the glow of animation, the faroff gaze that does not seem to include him' *OWC* 24), thus confirming some popular conceptions around the ageing process. Coetzee's attention to the vulnerability of the body in those pieces serves to interrogate the ethical implications of dependency.[14]

But these accounts of complex embodiment are informed by the distancing effects of irony in Coetzee's fiction. Literary accounts of irony include traditional types of irony and those that are specific to Coetzee's fiction. As regards the former group, the central premise of the plot of 'The Old Woman and the Cats' centres on the autotextual use of historical irony in one of the episodes of *Elizabeth Costello*, in which hindsight offers an ironic corrective on the statement made in the past. When irritated by her mother's confrontational style of addressing her audience and others around her, John wishes his mother were an obscure person living with her cats rather than an eccentric ageing public intellectual berating others for turning a blind eye on the industrial killing and mistreatment of animals: 'Why can she not be an ordinary old woman living an ordinary old woman's life? If she wants to open her heart to animals, why can't she stay home and open it to her cats?' (*EC* 83). As if in a gesture of a self-fulfilling prophecy, in 'The Old Woman and the Cats', Costello, after having retreated to a village in Spain, finds herself in precisely this situation. Her son's dismissive remark about her new lifestyle ironically brings to mind his former wish, which has come true to haunt and mock him: 'Where does it get you, mother, he says, sitting by yourself in this godforsaken village in the mountains of a foreign country [. . .] while wild cats [. . .] skulk under the furniture?' (*OWC* 10).[15]

Coetzee's interrogation of the exigencies of ageing can be subsumed under the concept of embodied irony. This iteration shows most vividly in *Slow Man*, where Costello's unsolicited arrival in Rayment's flat frustrates the reality-effect of the novel. The possible interpretation of Costello's appearance as the intrusion of the author figure into the text is an ironic reminder of the constructionism of a literary text. However, the irreducible embodiment of Costello also acts to disrupt, in turn, the suspension of the reality-effect, and the reinforcement of Costello's struggling with her ageing makes it problematic to dismiss her appearance as a facile formalistic trick. In this sense, the double function of Costello as a literary device and an embodied literary character renders the metafictional impulse of the novel unresolved. Her response to Rayment's question about whether she is real – 'Of course I am real. As real as you' (*SM* 233) – is both ironic (she is real, indeed, but on fictional terms, just as Rayment is) and indicative of the uncertain ontological status of a literary character that the text dramatises.[16]

As suggested above, the Costello fictions employ a dialogic narrative structure reflected in conversations between the characters (such as between Costello and her son John, daughter-in-law Norma, sister Blanche, her audience during public lectures, among others).[17] This structure allows Coetzee to develop a form of ironic dialogism, which, in my reading of it, denotes a situation in which a dialogue is staged as a platform for the characters to question received ideas through counterarguments. In the next stage, the finality of these counterarguments is deflated by an ironic situation. Ironic dialogism takes as its basis a form of liberal irony, which in Rorty's terms[18] involves resistance to finality and scepticism about the centrality of any opinion. Elizabeth's irritation at her sister Blanche's seizing of the moral high ground should be regarded with suspicion on the part of the reader, considering the confrontational tone of her own lectures on animals (*EC* 138); likewise Costello's censorial condemnation of Paul West's graphic depiction of the Holocaust atrocities should be regarded with suspicion in the light of her own use of the Holocaust metaphor to condemn the inhumane killing of animals in industrial slaughterhouses (*EC* 158). Furthermore, Paul West's refusal to respond to Costello's accusations is ironic in that his wilful silence stands for a disruption of the customary dialogic contract between the characters. Ironic is also the abundant and hyperbolic use of infernal metaphors in her contemplation of the banality and monstrosity of evil,[19] which seems to serve as a self-reflective corrective to Costello's confrontational style of addressing moral issues in her lectures. The formal devices that bring out ironic effects seem to hint at the possibility of Costello's pornographic obsession with evil ('she had gone on reading [West's novel], excited despite herself' *EC* 178), which compels the reader to pause to contemplate the veracity and finality of Costello's penchant for public proselytising. The purpose of ironic dialogism is thus less to affirm or deny an idea or a concept and more to deflate the authority of the speaker. Some narrative devices have the capacity to manipulate the reader into accepting the authority of those that control or dominate the narrative, such as implied authors, narrators, protagonists, or focalisers. When this happens, the reader risks acknowledging the speaker's opinions without question. Ironic dialogism serves to deny such claims for discursive authority.

Characteristic of Coetzee's dialogic devices is what could be termed as confrontational irony, typified by the use of an emphatic or provocative statement that usually leaves the interlocutors baffled or speechless. When asked by President Garrard to justify her vegetarianism, Costello responds that it 'comes out of a desire to save my soul' (*EC* 89). The response of her dining companions is one of puzzlement and the inability to fit the response within the framework of rational explanation or conventions of discourse: 'now there truly is silence' (89). Part of the ironic effect of these 'conversation stoppers' lies in the inability, on the part of the reader of the story or fictional interlocutors, to ascertain to what extent the speaker means what she or he says. Although not part of the Costello saga, *Age of Iron* and *Summertime* offer their examples of the use of confrontational irony between fictional interlocutors. When Elizabeth Curren compares her sense of historical shame to the 'cancer of the heart', the medical assistant only 'shook her head as if shaking off flies' (*AI* 156), unable to respond on Curren's terms. When Margot insists that her cousin John explain with whom he expects to communicate once he has learned Hottentot, a dead language, he replies, smirking, 'The dead. You can speak with the dead.' His response 'is more than enough to shut her up' (*ST* 104).

Akin to such ironic provocations of Coetzee's characters is what might be couched under the term of ironic defamiliarisation, which involves questioning the neutrality of linguistic constructions to attack moral certainties that these constructions reinforce. For Costello, meat products are nothing less than '[c]orpses, fragments of corpses that [people buy] for money' (*EC* 114). In a related scene of *Diary of a Bad Year*, JC encourages the implied readers of his 'Strong Opinions' to force themselves to consider eating meat 'with what Viktor Shklovsky would call an estranged eye' (*DBY* 63). JC's reference to the theorist who coined the concept of defamiliarisation is by no means accidental. When used ironically, that is, with the purpose of questioning received cultural assumptions, the defamiliarising optics can be a force for an undoing of unexamined certainties, such as the normalisation of eating meet. The use of defamiliarising terms is ironic in that it exposes a casual situation as other than it pretends to be. Such fragments often elicit an affective response from the reader to provoke her to rethink an otherwise unexamined assumption. On the part of the reader, such passages often lead to hermeneutic micro-epiphanies that shake the foundations of the reader's belief in final vocabulary. To achieve that effect, Elizabeth Costello often takes pains to demystify the ambiguity embedded in the conventions of language. When John tells his mother that 'for someone in your position' (*L*) it would be advisable to accept professional care, Costello insists that he unpack the euphemism for her, but he is reluctant to comply: 'Just for a change, just as an exercise, tell me the truth' (*L*). Elizabeth seems aware of the irony of the use of certain figures of speech that are conceived to confound what the speaker has in mind to attenuate the force of the statement. Consequently, the interrogative linguistic tactics of Elizabeth serve to compel the interlocutor to confront head-on what conventional language attempts to efface.

Confrontational irony plays a part in Coetzee's systematic refusal to debate ethical issues along the lines determined by the shibboleths of liberal and rationalistic thinking. Derek Attridge sees this sentiment as Coetzee's 'wider conception of rationality' (2017, 98). This form of rationality includes ethical thinking, which after all need not be extricated from reason, or even may need reason to work. As a subject of rationalistic debates, ethics can be all too easily entangled in preconceived and therefore restricting patterns of thinking. Once these patterns consolidate themselves, it is hard to recuperate the ethical core that has inspired them in the first place. Therefore, the question arises: how to create a dialogue between thinking interlocutors without reproducing these rationalistic patterns or without reproducing no less dualistic forms of anti-rationalistic transcendentalism? The clue may lie in the character construction of Elizabeth Costello. As suggested above, Costello gradually succumbs to physical and emotional symptoms of ageing, such as a gradual transition from intellectual to affective states. This transition is tentative in that Costello can also be a sharp and argumentative interlocutor, showing hardly any signs of senile intellectual decline (which somehow compromises an unproblematic, medically diagnostic reading of the character). However, some symptoms associated with ageing, such as a penchant for scepticism and sentimentalism, seem to serve as a platform for a critical re-evaluation of rationalistic forms of ethics. In this sense, senescence and the ironic dialogism of Coetzee's text offer joint countervoices to moral prescriptivism.

The central theme of 'The Old Woman and the Cats' is a dialogue between a woman and her son in which the ethical necessity to respond to the socially excluded other, as advocated by the mother, is pitted against the utilitarian notions of ethics championed by the son. When challenged by John as to why she refuses to sterilise the cats she keeps feeding, Costello responds thus:

> Then one day, as I was taking a walk, I spotted a cat in a culvert. It was a female, and she was in the act of giving birth. Because she could not see, she glared at me and snarled instead. A poor, half-starved creature, bearing her children in a filthy, damp place, yet ready to give her life to defend them. I too am a mother, I wanted to say to her. But of course she would not understand. Would not want to understand.
>
> That was when I made my decision. It came in a flash. It did not require any calculation, any weighing up of pluses against minuses. I decided that in the matter of the cats I would turn my back on my own tribe – the tribe of the hunters – and side with the tribe of the hunted. No matter what the cost. (OWC 22)

The encounter with the cat challenges Costello's rationalistic habits of thinking. Trying to connect with the cat on anthropocentric terms, she would be certain to fail. To overcome this impasse, she takes a leap of faith by responding unconditionally to the mute call of the other. However, Costello's non-consequentialist notion of ethics is embroiled in an irony that is not lost on John: 'Cats are hunters too. They stalk their prey – birds, mice, rabbits – and eat them alive. How did you solve that moral problem?' (OWC 22). So the cruel irony of responding to the singular other is that Costello sacrifices the well-being of other beings on which this other preys. What Costello must face at this point is the cosmic irony of ethics, which is that one ethical decision usually entails unethical side effects of this decision. From this it follows that the consequences of an ethical decision necessarily annul its claims for rightness. Utilitarian ethics addresses this contradiction by calculating the gains and losses of an ethical decision in order to choose the greater good or lesser evil of the outcome. However, Costello does not seem impressed by utilitarian calculations: 'I responded without question, without referring to a moral calculus' (22). She refuses the utilitarian solution her son advocates, with the implication being that the utilitarian morality rests on the sacrifice of others too, and for her ethics is a matter of substance rather than degree, that is, of the deontological duty to respond to the call of the other, rather than of the utilitarian impulse to calculate the moral implications of a decision: 'The other way I speak of is not a matter of choice. It is an assent. It is a giving-over. It is a Yes without a No' (25). Her turn to a singular ethics exposes the limitations of utilitarian ethics without, however, escaping the cosmic irony of the ethical principle itself. The irony of the ethical limitations and contradictions of her moral decisions remains unaffected by her refusal to succumb to moral rationalism.

But John does not tire too quickly of his Socratic baiting: 'It's a pretty picture but who is going to feed them all?' (*OWC* 24). Elizabeth retorts: 'God will feed them' (24), as if in a futile attempt to, characteristically, end the conversation with the use of confrontational irony. John responds to his mother's provocation thus:

> There is no God, mother. You know that.
>   No, there is no God. But at least, in the world I pray for, every soul will have a chance. There will be no more unborn beings waiting outside the gate, crying to be let in. Each soul will have a turn to taste life, which is incomparably the sweetest sweetness there is. And we will be able to hold up our heads at last, we masters of life and death, we masters of the universe. We will no longer have to stand barring the gate, saying, Sorry, you cannot come in, you are not wanted, you are too many. Welcome, we will instead be able to say, come in, you are wanted, you are all wanted. (24)

Costello's solution is unconditional and rests on a total suspension of utilitarian measures of population control that facilitate the maximisation of well-being. But where do these radical sentiments come from? Does Costello reveal some characteristics typical of people of a certain age, such as sentimentalism, scepticism towards authoritative explanations, a penchant for the transcendental, detachment and introversion? And does John intuit some of these symptoms?: 'He is not used to his mother in this rhapsodic mood. So he waits, giving her every chance to return to earth, to qualify herself' (24). As she grows older, Costello seems to acquire the characterological and attitudinal attributes that make her better disposed towards embracing the notions of ethics she champions: the ethics of giving-over rather than choosing. Deckard and Palm propose that Costello, through her '"ironic attitude" or, more precisely, an irony towards attitudes' represents a form of romantic irony, rather than Socratic, Rortian or verbal irony (2010, 343). Romantic irony involves a critique of reason mingled with the awareness of the impossibility of making such a critique outside of reason. This involves an ironic attitude founded on the awareness of irresolvability of the problem, in which the attitude or the demonstration of the impasse itself is a solution, if partial. The impulse of 'a Yes without a No' is one that does not rest on the liberal, triumphalist notions of choice that are consonant with claims for control, whereas the ethics of giving oneself over to the other implies a resignation of the self in favour of the other, allowing oneself to be apprehended by the ineffaceable call of the other. Costello might be anything but ironic in her attitude towards the other, but her 'giving-over' to the other is ironic in its implicit scepticism towards prescribed notions of morality.

The ironic effects of Coetzee's foregrounding of the aporetic nature of ethics are also mediated by the care of the ailing and ageing body. Such effects derive from the narrator's contemplation of the semantic ambiguity of the word 'care'. When John suggests that his mother seek professional assistance to 'take care of' the homeless cats, his mother responds: 'Take care of ... Be careful, John. In some circles take care of means dispose of, means put down, means give a humane death' (*OWC* 27). Following this thread, the reader of 'Lies', who is familiar with the ambiguity of the phrase introduced in one of the previous instalments of the Costello series, is likely to detect irony in Costello's son's assurance that his mother 'will be taken care of' if she submits to residential care (*L*). Nor does the semantic irony of the phrase escape Paul Rayment in another novel featuring Costello, *Slow Man*, as he recollects his father using this phrase as a euphemism for killing his dying dog: '*Je m'en occupe:* I'll take charge of it; I'll take care of it' (*SM* 44). Similarly, in *Diary of a Bad Year*, Anya's partner's repeated assurance 'I will take care of [JC and his finances]' (*DBY* 85, 137) rings resoundingly ironic given the attempted, if eventually thwarted, fraud he is about to commit later in the novel.

If, as proposed in Chapter 7, *Slow Man* dramatises a tension between Paul's deontological and Marianna's utilitarian conceptions of professional care, Elizabeth acts as an ironic interlocutor to Paul's notions of giving and receiving care. To Rayment's assurances that his financial offer to Marijana involves 'no strings attached', Costello responds ironically, in a manner characteristic of Coetzee's penchant for logomachy: 'What about heartstrings, Paul, strings of affection?' (*SM* 152). In these words, Elizabeth attempts to expose Paul's efforts to consolidate the reciprocal dependence between him and Marijana. Costello's justification of her intrusion ('You occurred to me – a man with a bad leg and no future and unsuitable passion' [85]) suggests that her function in the text is corrective. The phrase 'you occurred to me' seems to imply that she plays the role of a quasi-author-figure in the text. Seen in this light, the ultimate irony of Paul's attempts to implicate Marijana in the relations of care is that this process develops against the backcloth of the broader and somewhat elusive notion of care: the care of the author towards the characters of her making. The fact that Costello exercises her demiurgic agency in the novel by literally staging the farcical sex scene between Paul and her own candidate to substitute Mrs Jokić, the blind Marianna, is suggestive of her ambitions to take the helm of (take care of?) the plot of the story she partakes in as a character. Marianna's blindness figures here as an ironic device that helps Paul comprehend the authorial function of Costello, and Rayment's moment of consciousness is most forcefully spelled out in an early draft of *Slow Man*: 'She was not blind at all, he was' (HRC 39.2, 22). The appearance of Costello announces a form of cosmic irony in which 'forces outside the individual are in the driver's seat, rendering a person's actions unimportant or even irrelevant' (Kreuz 2020, 22). Nevertheless, the fact that the mystical meddler who changes the course of events is a seventy-two-year-old woman ('As old as that!' exclaims Rayment [*SM* 120]) complicates the relations of care further. Claim the position of Paul's carer she may, but being an older woman of sickly disposition means that she may also require professional care: rather than being a carer, she is a burden on Paul, and is seen as such in his eyes.

Like care, charity fails to elude the subversive grasp of irony in the Costello sequence. Nor is it the first time Coetzee toys with the ambiguities of the concept. In *Life & Times of Michael K*, the titular protagonist frowns upon an act of charity enacted upon him, seeing it as one of the forms of social dependence which he desperately seeks to escape from. In *Age of Iron*, Elizabeth Curren contemplates the etymology of the word *caritas* – 'Charity: from the Latin word for the heart' (*AI* 22) – and in her fierce diatribe against the atrocities of the political regime of the apartheid in South Africa, she bemoans that fact that 'the spirit of charity has perished in this country' (22). The irony, and one that does not escape Curren, is that 'charity, *caritas*, has nothing to do with the heart' (*AI* 22). It seems that the false etymology signals the essential ambiguity of the term:

what is the relationship between charity and love or caring? Is it as straightforward as the (false?) conceptions of collective imagination would have us believe? The irony of the term comes to light in *Elizabeth Costello*, where the charitable mission of Elizabeth's sister Blanche in her service to the frail is juxtaposed with Costello's own voluntary sexual favour to Mr Philips, an elderly bedridden cancer patient, as her own way of acting charitably or giving oneself over to the other. Her act foreshadows the thoughts of Paul Rayment: 'Does intercourse with the beautiful elevate us, make better people of us, or is it by embracing the diseased, the mutilated, the repulsive that we improve ourselves?' (*SM* 108). Is charity capacious enough to contain notions of ethics that depart from sanitised bounds of the Judaeo-Christian conception of *Caritas*? It is the ironic potential of the word, its capacity to mean more than it denotes, that makes it resonate with the capacity of ethics to operate beyond the collective master scripts of morality and prudence. As the perimeters of charity and ethics are broader than the limited proscriptions of morality allow, it is through irony that such limiting metanarratives can be dismantled.

As proposed by Alice Hall, 'Coetzee's later works explore a fascination with the ways in which the body mediates the process of writing and how this relationship changes according to different states of health and stages of life' (2012b, 130). As adumbrated above, the metaliterary aspects of *Slow Man* (such as irony and metafiction) are strongly keyed to the issues of senility and disability of the central characters in terms of the ethical implications of care and dependency. The ending of *Slow Man* and the last chapter of *Elizabeth Costello*, 'At the Gate', seem to reinforce the linking between writing, irony and old age. Rayment's refusal to spend the autumn of his life by Costello's side, as she suggests they should do, is, in fact, an ironic crypto-commentary on the nature of writing itself. Old age, as the final stage of life, helps one understand human life as a structure with a beginning, middle and end – a structure that is conventionally applied to the novel. However, old age is a process rather than an event, and one characterised by its protracted temporality and liminality between living and dying. In Coetzee's fictions, old age resists rather than reinforces narrative closure. Rayment's refusal to live with Costello is thus an ironic commentary on the lived-happily-ever-after novelistic convention that is premised on the principle of closure. Likewise, the ironic ending of *Elizabeth Costello* in which the eponymous heroine finds herself 'at the gate', reminiscent of a limbo between life and its hereafter, seems to offer a similar affinity between contemplation of the liminality of the ageing process and resistance to narrative closure. By doing so, Coetzee nurtures his ironic distance from both master scripts about ageing or illness and the literary conventions that sustain them. After all, 'in my line of work' – divulges Costello 'at the gate' – 'one must suspend belief' (*EC* 213).

Ironic Autogerontography

Diary of a Bad Year tells a story about the relationship between the ageing Australian author, known in the text variously as C, Señor C and JC, and his young and attractive amanuensis, told from the first-person narrative perspective of both protagonists. As is characteristic of Coetzee's later works, and particularly of the Costello saga, the dialogic dynamic of the encounters between the characters fosters a critique of received cultural assumptions. What shores up the ironic dialogism of *Diary of a Bad Year* is its formal construction. While in *Elizabeth Costello* one interlocutor is intended to question the opinions of another interlocutor, in *Diary of a Bad Year* the limitations of an opinion introduced in one layer of the text are exposed in another layer. This dialogic tension is intermodal rather than interpersonal. The layers do not 'speak' to each other directly. Instead, they unfold independently while inviting the reader to pit these disparate narrative strands against one another. If in a spoken dialogue (or a fictionalised spoken dialogue) the interlocutors typically assume symmetrical subject positions (such as those of speaker–hearer, lecturer–audience, mother–son, etc. in *Elizabeth Costello*), in *Diary of a Bad Year*, the intermodal, multi-layered utterances, when read vertically (layer by layer from page to page) rather than horizontally (section by section), are offset by other utterances expressed in a different mode or genre. For example, the first-person diaristic narrative of Anya occupying the third layer of the text often serves to downplay the credibility of the essays authored by JC occupying the first layer or the first-person diaristic entries of JC in the second layer, or vice versa. This narrative construction allows Coetzee to put into question the veracity of 'Strong Opinions', considering the claim for authority that the title of this section seems to make, or the authority of their author (and, ironically, the authority of the author of *Diary of a Bad Year*, J. M. Coetzee, by extension) through multimodal forms of what I referred to in the previous section as ironic dialogism. The polyphonic structure of the narrative allows Coetzee to adopt a form of 'ironic "*non*position,"' which on the one hand frustrates the claims for any narrative voice to claim centrality, and, on the other hand, exposes the inability of any narrator or author to speak from a wholly impartial position, or a position of non-authority (Geertsema 2011, 74). The fact that each section ends with a full sentence or ends abruptly in mid-sentence (thus hampering the layer-by-layer reading mode) means that Coetzee encourages the reader to alternate the two reading modes (layer-by-layer and section-by-section).

The elusive character of the novel's genre also casts some light on the links between form and irony. The novel both delivers and defers what the title promises. Although the narratives of JC or Anya could be considered as diaries of sorts (albeit the date references are missing), the novel seems to merge other genres, such as 'novel, autobiography, memoir, testimony, public opinion, and private confession' (Hall 2012a, 53). Similarly, while the character of JC is seemingly modelled on J. M. Coetzee, the differences (JC is older than J. M. Coetzee at the time of the novel's publication; JC, unlike Coetzee, is childless, etc.) seem to frustrate such unproblematic autobiographical ascriptions. Challenged by Anya to write a novel instead of a series of public opinions, JC responds: 'To write a novel you have to be like Atlas, holding up a whole world on your shoulders and supporting it for months and years while its affairs work themselves out. It is too much for me as I am today' (*DBY* 54). This remark implies that JC's justification for writing public opinions serves as a metafictional conduit through which Coetzee questions his own choice of multimodal narrative in place of a conventional novel, thus fuelling the autobiographical energy of the novel while keeping it subdued. In a similar vein, Derek Attridge proposes that '[a]lthough *Diary of a Bad Year* is far from being a memoir, it does at times read as an attempt on the part of Coetzee to see himself, unflatteringly but amusedly, from the outside: the elderly writer, finding novels more and more difficult to write, letting off steam in opinion pieces, and, perhaps, liable to inappropriate and unfulfillable passions' (2020, 94). Along these lines, Coetzee employs formal devices to nurture an ironic distance towards himself as an ageing writer while confounding the straightforwardly autobiographical status of his novel. Considering the far-reaching liberties with historical truth that Coetzee took in his semiautobiographical novel *Summertime*,[20] it could be argued that his third instalment of the trilogy *Scenes from Provincial Life* is a companion piece to *Diary of a Bad Year* in that in it Coetzee employs formal experimentalism as a way to forward a self-scathing account of the life the late writer 'John Coetzee'. For all the factual inconsistencies of *Summertime* and *Diary of a Bad Year*, both works seem to show Coetzee's auto-ironic impulses to intensify as he ages, and the resistance to historical accuracy manifested through the formal experimentation of the works partakes in the process of the ironic self-distancing of the author.

JC's complaint about his ostensible recalcitrance to writing a novel as an older man also gestures towards a larger thematic strand of the novel, one of the contemplation of the limitations of the ageing body. In this sense, *Diary of a Bad Year*, rather than a straightforward autobiography, could be termed an autogerontography, which term I use to refer to a literary account of the author's experience of ageing, or else 'auto/somatography', which 'highlight[s] the problem of narrative agency in relation to disabled or ill authors of autobiographies' (Hall 2012a, 57). In this respect, Coetzee's late fiction puts itself in the tradition of those writers of his generation, such as Philip Roth, A. S. Byatt and Doris Lessing, among many others, whose later fictions interrogate the pressures of senescence or reflect their authors' own experience of ageing. Roth's novels *Exit Ghost* and *The Dying Animal*, Byatt's collection of short stories *Little Black Book of Stories* and Lessing's essay collection *Time Bites* demonstrate the authors' enquiry into ageing in the ways that reflect their own life experience. That Coetzee took keen interest in the works of these writers is documented in his essay collections *Stranger Shores*, *Inner Workings* and *Late Essays 2006–2017*. Beckett's multiple accounts of ageing in his plays and novels are likely to have inspired Coetzee's in this direction as well. Attwell also mentions Saul Bellow among the writers whose reflections on ageing Coetzee studied (2015, 177).

While the references to old age abound in *Diary of a Bad Year* – JC's awareness of himself as an older man with the Parkinson's disease is compounded by the awareness of the futility of his veiled amorous advances to Anya – the structure of Coetzee's gerontography elicits some hermeneutic effects that resonate with the process of ageing. The text enjoins the reader to choose from at least two possible ways of approaching the text. Reading each of the three narratives of the novel separately allows the reader to follow their logical and linear structure unimpeded but at the cost of having to navigate one's way through the text back and forth. Following each page from top to bottom may hinder the reader's sense of the text's linear and logical progression and thus to disrupt her familiar habits of reading. When approached this way the text begins to appear as fragmented, disjointed, unfocused and elusive in the reader's perception. Various genres require different reading approaches. If the contemplative nature of the sections placed on the upper layers of the page 'Strong Opinions' and 'Second Diary' demands a decelerated reading process, the narrative of JC, a first-person diaristic narrative recounting JC's relationship with Anya, and the narrative of Anya (another first-person diaristic account replete with witty anecdotes, erotic teasers and a thwarted crime story) require a less engaged and more fast-paced reading involvement on the part of the reader. The effect of these modalities of reading is that the reader is compelled to modulate her reading abilities and process, especially when she follows the text page by page rather than narrative by narrative, which might lead to her failing to remember, if only momentarily, what she has read on the previous page or else losing track of one narrative when repeatedly interrupted by another. This disruptive reading experience might be meant to evoke, and hence encourage the reader to ponder on, some effects associated with ageing (or specifically the protagonist's experience of Parkinson's disease), such as distractibility, forgetfulness, confusion, slowed thinking or disorientation. In this sense, Coetzee's formal tactics serve to amplify the novel's sustained contemplation of embodied experience.

If one of the functions of irony is to allow the narrator, character or the reader to come to realise something they did not know before, the ironic function of *Diary of a Bad Year* is to help the reader revise her received assumptions about ageing. At the narrative rather than the structural level of the novel, however, the revision of ageist metanarratives develops through an ironic interplay between the younger characters' (specifically Anya's and Alan's) stereotyping of JC on account of his age, and JC's own internalised ageism or its rebuttal. The polyperspectivity of the novel permits the competing narratives to create ironic effects which result in a reciprocal undermining of the fixed opinions held by the narrators and characters. Conscious of her alluring looks, Anya accepts her role of a young secretary desired by her older employer: 'That is the game between him and me. I don't mind' (*DBY* 28). Although JC does not deny having indecent thoughts about Anya ('God, grant me one wish before I die, I whispered; but then was overtaken with shame at the specificity of the wish and withdrew it' [8]) on many occasions, such improper intentions are elsewhere imputed to JC on the basis of stereotypical assumptions about the sexual behaviour of older people, as indicated by Anya's patronising remark: 'For an old man, after all, what is there left in the world but wicked thoughts?' (97). Similarly, Alan attempts to persuade Anya that JC has employed her to trick her into typing his sexual fantasies about her, which according to Alan is JC's roundabout way of 'exercising power over a woman when you can't fuck anymore' (60).

JC's own response to his relationship with his ageing body rests on his inner struggle between the refusal to embrace ageistic metanarratives and their internalisation. JC often resorts to ageistic metaphors or stereotypes when referring to his opinions or writing: 'I should thoroughly revise my opinions, that is what I should do. I should cull the older, more decrepit ones, find newer, up-to-date ones to replace them' (*DBY* 143). Later, JC complains that his opinions have been nurtured in the 'spirit of impotent scorn' (146). The choice of the metaphors of population control and experience of senility in reference to his creative powers are telling. JC attempts to euthanise the old man in him to reduce the distance between himself and Anya. The rejuvenation of his creative powers would entail the rebirth of himself as a writer, and, in turn, as a man. Not without reason does this fragment coincide with his attempts to plead with Anya to resume her duties as a typist. Having admitted that his opinions have grown 'obdurate, stony, bullish' with age (126), JC revises his opinions through the lens supplied by Anya: 'I can see these hard opinions of mine through her eyes – see how alien and antiquated they may seem to a thoroughly modern Millie' (136–7). This new optic via which JC has acquired an ironic distance to his own opinions is instrumental in JC's overcoming of the prejudicial opinions accruing as a result of the generation gap. On the other hand, and ironically so, this comes at the cost of reinforcing another form of prejudice: JC's internalised ageism.

The process of renouncing the old in JC comes through the neoliberal principle that everything can be bought: 'Can one buy fresh opinions in the marketplace?' (*DBY* 143). Although critical of neoliberalism in his 'Strong Opinions', JC is now clinging to the neoliberal logic of commodification of human experience as a last-resort attempt to win Anya back. The turn of the phrase is, however, ironic, if partly. It seems to mock the neoliberal false consciousness that exploits the psychological vulnerability of consumers in order to capitalise on it. JC concludes: 'Are old men with doddering intellect and poor eyesight and arthritic hands allowed on the trading floor, or will we just get in the way of the young?' (144). At this point, JC's internalisation of ageism, which is in line with the neoliberal culture of productivity, is shortly offset by a counternarrative that puts into question this cultural logic of exclusion. Although 'Strong Opinions' serve to criticise 'what is wrong with today's world' (21), they are a mere sideshow to the dynamic between Anya and JC related in their separate first-person narratives. The irony of 'Strong Opinions' is that their claim for rational authority (as demanded by the laws of the public opinion genre) only conceals the fact that JC's real focus is on the bodily and the erotic, rather than rational or political. Not that JC fails to see the irony of it. It is the ageing narrator himself who sees his own attempt to discredit the world that discredits people like him on account of their age as a symptom of senile insecurity. JC self-reflectively admits that by mounting his critique of the current order of the world, he is 'taking a revenge on the world for declining to conform to my fantasies' (22). One of the major narrative strands of the novel, the public opinions, rests on JC's inability to come to terms with his feeling of being redundant as an older man: 'We find that we are too old and infirm to enjoy the proper fruits of our triumph' (22). JC's critical defiance may be part of his refusal to come to terms with the cultural prohibitions associated with personal manners and sexual behaviour imposed on the elderly (Theris and Jett 2013), which is indicative of Coetzee's systematic critique of oppressive cultural narratives.

The critique of ageism ingrained in the neoliberal culture of productivity reverberates most forcefully in the grotesque, to the point of being auto-ironic, diatribes of Alan against JC and the apparently outdated values the ageing author promulgates in his public opinions. Alan explains to Anya why in the English-speaking world of common sense, writers like JC, 'whose sole achievement lies in the sphere of the fanciful' (*DBY* 206), have no currency as public speakers, ironising, '[w]hereas in places like Germany and France people still tend to drop to their knees before the sages with white beards' (207). Alan, a steadfast neoliberal individualist, mocks the idea of looking up to wise men as a source of knowledge. By trading knowledge for information, the neoliberal order has finally dismissed the figure of an old sage as impractical and redundant. In her *The Right to Main* (2017), Jasbir K. Puar expounds on how neoliberal states exploit and manage human capacities to sustain their power structures. If the state wields biopolitical power to mobilise the capacities that legitimise the system, those capacities that threaten the power can be debilitated and vice versa. Therefore, for Puar, ability and disability are not the essential attributes of the body. Instead, they are specific functions within the system that can be manufactured and tailored according to the specific demands of the state. It follows from this that the state has the power to capacitate a disabled body 'through circuits of (white) racial and economic privilege, citizenship status, and legal, medical and social accommodations' and to debilitate a non-disabled body through various forms of institutional and military practices (Puar 2017, 20). By uncritically extolling the virtues of the neoliberal state, Alan subscribes to attitudinal ageism ('*Oldies need not apply*' [*DBY* 208]), reinforced by the triumphalist narratives of neoliberal individualism calculated to denigrate, and therefore socially debilitate, those individuals whose capacities are seen as unprofitable for the system. Alan ironises: 'Wanted: Senior Guru. Must have lifetime of experience, wise words for all occasions. Long white beard a plus' (209). To Alan, JC's efforts to publish his critique of the ills of the neoliberal state are a desperate, last-resort attempt to reassert his authority in the teeth of his waning mental and motor capacities: 'You have decided to try your hand at being a guru, Juan' (208). What JC objects to in his 'Strong Opinions' is the cultural euthanasia of older people as well as the social logic of 'the biopolitics of debility' conceived to devalue the capacities of the elderly (Puar 2017, 20). Such social and cultural debilitation of the aged is due to the conflation of disability and old age prevalent in the cultural metanarratives around senility. By stressing the social constructionism of old age and delinking senility from disablement, Jessica Kelley-Moore disputes the reliance on 'organismic ageing' as a cause of disability (2010, 99).

In discussing the notion of 'ablenationalism' Sharon L. Snyder and David T. Mitchell point to the ways in which neoliberal nation-states combine the principles of nationalism and norms of ability to forge normative standards of citizenship (2015, 13). Within such a framework disability, which does not live up to these normative standards of embodiment and productivity, is contained through various forms of institutionalisation and segregation (such as involuntary hospitalisation and sterilisation, inaccessibility of public spaces, segregated education, to list a few). What is socially discredited and excluded must now be politically included and contained within the confines of the state. Therefore, neoliberal states allow a form of 'inclusionism' which, however, 'requires that disability be tolerated as long as it does not demand an excessive degree of change from relatively inflexible institutions, environments, and norms of belonging' (Mitchell and Snyder 2015, 14). What may appear as an inclusionary policy of nation-states, implemented to activate and empower people with disabilities, is, along these lines, merely an oppressive tactic conceived to compel disabled citizens to conform to the norms of productivity determined by the injunctions of market capitalism. In this sense, the liberal shibboleths of inclusion, choice and independence are better defined as the regimes of incorporation.

In his 'Strong Opinions', JC maintains an ironic distance from these liberal catchcries by exposing the double standards of modern nation-states. Although democracy is premised on the basic principle of the freedom of choice, the only choice that citizens are allowed to exercise is reduced to electing a candidate from within the system. The citizen is not allowed, however, to choose the system itself: 'Democracy does not allow for policies outside the democratic system. In this sense, democracy is totalitarian' (*DBY* 15). Born into the system, the citizen is merely a 'subject presented with the accomplished fact' (8). This system is capable of incorporating all forms of defiance and criticism, which 'are quite comfortably accommodated within' it (15). The irony of the cynical view of democracy is that democracy annuls any attempts to discredit the system within its limits, thus rendering the cynical view futile. One can take the ironic view, but this does not help one subvert the system. It seems then that for all the cynicism, the tragedy of the way the democratic system works is that the 'people engaged in spreading freedom see no irony in the description of the process just given' (9). JC's critique of the constraints of citizenship in a democratic state echoes and sheds light on the position of a disabled person within the structure of ablenationalism, in which the biopolitics of disability serves to manufacture the regimes of dependency masquerading as the culture of inclusion. JC's ironic distance towards neoliberal politics, together with his cynical view of the modern world, follows from the recognition of the paradoxes of inclusionism. Invited to comment on 'an unfair state of affairs' (22) of the modern world he may have been, he realises nonetheless that his public pronouncement is only 'an opportunity to grumble in public' (23), and the fact that he 'jumped to accept it' (23) only reveals a sense of desperation prompted by the futility of defying the normative narratives of embodiment and age from within the structures that sustain these narratives; structures capable of containing the irony that attempts to undermine them.

The ironic countervoice to the triumphalist master scripts of neoliberalism is rooted not only in JC's 'Strong Opinions' but also in the second section of the novel, 'Second Diary', which provokes a meditation on ethics and end-of-life care. The dynamic between the characters in the second part of the novel is dialogic, in that both Anya and JC find their opinions or attitudes revised as a result of their mutual influence. Alert to Anya's view of 'Strong Opinions' as being too judgemental and disparaging, JC now offers a 'Second Diary', which serves as a corrective to the previous set of opinions.

In this part, inspired by his conversations and encounters with Anya, JC discusses miscellaneous matters without the judgemental tone prevalent in the previous section. What pervades the second section is its suspicion of the utilitarian notion of ethics. JC finds prescriptive concepts of morality – such as 'Which is worse, the death of an albatross or the death of an insentient, brain-damaged infant hooked up to life-support machine?' (*DBY* 205) – inconsequential. What sets the course for this section is a rethinking of the ethics of care, disability and ageing, beyond such binary contestations. His meditation on saving the keepsakes of his departed father, as recounted by JC in the section 'My father', signals a gesture towards singular ethics in relation to those consigned to oblivion by the culture of productivity: 'Anyhow, here he is reduced to this pitiful little box of keepsakes; and here I am, their ageing guardian. Who will save them once I am gone?' (166).

If 'Strong Opinions' may be read as an attempt on the part of JC to reclaim his youth and masculine prowess through writing, thus to fend off the (socially rather than physically) debilitating effects of ageing, in 'Second Diary' JC not only embraces his ontological status of an 'ageing guardian', but also uses this position to reach out to those who find themselves on the farthest end of the continuum of life – that is, the terminally ill and the dead. In a manner reminiscent of Elizabeth Costello's self-proclaimed role of the 'secretary of the invisible' (*EC* 210), or Magda's as the 'poetess of interiority' (*HC* 38),[21] 'JC refers to himself as the 'guardian and protector of the unloved and unlovable, of what other people disdain and spurn' (*DBY* 188). JC's ethical impulse does not, however, belong in the liberal culture of choice. Like Costello, whose resolution to take care of the cats is an act of 'a giving-over [. . .] a Yes without a No' (*OWC* 25), JC does not get to choose his vocation: 'It is a role I resist; but every now and then the mute appeal of the unwanted overwhelms my defences' (*DBY* 188). Nor does it escape JC that he is soon likely to find himself on the receiving end of the ethics of hospitality and care he advocates, at the threshold of life and death: 'Inexorably, day by day, the physical mechanism deteriorates' (181). This is foretold in one of the dreams he recounts in the first story of his 'soft opinions', as Anya calls them, about his own dying day and the care he receives during that day from a younger woman (157). Anya, for whose eyes the relation of this dream is meant, responds to the call as she vows to take care of him and his affairs on his deathbed: 'I will hold his hand. I can't go with you, I will say to him [. . .] but what I will do is hold your hand as far as the gate' (226).

Nevertheless, characteristically, irony is lurking behind JC's revision of his strong opinions. If 'Second Diary' is meant to be read by Anya – it has been written, and therefore shaped, with her in mind and for her – to what extent can the reader of *Diary of a Bad Year* trust the veracity and impartiality of JC's second account? Is the reader presented with an account of an ageing author who has overcome his ironic distance towards the world, courtesy of Anya's criticism and influence? Or else is JC a crafty ironist who revises his opinions to compensate for his senile insecurities or with an eye to pull Anya into the ambit of his desire? 'Were [Strong Opinions] intended for Anya's eyes only, written for her and her alone' too? – asks Stuart J. Murray in a similar vein (2014, 324). And if so, what story lies behind this partiality? What has been lost in the process of JC's dictation, Anya's transcription and the publisher's translation?[22] Does the ultimate irony of *Diary of a Bad Year* lie in the potentiality of what has been concealed and what must remain forever deferred? Finally, what is the relation between the author of 'Strong Opinions' and the author of *Diary of a Bad Year*? The text refuses to yield definitive answers, and the force of Coetzee's ironic autogerontography lies precisely in these distancing strategies of the text.

Notes

1. In the short story 'A House in Spain', the nameless ageing protagonist contemplates his relationship with the eponymous medieval house he owns as a 'form of marriage between a man growing old and a house no longer young' (*HS* 20). This strange conviviality between a man and a house, wedded to each other not only by the rights of property ownership but also through age, is symptomatic of Coetzee's expansive notion of ethics, based on sympathetic imagination, that extends beyond traditional humanistic confines towards non-human species (as amply illustrated in *Disgrace* and *Elizabeth Costello*) and inanimate objects.
2. Irony is often equated with cynicism because the ironist's detachment often signals his or her refusal to commit oneself to the matter at hand. Along these lines, irony is associated with moral cowardice, lack of moral integrity or responsibility, or a refusal to respond ethically to a person or a cause that might call for a morally unambiguous response, which the ironist refuses to do.
3. Coetzee employs the stereotype of the lewd old man in one of the scenes of *Life & Times of Michael K*, in which hospitalised Anna is 'stopped by an old man in grey pyjamas who spoke filth and exposed himself' (*MK* 5). However, the figure of an older man is rendered nuanced in

Slow Man and *Diary of a Bad Year*, in which novels the aged protagonists show much more restrained (albeit not asexual) attitude to attractive young women.
4. The vulnerability and precariousness of Anna's position is best summarised by the third-person narrator of the novel: 'Her nights among the dying in the corridors of Somerset Hospital had brought it home to her how indifferent the world could be to an old woman with an unsightly illness in time of war' (*MK* 7).
5. In a biomedical reading of Cruso's state, it is not unjustified to argue that the contradictory accounts of his and Friday's life on the island which he recounts to Barton, together with his outlandish, purposeless ideas of building terraces for further generations of farmer-colonisers, may be attributed to mental states associated with senile dementia. See, for instance, *F* 11–12, 18, 33. Barton repeatedly refers to Cruso as an old man (53, 55).
6. I discuss Jacobus Coetzee's disabling ailments at length in Chapter 1.
7. 'I carry my father out of his room and seat him on the stoep, propped up with cushions in his old armchair, so that he can once again face out over the old acres, which he no longer sees, and be exposed to the birdsong, which he no longer hears' (*HC* 147).
8. The caveat, however, is that Magda's assertion about her age may be, as her other accounts, unreliable.
9. The death of Cruso or Anna K on the way to their destination foreclose the prefigured resolution of these novels: a triumphant return in England, and the happy life of Michael K with his mother at Prince Albert, respectively.
10. 'You charged me, and I pleaded guilty to the charges. That is all you need from me.' / 'No. we want more. Not a great deal more, but more. I hope you can see your way clear to giving us that. / Sorry, I can't' (*D* 58).
11. *Elizabeth Costello* comprises previously published fictions and lectures. An early version of 'Realism' appeared as 'What is Realism?' in *Salmagundi* (1997). 'The Novel in Africa' was published under the same title in *Occasional Papers of the Doreen B. Townsend Center for the Humanities*, University of California at Berkeley (1999). 'The Lives of Animals' (Parts One and Two) were published by Peter Singer, Marjorie Garber, Wendy Doniger and Barbara Smuts as *The Lives of Animals* (1999). 'The Humanities in Africa' is a revised version of 'Die Geisteswissenschaften in Afrika' published by the Munich-based Siemens Stiftung (2001). 'The Problem of Evil' was previously published in *Salmagundi* (2003a). 'Letter of Elizabeth, Lady Chandos' was published by Intermezzo Press, Austin, Texas (2002) (see the Acknowledgements to *Elizabeth Costello* for details). After the publication of *Elizabeth Costello*, the eponymous character also featured in 'As a Woman Grows Older', published in *The New York Review of Books* (2004), the novel *Slow Man* (2005), Coetzee's contribution

to Berlinde De Bruyckere's project *Cripplewood/Kreupelhout* at the Belgian Pavilion for the Venice Biennial of 2013, published under the title 'The Old Woman and the Cats' (2013), and in the short story 'Lies' published in *The New York Review* (2017). What binds all of these contributions together is Coetzee's reluctance to follow the conventional format of a public speech or the curator's contribution – a practice he was loyal to in his 2003 Nobel Lecture in which, instead of a traditional lecture, he read out his fictionalised account of the Robinson Crusoe story 'He and His Man' (2003).

12. In *Elizabeth Costello*, the titular protagonist is sixty-six while in *Slow Man* and 'As a Woman Grows Older' she is seventy-two. Although in 'The Old Woman and the Cats' and 'Lies' neither her age nor her name is specified, the sense of continuity with the previous Costello appearances allows the reader to assume that the aged protagonist of the stories is none other than Costello in the final years of her life. Costello also appears in two short stories in the collection *The Pole and Other Stories* (2023). In 'The Glass Abattoir', where she is unnamed too, and in 'Hope' she goes through various stages of senile dementia and physical infirmity.
13. Kannemeyer implies that this accident inspired the central plot of *Slow Man* (2012, 584).
14. For a nuanced reading of the 'dialectics of dependency' in Coetzee's later fiction, see Hall (2012).
15. The basic plot of 'The Old Woman and the Cats' carries an echo of Beckett's 'Ill Seen Ill Said' which relates a story of an old woman living her dying days in a sequestered cottage.
16. See Chapter 7 for further reference on Costello's ontological status – located between metafiction and realism – in *Slow Man*.
17. For further reference on the dialogic structure of Coetzee's late works, see Wilm (2016, chap. 7).
18. On the liberal notions of irony, see Rorty (1993).
19. Paul West is described as 'a dupe of Satan' (*EC* 164), 'Satan in one of his disguises' (169). About herself, Costello says, 'The devil is leading me on' (178), 'Satan is still feeling his way' (180).
20. See Attridge (2020, 95) on the list of counterfactual biographical details in *Summertime*.
21. Costello explains that a 'secretary of the invisible' is someone 'waiting' and responding to 'the call' of those that are incapable of speaking for themselves or itself (*EC* 199–200). Magda speaks of herself as 'a poetess of interiority, an explorer of the inwardness of stones, the emotions of ants, the consciousness of the thinking parts of the brain' (*HC* 43).
22. As Strong Opinions are to be submitted to translation and published in German by the publisher Mittwoch Verlag GmbH, which version is the reader reading? The one typed by Anya in English or another version, perhaps one translated back from German into English?

Chapter 9

Negative Capabilities: Illness Narrative as Bibliotherapy in the *Jesus* Novels

There is a reason why J. M. Coetzee has not built a reputation for writing feel-good novels. Inexorably exploring heavyweight philosophical and ethical issues, such as human and animal suffering, physical debilitation, mental and terminal illness, death, mourning, political oppression and torture, exploitation of the dispossessed (women, children, people with disabilities and animals), Coetzee's novels are known for standing firmly on the bleak side. If the word 'Coetzeean' might not be easily defined,[1] it is most often associated with the writer's penchant for reclusiveness in private life, the sparseness of his writing style, as well as the exploration of hostile settings and pessimistic themes. On top of that, Coetzee's formal experimentalism and scepticism towards narrative resolution and closure may be seen as disrupting the reader's conventional reading habits. On the other hand, Coetzee's acute examination of serious existential issues steeped in the text's philosophical self-reflection will prove rewarding for the more committed readers. Rather than sealing 'Coetzee's reputation as a master of bleakness' (Cummins 2013), the recurrent tropes of violence, illness and suffering permeating Coetzee's fictions are likely to produce certain effects on the reader that may be called, as I shall propose, therapeutic.

Coetzee's series of novels, *The Childhood of Jesus*, *The Schooldays of Jesus* and *The Death of Jesus*, often referred to jointly as the *Jesus* novels, explores the characters' coming to terms with a reality that is void of history. Deprived of temporal framework via which to construct his understanding of himself, David, the quasi-eponymous protagonist of the trilogy, invariably resorts to fiction as a point of reference, thus rendering the processes of fiction reading and making as well as identity construction inextricable. Telling a story is a vital part of bibliotherapy because it 'helps to shape experience by placing a structure on to it' (Brewster 2018, 43). The shaping of David's sense of who he is through fiction metafictionally reports on the processes involved in the reader's struggle to restore their sense of themselves through bibliotherapy. But David's illness and death, together with his ambiguous ontological status, frustrate a conventional story of restitution based on narrative closure. The aim of this chapter, therefore, is not as much to demonstrate the definitive therapeutic qualities of Coetzee's text along biomedical or psychotherapeutic lines, as to show the affinities between Coetzee's fictional staging of the relation between fiction and identity construction in his illness narratives and the effects of storytelling on a patient in bibliotherapy. I will also seek to demonstrate the extent to which Coetzee's fiction lends itself for bibliotherapy despite failing to meet the standards of traditional books for prescription.

(St)illness and Bibliotherapy

Can reading be used as therapy? Coetzee's stance on this matter is curiously unequivocal. In his exchanges with psychologist Arabella Kurtz on the relationship between fiction and psychotherapy, Coetzee states it plainly that 'any analogy between writer and therapist [. . .] must break down' for the simple reason that '[i]n the therapeutic situation there must be two persons, whereas stories are written [. . .] by one person' (*GS* 52). Therapy relies heavily on a dialogue, a process involving a projection of oneself onto the other. Although fiction may serve as a site of such a projection, the fictional other is imagined rather than actual. If for Coetzee the actuality of the other is a prerequisite for a dialogue to take place, fiction must fail to reconstruct a dialogic, and psychotherapeutic by extension, situation.

None, I think, would disagree with this statement more than one of Coetzee's own most outspoken characters – one that, ironically, is most often hailed as her author's alter ego – Elizabeth Costello. In her oft-quoted statement, '[t]here are no bounds to sympathetic imagination', Costello strongly supports the notion that the writer has the capacity to 'think [her] way into the existence of a being' real or imagined (*EC* 80). Fiction may not be a site of the writer's actual encounter with the other, but it is a conduit via which she annuls the distance between herself and her imagined object, no matter how ontologically remote from herself it may be. Witnessing the process of penetrating the ontological boundary between the writer's self and the being of the imagined other, the reader is prompted to respond to this imaginative challenge. On a similar note, Martha Nussbaum argues that, as 'an essential ingredient of an ethical stance that asks us to concern ourselves with the good of other people whose lives are distant from our own' (Nussbaum 1995, xvi), literary imagination is instrumental in shaping the reader's ethical views and standards. To Nussbaum, literature elicits from the reader a form of self-examination that activates her decision-making processes (2001). It follows from Nussbaum's theorisation that literary texts influence the reader's capacity for self-reflection and empathy.

Whereas the contemplation-inducing quality of a text can be referred to as 'cognitive empathy', which involves the reader's capacity to comprehend the character's point of view, a literary text can also activate 'emotional empathy', denoting the reader's emotional identification with the character (Davis 1980, 3). The latter type of response to a text, which is also referred to as *affective*, involves effects that are intellectual, emotional and somatic in kind (Attridge 2015, 190), and the intensity of these reactions may vary from relative indifference to strong investment with the matter at hand. Although the literary text's intellectual and emotional impact on the reader is usually a short-time affair – the reader is often moved by a novel or poem so long as the process of reading lasts, or not long thereafter – the sum of reading experiences actively partakes in the shaping of the reader's character and inner life. Many readers are indeed aware of the transformative agency of lifelong reading. Some would go so far as to testify to a life-changing impact of reading a single book (regardless of how reliable such assurances are). Instances like these provoke questions about the limits that the reading practice can have on the subjective experience and well-being of the reader. Or, to put it simply, if the reader can be variously affected by the text, can she be also cured by it?

The central premise of bibliotherapy – broadly defined as 'the guided reading of written materials' for the purpose of 'gaining understanding or solving problems relevant to a person's therapeutic needs' (Riordan and Wilson 1989, 506), and one of its variants, creative bibliotherapy, which centres on the guided reading of imaginative literature, such as poetry, dramatic works, short stories and novels, for curative purposes (Glavin and Montgomery 2017) – is that reading can be used to support or restore the mental health of the reader-patient. While more often used to provide support and guidance around diagnosed conditions, therapeutic reading has been applied – albeit with varying degrees of measurable success – for the treatment of clinical mental disorders, such as depression, anxiety and PTSD.[2] What is often at stake in such a treatment is an attempt to restore the patient's ruptured sense of self caused by traumatic events or illness.

Although reading for therapeutic purposes may involve an extent to which the reader responds affectively to the text, reading as a therapy in large part also depends on tempering emotional reading responses – a process that could be tentatively called a distancing effect of reading. This process involves the reader's contemplation of the text that helps her rethink values, norms and prejudices, especially those that have caused her to develop negative emotions leading to traumatic experiences. The ability of the reader to comprehend and obtain an emotional distance from a given problem via fiction can be then transposed onto her real-life experience. The goal of reading in this case is to confront the memory of a distressing experience taking place in the aftermath of the reading process. For this purpose, bibliotherapy relies on texts that 'provide a perspective on a topic not previously considered', give 'opportunities for the recognition of common human experience and individual feelings in a text', 'help with meaning-making and improving understanding of human experience', and provide a stimulus for the reader to take stock of her life experience and face the causes of distress or mental disorder (Brewster 2018, 42–3). This can be achieved when a story provides a fictional counterpart to the events in the reader's life or when a text, which may be unrelated to her singular experience, helps her rationalise the problem she is grappling with. An active contemplation of the causes of the traumatic feelings may be a means to offsetting the negative effects they make on the patient. A text that evokes such a self-searching response can be called dialogic because it necessitates hermeneutic processes that are not purely receptive but fundamentally responsive or performative.

Coetzee's fictions have been widely known to provoke similar self-reflexive reading effects. As discussed above in Chapter 2, for Jan Wilm, Coetzee's texts demand from their readers to 'weigh down conflicting ideas, to qualify, to backtrack, and to reconsider formed opinions about the text' (2016, 14). Calculated to hinder the reader's superficial engagement with the text's ideas and representation as well as to complicate orthodox meaning-making impulses, the use of formal devices in Coetzee's fiction forces the reader to decelerate her reading process – which Wilm calls slow reading – and encourages her to meditate on the text's ambiguities and the nature of textual interpretation alike. For Wilm, these immersive tactics serve to 'pu[t] the reader on the same level with characters, whose searching, ruminating doubting makes them thinkers [. . .] and makes Coetzee's works thinking texts' (ibid.). Central to Wilm's theorisation of slow reading is the assumption that Coetzee's self-reflective texts pull the reader into the orbit of critical meditation on the text's themes and form which, in turn, elicits from her a form of heightened identification and engagement with the characters or narrators and their reflexive preoccupations.

It is the latter aspect that is also paramount in bibliotherapy, which relies on the '"affiliation" between the reader and character as a type of therapeutic transference relationship' (McNicol 2018, 27). Bibliotherapy is a three-stage process involving: 1) the reader's empathetic identification with the character; 2) catharsis – the reader's intense emotional engagement with the character; 3) insight – marking the reader's deep reflection on her relationship with the character which in turn helps her 'deal more effectively with their own personal issues' (ibid., 29). At the basic level, this stage of identification involves various ways in which the reader develops a bond with the protagonists, which helps her grapple with the complexity of her own experience. The role of the character vis-à-vis the reader in this scenario may be that of a role model or a fellow sufferer. Although Coetzee's characters can rather unproblematically fit in both of these moulds (many readers may find Elizabeth Costello a role model in respect of animal ethics, cancer patients are likely to find affinities with Elizabeth Curren's handling of terminal illness, just as well as political migrants may sympathise with Michael K's nomadic experience or resistance to political oppression), the ethical demands that Coetzee's texts make on the reader occasion a more nuanced form of affiliation on the axis of reader and text. While Wilm is correct in locating the thrust of Coetzee's formal engagements in his ability to compel the reader to reflect on the text, part of this self-reflexive impulse is to do with the suspension of the rational in favour of the ethical engagement with certain issues. As discussed in the previous chapters, the ethical import of Coetzee's novels heavily depends on their ability to challenge the received cultural assumptions of the reader.

In bibliotherapy, the patient-reader's mental state, such as depression or anxiety, may be a consequence of her subscription to oppressive cultural standards and values legitimising social prejudice (such as an affirmation of the desirability of normalcy by people with disabilities, or many women's unconscious internalisation of male superiority) which undermine her social position or sense of self-worth.[3] Nevertheless, a suspension of one's biases and beliefs marks the moment in which one temporarily betrays one's intellectual position that fuels and completes one's sense of self. The overcoming of one's views and dogmas – no matter how ungrounded – involves allowing to put oneself in the position of intellectual and emotional vulnerability, a process that may prove challenging but eventually rewarding. When Elizabeth Costello in 'The Old Woman and the Cats' justifies her – by many standards – incomprehensible and impractical decision to keep countless cats in her home in the following words: it 'is not a matter of choice. It is an assent. It is a giving-over. It is a Yes without a No' (OWC 25), the logically trained reader is implicitly invited to suppress an inclination for a rational explanation. Similarly, the various evocative silences of the characters of other Coetzee novels, such as Michael K, Friday, the barbarian woman, Vercueil, among others, pose a similar cognitive challenge, thus asking the reader to pause, reflect and suspend her rationalistic habits of reading as well as other forms of interpretative shortcutting. The ethical impulse of the above passage does not so much derive from the protagonist's decision to care for the cats – although this does count as an ethical act by most humanistic standards – as the text's capacity for transference into the reader's experience.

If Coetzee's works produce hermeneutic effects that can be called therapeutic, Coetzee also often thematises therapeutic situations in his works. This impulse traces back to his earliest novelistic efforts. A discarded first sketch of 'The Vietnam Project' consists fully of an exchange between a 'Mrs C—' (who in later drafts and the published version of *Dusklands* is known as Marilyn, Eugene Dawn's wife) and a counsellor discussing the former's marital problems (HRC 33.2). Although in the second sketch for 'The Vietnam Project', titled 'Lies',[4] selected and revised fragments of this exchange are incorporated into Dawn's first-person narrative (HRC 1.1) and are eventually removed from the published version of the novel, this scene foreshadows Coetzee's tendency for staging a dialogic situation as a platform for exposing various forms of injustice, violence and uneven relations of power. The fact that Marilyn discusses her marriage with a counsellor during a therapy session means that, before Coetzee is able to develop his first-person unreliable narrator in later drafts, he must bring an external perspective to bear on the narrator's biases. But the stakes of Coetzee's first novel are higher still. It is not only the 'neurotic'[5] Marilyn and 'psychotic' Dawn[6] that need healing, but their author in the first place. The character Julia, John's former lover in Coetzee's semiautobiographical novel *Summertime*, written three decades after Coetzee's first novel, has this to say about *Dusklands*: 'The best interpretation I can give of the book is that writing it was a project in self-administered therapy' (*ST* 58). Although the therapy session scene disappears from the final version of *Dusklands*, it is not by chance that the author uses it as a point of departure for further drafts. It is as if the scene has to disappear from the drafts to make room for a therapy of a higher order. As a bearer of colonial guilt, an 'heir of an expansionist colonial philosophy of violence fuelled by Western rationalism and the delusion of [his] own election', Coetzee must first subject himself to the curative and purgative ordeals of writing (Atwell 2015, 30). In this sense, therapy becomes a pattern of Coetzee's becoming as a writer.

A therapeutic dialogue creates a venue in which characters, in working through their problems and negotiating their disagreements, develop a basis for ethical communication between each other. But a dialogue for healing purposes does not need to take place in a medical setting. Sometimes Coetzee's characters strive to create therapeutic situations by other means. Elizabeth Curren's letter to her daughter, Dostoevsky's heretical rewriting of his son's notes, or Simón's persistent attempts to confide in his Spanish composition teacher in his written assignments mark different ways in which protagonists resort to writing as a way to work through personal problems that surpass their comprehension or to achieve (often unsuccessfully) a sense of closure.

By both thematising therapeutic situations and drawing attention to the curative function of fiction, Coetzee's works and opinions have attracted vivid interest among bibliotherapists and scholars. Coetzee's own conversations with the psychotherapist Arabella Kurtz published in *The Good Story*, quoted above, are a worthy contribution to debates around the relationship between fiction and psychotherapy. The joint publication of the bibliotherapists Ella Berthoud and Susan Elderkin, *The Novel Cure* (2013), includes *Disgrace* and *Diary of a Bad Year* in the list of books recommended for self-healing. Similarly, Chris N. van der Merwe and Pumla Gobodo-Madikizela read *Disgrace* 'as an example of a text that portrays individual and communal traumas and suggests ways of healing' in their monograph on the therapeutic effects of trauma narratives (2007, 72). Also, Sam Durrant mentions his book on Coetzee, *Postcolonial Narrative and the Work of Mourning: J. M. Coetzee, Wilson Harris and Toni Morrison* (2004), among the publications and outputs used for the purposes for his decade-long (2010–20) project based in the University of Leeds and offering bibliotherapy for refugees and asylum seekers.[7] Coetzee's texts are also often put on the list of books on prescription for bibliotherapy offered by various state and university libraries.

However, the therapeutic effects of Coetzee's texts may not always appear as straightforward. Because lists of books on prescription are commonly populated with self-help publications and other texts intended to console, inspire or guide the reader-patient through a life crisis, many readers may hold a rather superficial (albeit not necessarily incorrect) view about bibliotherapy as a practice that is specifically oriented at providing solace, comfort and closure. As has been mentioned, by tackling difficult issues or challenging the reader's assumptions about the world, Coetzee's texts often push their readers beyond their comfort zone, and by doing so may make them feel unhappy about the way things are in the world, even if the deeper understanding that follows from reading Coetzee's texts may offset these adverse feelings in the long run. Indeed, one would be hard pressed to find the endings of such novels as *Dusklands, Age of Iron, The Master of Petersburg, Disgrace* or indeed most of other Coetzee's novels, reassuring in the traditional sense of the word. By constantly frustrating his novels' capacity for redemption, Coetzee 'both trials and erases the emergence of solace' (James 2019, 190). Such forms of resistance to consolation – which David James calls 'discrepant solace' (ibid., 5) – are often manifested in Coetzee's texts through their refusal to offer a clear sense of an ending (which typically gives the reader a form of closure), the sparseness of style and other meaning-deferring tactics.

For all their suspicion of ameliorative reading effects, Coetzee's fictions subversively derive their therapeutic strength from that which seemingly belies their capacities for healing. To Ceridwen Dovey, Coetzee's works teach the reader 'how to manage uncertainty, how to live with complexity: the project of a lifetime' (2018). Some aspects of the cruel complexity of life are often catered for in Coetzee's novels through representations and contemplation of suffering, humiliation, grief, illness, and other extreme or complex states of existence, aspects that are an integral part of – rather than inimical to – therapeutic practices. In fact, the Freudian notion of the 'abreaction theory' or 'the talking cure' assumes that 'talking about traumatic experiences is therapeutic' (Pett 2014, 33). Trauma survivors often experience a conflicting compulsion to both withhold a traumatic memory and to talk about it. Although talking about a traumatic situation might entail 'an extremely painful reliving of the event', it is the 'confrontation of the suppressed memory that is needed for inner healing' (van der Merwe and Gobodo-Madikizela

2007, viii). Along these lines, the reader's identification with those Coetzee's characters that experience various existential crises can bring consolation of sorts. Moreover, Coetzee's characteristic moments of textual ambiguity and deferral of redemption often force the reader to challenge their presuppositions in order to defamiliarise some aspects of their experience, including potentially those that are a source of their distress or anxiety. The patient's critical reassessment of her experience – a process which involves both serious meditation on and sympathetic imagination towards that which has so far eluded comprehension – may offer a way towards a recognition of the complexity of the problem she has been dealing with. Coetzee's critique of reason manifested in many of his novels invites the reader to open herself empathetically to alternative ways of living and thinking that often go against the grain of conventional wisdom – an opening that may have a liberating effect on a person whose mental state is caused by an overreliance on normative cultural narratives.

Coetzee's novels offer diverse ways via which the reader can work through her problems. While through Elizabeth Costello the reader comes to intuit some therapeutic aspects of reading implicitly, other characters address this matter more openly. In the 'Second Diary' section of *Diary of a Bad Year*, the established author JC ruminates on the affective agency of reading. He is specifically puzzled at why a familiar scene from *The Brothers Karamazov* has an unabating capacity to move him to tears: 'These are pages I have read innumerable times before, yet instead of becoming inured to their force I find myself more and more vulnerable to them. Why?' (*DBY* 224). In a gesture that is typical of Coetzee's suspicion of reason, JC concludes that the cathartic impact of this passage derives from its rhetorical rather than rational force: 'Far more powerful than the substance of his argument, which is not strong, are the accents of anguish, the personal anguish of a soul unable to bear the horrors of this world. It is the voice of Ivan, as realised by Dostoevsky, not his reasoning, that sweeps me along' (225). JC's opinions on the nature of the literary affect as well as the non-rationalistic aspects of reading in this passage seem to foreshadow a more extensive probing of the impact of reading on the reader's sense of self as demonstrated in the series of *Jesus* novels.

As all of the instalments of the trilogy, that is *The Childhood of Jesus* (2013), *The Schooldays of Jesus* (2016) and *The Death of Jesus* (2019), are part of the same storyline, I will be referring to all of them, with a special focus on the final instalment of this series. The titles of these novels signpost the basic plotline of the trilogy. In the first novel, the boy David and his middle-aged guardian Simón arrive by boat in the town of Novilla, located in a Spanish-speaking country, in search for the boy's mother. Despite the odds – the protagonists have no memory of the place they have come from and the letter that explains who David's mother is has got lost – Simón intuits a woman called Inés to be the boy's mother and leaves him under her care. In the 2016 sequel, Simón, Inés and Davíd[8] arrive in the town of Estrella, where the boy attends a dance academy, begins to demonstrate his unorthodox talents and harbingers of precociousness, and falls under the influence of diabolical Dmitri, a future murderer of his headmistress. In the final novel, David leaves his parents against their will to live at the orphanage of one Dr Fabricante, where the boy comes down with a mysterious illness and dies in unexplained circumstances soon after, having gathered a number of devoted followers prior to his decease.

Following the terms and concepts of bibliotherapy, the trilogy at large (and *The Death of Jesus* in particular) falls within the category of the illness narrative. According to Arthur Frank, stories about illness follow three basic narrative patterns: 1) the restitution charts the protagonist's progress from the debilitating state of illness to her successful recovery; 2) in the chaos narrative the protagonist fails to recover from the illness; 3) and finally the quest narrative centres on the inner transformation of the protagonist as opposed to the physical outcomes of the illness (2013, 187). As David never recovers from the fictional disease – 'Saporta syndrome [. . .] a pathology of the neural pathways' (*DJ* 60)[9] – and the final novel centres on the boy's self-development in illness as well as the effects it has on those around him, the trilogy occupies a middle ground between the chaos and quest narrative. The balance, however, tips more decisively to the former category. Because in a traditional quest narrative the person takes an active interest in the illness and often uses this knowledge for social change, the extent to which *The Death of Jesus* qualifies as a quest narrative is limited. If the chaos narrative typically 'runs counter to the restitution narrative by removing all sense of certainty and resolution' (Brewster 2018, 47), Coetzee's final *Jesus* instalment fits in this framework as it reinforces the effects of ambiguity on several textual planes.

The novel evokes these effects in the moments that cause the reader to halt her reading process. These decelerative reading tactics can produce a sense of 'stillness', allowing a space in which 'the slowing down of readers' perceptions of the fictional world, caused by defamiliarization' takes place (Koopman and Hakemulder 2015, 80).

Eva Maria Koopman and Frank Hakemulder propose that stillness is a form of aesthetic distance that fosters empathic thinking by inducing the reader's self-reflection and suspension of judgement (ibid.). As suggested above, the ethical implications of reading are crucial for therapeutic purposes to the extent that they lend themselves for a transference of affective and intellectual outcomes of reading into the reader-patient's personal experience. The *Jesus* novels are likely to evoke the defamiliarising effects of stillness via the scenes and narratives strategies that serve to put on hold the familiar protocols of meaning-making and interpretation, such as those relating to the notions of historical memory, allegory, relationship between reality and fiction, the cause and role of illness and its disabling effects, as well as the ambiguous ontological status of the quasi-eponymous protagonist.

As mentioned above, the main plot of the *Jesus* novels is based on the premise that for reasons unknown Simón and David, together with all inhabitants of Novilla (which etymologically stands for 'new home'), have no memory of their previous lives and identity. The unknowability around the town inhabitants' collective dissociative amnesia serves as one of the central moments of defamiliarisation that evokes a sense of stillness. Although not stated explicitly, it is not unreasonable to conclude that the loss of memory may be related to a trauma, from which it entails that historical amnesia is a form of collective repression. Jean-Michel Rabaté seems to support this conjecture by stating that 'Novilla is predicated on a consensus that one will live better if one abandons any memory of a past marked by disaster and trauma' (2017, 194). While Simón does not entirely give up on his memories of the past, thus accepting his present condition as unfortunate – 'I know we are all supposed to be washed clean by the passage here [. . .]. But the shadows linger nevertheless [. . .]. I hold onto them, those shadows' (*CJ* 77) – the inhabitants of Novilla seem to consider forgetting as an active, deliberate and hard-won process: 'Forgetting takes time [. . .] Once you have properly forgotten, your sense of insecurity will recede and everything will become much easier' (169). As the experience of trauma impairs the 'ability to integrate the objective events with the affective component of the experience', it may lead to misremembering events as they occurred. This in turn results in a form of an 'undoing of the self' through a multiple sense of loss: 'loss of control, loss of one's identity, loss of the ability to remember, and loss of language to describe the horrific events' (van der Merwe and Gobodo-Madikizela 2007, vii). Along these lines,

The Childhood of Jesus can be read as a novel that explores the traumatic experience of migration.

Indeed, it is possible to read the trilogy as a political allegory on the plight of refugees and an implicit critique of Australian government's anti-migration regulations. As an immigrant to Australia himself, Coetzee has remained attentive to the complexity of migration or cultural assimilation in most of his late fictions: while Paul Rayment, the Jokić family (*Slow Man*) and JC (*Diary of a Bad Year*) are immigrants to Australia, Elizabeth Costello ('The Old Woman and the Cats') emigrates to Spain in her old age. The fact that Coetzee himself 'was forced to return to South Africa from self-imposed exile in 1971 and never got over it until he left for Australia in 2002' explains why the theme of migration figures prominently in Coetzee's semi-autobiographical works comprising the trilogy *Scenes from Provincial Life* (Attwell 2015, 26). In *Youth* (2002), John spends a year working in London, while the interviewees of *Summertime* (2009) are all migrants to various countries, such as France, Brazil, the United Kingdom and Canada. JC's 'strong opinions' on 'the Australian way of handling refugees' in his essay 'On Asylum in Australia' – 'How can a decent, generous, easygoing people close their eyes while strangers who arrive on their shores pretty much helpless and penniless are treated with such heartlessness, such grim callousness?' (*DBY* 111) – sail very close to Coetzee's own stance on the matter. In his evocatively titled *The New York Review* article 'Australia's Shame' (2019), Coetzee mounts a pungent critique of Australia's treatment of immigrants, and specifically laws mandating indefinite detention of asylum seekers by government authorities.[10]

Nevertheless, *The Childhood of Jesus* subtly departs from the genre of political allegory in the traditional sense of the term. Rather than a raging diatribe against the plight of refuge seekers, the novel tackles social issues in a way that matches some of its formal effects, such as the sparsity of language and minimalism of expression. 'There is thus a sense', argues David Hartley, 'in which Coetzee has managed formally to reproduce the atmosphere of worldlessness' which is concomitant with 'depersonalised refugee experience' (2020, 508). As mentioned above, Coetzee also uses some distancing narrative techniques, such as textual elisions and ellipses, which serve to reinforce the effects of indeterminacy indicative of the migrant experience. These distancing narrative devices resonate with the liminal position of the migrant subject who 'is articulated in the break between home country and host county, in a precarious space between a fading past and an imagined future' (Jacobs 2017, 62). Coetzee's resistance to overt or generic forms of relating migrant experience realised through narrative defamiliarisation results in the moments of stillness that prompt the reader to critically reflect on the event rather than only to register it. While the sense of closure achieved in the moment of registering an event allows the reader to comfortably read on, thus taking the event at face value, the reflexive and self-reflexive effects arising out of a deceleration of reading result in identification and transference, which is a substantial factor in the process of the restitution of self in bibliotherapy.

Other meaning-delaying tactics of Coetzee's late novels include the ways in which Coetzee uses paradoxical statements or defamiliarises everyday speech patterns to both hint at and undermine the allegorical framework of the text. When Simón appoints a seemingly random woman, Inés, her name meaning 'virgin', to become David's 'natural mother', even though he 'cannot explain how that happens' (*CJ* 96), the reader is invited to find in this moment of ambiguity correspondences with the biblical or apocryphal stories of the early years of Jesus' life. However, as biblical allusions are often derailed by other hermeneutic possibilities – such as the one suggested above, that the *Jesus* novels, by reporting on the trauma of migrant experience, are a form of political rather than biblical allegory – the reader is forced to halt the reading process to come to terms with the text's indeterminacies. These hermeneutic effects also derive from linguistic estrangements that underpin the ambiguity. Simón's striking justification of his choice of the boy's mother, 'he needs a mother, he needs to be born to a mother' (94), carries within itself an impossible modality (the grammatically and lexically correct alternatives could be: 'he could/must/not have been born to a mother', or 'needs to be adopted/accepted by a mother'), which should not be dismissed as a simple metaphor in view of Simón's multiple assertions that Inés is not a surrogate mother, but the natural mother – that is, the only mother that the boy has ever had. Instead, the phrase is calculated to pose a certain cognitive challenge that suspends a single line of interpretation (including any single line of interpretation suggested above).

The above interpretative doubling, which involves a reading of Coetzee's *Jesus* novels along the lines of religious or political allegory, is further complicated by the novels' staging of their own fictionality. When, in *The Schooldays of Jesus*, Davíd inquires Simón further about his origins, the latter responds irritably:

> Either I can reply, 'Yes, you were born out of Inés's tummy,' or I can reply, 'No, you weren't born out of Inés's tummy.' But neither reply will bring us any closer to the truth. Why not? Because, like everyone else who came on the boats, you can't remember and nor can Inés. Unable to remember, all you can do, all she can do, all any of us can do is to make up stories. (*SJ* 18)

Although Simón seems to be making a general point about the role of fiction in the process of filling in the factual gaps caused by a loss of memory or impairment of the memory function, the fragment also hints at another possibility. The characters cannot remember their lives before the arrival simply because, being fictional characters, they have never had any life before the fictional events they are part of. Following this line of reasoning, the 'atmosphere of worldlessness' that Hartley proposes may have less to do with reproducing the migrant experience and more with calling attention to the fictionality of the novel. Rather than annulling the other ways of interpreting the *Jesus* series suggested above, this metafictional reading only offers another layer of interpretation and reinforces the effects of stillness by mounting resistance to closure or traditional meaning-making patterns. As will be argued below, the *Jesus* trilogy, as a kind of illness narrative, prompts meditation on the relationship between fiction and self-understanding, or else self-understanding through fiction (together with the therapeutic effects that this self-understanding brings about). A fiction so constructed contains within itself a certain capacity to trigger the reader's (self-)reflection through withholding its meanings. This problematic 'capacity' of fiction is coupled with the complicated ontological and fictional status of the protagonist, David, together with his understanding of his (dis)abilities as well as sense of self in illness.

Negative Capabilities

Proclaiming the *Jesus* novels 'ruminative, meandering, and open-ended', William Deresiewicz underscores the essential capacity of the trilogy to lend itself to various, often conflicting, interpretations (2020). What appears to irk some critics is the resistance of these novels to succumb to any possible reading script conclusively. 'I've given up trying to force meaning into these novels,' complains critic Alex Preston, 'I'm increasingly convinced that this trilogy is an elaborate joke by its author at the expense of the exegetes attempting to "translate" his work' (2019). In a review that resonates with

Preston's criticism, Susan Balee writes that in *The Childhood of Jesus* – an example of 'literature of the absurd' – 'the laugh is on the reader' (2013). The sense of inconclusiveness of these novels that has perplexed many critics may have been further aggravated by the context in which they were written and the readers' possible expectations. After all, the readers had waited for the best part of the past decade for Coetzee to tie up all of the loose ends of his first ever fictional trilogy and offer closure, which, as the critics are right to point out, he characteristically chose not to do.

But Preston and Balee miss some crucial points. Rather than mocking the reader, Coetzee brings to fruition through formal and narrative devices that which Costello's and JC's overt diatribes foreshadow in the preceding Australian novels and short fictions: a failure of the philosophical reason to address the ethical complexities of human experience. The critique of reason is inextricable from Coetzee's misgivings about the medium which, for him, is liable for sustaining the bourgeois myth of rationalistic triumphalism – that is, literary realism (Woessner 2017, 143). As Coetzee confesses to Kurtz: 'I don't have much respect for reality. I think of myself as using rather than reflecting reality in my fiction' (*GS* 69). If these sentiments have been variously practised in Coetzee's previous fictions,[11] they seem to have crystalised in his *Jesus* novels into an exploration of the transcendental as a way of probing the limits of reason, and, by extension, the real – an exploration that encompasses both the reality of the world and realism of fiction. It is along these lines that Martin Woessner reads the *Jesus* novels as an expression of what he calls Coetzee's 'post-secular imagination' (2017, 143). In my reading of it, Coetzee's deliberate rupturing of both rationalistic and realistic patterns of literary representation, as documented in the trilogy, can be explained in terms of certain 'capabilities' (and therefore incapabilities too) that the text displays on several narrative levels.

Coetzee's recalcitrance to the ideological and formal constraints of literary realism and philosophical rationalism resonates with John Keats's famous formulation of 'Negative Capability, that is, when a man is capable of being in uncertainties, mysteries, doubts, without any irritable reaching after fact and reason' (1994, 232). In his preference for creative ambiguity over philosophical certainty in the poet's pursuit of artistic beauty, Keats stresses the primacy of individual perception at the expense of calculated reasoning in the creative process. Because negative capability, both in terms of the concept's phrasing and definition, intimates a critique of reason and normative notions of ability, some scholars and poets have used this concept to account for the singularity of disability experience. Tom Shakespeare finds affinities between negative capability and Erik Parens's notion of 'binocularity', which, 'beginning with "a hermeneutics of suspicion," oscillating between different lenses, but ending up in a decision', denotes the ability of seeing a phenomenon from more than one perspective rather than from a single authoritative standpoint sanctified by 'High Reason' (Shakespeare 2015, 521). Similarly, for the poet Sheila Black negative capability informs 'disability poetics [...] in all the ways John Keats may have intended it – an upheaval, a defamiliarization, an ability to remain open and, because [...] disability poetics is inextricably bound up with the trauma of having been categorized and mistreated by an ableist world – it is profoundly a poetry of vulnerability' (Black, n. d.). For Black, it is in its defiance of both formal and social protocols of normativity that disability poetics can be defined along the lines of negative capability.

This cross-fertilisation of the poetics of disability and negative capability helps account for the ability of certain texts to combine defamiliarising formal effects and narrative binocularity (or multi-perspectivity) as a way to reproduce the complexities of vulnerability and resistance. Although the *Jesus* trilogy can be classified, as I have proposed to do it, as a type of illness narrative, how exactly it fits within the framework of disability narrative, and, further, how this theme chimes with the novel's multiple narrative ambiguities, may be less transparent. Among the many enigmas of the *Jesus* trilogy, Deresiewicz counts the following:

> Davíd, who both is and isn't Jesus, lives with Simón and Inés, who both are and aren't his parents, in a world that both is and isn't our own. And Davíd both is and isn't his name. It is the name that was assigned to him when he and Simón arrived in the country, or sphere, where the action takes place. Arrived from where? [...] Another country? Another life? Another plane? [...] Are they refugees? Immigrants? Souls transported to a kind of blandly social-democratic afterlife? [...] Or is it only another life—lust and pain and death and even evil, it transpires, have not been banished—one, perhaps, in an endless succession of lives? (2020)

If the uncertainty around David's ontological status (is he an allegorical representation of Jesus or perhaps Don Quixote?) may be a crucial point of the novels' pervasive poetics of ambiguity, what is intimately associated with this question is the confusion around the boy's intellectual status. By referring to David as 'a young Jesus with Asperger's', Balee offers a diagnostic reading that apparently accounts for a combination of the boy's social maladaptation and exceptionalism (2013). Although she may have used the term Asperger's playfully rather than literally (or not), there are reasons to suspect the novel can be read along these biomedical lines. Indeed, David is considered by some characters as having learning difficulties. In *The Childhood of Jesus*, what later turns out to be David's obstinacy rather than lack of literacy and numeracy skills is seen by Señor León as a symptom of a 'specific deficit linked to symbolic activities' (*CJ* 243), which is in need of a cure. Similarly, in *The Schooldays of Jesus*, Davíd's would-be tutor claims that the boy 'may be suffering from [. . .] a cognitive deficit', before the boy proves capable of doing sums (*SJ* 30). But even when he does, Simón later admits that 'David has a blind spot for arithmetic' (*DJ* 79), which may be a symptom of dyscalculia. The fact that Señor León recognises that the boy may be gifted only strengthens the doctor's resolution to submit the boy to corrective practices at the Special Learning Centre at Punto Arenas: 'A specialist may be able to tell us whether there is some common factor underlying the deficit on the one hand and the inventiveness on the other' (*CJ* 243). Señor León's diagnosis resonates with a general medical consensus that confirms a correlation between certain neurodevelopmental states and high intellectual potential, such as in people with Asperger's syndrome. The standard manual of mental disorders *DSM-5* states that 'specific learning disorder[s] may occur in individuals identified as intellectually "gifted"' (*Diagnostic and Statistical Manual of Mental Disorders* 2013, 32). Similarly, David's excessive attachment to *Don Quixote*, the only book he has ever read, may be a symptom of the restrictive-repetitive behaviour that typifies some forms of autism.

Further on in the novel, the psychologist Señora Otxoa suggests that the causes of the boy's 'unsettled behaviour' – which to her may be a symptom of dyslexia – are oedipal at their roots: 'David's learning difficulties stem from a confusion about a world from which his real parents have vanished' (*CJ* 246). The psychological and oedipal causes of a child's neurological states, similar to those mentioned by Señora Otxoa, have long been pursued by medical researchers. The 'refrigerator mother theory', for instance, maintains that autism is 'caused by a mother's subliminal rejection of their child, which the child sensed, and responded to by rejecting both the mother and people at large' (Tweed 2020, 367). The boy's uneasy relationship with his adopted mother – as registered in the fragment that brings to mind a biblical passage: 'You are not my mother!' (*DJ* 38) – carries some echoes of this now long-discredited medical theory. There are also hints to suppose that the boy is an example of a person with narcissistic personality disorder. David, who 'feels himself to be special' (*CJ* 247), seems to meet some diagnostic criteria of this state, such as having 'a grandiose sense of self-importance', 'a sense of entitlement' or being 'interpersonally exploitative' (*Diagnostic and Statistical Manual of Mental Disorders* 2013, 669–70).[12] As 'the narcissistic theme of entitlement is uniquely related to narcissistic fantasy', David's mystical relationship with numbers through dancing may be a further indication of this state (Raskin and Novacek 1991, 490). On top of that, the novel's potential for allegory also invites questions about an extent to which the relationship between David and Simón should be read vis-à-vis that of the 'mad' Don Quixote and rational Sancho respectively.

Although David's intellectual status lends itself to various medical diagnoses, there is not much benefit to be had from such definitive prescriptive interpretations. While David may at first glance demonstrate some savant abilities, not only is he not socially withdrawn, but he has an ability – as befits a modern incarnation of Jesus – to attract followers. Although fantasy-prone personality or narcissism may in specific forms be considered pathological in adults, they rarely are – unless in considerable excess – in children. Furthermore, Señora Otxoa's initial diagnosis of dyslexia is dismissed the moment the boy demonstrates his reading proficiency, just as Señor León's vague references to David's intellectual 'deficit' may be signs of his nonconformity and exceptionalism – qualities that tend to be pathologised in such normatively inclined socialist utopias as Novilla – rather than cognitive atypicality. To put it in Deresiewicz's words, the boy is 'simply an exceptionally gifted child, the kind of kid with whom the world in general, and the education system in particular, does not know how to deal' (2020). Speaking in terms proposed by the social constructionist model of disability, David is disabled by the education system and politics of the state rather than his body or mind. But Coetzee does not deal in plausibilities. Medical interpretations are neither entirely unfounded, nor should they serve as a passkey to the text's meanings. What is at stake in the trilogy is that Coetzee hints at biomedical explanations of the novel's hidden meanings only to withdraw them the moment when their meanings begin to assert themselves as authoritative.

However, whether David is or is not neuroatypical may be secondary to the question about the ways in which the boy's uncommon characteristics and abilities are accommodated within the biopolitics of Novilla. As a kind of socialist, consumption-free utopia, Novilla is a place in which all forms of excess are frowned upon. Even for rationally disposed Simón, later referred to as 'señor Normal' (*DJ* 189) and 'the man of reason' (*DJ* 102), the inhabitants' customs, such as their indifference to erotic desire, inability to grasp irony, and vegetarian diet, seem puritanical. Constructed along these lines, the biopolitics of Novilla is inimical to forms of cultural diversity. As noticed by Jarad Zimbler, the bureaucratic character of Novilla is hostile to 'exceptional children and unsanctioned desires' (2020, 50). Whether for the boy's well-being or to satisfy his own conceptions of intellectual normalcy, Simón often attempts to curb the boy's peculiar habits. When David refuses to read in a traditional way, Simón abides the boy's idiosyncrasies until the point when school authorities draw his attention to his apparent deficiencies – 'you are going to learn to read and write and count like a normal person' (*CJ* 255) – thus joining the chorus of those who seek to subject the apparently exceptional boy to normative standards. Although not an authoritarian state as such, Novilla can be characterised by what Lennard J. Davis calls 'an enforcing of normalcy' in that 'the deviations in society [. . .] must be minimized' (1995, 29). For this reason, as suggested by Kai Wiegandt, '[t]he imminent census puts David at risk of being [. . .] sorted into a category – disabled, lacking in the cognitive ability to think abstractly – with other numbered citizens' (2019, 215). In Novilla, 'where humans [are] treated as objects to be measured, ordered and controlled', human exceptionality and singularity give way to collective normative standards (Preston 2016). Similarly, by stating that 'Simón's discouraging of David's fantastic reading inhibits rather than opens up the child's learning', Apanra Mishra Tanc seems to confirm the supposition that it is the social factors rather than an intellectual state that has a debilitating effect on the boy's functioning and educational progress (2020, 102). Although Inés seems to be the only one to approve of the boy's vivid imagination, by overindulging the child rather than offering pedagogical guidance, she only manages to infantilise the child. Whether David is neurodiverse or gifted, or a combination of the two, he finds himself in a social environment that is fundamentally inhospitable for nurturing social or intellectual diversity.

As stated above, David is consistently referred to as an exceptional child by those who know him. This consensus in large part derives from the child's reluctance to follow formal or rational protocols of learning. In this sense, Keats's formulation of negative capability as one's capacity to embrace 'uncertainties' without having recourse to 'reason' lends itself as a modus operandi of David's character development. Interestingly enough, the only sceptics about David's unique abilities are the state school authorities and functionaries, who not only discredit the boy's precociousness but suggest the child should be subjected to segregated education in an attempt to correct his unorthodox behaviour.[13] Deterred by the traditional education system of Novilla, after relocating to Estrella, David is drawn to people or institutions implementing unorthodox teaching methodologies, such as the quasi-mystical philosophy of 'number-dancing' (*SJ* 234) championed by Juan Sebastián Arroyo and his wife, Ana Magdalena, at their Academy of Dance or the 'practical education' advocated by Dr Julio Fabricante, 'a foe of book learning', in his orphanage (*DJ* 29). Simón's role in the shaping of the boy's unconventional way of thinking is awkward because for all his efforts to temper the boy's penchant for excessive fantasising, it is him who teaches the boy the rudiments of reading and critical thinking through a series of conversations that resemble Socratic dialogues. Simón is also the one who never lets the boy forget about his special status – 'You are an exceptional child' (*CJ* 253) – and who 'is confident that a child with such clear inborn intelligence can do without formal schooling' (*DJ* 7).

While the boy occasionally questions this special role assigned to him by those around him ('Why am I exceptional?' *CJ* 253), it is only when he comes down with the mysterious illness that he begins seriously to contemplate and put into question his abilities and ontological status. Also, the incomprehensible, debilitating effects of the illness become a structure of the boy's inexplicable sense of mission. Shortly before David suffers the first symptoms of a combination of muscle inflammation and seizures, he inexplicably resolves to leave home for the local orphanage, pleading with his remonstrating foster father in a way that directly invites parallels with biblical Jesus' own sense of ministry: 'You must leave me to what I have to do' (*DJ* 43), 'I am who I am' (*DJ* 35). The allegorical undertones begin to gather strength when David confronts his own disabilities. The repetitive seizures, which the boy subjectively experiences as 'falling', call to mind Jesus' falls under the weight of the cross. There is an indication that the boy intuits that his disablement is intimately related with his mission: 'I am the only one who falls' (*DJ* 57). Similarly, David's repeated diatribes against his fate when bedridden – 'Why does it have to be me?' (*DJ* 52), 'Why do I have to be this boy?' (*DJ* 103), 'But I don't want to be this boy [. . .]', 'He gestures toward his body, with its wasted legs' (*DJ* 110), 'I would prefer to be normal' (*DJ* 112) – are reminiscent of Jesus' agony in the Garden of Gethsemane.

Apart from strengthening the allegorical structure of the trilogy, the inexplicability of illness and disability partakes in the final novel's foregrounding of its uncertainties, or negative capabilities. David's reluctance to succumb to Simón's rationalistic teaching instructions begins to show in their early encounters, when the boy insists on following his own reading methods: 'The boy closes his eyes. "I'm reading through my fingers," he announces' (*CJ* 191). The boy would remain committed to resisting rational explanations until the end. Envisaging his own death, the boy accepts Simón's offer to write a book about his life and deeds on one condition: 'But then you must promise not to understand me. When you try to understand me it spoils everything' (*DJ* 103–4). Nor does the boy give much reason to his followers to understand him and his legacy. They expect a message that would explain everything, a message, which, however, would never come: 'David was carrying a message, though the content of the message is still obscure' (*DJ* 183). Resigned to the inexplicability of this lack, Dmitri, the boy's apostle of sorts, concludes: 'David himself may have been the message. / The messenger was the message' (*DJ* 183). Nevertheless, Simón is presented with one last chance to receive the boy's message when he finds a slip of paper at the back cover of David's lost copy of *Don Quixote* on which the editor encourages his children readers to respond in writing to the question: 'What is the message of this book?' (*DJ* 196). Simón hopes to find David's response, his ultimate message, among a number of other children's handwritten notes. In vain.

In these final moments, the boundary between the child protagonist and the novel he inhabits begin to blur. Like David himself, the novel refuses to yield its messages or resolve its uncertainties. Paraphrasing Dmitri's formulation, the novel itself is the message. If the presupposition that David is an allegory of the novel holds, then it follows from this that the reader, like Simón, must now 'promise not to understand' it and leave the novel's mysteries forever unresolved. Following this thread, David's illness narrative becomes a story of negative capabilities that metafictionally reports on the processes involved in bibliotherapy, that is therapy through storytelling. In their last moment together, in a scene that resembles a deathbed confession, David tries to understand the nature of afterlife as well as the relationship between life and fiction. As usual, it is through *Don Quixote* that the boy attempts to probe these philosophical issues: 'Will I see Don Quixote in the new life?' (*DJ* 108), 'And why is Don Quixote not allowed to come here?' (*DJ* 109). In bibliotherapy, guided reading is used to help the patient come to terms with the difficult experience she is going through. Just as, in the early days in Novilla, Simón resorts to fiction to help the child understand the new reality void of memory and identity, it is through the guided reading of *Don Quixote* that he attempts to explain heavyweight existential issues during David's dying days to ameliorate the boy's, and his own, sense of incomprehensibility of illness and death. This leads Apanra Mishra Tanc to conclude that '[w]here he fails as a parent, as a teacher of literacy Simón excels. He reads animatedly and stops to respond to his student's questions' (2020, 100). Fail to understand David on his own terms as he may, Simón's commitment to fostering David's critical thinking through dialogic exchanges and guided reading of fiction has helped shape the boy's vivid imagination and the sense of self in the moments of deep existential crisis, such as migration and illness. The role of fiction and reading in the novel is in this sense both educational and psychotherapeutic, and Simón's role, consequently, is one of a creative bibliotherapist. If bibliotherapy involves a use of fiction for therapeutic purposes or restitution, 'enabl[ing] the restoration of self-identity', the *Jesus* trilogy lends itself to bibliotherapy because it dramatises the boy's self-development through his conscious identification with a fictional character, and shows how the text's obscurities and limitations help the reader come to terms with the complexity of traumatic experience, which should be understood as a long-term process rather than an obstacle to be overcome (Brewster 2018, 46). Whether David's reclamation of the story of himself has materialised, the reader has no way of knowing. The message is not revealed to her after all. Or perhaps this aspect of textual ambiguity has less to do with the novel's reluctance to deliver a message, and more with Simón's incapacity to register it.

As Simón, not David, is the main focaliser in the novel, it is through his consciousness that the novel's meanings are mediated. Simón, who works in Estrella as a bicycle messenger, doubles as the implicit messenger of David's story. It follows from this that it is not David or his message that the reader fails to understand. Rather, the reader bears witness to Simón's inability to understand his foster child. Simón is an unreliable focaliser of sorts, one who attempts but always fails to grasp the meanings he is after, and therefore fails to deliver them through the narrator to the reader. This final act of the novel's resistance to yield to a satisfying closure is intimately linked with the novel's capacity for healing. Indeed, Simón's focalisation expands the possibilities of the novels' therapeutic function. While people with muscular dystrophy or the terminally ill may identify with David's struggle with the illness, the novel invites the reader to sympathise with Simón's inability to rationalise the boy's death. At this point, the novel's tactical deferral of rational explanation of events is a formal strategy of reproducing the mourner's sense of incomprehensibility of the beloved's illness and death. Coetzee's tenacity to keep his explanations close to his chest is not gratuitous. The fact that the reader is left with plenty of questions and few answers (What is the cause of David's medical illness and death? And why does Coetzee choose a fictional illness rather than an existing one?, etc.) is because the incomprehensibility of one's death has nothing or little to do with medical explanations. The failure of comprehending death is not a failure of rationalisation, but a failure of accommodating the incomprehensible event within the deeper structures of the self, of forcing the self to comprehend the other's impenetrable suffering, as well as come to terms with the irreducible otherness of death. One of the reasons why Coetzee resorts to an illness narrative as a way to formally conclude the trilogy is that yearning for transcendence, such as one registered in the need to account for one's own or the other's death, is particularly pertinent for the terminally ill. Read along these lines, the title does not explain the plot (as stated above, the novel's allegorical possibilities are only limited) but documents Coetzee's preoccupation with helping the other answer the unanswerable: how does one comprehend the cosmic injustice of the heartlessness of the world and inconceivability of dying?

Nor is rationalisation of one's experience irrelevant in self-healing. In fact, narrative closure in traditional books on prescription provides the reader with a blueprint by which they also can hope to achieve a closure in their lives through transference. Understandably, many readers prefer to have their difficult experience spelled out for them clearly and with no delays, and for many this narrative strategy works. Coetzee offers no such comforts, however. 'When Coetzee withholds back story,' says critic Judith Shulevitz, 'the reader must learn to tolerate mystery' (2020). Coetzee is a master of the withholding of meaning, and in doing so he asks the reader to put into question her reading habits and prejudices. Coetzee's fiction does not fit neatly within the corpus of books on prescription. Its therapeutic powers lie in what he does not show rather than in a revealed truth that offers a catharsis. Coetzee's narrative uncertainties elicit the moments of stillness and contemplation that have the capacity to heal in ways that elude the standard protocols of bibliotherapy. And it is in the strategic textual elusions that the negative capabilities of Coetzee's (st)illness narrative – one that occupies the uneasy juncture between stillness and chaos, one that is decelerative, self-reflexive and closure-resisting – are at their most robust.

Disability Life Writing

While the *Jesus* novels comprise the first trilogy of novels in Coetzee's oeuvre, they were preceded by a trilogy of a different kind. Not long before settling down to write *The Childhood of Jesus*, Coetzee had published the third and last instalment of his fictionalised memoirs *Scenes from Provincial Life*, consisting of *Boyhood* (1997), *Youth* (2002) and *Summertime* (2009), an ambitious project taking Coetzee more than two decades to complete from its early drafts of 1987 to the publication of the final memoir in 2009. But the tripartite structure of both series is not the only common thread between them. Both trilogies are defined by the structural pattern of childhood, education and death of their protagonists. These parallels between the lives of John and David give rise to questions about the relationship between fiction and autobiography in both series. Quoting Coetzee's famous formulation: 'All autobiography is storytelling, all writing is autobiography' (*DP* 391), David Attwell argues that, while Coetzee scholars and critics have often referred to these words to account for 'third-person treatments of the autobiographical persona' in Coetzee's fictionalised memoirs, 'they have not been much discussed in relation to Coetzee's fiction' (2015, 7–8).

But there is a middle way not mentioned in Coetzee's oft-quoted statement, which is to do with the autotextual aspect of his writing, that is with the ways in which Coetzee's texts take after or respond to each other.[14] Having committed the facts of his life to writing, what kind of life emerges from the process of the fictionalisation of life and what impact does this process have on Coetzee's further fictions? In other words, if the John of *Scenes from Provincial Life* is a fictional figure by virtue of being subjected to the laws of storytelling, how does this character translate into the construction of Coetzee's *Jesus* novels? Emerging from this process is an entanglement of not only fiction and storytelling but also of autotextual relations further obliterating the established limits between fiction and its outside. However, accepting the implication that the *Jesus* trilogy positions itself in a relation with *Scenes from Provincial Life*, the question about what kind of relation it yields remains unresolved. Did the *Jesus* novels carry on where the memoirs had left off, or, consistent with Coetzee's penchant for redrafting his novels, did

Coetzee go so far as to rewrite the life of John through the life of David? In other words, did David's story bring to conclusion what its predecessor had striven to accomplish?

Read along these lines, the *Jesus* trilogy would be a repository of its author's accumulated experience of sorts. Considering the prevalence of the themes of illness and disability in Coetzee's late fiction, as well as their relation to the author's life, Alice Hall refers to Coetzee's works of this period as examples of 'disability autobiography' (2012a, 57). Hall is correct to assume that as works depending on an imbrication of disability representation, formal experimentation and autobiographical references in equal measure, *Slow Man* and *Diary of a Bad Year* can be considered along the lines of disability life writing. In their focus on the debilitating effects of senescence, some of which may be inspired by the then sexagenarian author's own grappling with ageing, these novels, together with other late fictions such as *Elizabeth Costello* or *Summertime*, can also be couched under the term of gerontography or autogerontography.[15] Centring on the illness of their quasi-eponymous protagonist in their finale, the *Jesus* novels can be read as examples of illness narrative, as I propose to do in the previous section, or pathography, as well as, bearing in mind the incapacitating effects of David's mysterious illness, disability narrative. Taking these distinctions as a starting point, I will study the extent to which the events associated with Coetzee's life, especially those that found their way to the author's fictionalised memoirs, inform the *Jesus* novels, thus reading them as instances of (auto)pathography or disability life narrative.

The clue to legitimising the bond between fiction and storytelling is also ingrained in Coetzee's own concept of '*autre*biography' (*DP* 384) denoting the author's strategic detachment from himself through a displacement of the grammatical subject position, which tactic accounts for the shift from first- to third-person narrative in Coetzee's fictionalised memoirs. As the archive of Coetzee's private papers at The Harry Ransom Center reveals, Coetzee adopted a conventional first-person narrative perspective in the early drafts of what was originally conceived as an 'autobiography'.[16] The shift from first- to third-person narrative, which occurs on 8 August 1993, is preceded by the author's rather striking and game-changing resolution: 'Not a memoir but a novel, a slim novel' (HRC 27.2, 8-8-1993). This turn sets the stage for an *autre*biographical programme involving two forms of distancing: 1) the story of the self must be related from the narrative position of the other; 2) historical facts must yield to the laws of storytelling. Consequently, 'What I have to do is to invent a position', writes Coetzee in his notebook nearly two years later, 'that does not belong to realism, that is in effect a fictional construct' (HRC 35.2, 5-12-1994). Although these words refer to Coetzee's semi-autobiographical work in progress, in which the author resists realist impulses by manipulating biographical facts and 'collaps[ing] the chronology',[17] they also prefigure more complex and far-reaching self-reflexive strategies developed in his other late fictions, such as *Slow Man* and the *Jesus* novels, where Coetzee's autobiographical impulses partake in the novels' disruption of the realist effect.[18] While in *Slow Man* the suspension of realism comes through an unsolicited incursion of Elizabeth Costello, whose function is both autobiographical (as she acts as an author figure and is often believed to be Coetzee's alter ego) and autotextual (as a character in Coetzee's other fictions), in *The Childhood of Jesus* the defamiliarising effects of protagonists' historical amnesia echo Coetzee's own problematic relationship with South Africa.

In the opening note of one of Coetzee's early drafts of *Boyhood*, Coetzee spells out the role of South Africa in his memoir thus: 'Deformation. My life as deformed, year after year, by South Africa. Emblem: the deformed trees on the golf links in Simonstown' (HRC 27.2, 11-5-1993). Six years earlier, in his 1987 'Jerusalem Prize Acceptance Speech', Coetzee remarks along similar lines that '[t]he deformed and stunted relations between human beings' in apartheid South Africa result in 'a deformed and stunted inner life', and that '[a]ll expressions of that inner life [. . .] suffer from the same stuntedness and deformity' (*DP* 98). Coetzee's use of disability metaphors and symbolism in both of these excerpts underscores his unambiguous position about the incapacitating impact of South Africa's ecosystem of oppression on the life of an individual in general and his own life particularly. For Coetzee, South Africa becomes metonymic of what Jasbir Puar refers to, albeit in a different political context, as 'the biopolitics of debilitation', foregrounding a 'slow wearing down of populations instead of the event of becoming disabled' as such (2017, xiii–xiv). Such stultifying conditions must press heavily on the boy's formative process. Consequently, 'whoever the true "I" is that ought to be rising out of the ashes of his childhood [. . .] is being kept puny and stunted' (*BH* 140). This sentiment is later highlighted in *Youth*, where John as a young man looks back on his South African experience as 'a handicap' (62), 'an albatross around his neck' (101) and 'a wound within him' (116).

In view of the heavy psychological toll that living in South Africa takes on the protagonist and the author by association, disability should be accepted as more than just a rhetorical device. Coetzee's fictionalised memoirs may be considered alongside G. Thomas Couser's concept of 'disability autoethnography' foregrounding the story of a disabled self in relation to her resistance to political subjection (2009, 92). While Coetzee's autobiographical works may not strictly fit into this category in generic terms, they variously force the reader to ponder on the link between disability and forms of political oppression by militating against the incapacitating impact of colonialism. *Scenes from Provincial Life*, therefore, marks Coetzee's attempt to take stock of his childhood experience in South Africa and come to terms with its debilitating effects on his formative years: 'He is the product of a damaged childhood, that he long ago worked out; what surprises him is that the worst damage was done not in the seclusion of the home but out in the open, at school' (*ST* 252). This autobiographical thread is echoed in the staging of Novilla's normative politics as fundamentally inimical to David's unorthodox educational needs in *The Childhood of Jesus*. As I argue in the previous section, although the school authorities of Novilla suspect David of having 'learning difficulties' (*CJ* 246) or an intellectual 'deficit' (*CJ* 242) caused by the boy's inability to root his young self in a secure sense of the past, it is, conversely, the constricting conditions of Novilla that do not allow the boy to thrive intellectually. Consequently, both John and David are figures of the social model of disability – which presumes disability as an effect of social barriers rather than an individual's inherent intellectual, physical or sensory deficit – in that the intellectual or psychological state of the two boy protagonists is presented as a consequence of the disabling social conditions they are exposed to.

Through its perplexing politics of forgetting, the *Jesus* trilogy can be in a sense read as Coetzee's attempt to offset the weight of the memory of childhood, which to him is 'a time of gritting the teeth and enduring' (*BH* 14). The protagonists of the *Jesus* trilogy 'are all washed clean of memory' upon their arrival in Novilla (*CJ* 246). Incapable of rooting their present selves in the forgotten past, they are forced to shape their experience and history anew: 'Unable to remember [. . .] all any of us can do is to make up stories' (*SJ* 18). Considered along these lines, the *Jesus* novels bring to fruition Coetzee's fantasy of wiping clean his past as a kind of coping mechanism, a sentiment articulated in the following passage of *The Childhood of Jesus*: 'Once you have properly forgotten, your sense of insecurity will recede and everything will become much easier' (*CJ* 169). The *Jesus* novels' enigmatic ecosystem of historical amnesia, which is a marker of the novels' suspension of realism characteristic of Coetzee's other late fictions, may be said to partake in Coetzee's programme of rewriting the story of the 'deformed' self through fiction – a programme that, to recall the words of Julia in *Summertime*, presupposes writing as the author's 'self-administered therapy' (*ST* 58).

Coetzee's meditation on the intellectual abilities of his protagonists as well as their normative status invites comparisons between the John of the memoirs and David of the *Jesus* novels. David is both gifted and yet strangely detached and socially deficient, which is much in line with the ways in which Coetzee presents his younger self – in a characteristically self-deprecating manner – in the memoirs. Both John and David show signs of narcissistic personality or self-entitlement issues. Reminiscent of John's 'sense of himself as prince of the house' (*BH* 12), David's claim to be 'the prince' is acknowledged by Inés (*CJ* 309). While both boys are depicted as surpassing their peers intellectually, they also share anxiety about their sense of normalcy. John 'is grateful to his mother for protecting him from his father's normality', but he also resents her 'for turning him into something unnatural' (*BH* 8), as he sees himself as 'stupid and self-enclosed [. . .] childish; dumb; ignorant; retarded' (160–1). The early drafts of *Boyhood* reinforce these sentiments. Since John 'would like to be normal' (HRC 27.2, 11-9-1993), he blames his mother for the fact that 'her abnormality [. . .] made him abnormal' (HRC 27.2, 23-8-1993). Similarly, David 'feels himself to be special, even abnormal' (*CJ* 247), but he 'would prefer to be normal' (*DJ* 112).

In a similar manner, allusions and direct references to the adult John's 'autistic quality' in *Summertime* play the double role of underscoring the protagonist's exceptionality and social ineptitude (*ST* 52). Coetzee's notebooks show that he intended the protagonist's neuroatypicality to be meant literally rather than figuratively. In an early sketch of the final part of his semi-autobiographical trilogy, he writes: 'Theme: objectively speaking, he is happiest and most productive when he is living alone. [. . .] Link this to [. . .] Asperger's syndrome' (HRC 46.1, 29-7-2005). Hannah Tweed lists 'a lack of self-reflexive thought; interests in set topics (maths, numbers and patterns); the inability to communicate with neurotypical characters' as typical characteristics of autistic characters as represented in literary works and film (2020, 367). Described in *Summertime* by his former lovers and cousin as a 'loner' (*ST* 20, 133), '[s]ocially inept' (20), '[r]epressed' (20), a 'life's failur[e]' (37), characterised by 'a narrow, myopic kind of cleverness' (24), 'too preoccupied with himself' (46), 'autistic' (53), 'treat[ing] other people as automata' (53), with '[h]is mental capacities [...] overdeveloped, at the cost of his animal self' (58), the over-thirty-year-old John checks at least several boxes of the cultural representations of neuroatypical characters.[19] In the novel's drafts, Julia makes the point about John's social ineptitude even more emphatically: 'It quite takes her breath away, how stupid a man can be. More than stupid, she wonders whether in this case the man might not be autistic. Autistic people have no appreciation of what is going on in the hearts of the people around them. To autistics, other people have no heart, no inner life' (HRC 46.3, 6-7-12-2005).

To this effect, Coetzee's memoirs could be read along the lines of what some disability scholars term 'autie-biography', which refers to 'first-person narratives by people with autism' (Couser 2009, 5). Although this possibility may be purely hypothetical, as no Coetzee biographer confirms this supposition, Coetzee's own contemplation of the mental state of his counterpart, be it directly in his notes or by proxy through other characters and narrators, invites the reader to consider Coetzee's autobiographical fictions in the light of these biomedical categories. It should also be noted that Coetzee's autie-biography is inextricable from his autre-biography in that Coetzee's meditation on John's mental capacities comes through a combination of the third-person narrative and fictionalisation of events, by which the author can achieve the position of the other when relating the story of his self. Without pushing this argument too far into the medical territory, these distancing formal devices of Coetzee's autobiographical fictions call to mind a phenomenon referred to as 'pronoun atypicality' which denotes a tendency among autistic people 'to use the second-person pronoun *you* or third-person pronoun *he/she* to refer to themselves, as well as to use the first-person pronoun *I* to refer to the person addressed' (Sterponi, de Kirby and Shankey 2015, 273). Taking biomedical scholarship on neurodiversity as a clue, what Coetzee achieves in *Scenes from Provincial Life* is not only the representation of atypicality, manifested in the explicit references or allusions to the protagonist's mental state, but also the poetics of atypicality, in that the strategy of subject displacement that is associated with pronoun reversal among autistic people underpins the narrative mode of the novel.

The autie-biographical allusions of Coetzee's memoirs also extend to the *Jesus* novels' staging of the characters' peculiar abilities. The combination of social maladaptation and intellectual precociousness that John and David share attracts considerations about the boys' symptoms of neurodiverse states, such as Asperger's syndrome. But if the young John acts as an autobiographical prototype of David regarding the latter's ambiguous intellectual and psychological state, so the tricenarian John finds his counterpart in Simón in the same respect. These characters, as I argue above, are often shown to contemplate or question their normalcy. It is often their ability to dance, which is a recurrent theme in both trilogies, that becomes a measure of their sense of being normal. As a result, while the inability to dance is a marker of abnormality, unconventional forms of dancing foreshadow abilities transcending the protocols of normalcy – that is, super-abilities. David's profound aptitude for dancing the numbers, a philosophy championed by the Arroyos in their unorthodox dancing academy, serves to fortify the aura of inscrutability or even divinity about the boy. Simón is acutely aware of the correlation between dancing and normalcy. When the boy boasts to his guardian that he 'can dance all the numbers', the latter, somehow nonplussed, asks if the boy can 'do human dancing' as well (*SJ* 234). Simón's tacit admonition implies that he presupposes dancing as an important component of human socialisation, a proof of normality if performed according to certain cultural standards, but also of aberration if these standards are contravened by the dancer. Therefore, 'until you learn to do what human beings do', he presses on, 'you can't be a full human being' (*SJ* 234).

These pedagogical meditations on the social role of dancing in the child's normal development compel Simón to revise his relation to dancing, and in doing so contemplate his own normalcy. As a dancer 'without any gifts', Simón 'plays the gramophone' and 'does his dancing in private, in the evenings, alone' (*DJ* 7). Dancing for Simón is an intensely intimate act and as such it is a symptom of his social withdrawal. If dancing is a marker of normal social functioning, dancing in private or else the inability to dance must therefore be seen as socially aberrant. When Simón resents his role in the family as 'the stupid one, the blind one, the danceless one' (*SJ* 257), his choice of disability metaphors – such as blindness as ignorance, or stupidity connoting a form of intellectual atypicality – reveals that for him the inability to dance is socially inhibiting or even disabling. In an early draft of *Life & Times of Michael K*, Coetzee contemplates a scene foreshadowing Simón's private ritual of dancing, in which, 'when alone', Michael 'dances to the radio in the flat' (HRC 33.5, 22-5-1981). While this scene was abandoned in the later drafts and published version of the novel, Coetzee continued to explore the theme of the inability to dance as a sign of the character's social exclusion before it was brought to fruition in the *Jesus* novels. John in *Youth*, for example, 'enrolled for a package of lessons at a dance school [...] [w]hen as a university student he found it too much of an embarrassment to go to parties and not know how to dance' (*Y* 89).[20] The dancing class scene is later retold in *Summertime*, where this particular failing of John's partakes in what Robert Kusek calls 'the attitude of deprecation that the narrative displays towards its central protagonist' (2017, 195). When, by Adriana's account, John enrols in her dancing class to pursue her as a lover, he shows 'no aptitude' (*ST* 182), '[h]e was not at ease in his body' (183), he was 'unteachable' (183), 'disembodied' (198), 'not human' (198), thereby suggesting that Coetzee's biographer interviewing her title his book '*The Wooden Man*' (198).[21] Dancing as a necessary component of socialisation is also hinted at in the scene in which John recollects his mother attending weekend night dances in an act of defiance against her domestication: 'I will not be a prisoner in this house!' (*Y* 88). John's ineptitude as a dancer, therefore, acts as a metonymy for his failure to overcome his limitations. It is a handicap that impedes his access to normalcy. In this sense, the awareness of his failure to follow the protocols of this important social ritual helps shape Coetzee's double vision of privilege and vulnerability.

As an accomplished dead white male author in *Summertime*, an emblematic figure of western power, Coetzee probes his weaknesses and limitations as a way to undercut the narrative of entitlement. These concerns have preoccupied Coetzee since his early fictions. In his 1980 private notebook, Coetzee confesses his complicity with the class of the rulers: 'I am outraged by tyranny, but only because I am identified with the tyrants, not because I love (or "am with") their victims. [...] There is a fundamental flaw in my novels: I am unable to move from the side of the oppressors to the side of the oppressed' (HRC 33.5, 16-6-80). If Coetzee laments his inability to put himself in the position of the victim in his earlier fiction, in his later novels and autobiographical works, he finally figures out how to take this leap. In these works, the characters that invite comparisons with their author, such as Elizabeth Costello, JC, Paul Rayment, John Coetzee from the autobiographies, as well as both Simón and David from the *Jesus* novels, often have their exceptional abilities tested by a disabling state. While these vulnerabilities often manifest themselves as a physical or intellectual state, such as illness, disability or senescence, they are also conveyed through a symbol, such as dancing as a pointer of social normalcy.

Similarly, in *Boyhood*, John's timidity to expose his feet in front of his peers is a socially estranging experience for him. Although this episode is depicted in the published version of the novel too, an early draft communicates this point more forcefully: 'He knows there is something strange about this. He has a secret which is truly shameful because it is unlike the secrets of other people. Something has become displaced in him [...] in a shameful way' (HRC 27.2, 9-8-1993). Dancing and the feet count among Coetzee's private symbols of abnormality, ones that prevent him an entry into this incomprehensible, part despised and part desired, domain of normalcy. The allegorical force of dancing manifests itself also in David's dying days in *The Death of Jesus*. As remarked by Alyosha: 'But it always struck me as odd that the disease that killed him began by crippling him. Odd or sinister. As if the disease had a mind of its own. As if it wanted to stop him from dancing' (*DJ* 178). Physically incapacitated by the mysterious illness, David is now unable to convey his message through number-dancing. While their inability to dance is for John and Simón a symptom of their abnormality, for David his unique ability in this department is an indication of his deeper mystical insight (although, as is characteristic of Coetzee's fiction, this mystical ability is hinted at rather than brought to a logical conclusion) or super-ability. Reading along the biblical lines suggested by the trilogy's title, if illness and death stand for the way of the cross and the crucifixion, dancing epitomises David's miraculous ministry. The debilitation of the boy's physical faculties, ending in his literal death and the figurative death of the saviour he represents, mirrors Coetzee's own sense of the inability to function and flourish, especially socially.

Coetzee's relationship with his mother tongue, or rather his inability to claim or own a mother tongue, is, as in the autobiographical episodes about dancing and the feet, another cause of social estrangement for him. In an early draft of *Summertime*, Coetzee writes:

> He was born into English, it was 'his,' though without a thought. Then gradually in adulthood he has lost that happy unawareness. More and more the language becomes a foreign body which he has to enter. He becomes, in his mind, a person without a language, a disembodied spirit. (HRC 46.1, 18-3-2005)

Although, as Coetzee reminisces in *Boyhood*, 'he could not pass for a moment as an Afrikaner' (*BH* 124), English is increasingly becoming a foreign language to him. As the capacity to produce language is a basic proof of being human, John's alienation from language renders him a 'disembodied spirit' and 'unnatural' (*BH* 6). The passage about John's languagelessness did not survive in the published version of *Summertime*, but Coetzee revisited this idea in his exchange of letters with writer Paul Auster, later collected and published as *Here and Now*, where Coetzee writes about his reservations about claiming English as his mother tongue (*HN* 65–6). In the same inquisitive spirit, another of Coetzee's characters-cum-alter-egos, who also bears his author's initials, JC from *Diary of a Bad Year*, has this to say to his amanuensis Anya: 'What does that mean, mother tongue? [. . .] Do I have to have learned language at a woman's knee? Do I have to have drunk it from a woman's breast?' (*DBY* 51). Born and raised in an English-speaking family but mixing with Afrikaans-speaking peers, Coetzee developed a strained relationship with English, one that resembles his attitude to the country of his birth. Like South Africa, for Coetzee, English is a handicap, a marker of his limited sense of belonging, and therefore of exclusion. Coetzee's sense of languagelessness takes us back to the theme of historical amnesia in *The Childhood of Jesus*. One of the novel's implausibilities is to do with the fact that the inhabitants of Novilla have no sense of memory, which includes no memory of the language they spoke before the arrival, no memory of their mother tongues. As they are languageless in the strict sense of the term, they unambiguously epitomise and bring to fruition Coetzee's complex and tortured relationship with his mother tongue, which he was at a loss to comprehend or verbalise in his various (semi) autobiographical writings.

Other autobiographical symmetries between the protagonists of both trilogies under discussion abound. The role of Inés, David's mother, who is at the same time not the boy's biological mother – which the boy occasionally reminds her of by exclaiming: 'You are not my mother!' (*DJ* 38) – and, by Simón's admission, 'his full mother [. . .] that one and only mother' (*CJ* 90), mirrors Coetzee's own strenuous relationship with his mother, Vera, whose attention he both craved and found supremely stifling. She is a mother both passionately claimed and disowned by her son.[22] Some echoes of this paradox are heard in *Boyhood* in scenes portraying Coetzee's accounts of his brother David Coetzee. When jealous of the attention his younger brother receives from their mother, John 'wants her to behave towards him as she does towards his brother' (*BH* 12–13). Although, as suggested above, David of the *Jesus* books is in some ways modelled on J. M. Coetzee's own childhood self, it appears that the choice of his protagonist's name might derive from Coetzee's childhood relationship with his brother. It is as if Coetzee seeks to claim the position of his brother to complete his project of the appropriation of the mother. Or else, considering that *The Childhood of Jesus* was published only three years after David Coetzee's untimely death from cancer in 2010, the choice of the protagonist's name might be seen as Coetzee's silent tribute to the memory of his deceased brother, who like the young hero of the trilogy succumbed to a terminal illness.[23]

Finally, the fictional David's recurrent sensation of falling during his illness evokes some autobiographical and autotextual references. Falling is a pervasive theme in *The Master of Petersburg*. It serves as an allusion to Dostoevsky's epilepsy, an illness that the writer is reported to have had. But the autotextual thread does not fully account for the prevalence of the theme. The fictional Dostoevsky's son's death from being pushed from a shot tower strikingly resembles Coetzee's own son's death from a fall from the balcony of his flat in Johannesburg at the tender age of twenty-three.[24] This theme of the death of the son marks Coetzee's 'empathic leap', as David Attwell calls it, via which the author 'imagin[es] his own grief as Dostoevsky's' (2015, 194). By revisiting the theme of falling as a symptom of David's illness in *The Death of Jesus*, Coetzee appears to close off another of his intensely private autobiographical circles that indicate his profound awareness of the subtle links between life, writing and vulnerability.

In this final section of my book, I have been attempting to demonstrate an extent to which Coetzee's *Jesus* fiction carries within it a complex cumulative experience of the writer's life as registered in both of his factually unreliable memoirs and deeply autobiographical fictional works. This tangled imbrication of writing and life is strongly mediated by the author's experience, both at first hand and through those close to him, of vulnerability, illness and disability. Coetzee is, however, not a disability life writer. Not in the traditional sense of the term. He is committed to confounding any references to his own life, to submit them to the pressures and ambiguities of writing – just as he makes writing answerable to the gravity of lived experience, one often defined by anxiety, suffering, or one's confrontation with their limitations, incapacities or disabilities. In this sense, disability is a structural thread that runs consistently through Coetzee's all writings. And it is on these conditions alone that Coetzee's texts can be deemed the works of disability autobiography. In other words, it is in this sense that Coetzee's autre-biography is always also an autie-biography, a study of the writer's uncertain and distant relation with himself through writing.

Notes

1. For more information, see Johnston's discussion on the meanings of the word 'Coetzeeean' (2021).
2. See Glavin and Montgomery (2017) on the use of bibliotherapy for the treatment of PTSD.
3. See, for example, Cox et al. (2012) for a discussion on the 'integrated perspective', which denotes various forms of social prejudice as a cause of depression.
4. The early draft of *Dusklands* titled 'Lies' is not to be confused with Coetzee's later short story of the same title published in 2017 in *The New York Review*.
5. In both the first sketch and first draft of *Dusklands*, Marilyn refers to herself in these terms: 'I'm just neurotic' (HRC 33.2); 'That's all there is to it [...] just a touch of neurosis' (HRC 1.1, 20-8-1972).
6. See Chapter 1 for details about Dawn's psychosis and hospitalisation.
7. See the project's description at the University of Leeds' official website ('Bibliotherapy for Refugees and Asylum Seekers').
8. The spelling of the boy's name changes in the second novel into 'Davíd' and is restored to 'David' in the last part of the trilogy. I will alternate the spelling in this chapter to fit the original spelling used by Coetzee. If I refer to the boy in general rather than to his appearance in any particular part of the trilogy, I use the unaccented variant: David.
9. In etymological terms, the word 'Saporta' derives from Old French and denotes the door, which, by connoting a passage from one world to another, is an important part of the allegorical framework of the novel.
10. Since his migration to Australia in 2002, Coetzee has been witness to events that were a consequence of the anti-migration policies upheld by the Australian government, such as the hunger strike of seventy asylum seekers in Woomera Detention Centre in 2002, the death of over thirty asylum seekers after a boat hit the rocks at Christmas Island in 2010, and the indefinite detention of Behrouz Boochani in an Australian offshore detention facility at Manus Island between 2013 and 2017, to name a few.
11. In some of his works, such as *In the Heart of the Country*, *Age of Iron*, *Elizabeth Costello* and *Slow Man*, Coetzee tests the limits of literary realism.
12. Although NPD is typically diagnosed in early adulthood, it can also be identified as early as in childhood and adolescence (Kernberg 1989, 671). The trilogy documents David's life between the ages of five and ten.

13. 'Refusing to listen to his teacher does not mean a child is exceptional, it just means he is disobedient. If you insist the boy must have special treatment, let him go to Punto Arenas. They know how to deal with exceptional children there' (*CJ* 267).
14. I use the term 'autotextuality', following Radosvet Kolarov, 'to mean the dialogue between texts written by the same author' (2021, 1).
15. As discussed in depth in Chapter 8.
16. The early draft of 1987 contains a title page including the following list of contents: 'Scenes from Provincial Life', 'Notes for autobiography' and 'Autobiography ("Boyhood")', which confirms that what was later published as the first part of the *Scenes from Provincial Life* trilogy, *Boyhood*, was originally conceived as an autobiographical work (see HRC 27.1).
17. As Coetzee writes in his notes for *Summertime* (HRC 46.1).
18. See Chapter 7 for a discussion on the suspension of realism through disability aesthetics in *Slow Man*.
19. I hereby limit myself to literary representations of autism and Asperger's. I am purposefully avoiding a discussion about how these cultural assumptions and narratives reflect biomedical consensus and discourse on the matter, which is not a subject of my study in this chapter.
20. In his biography of J. M. Coetzee, Kannemeyer confirms that Coetzee took 'a few dance lessons to make it easier to socialize with women at gatherings' (2012, 79), but only quotes Coetzee's *Youth* to support this fact.
21. This title echoes Coetzee's *Slow Man*, a novel about an unsociable leg amputee, thus implicitly linking John's inability to dance with not only physical dysfunction of the body but also lack of social skills.
22. In the early drafts of *Boyhood*, Coetzee negotiates a tension between these extremes. He asks himself through the narrator, 'Does he love his mother?' (HRC 27.2, 13-1-1995). He admits that, if he does, he does not love her in the traditional sense that can be seen in films. What 'he means by love is' a 'wish to break away from her without hurting her' (ibid.).
23. With no biographical evidence to corroborate the link between David Coetzee and the David of the *Jesus* novels at my disposal, I would like to propose this line of interpretation in the spirit of critical speculation rather than a fact.
24. See Chapter 6 for my discussion on the (auto)biographical aspects of *The Master of Petersburg*.

Epilogue: Positive Incapabilities

Throughout this book, I have discussed the ways in which Coetzee's fictions respond to the complexities of embodiment. His novels are populated by characters who negotiate their ways in the world founded on norms they cannot or will not fit into. The strained relationship between these characters' non-conforming bodies and the worlds they inhabit bars them from normal functioning. Whether physically debilitated by oppressive politics of the state or socially excluded, these characters embody, contemplate or resist forms of incapacitation foisted upon them. Ever committed to examining the entanglement between fact and fiction, as well as form and representation, Coetzee demonstrates in his novels how the narrative operations of the text tie in with fictional representations of disability and the ways in which some of these representations intimate the author's life experience. But what these novels conceal, or reveal implicitly, is that Coetzee's reflections on disability and incapability mirror the author's personal relationship with writing.

Coetzee's remarks on the incapacitating experience of writing from his early writer's notebooks seem to be written in the spirit of 'self-administered therapy', to recall the words of one of his characters (*ST* 58). That Coetzee should heal the effects of writing with writing is perhaps ironic, but also symptomatic of his preoccupation with the possibilities and limitations of the creative process. Writing has the capacity to facilitate reflection; it 'reveals to you what you wanted to say in the first place', or even 'sometimes constructs what you want or wanted to say' (*DP* 18). To reap these rewards, one must first commit oneself unconditionally to the task. But there is a price to pay for negligence: 'I must write every day' – writes Coetzee in his writer's notebook for *Life & Times of Michael K* – 'The nausea mounts as one is absent from the story and it begins to look thin & remote' (HRC 33.5, 7-2-1981). Following from this is an image of a writer who can be physically affected by his creative labours. Nor is one's dedication to the work a formula to success: 'Every morning since 1 Jan 1970 I have sat down to write. I HATE it' (HRC 33.3, 30-5-78). Apart from being affective, writing can also take a heavy psychological toll on the writer. Drafting *Waiting for the Barbarians* in 1977, Coetzee checks himself when he is beginning to approach the point of descent into the 'drama of consciousness' characteristic of his previous novel, *In the Heart of the Country*: 'I cannot face the project of writing at that hysterical intensity again' (HRC 33.3: 10-10-1977). As the phrase 'hysterical intensity' might accurately describe Magda's own state of mind when narrating or writing her impassioned account, it is revealing that Coetzee claims to have shared his protagonist's mental and emotional experience when writing her story.

These sentiments and sensations refuse to abate with further novels. The early drafts of *Foe* do not yield easily to the writer's designs: 'Ground down by the tedium of writing the opening section. Cannot possibly go on to a middle section' (HRC 33.6, 23-2-1984). Nearing a halfway point in the drafting, Coetzee complains again: 'Reached my lowest point yet, yesterday. Thought I would give it all up. Headache, depression' (HRC 33.6, 5-4-1984). Again, Coetzee's body reacts with adverse physical symptoms to the exigencies of his creative endeavours. And conversely, at a certain point Coetzee interrupts drafting with a remark on the impact of his ailing body on writing:

> This was not intended to be a diary.
> BUT.
> An obstruction within the heart. Hence the lassitude, dizziness, exhaustion, stupidity. [...]
> The reason why I have been unable to work this year.
> Plus an infected pancreas. (HRC 33.6, 26-4-1984)

Coetzee suspects that his writing anxiety has a source: 'I am trying to write a book for which I have neither inclination nor talent – a story of "ideas"' (HRC 33.6, 6-9-1983). Readers familiar with Coetzee's oeuvre might be surprised by the author's assessment of his creative incapacities, considering that over years Coetzee has built a reputation as a novelist of ideas. And yet, admittedly, Coetzee would bring to fruition his interest in ideas in his later Australian fiction, such as *Elizabeth Costello*, *Diary of a Bad Year* and the *Jesus* novels, which maximise the role of the philosophical dialogue at the expense of the intricacies of plot. These self-effacing sentiments expressed in Coetzee's notes might thus be evocative of his determination to counterbalance his creative limitations. Attwell suggests that '[s]uch methods are built on [. . .] tenaciously working through the uncertainties [. . .] towards a distant goal until an illumination arrives, providing direction and momentum for the next phase' (2015, xx). In a similar vein, David Isaacs proposes that Coetzee 'allows his texts to construct themselves from the doubts, anxieties and obstructions of composition' (2021, 134). 'When the narrative founds on contradiction or incapacity,' affirms Coetzee, 'new versions are tried' (HRC 33.3, 26-4-1978). To refine this strategy, Coetzee would develop a punishing work ethic involving relentless revising and rewriting, 'tuning and tightening each sentence till it resonated like timpani' (Rutherford 2021, 221). It was common for Coetzee to have completed more than ten draft versions of some novels before they acquired the intended shape. Coetzee's struggle against the demands of writing and his own self-confessed creative limitations was, therefore, hard-won.

Sometimes, Coetzee's determination to get his story right meant that when faced with an inability to move on with the project, he abandoned it altogether. An impasse of this kind occurred during the outlining of what was to be Coetzee's second novel, provisionally titled 'Burning the Books', a story about a book censor employed by the Department of the Interior in Cape Town. On another level, the story discusses the writer's ineptitude to construct a new character, with the narrator taking the role of the creator, that is, of creating himself and of projecting this self-creation onto the text. The narrator addresses the reader about this fact directly: 'You will notice that there is something unsatisfactorily schematic about all the lives I can envisage for myself' (HRC 33.1, 29-6-1974). The draft leaves a number of self-reflexive clues about the narrator's awareness of (and anxiety about) his fictionality: 'In this incarnation I am a censor' (HRC 33.1, 27-6-1974). When describing his mother, the narrator states: 'I have difficulty focussing on her face, but it will come, do not rush me', thus dropping hints, again, about the demands of the creative process (HRC 33.1, 3-7-1974). But the moment of crisis for Coetzee arrives after only several pages into the drafting: 'When I think of a man sitting and censoring books, my heart sinks' (HRC 33.1, 18-6-1974). Characteristically, the writer's block announces itself through a bodily reaction. It seems that Coetzee quickly exhausted the resources of the metafictional premise on which the novel was built. In doing so, his rejection of the story prefigures the author's sentiments expressed in later notebooks and interviews about his scepticism towards pure metafiction, which 'is obviously another capability of writing. But its attractions soon pall: [...] writing-about-writing hasn't much to offer' (*DP* 204). Nor does Coetzee feel comfortable in a genre that nurtures this limiting device: 'I don't have it in me to carry off the light irony of the postmodern novel' (HRC 33.6, 16-12-1983).

Chiming with Coetzee's contemplation of his writing limitations and their somatosensory effects are the author's self-searching remarks on the representation of atypicality in his works. In the drafts for *Waiting for the Barbarians*, after having satisfactorily established the form and plotline of his novel, Coetzee writes: 'Disturbed by having pleasure with an incomplete object' (HRC 33.3, 4-1-1978). Although this enigmatic entry likely refers to the account of the novel's protagonist after his intimate encounter with the blinded and physically incapacitated barbarian woman, it also throws some light on Coetzee's own preoccupation with disability in his works. After toying with the idea of making Magda 'a mad old tramp-woman', Coetzee checks himself in his meditations on the first draft of what would become *In the Heart of the Country*: 'Why the attraction of/to craziness?' (HRC 33.3, 25-11-1975). Elsewhere, he also often challenges himself to revise his own ideas: 'What if Friday's blankness is all <u>learned</u>?' or 'Has she ever looked in Friday's mouth? Perhaps the story of the missing tongue was made by Cruso and it suits Friday to maintain it' (HRC 33.6, 30-9-1985). These moments of creative introspection allowed Coetzee to refine his depictions of these characters' relationship with their bodies and minds. As a result, Magda progresses in the drafts from the mad old woman stereotype to a character whose mental state does not fit into biomedical categories. Similarly, by keeping at bay the possibility of Friday's muteness, Coetzee refuses to reduce the character to a default position of the oppressed other characteristic of postcolonial narratives. The uncertainty about the characters' mental or physical state mirrors the internal operations of the text: 'I am inexplicable, unforgivable [...] why can I not be one of those narratives that finds its significance in the explanation of its action? Would it not be simpler for me if I were, say, a psychological thriller?' (HRC 3.1, 10-12-1974). Rather than descending into madness, Magda epitomises an inscrutability of a text that eludes familiar modes of interpretation. Magda's 'drama of consciousness' manifests itself in her failure to fit into the cultural standards she has imbibed and accepted as authoritative; it is a drama of the protagonist's inability to tell her story on the terms imposed on her by culture and history, or to embrace the story on its own – complex, inexplicable, ambiguous – terms.

Coetzee's introspective meditations on his creative choices prefigure the self-reflexive processes involved in the fictional staging of disability in his works of the early period. While Coetzee often depicts characters with various physical, cognitive and sensory disabilities in his fictions, he also often confounds their disabled status. In doing so, he refuses to read disability as a text with a single meaning. His works consistently show that the disruptive potential of disability resides in its resistance to interpretation. When Coetzee does the opposite, that is when he instrumentalises the role of disabled characters in the narrative – by presenting them as stereotypical figures of pity, victims of violence, or mysterious outcasts – he aims to highlight in so doing the complicity of literary authors (and he counts himself in that company) in denigrating disability in their works. Coetzee challenges such forms of epistemic injustice by undermining normative narratives (the culture of ableism) and narrative normativity (literary norms that reinforce ableism) on which they thrive. His works often employ formal innovation to impugn some cultural narratives' claims for universality. The modernist forms of *Dusklands* and *In the Heart of the Country* parallel the characters' physical and psychological states (Jacobus, Eugene, Magda) and their inability to conform to the injunctions of political and patriarchal power despite their best efforts to internalise these socially disabling narratives (Eugene, Magda). In *Waiting for the Barbarians*, Coetzee's meditation on closeness and tactile experience, together with the ways the text formally reproduces these somatosensory effects, aims to provoke the reader to question the centrality of the sight-centred view which legitimates the seer's subjugation of the unseeing object of the gaze through optical forms of control. Similarly, the ambiguity around Friday's disability in *Foe*, achieved through the text's tactical withholding of its meanings, helps Coetzee suspend the binary of speech and silence, on which western normativity has founded its uneven relations of power. In its foregrounding of the natural environment as a space that allows the protagonist to revise his relationship with his body and abilities, *Life & Times of Michael K* brings to light the exclusionary effects of institutionalisation as well as anthropocentric underpinnings of ableism.

Coetzee's South African novels of the later period show complex entanglements of the themes of illness, ethics of subjectivity and writing. In *Age of Iron*, the protagonist's experience of terminal illness – a transitional state between living and dying – becomes a signifier of the novel's 'inability to conceive of a possible future, [...] inability to project the self', which accounts for its epistolary status as well as resistance to narrative closure: like the dying self that cannot foresee what lies ahead, the letter's sender cannot know if the letter will reach its addressee (HRC 33.7, 6-5-1987). In *The Master of Petersburg*, epilepsy, or the falling sickness, prefigures Dostoevsky's moral downfall, which he brings to fruition through his heretical rewriting of the story of his stepson's life. If Coetzee's illness narratives refuse to offer redemption it is because for Coetzee ethics, like a text, produces contradictions that cannot be resolved by collective forms of moral reasoning.

While in Coetzee's early South African fictions disability partakes in the text's indictment of the narratives and systems of power legitimating political violence (such as colonialism, patriarchy, authoritarianism and anthropocentrism), his Australian novels focus on systemic injustices in neoliberal economies founded on the principles of social inclusionism. Again, Coetzee's examination of the vulnerability of the body or a critique of normativity is mediated by the text's formal operations. In *Slow Man*, the shattering of the realist veneer of the novel through the intrusion of Elizabeth Costello (a character epitomising an author-figure in the novel) mirrors Rayment's own sense of loss of his former self after the accident that has left him permanently physically disabled. In this sense, the novel acts as a reminder that the narrative's operations cannot be easily distinguished from disability representation, that '[f]orm follows dysfunction' (Davis 2002, 27). Similarly, in *Diary of a Bad Year*, the novel's experimental form facilitates the effects of ironic dialogism and has the capacity to obstruct the reader's familiar reading habits in a way reminiscent of cognitive disruptions attendant on senescence, thus bringing the reader closer to the state of mind of the ageing protagonist.

Some Coetzee scholars have noticed that the formal innovations of Coetzee's text have the capacity to challenge her to question her cultural assumptions (Attridge 2004), and ableist biases (Quayson 2007), thus eliciting from her an ethical response. If Coetzee's text can improve the reader's reading habits and help them become more informed citizens, it also can, in my reading of it, evoke affective responses that can be called therapeutic. But Coetzee's fictions do not lend themselves too easily for healing purposes due to their refusal to offer straight moral guidance and closure, as befits traditional books for prescription. And yet, it is precisely from this subversive quality that Coetzee's novels derive their psychotherapeutic effects.

Coetzee's *The Death of Jesus* is an example of illness narrative that can offer comfort through its withholding of meanings and narrative closure, as well as other (as I have called them after Keats) 'negative capabilities' of the text.

In the closing section of this book I argued that the protagonist of the *Jesus* novels, David, is partly modelled on Coetzee's own childhood self. From his earliest novels, Coetzee has kept reminding his readers that fiction is always somehow embroiled in the life of its creator. This brings me back to the opening point of this epilogue. If Coetzee's narratives of disability and illness compel the reader to put on hold her ableist biases through the text's use of formal innovations, disruptions and uncertainties, or negative capabilities, Coetzee's private notebooks reveal that the author's own embodied relationship with writing involves creative disruptions of another kind. As demonstrated above, Coetzee's struggle with his self-proclaimed limitations and ailments that have revealed themselves in the creative process, including adverse physical and cognitive reactions to writing, has influenced the final shape of his works. Considering Coetzee's penchant for confounding the limits of sorts in his fictions – between representation and form, between fiction and autobiography, or between ability and disability – these creative embodied interferences, or positive incapabilities, must be acknowledged as an integral part of the disabled textuality of Coetzee's works.

Works Cited

Archival Material

All archival materials used in this book have been adopted from the J. M. Coetzee Papers collection at The Harry Ransom Center, The University of Texas at Austin.

Container 1, folder 1, Long Works, 1960s–2012. *Dusklands* (Fiction, 1974). 'Lies', handwritten draft with revisions and notes, 11 June 1972 – 13 February 1973.

Container 1, folder 2, Long Works, 1960s–2012. *Dusklands* (Fiction, 1974). 'The Vietnam Project', early handwritten draft with revisions and notes, 21 December 1972 – 26 April 1973.

Container 1, folder 3, Long Works, 1960s–2012. *Dusklands* (Fiction, 1974). 'The Vietnam Project', handwritten draft with revisions and photocopy, 4 April – 24 May 1973.

Container 1, folder 5, Long Works, 1960s–2012. *Dusklands* (Fiction, 1974). 'Narrative of Jacobus Coetzee', handwritten draft with revisions, 1 January 1970 – 18 January 1971.

Container 3, folders 1–3, Long Works, 1960s–2012. *In the Heart of the Country* (Fiction, 1977). Handwritten first draft with revisions, 12 January 1974 – 26 January 1976.

Container 3, folders 4–5, Long Works, 1960s–2012. *In the Heart of the Country* (Fiction, 1977). Handwritten final draft with extensive revisions, 26 November 1975 – 26 January 1976.

Container 5, folder 1, Long Works, 1960s–2012. *Waiting for the Barbarians* (Fiction, 1980). Early handwritten drafts, 20 September 1977 – 26 March 1978.

Container 7, folder 1, Long Works, 1960s–2012. *Life & Times of Michael K* (Fiction, 1983). 'Versions 1-4', handwritten draft with revisions, 31 May 1980 – 14 January 1981.

Container 7, folder 2, Long Works, 1960s–2012. *Life & Times of Michael K* (Fiction, 1983). 'Versions 5', handwritten draft with revisions, 16 January – 25 April 1981.

Container 7, folder 3, Long Works, 1960s–2012. *Life & Times of Michael K* (Fiction, 1983). 'Version 6', handwritten draft with light revisions, 27 April – 27 August 1981.

Container 7, folder 4, Long Works, 1960s–2012. *Life & Times of Michael K* (Fiction, 1983). 'Version 6-6a', handwritten draft with revisions, 28 August 1981 – 12 July 1982.

Container 7, folder 5, Long Works, 1960s–2012. *Life & Times of Michael K* (Fiction, 1983). 'Version 7', handwritten draft with extensive revisions, 28 April – 28 July 1982.

Container 8, folders 1-2, Long Works, 1960s–2012. *Life & Times of Michael K* (Fiction, 1983). 'Version 9', typed draft with revisions, 1982.

Container 8, folders 3, Long Works, 1960s–2012. *Life & Times of Michael K* (Fiction, 1983). Typed late draft with corrections, 1983.

Container 10, folder 1, Long Works, 1960s–2012. *Foe* (Fiction, 1986). 'Versions 1–3', handwritten draft with revisions, 1 January – 14 September 1983.

Container 10, folder 2, Long Works, 1960s–2012. *Foe* (Fiction, 1986). 'Versions 4, 5a–b', handwritten draft with revisions, 16 September 1983 – 25 January 1984.

Container 14, folder 1, Long Works, 1960s–2012. *Age of Iron* (Fiction, 1990). Handwritten drafts '0–2' and 'fragments' with light revisions, 19 May – 26 October 1987.

Container 14, folder 2. Long Works, 1960s–2012. *Age of Iron* (Fiction, 1990). Handwritten drafts 3–5 with revisions, 31 October 1987 – 8 March 1988.

Container 17, folder 2, Long Works, 1960s–2012. *Age of Iron* (Fiction, 1990). Composite notes, fragments and photocopied research articles, 1988–1989.

Container 19, folders 1–2, Long Works, 1960s–2012. *The Master of Petersburg* (Fiction, 1994). Handwritten draft 1 part A, 21 February 1991 – 4 February 1992.

Container 27, folder 1, Long Works, 1960s–2012. *Boyhood* (Fictionalised autobiography, 1997). 'Scenes from Provincial Life', early handwritten draft, 20 March – 12 June 1987.

Container 27, folder 2, Long Works, 1960s–2012. *Boyhood* (Fictionalised autobiography, 1997). 'Autobiography', early handwritten draft with revisions and notes, 1993–1995.

Container 33, folder 1, Long Works, 1960s–2012. 'Burning the Books' (unrealised). Handwritten notes and unfinished draft, 19 October 1973 – 4 July 1974.

Container 33, folder 2, Long Works, 1960s–2012. *Dusklands* (Fiction, 1974). Discarded first sketch of 'Vietnam Project', handwritten draft, 11–27 May 1972.

Container 33, folder 3, Long Works, 1960s–2012. *In the Heart of the Country* (Fiction, 1977). Small notebook, 16 March 1974 – 9 February 1976. Small spiral notebook, 11 July 1977 – 28 August 1978.

Container 33, folder 5, Long Works, 1960s–2012. *Life & Times of Michael K* (Fiction, 1983). Gray casebound notebook, includes notes on other subjects, 1979–1982.
Container 33, folder 6, Long Works, 1960s–2012. *Foe* (Fiction, 1986). Green casebound notebook with gilt edges, 1982–1985.
Container 33, folder 6, Long Works, 1960s–2012. *Age of Iron* (Fiction, 1990). Small red notebook, June 1986 – June 1988. Small black-and-red notebook, 2 July 1988 – 5 May 1989. Small yellow notebook, 15 May 1989 – 31 August 1989.
Container 33, folder 7, Long Works, 1960s–2012. *Age of Iron* (Fiction, 1990). 'Scenes', typed notes with photocopied research materials, 5–18 May 1987.
Container 35, folder 2, Long Works, 1960s–2012. *Boyhood* (Fictionalised autobiography, 1997). Casebound notebook (includes other subjects), 1994–1995.
Container 39, folder 2, Long Works, 1960s–2012. *Slow Man* (Fiction, 2005). Notes and draft fragments, 2003–2004.
Container 39, folder 5–6, Long Works, 1960s–2012. *Slow Man* (Fiction, 2005). Draft 20 with corrections and composite notes and fragments, 13 July – 16 August 2004.
Container 46, folder 1, Long Works, 1960s–2012. *Summertime* (Fictionalised autobiography, 2009). Notes, 2002–2006.
Container 46, folder 3, Long Works, 1960s–2012. *Summertime* (Fictionalised autobiography, 2009). Draft 2 with later revisions, September 2005 – April 2007.

Works by J. M. Coetzee

Novels and memoirs

Coetzee, J. M. [1974] 2004. *Dusklands*. London: Vintage.
Coetzee, J. M. [1977] 2004. *In the Heart of the Country*. London: Vintage.
Coetzee, J. M. [1980] 2004. *Waiting for the Barbarians*. London: Vintage.
Coetzee, J. M. [1983] 2004. *Life & Times of Michael K*. London: Vintage.
Coetzee, J. M. [1986] 2010. *Foe*. London: Penguin Books.
Coetzee, J. M. [1990] 1998. *Age of Iron*. New York and London: Penguin Books.
Coetzee, J. M. [1994] 2007. *The Master of Petersburg*. London: Vintage.
Coetzee, J. M. [1997] 1998. *Boyhood*. London: Vintage.
Coetzee, J. M. [1999] 2000. *Disgrace*. London: Vintage.
Coetzee, J. M. [2002] 2003. *Youth*. London: Vintage.
Coetzee, J. M. 2003. *Elizabeth Costello*. London: Vintage.
Coetzee, J. M. [2005] 2007. *Slow Man*. London: Vintage.

Coetzee, J. M. [2007] 2008. *Diary of a Bad Year*. London: Vintage.
Coetzee, J. M. [2009] 2010. *Summertime*. London: Vintage.
Coetzee, J. M. [2013] 2014. *The Childhood of Jesus*. London: Vintage.
Coetzee, J. M. 2016. *The Schooldays of Jesus*. London: Harvill Secker.
Coetzee, J. M. 2019. *The Death of Jesus*. London: Harvill Secker.

Essays, short fiction and collaboration

Coetzee, J. M. 1986. 'Farm Novel and "Plaasroman" in South Africa.' *English in Africa* 13 (2): 1–19.
Coetzee, J. M. 1997. 'What is Realism?' *Salmagundi* 114/115: 59–81.
Coetzee, J. M. 1999. 'The Novel in Africa.' *Occasional Papers of the Doreen B. Townsend Center for the Humanities* 17: 1–19.
Coetzee, J. M. 1999. *The Lives of Animals*, edited by Peter Singer, Marjorie Garber, Wendy Doniger and Barbara Smuts. Princeton: Princeton University Press.
Coetzee, J. M. 2001. 'Dostoevsky: The Miraculous Years.' In *Stranger Shores: Literary Essays 1986-1999*, 114–26. London and New York: Viking Penguin.
Coetzee, J. M. 2001. *Stranger Shores: Literary Essays*. London and New York: Viking Penguin.
Coetzee, J. M. 2001. *The Humanities in Africa / Die Geisteswissenschaften in Afrika*. Munich: Carl Friedrich von Siemens Stiftung.
Coetzee, J. M. 2002. *Letter of Elizabeth: Lady Chandos, to Francis Bacon*. Austin, TX: Press Intermezzo.
Coetzee, J. M. 2003a. 'Elizabeth Costello and the Problem of Evil.' *Salmagundi* 137-8: 48–64.
Coetzee, J. M. 2003b. 'Fictional Beings.' *Philosophy, Psychiatry, & Psychology* 10 (2): 133–4.
Coetzee, J. M. 2004. 'As a Woman Grows Older.' *New York Review of Books*, 15 January 2004. www.nybooks.com/articles/2004/01/15/as-a-woman-grows-older/.
Coetzee, J. M. 2007. *Inner Workings: Essays 2000–2005*. With an Introduction by Derek Attridge. London: Vintage Books.
Coetzee, J. M. 2013. 'The Old Woman and the Cats.' In Berlinde de Bruyckere and J. M. Coetzee, *Cripplewood/Kreupelhout*, 7–28. Brussels: Mercatorfonds.
Coetzee, J. M. 2014. 'A House in Spain.' In *Three Stories*, 1–22. Melbourne: The Text Publishing Company.
Coetzee, J. M. 2014. 'He and His Man.' In *Three Stories*, 45–71. Melbourne: The Text Publishing Company.
Coetzee, J. M. 2014. *Three Stories*. Melbourne: Text Publishing.
Coetzee, J. M. 2017. 'Lies.' *The New York Review*, 21 December 2017. www.nybooks.com/articles/2017/12/21/lies/.

Coetzee, J. M. 2019. 'Australia's Shame.' *The New York Review*, 26 September 2019. www.nybooks.com/articles/2019/09/26/australias-shame/?lp_txn_id=1273993.

Coetzee, J. M., and Arabella Kurtz. [2015] 2016. *The Good Story: Exchanges on Truth, Fiction and Psychotherapy*. London: Vintage.

Coetzee, J. M., and Berlinde de Bruyckere. 2013. *Cripplewood/ Kreupelhout*. Brussels: Mercatorfonds.

Coetzee, J. M., and David Attwell. 1992. *Doubling the Point: Essays and Interviews*. Cambridge, MA: Harvard University Press.

Coetzee, J. M., and Paul Auster. 2013. *Here and Now. Letters: 2008–2011*. London: Faber & Faber and Harvill Secker.

Media material

Coetzee, J. M., and Wim Kayzer. 2000. 'Van de Schoonheid en de Troost (Of Beauty and Consolation).' Episode 17. Produced by VPRO. TV Series. Video, 1:19:32. Accessed 30 October 2022. www.austlit.edu.au/austlit/page/7979480.

Coetzee, J. M. 2003. 'Banquet speech.' NobelPrize.org. Accessed 10 April 2020. www.nobelprize.org/prizes/literature/2003/coetzee/speech/.

Further Works Cited

Agamben, Giorgio, and Daniel Heller-Roazen. 1998. *Homo Sacer: Sovereign Power and Bare Life*. Stanford, CA: Stanford University Press.

American Optometric Association. 2018. 'Visual Acuity: What is 20/20 Vision?' Accessed 12 August 2019. www.aoa.org/patients-and-public/eye-and-vision-problems/glossary-of-eye-and-vision-conditions/visual-acuity.

American Psychiatric Association. 2013. *Diagnostic and Statistical Manual of Mental Disorders: DSM-5*. 5th ed. Washington, DC: American Psychiatric Publishing.

Anolik, Ruth Bienstock, ed. 2010. *Demons of the Body and Mind: Essays on Disability in Gothic Literature*. Jefferson: McFarland.

Ashcroft, Bill. 2011. 'Silence as Heterotopia in Coetzee's Fiction.' In *Strong Opinions: J. M. Coetzee and the Authority of Contemporary Fiction*, edited by Chris Danta, Sue Kossew and Julian Murphet, 141–57. London and New York: Continuum.

Attridge, Derek. 2004. *J. M. Coetzee & the Ethics of Reading: Literature in the Event*. Chicago: University of Chicago Press.

Attridge, Derek. 2015. *The Work of Literature*. Oxford: Oxford University Press.

Attridge, Derek. 2017. '"A Yes without a No": Philosophical Reason and the Ethics of Conversion in Coetzee's Fiction.' In *Beyond the Ancient Quarrel*, edited by Patrick Hayes and Jan Wilm, 91–106. Oxford: Oxford University Press.

Attridge, Derek. 2020. 'Genres: *Elizabeth Costello, Diary of a Bad Year, Summertime*.' In *The Cambridge Companion to J. M. Coetzee*, edited by Jarad Zimbler, 84–99. Cambridge: Cambridge University Press.

Attwell, David. 1993. *J. M. Coetzee: South Africa and the Politics of Writing*. Berkeley, Los Angeles and Oxford: University of California Press.

Attwell, David. 1998. '"Dialogue" and "fulfilment" in J. M. Coetzee's *Age of Iron*.' In *Writing South Africa*, edited by Derek Attridge and Rosemary Jolly, 166–79. Cambridge: Cambridge University Press.

Attwell, David. 2015. *J. M. Coetzee and the Life of Writing: Face to Face with Time*. Oxford: Oxford University Press.

Attwell, David. 2016. 'Reading the Coetzee Papers.' *Texas Studies in Literature and Language* 58 (4): 374–7.

Balee, Susan. 2013. 'J. M. Coetzee's *The Childhood of Jesus*: Literature of the Absurd.' *Pittsburgh Post-Gazette*, 22 September 2013. www.post-gazette.com/ae/book-reviews/2013/09/22/J-M-Coetzee-s-The-Childhood-of-Jesus-Literature-of-the-absurd/stories/201309220107.

Barker, Clare. 2011. *Postcolonial Fiction and Disability: Exceptional Children, Metaphor and Materiality*. Basingstoke: Palgrave Macmillan.

Barker, Clare. 2018. '"Radiant Affliction": Disability Narratives in Postcolonial Literature.' In *Literature and Disability*, edited by Clare Barker and Stuart Murray, 104–19. Cambridge: Cambridge University Press.

Barker, Clare, and Stuart Murray. 2010. 'Disabling Postcolonialism. Global Disability Cultures and Democratic Criticism.' *Journal of Literary & Cultural Disability Studies* 4 (3): 219–36.

Barnes, Elizabeth. 2016. *The Minority Body: A Theory of Disability*. Oxford: Oxford University Press.

Barton, Ellen L. 2001. 'Textual Practices of Erasure.' In *Embodied Rhetorics: Disability in Language and Culture*, edited by James C. Wilson and Cynthia Lewiecki-Wilson, 169–99. Carbondale, Edwardsville: Southern Illinois University Press.

Beckett, Samuel. 2009. *Company, Ill Seen Ill Said, Worstward Ho, Stirrings Still*. London: Faber & Faber.

Beckett, Samuel. 2015. *Molloy, Malone Dies, The Unnameable*. With an Introduction by Gabriel Josipovici. New York, London and Toronto: Everyman's Library, Alfred A. Knopf.

Baudrillard, Jean. 1988. 'Simulacra and Simulations.' In *Jean Baudrillard, Selected Writings*, edited by Mark Poster, 166–84. Stanford; Stanford University Press.

Baudrillard, Jean, and Marc Guillaume. 2008. *Radical Alterity*. Los Angeles: Semiotext(e).

Bauman, H-Dirksen. 2008. 'Listening to Phonocentrism with Deaf Eyes: Derrida's Mute Philosophy of (Sign) Language.' *Essays in Philosophy* 9 (1): n. pag.

Benjamin, Walter. 2010. 'The Work of Art in the Age of Its Technological Reproducibility.' In *The Norton Anthology of Theory and Criticism*, edited by Vincent B. Leitch et al., 1051–71. New York: W. W. Norton and Company.

Berman, Jessica Schiff. 2012. *Modernist Commitments: Ethics, Politics, and Transnational Modernism*. New York: Columbia University Press.

Berthoud, Ella, and Susan Elderkin. 2013. *The Novel Cure: From Abandonment to Zestlessness*. New York: The Penguin Press.

Bertmann, Isabella. 2018. *Taking Well-Being and Quality of Life for Granted? An Empirical Study on Social Protection and Disability in South Africa*. Wiesbaden: Springer.

Bérubé, Michael. 2016. *The Secret Life of Stories: From Don Quixote to Harry Potter, How Understanding Intellectual Disability Transforms the Way We Read*. New York & London: New York University Press.

Białas, Zbigniew. 2022. 'Hunter's Drift and Far-Off Places: South African Fiction and the Failure of the Literary Western Tradition.' In *The Western in the Global Literary Imagination*, edited by Christopher B. Conway, Marek Paryż and David Rio, 300–14. Leyden: Brill.

Bibliotherapy for Refugees and Asylum Seekers. n. d. *University of Leeds*. Accessed 21 August 2021. https://ahc.leeds.ac.uk/english/dir-record/research-projects/1432/bibliotherapy-for-refugees-and-asylum-seekers.

Black, Sheila. n. d. 'Disability Poetics.' *Poetry International*. Accessed 16 September 2021. www.poetryinternationalonline.com/disability-poetics-conversation-with-sheila-black/.

Blamires, Cyprian P. 2006. *World Fascism: A Historical Encyclopedia*. Oxford: Abc-clio.

Boehmer, Elleke. 2011. 'J. M. Coetzee's Australian Realism.' In *Strong Opinions: J. M. Coetzee and the Authority of Contemporary Fiction*, edited by Chris Danta, Sue Kossew and Julian Murphet. New York and London: Continuum. 2011.

Bolt, David. 2016. *The Metanarratives of Blindness: A Re-reading of Twentieth-Century Anglophone Writing*. Ann Arbor: The University of Michigan Press.

Borowska-Beszta, Beata. 2012. *Niepełnosprawność w kontekstach kulturowych i teoretycznych*. Kraków: Impuls.

Botting, Fred. 1996. *Gothic*. London: Routledge.

Bradstreet, Tom Z. 2017. '"The Coming of the Storm": Imperial Empiricism and Ecological Indifference in *Waiting for the Barbarians*.' *A Review of International English Literature* 48: 1–23.

Brewster, Liz. 2018. 'Bibliotherapy, Illness Narratives and Narrative Medicine.' In *Bibliotherapy*, edited by Sarah McNicol and Liz Brewster, 41–58. London: Facet Publishing.

Brontë, Charlotte. [1847] 1999. *Jane Eyre*. London: Wordsworth Classics.

Brittain, Christopher Craig. 2012. 'Between Necessity and Possibility: Kierkegaard and the Abilities and Disabilities of Subjectivity.' In *Disability in the Christian Tradition: A Reader*, edited by Brian Brock and John Swinton, 286–320. Cambridge: William B. Eerdmans Publishing Company Grand Rapids, Michigan.

Bronwen, Thomas. 2016. *Narrative: The Basics*. London and New York: Routledge.

Bruhm, Steven. 2002. 'The Contemporary Gothic: Why We Need It.' *The Cambridge Companion to Gothic Fiction*, edited by Jerrold E. Hogle, 259–76. Cambridge: Cambridge University Press.

Bukowski, Danielle. 2014. 'Paranoia and Schizophrenia in Postmodern Literature: Pynchon and DeLillo.' *Vassar College Digital Library*. Accessed 30 October 2022. https://digitallibrary.vassar.edu/collections/institutional-repository/paranoia-and-schizophrenia-postmodern-literature-pynchon-and.

Carusi, Annamaria. 1990. 'Post, Post and Post. Or, Where is South African Literature in All This?' In *Past and the Last Post: Theorizing Post-Colonialism and Post-Modernism*, edited by Ian Adam and Helen Tiffin, 95–108. Calgary: University of Calgary Press.

Caruth, Cathy. 1996. *Unclaimed Experience: Trauma, Narrative, and History*. Baltimore: Johns Hopkins University Press.

Cella, Matthew J. C. 2013. 'The Ecosomatic Paradigm in Literature: Merging Disability Studies and Ecocriticism.' *Interdisciplinary Studies in Literature and Environment* 20 (3): 574–96.

Cheyne, Ria. 2019. *Disability, Literature, Genre: Representation and Affect in Contemporary Fiction*. Liverpool: Liverpool University Press.

Clarkson, Carrol. 2013. *J. M. Coetzee: Countervoices*. London and New York: Palgrave MacMillan.

Cohen, Lawrence. 2003. 'Senility and Irony's Age.' *Social Analysis: The International Journal of Anthropology* 47 (2): 122–34.

Collin, P. H. 2005. *Dictionary of Medical Terms*. London: A & C Black.

Conrad, Joseph. [1907] 2016. *The Secret Agent*. London: Penguin Books.

Conway, Kathlyn. 2013. *Beyond Words: Illness and the Limits of Expression*, University of New Mexico Press. ProQuest Ebook Central. Accessed 1 March 2018. http://ebookcentral.proquest.com/lib/york-ebooks/detail.action?docID=1172734.

Couser, G. Thomas. 2009. *Signifying Bodies: Disability in Contemporary Life Writing*. Ann Arbor: The University of Michigan Press.

Cox, William T. L., Lyn Y. Abramson, Patricia G. Devine and Steven D. Hollon. 2012. 'Stereotypes, Prejudice, and Depression: The Integrated Perspective.' *Perspectives on Psychological Science* 7 (5): 427–49.

Cuddon, J. A. 1999. *The Penguin Dictionary of Literary Terms and Literary Theory*. London and New York: Penguin Books.

Cummins, Anthony. 2013. 'The Childhood of Jesus by J. M. Coetzee, and A Life in Writing by J. C. Kannemeyer: Review.' The Telegraph, 11 March 2013. www.telegraph.co.uk/culture/books/bookreviews/9914820/The-Childhood-of-Jesus-by-J-M-Coetzee-and-A-Life-in-Writing-by-J-C-Kannemeyer-review.html.

Davenport, John J. 2013. 'Selfhood and "Spirit."' In The Oxford Handbook of Kierkegaard, edited by John Lippit and George Pattison, 230–51. Oxford: Oxford University Press.

Davidson, Michael. 2008. Concerto for the Left Hand: Disability and the Defamiliar Body. Ann Arbor: The University of Michigan Press.

Davidson, Michael. 2018. 'Paralyzed Modernities and Biofutures: Bodies and Minds in Modern Literature.' In The Cambridge Companion to Literature and Disability, edited by Clare Barker and Stuart Murray, 74–89. Cambridge: Cambridge University Press.

Davies, David. 2007. Aesthetics and Literature. London: Continuum.

Davis, Lennard J. 1995. Enforcing Normalcy: Disability, Deafness, and the Body. London and New York: Verso.

Davis, Lennard J. 2002. Bending over Backwards: Disability, Dismodernism & Other Difficult Positions. New York and London: New York University Press.

Davis, Lennard J. 2007. 'Dependency and Justice.' Journal of Literary Disability 1 (2): 1–4.

Davis, Mark. 1980. 'A Multidimensional Approach to Individual Differences in Empathy.' JSAS Catalogue of Selected Documents in Psychology 10: 85.

Dean, Andrew. 2020. 'Lives and Archives.' In The Cambridge Companion to J. M. Coetzee, edited by Jarad Zimbler, 221–33. Cambridge: Cambridge University Press.

De Boever, Arne. 2014. Narrative Care: Biopolitics and the Novel. London: Bloomsbury.

De Sousa, Avinash, Shibani Devare and Jyoti Ghanshani. 2009. 'Psychological Issues in Cleft Lip and Cleft Palate.' Journal of Indian Association of Pediatric Surgeons 14 (2): 55–8. DOI: 10.4103/0971-9261.55152.

Deckard, Michael Funk, and Ralph Palm. 2010. 'Irony and Belief in Elizabeth Costello.' In J. M. Coetzee and Ethics, edited by Anton Leist and Peter Singer, 337–56. New York and Chichester: Columbia University Press.

Deresiewicz, William. 2020. 'J. M. Coetzee's Unsettling Trilogy about a Possibly Divine Boy.' The Atlantic, June 2020. www.theatlantic.com/magazine/archive/2020/06/coetzee-death-of-jesus/610585/.

Derrida, Jacques. 1993. Memoirs of the Blind: The Self-Portrait and Other Ruins, translated by Pascale-Anne Brault and Michael Naas. Chicago and London: The University of Chicago Press.

Derrida, Jacques. 1998. Of Grammatology. Baltimore: Johns Hopkins University Press.

Derrida, Jacques, and Peggy Kamuf. 1994. *Specters of Marx*. New York: Routledge.

Derrida, Jacques, and David Wills. 2002. 'The Animal That Therefore I Am.' *Critical Inquiry* 28 (2): 369–418.

Dolcerocca, Özen Nergis and Meliz Ergin. 2017. 'Crippling Story: Disability and Storytelling in J. M. Coetzee's *Slow Man*.' *Mediterranean Journal of Humanities* 7 (2): 211–21.

Dolmage, Jay. 2018. 'Disability Rhetorics.' In *The Cambridge Companion to Literature and Disability*, edited by Clare Barker and Stuart Murray, 212–26. Cambridge: Cambridge University Press.

Dooley, Gillian. 2010. *J. M. Coetzee and the Power of Narrative*. New York: Cambria Press.

Dovey, Ceridwen. 2018. *On J. M. Coetzee: Writers on Writers*. Melbourne: Black Inc.

Dovey, Teresa. 1989. 'The Intersection of Postmodern, Postcolonial and Feminist Discourse in J. M. Coetzee's *Foe*.' *Journal of Literary Studies*, 5 (2): 119–33. DOI: 10.1080/02564718908529908.

Durrant, Sam, ed. 2004. *Postcolonial Narrative and the Work of Mourning: J. M. Coetzee, Wilson Harris and Toni Morrison*. Albany: State University of New York Press.

Easton, Kai, Marc Farrant and Herman Wittenberg (eds). 2021a. *J. M. Coetzee and the Archive: Fiction, Theory, and Autobiography*. London, New York and Dublin: Bloomsbury.

Easton, Kai, Marc Farrant and Herman Wittenberg. 2021b. 'Introduction: Fiction, Theory, and Autobiography.' In *J. M. Coetzee and the Archive: Fiction, Theory, and Autobiography*, edited by Kai Easton, Marc Farrant and Herman Wittenberg, 1–14. London, New York and Dublin: Bloomsbury.

Evans, Suzanne E., 2004. *Forgotten Crimes: The Holocaust and People with Disabilities*. Chicago: Ivan R. Dee.

Eze, Chielozona. 2011. 'Ambits of Moral Judgement: Of Pain, Empathy and Redemption in J. M. Coetzee's *Age of Iron*.' *Journal of Literary Studies* 27 (4): 17–35. DOI: 10.1080/02564718.2011.629441.

Farrant, Marc. 2021. '"The Aura of Truth": Coetzee's Archive, Realism and the Problem of Literary Authority.' In *J. M. Coetzee and the Archive: Fiction, Theory, and Autobiography*, edited by Kai Easton, Marc Farrant and Herman Wittenberg, 163–77. London, New York and Dublin: Bloomsbury.

Flaugh, Christian. 2010. 'Of Colonized Mind and Matter: The Dis/Abilities of Negritude in Aimé Césaire's *Cahier d'un retour au pays natal*.' *Journal of Literary & Cultural Disability Studies* 4 (3): 291–308.

Foley, Matt. 2011. 'Living with Lawrence's Silent Ghosts: A Lacanian Reading of "Glad Ghosts."' *The Linguistic Academy Journal of Interdisciplinary Language Studies* 1 (1): 19–32.

Foucault, Michel. 1995. *Discipline and Punish: The Birth of the Prison*, translated by Alan Sheridan. New York: Vintage.

Foucault, Michel. 1998. *The History of Sexuality: The Will to Knowledge: The Will to Knowledge*, translated by Robert Hurley. London and New York: Penguin Books.
Foucault, Michel. 2006. *Madness and Civilization: A History of Insanity in the Age of Reason*, translated Richard Howard. New York: Vintage.
Foucault, Michel. 2010. 'What is an Author?' in *The Norton Anthology of Theory and Criticism*, edited by Vincent B. Leitch, 1475–90. New York and London: W. W. Norton & Company.
Frank, A. W. 2013. *The Wounded Storyteller: Body, Illness and Ethics*. 2nd ed. Chicago: University of Chicago Press.
Freud, Sigmund. 2004. *Totem and Taboo: Some Points of Agreement between the Mental Lives of Savages and Neurotics*, translated by James Strachey. Routledge: London and New York.
Fricker, Miranda. 2010. *Epistemic Injustice: Power and the Ethics of Knowing*. New York: Oxford University Press.
Garff, Joakim. 2005. *Søren Kierkegaard: A Biography*, translated by Bruce H. Kirmmse. Princeton and Oxford: Princeton University Press.
Garland-Thomson, Rosemarie. 1997. *Extraordinary Bodies: Figuring Physical Disability in American Culture and Literature*. New York: Columbia University Press.
Garland-Thomson, Rosemarie. 2005. 'Disability and Representation.' *PMLA* 120 (2): 522–7.
Geertsema, Johan. 1997. '"We embrace to be embraced": Irony in an Age of Iron.' *English in Africa* 24 (1): 89–102.
Geertsema, Johan. 2011. 'Coetzee's *Diary of a Bad Year*, Politics, and the Problem of Position.' *Twentieth Century Literature* 57 (1): 70–85.
Gibson, Andrew. 2022. *J. M. Coetzee and Neoliberal Culture*. Oxford: Oxford University Press.
Glavin, Calla E. Y., and Paul Montgomery. 2017. 'Creative Bibliotherapy for Post-Traumatic Stress Disorder (PTSD): A Systematic Review.' *Journal of Poetry Therapy* 30 (2): 95–107. DOI: 10.1080/08893675.2017.1266190.
Goffman, Erving. 1963. *Stigma: Notes on the Management of Spoiled Identity*. Englewood Cliffs, New Jersey: Prentice-Hall.
Gordimer, Nadine. 1998. 'The Idea of Gardening: *Life and Times of Michael K* by J. M. Coetzee [Review].' In *Critical Essays of J. M. Coetzee*, edited by Sue Kossew, 139–44. New York: G. K. Hall & Co.
Gordimer, Nadine. 2005. *Get a Life*. London: Bloomsbury.
Grayson, Kyle, and Jocelyn Mawdsley. 2018. 'Scopic Regimes and the Visual Turn in International Relations: Seeing World Politics through the Drone.' *European Journal of International Relations* 25 (3): 1–27.
Gullette, Margaret Morganroth. 2017. *Ending Ageism Or, How Not to Shoot Old People*. New Brunswick: Rutgers University Press.
Gwyther, Liz, Sue Boucher and Richard Harding. 2016. 'Development of Palliative Medicine in Africa.' In *Textbook of Palliative Medicine and Supportive Care*, edited by Eduardo Bruera, Irene Higginson, Von

Gunten Charles F. and Tatsuya Morita, 49–58. Boca Raton: Taylor & Francis Group.

Hall, Alice. 2012a. 'Autre-biography: Disability and Life Writing in Coetzee's Later Works.' *Journal of Literary & Cultural Disability Studies* 6 (1): 53–67

Hall, Alice. 2012b. *Disability and Modern Fiction: Faulkner, Morrison, Coetzee and the Nobel Prize for Literature.* London and New York: Palgrave Macmillan.

Hall, Alice. 2014. 'Aging and Autobiography: Roth's *Exit Ghost* and Coetzee's *Diary of a Bad Year*.' In *Philip Roth and World Literature: Transatlantic Perspectives and Uneasy Passages*, edited by Velichka D. Ivanova, 289–304. New York: Cambria Press.

Hall, Alice. 2016. *Literature and Disability.* London and New York: Routledge.

Hallemeier, Katherine. 2016. 'J. M. Coetzee's Literature of Hospice.' *MFS Modern Fiction Studies* 62 (3): 481–98.

Hamel, Nic. 2021. 'Paradoxical Dramaturgies: Disability, Ritual, and Resistance in the Plays of Wole Soyinka.' In *Disability in Africa: Inclusion, Care, and the Ethics of Humanity,* edited by Toyin Falola and Nic Hamel, 185–208. Rochester: University of Rochester Press.

Hannay, Alastair. 2009. 'Introduction.' In Søren Kierkegaard, *The Sickness unto Death.* Translated with an Introduction and Notes by Alastair Hannay, 1–32. London and New York: Penguin Books.

Hartley, Daniel. 2020. 'Home and Law: Impersonality and Worldlessness in J. M. Coetzee's *The Childhood of Jesus* and Jenny Erpenbeck's *Gehen, Ging, Gegangen*.' In *Refugee Imaginaries: Research across the Humanities*, edited by Emma Cox, Sam Durrant, David Farrier, Lyndsey Stonebridge and Agnes Woolley, 503–17. Edinburgh: Edinburgh University Press, 2020.

Head, Dominic. 1997. *J. M. Coetzee.* Cambridge, New York and Melbourne: Cambridge University Press.

Hegel, Georg Wilhelm Friedrich. 1998. *Phenomenology of Spirit.* Delhi: Motilal Banarsidass.

Helgesson, Stefan. 2004. *Writing in Crisis. Ethics and History in Gordimer, Ndebele and Coetzee.* Scottsville: University of KwaZulu-Natal Press.

Houser, A. Marie. 2020. '"There, there": Disability, Animality, and the Allegory of *Elizabeth Costello*.' In *Disability and Animality: Crip Perspectives in Critical Animal Studies*, edited by Stephanie Jenkins, Kelly Struthers Montford and Chloë Taylor, 235–55. London and New York: Routledge.

Howell, Colleen. 2006. 'A History of the Disability Rights Movement in South Africa.' In *Disability and Social Change. A South African Agenda*, edited by Brian Watermeyer, Lesie Swartz, Theresa Lorenzo, Marguerite Schneider and Mark Priestley, 46–84. Cape Town: HSRC Press.

Hughes, Bill, and Kevin Paterson. 1997. 'The Social Model of Disability and

the Disappearing Body: Towards a Sociology of Impairment.' *Disability & Society* 12 (2): 325–40.
Hutcheon, Linda. 1980. *Narcissistic Narrative: The Metafictional Paradox.* Waterloo, Ontario: Wilfrid Laurier University Press.
Hutcheon, Linda. 1992. 'The Complex Functions of Irony.' *Revista Canadiense de Estudios Hispánicos* 16 (2): 219–34.
Hutcheon, Linda. 2010. *A Poetics of Postmodernism: History, Theory, Fiction.* New York: Routledge.
Innis, Robert E. 1984. 'Technics and the Bias of Perception.' *Philosophy and Social Criticism* 10 (1): 67–89.
Isaacs, David. 2021. 'Archival Realism: *Elizabeth Costello*, *Disgrace* and the Realm of Revision.' In *J. M. Coetzee and the Archive: Fiction, Theory, and Autobiography*, edited by Kai Easton, Marc Farrant and Herman Wittenberg, 133–48. London, New York and Dublin: Bloomsbury.
Iser, Wolfgang. 1978. *The Act of Reading: A Theory of Aesthetic Response.* Baltimore: John Hopkins University Press.
Jackson, Paul. 2006. 'The New Man.' In *World Fascism: A Historical Encyclopedia*, vol. 1, edited by Cyprian P. Blamires, 465–6. Oxford: Abc-clio.
Jacobs, J. U. 2017. 'A Bridging Fiction: The Migrant Subject in J. M. Coetzee's *The Childhood of Jesus*.' *Journal of Literary Studies* 33 (1): 59–75.
James, David. 2011. '*Dusklands* (1974).' In *A Companion to the Works of J. M. Coetzee*, edited by Tim Mehigan, 39–55. Rochester and New York: Camden House.
James, David. 2019. *Discrepant Solace: Contemporary Literature and the Work of Consolation.* Oxford: Oxford University Press.
Janes, Regina. 1997. '"Writing without Authority": J. M. Coetzee and His Fictions.' *Salmagundi* 114/115: 103–21.
Jay, Martin. 1988. 'Scopic Regimes of Modernity.' In *Vision and Visuality*, edited by Hal Foster, 3–27. Seattle: Bay Press.
Jay, Martin. 1994. *Downcast Eyes: The Denigration of Vision in Twentieth-Century French Thought.* Berkeley, Los Angeles and London: University of California Press.
Jędrzejko, Paweł. 2011. 'The Dangerous Prefix.' In *Inside(Out). Discourses of Interiority and Worldmaking Imagination*, edited by Zbigniew Białas, Paweł Jędrzejko and Karolina Lebek, 13–18. Bielsko-Biała: WSEH.
Johnston, Peter. 2021. '"Humming with fear of sincerity and fabulator": First Observations from the Coetzee Corpus and the Coetzee Bot.' In *J. M. Coetzee and the Archive: Fiction, Theory, and Autobiography*, edited by Marc Farrant, Kai Easton and Hermann Wittenberg, 95–116. London, New York and Dublin: Bloomsbury.
Jolly, Rosemary Jane. 1996. *Colonization, Violence, and Narration in White South African Writing: André Brink, Breyten Breytenbach, and J. M. Coetzee.* Athens: Ohio University Press.

Johnson, Merri Lisa and Robert McRuer. 2014. 'Cripistemologies: Introduction.' *Journal of Literary & Cultural Disability Studies* 8 (2): 127–47.

Jordaan, Eduard. 2005. 'A White South African Liberal as a Hostage to the Other: Reading J. M. Coetzee's *Age of Iron* through Levinas.' *South African Journal of Philosophy* 24 (1): 22–32.

Kafer, Alison. 2017. 'Bodies of Nature: The Environmental Politics of Disability.' In *Disability Studies and the Environmental Humanities: Toward an Eco-Crip Theory*, edited and with an introduction by Sarah Jaquette Ray and Jay Sibara, 201–41. Lincoln and London: University of Nebraska Press.

Kannemeyer, J. C. 2012. *J. M. Coetzee: A Life in Writing*. Melbourne and London: Scribe.

Keats, John. 1994. *Poems*. New York, London and Toronto: Alfred A. Knopf:

Kelley-Moore, Jessica. 2010. 'Disability and Ageing: The Social Construction of Causality.' In *The SAGE Handbook of Social Gerontology-SAGE Publications Ltd*, edited by Dale Dannefer and Chris Phillipson, 96–110. Los Angeles, London, Delhi and Washington, DC: Sage.

Kelly, Michelle. 2011. 'The Master of Petersburg (1994).' In *A Companion to the Works of J. M. Coetzee*, edited by Tim Mehigan, 132–47. Rochester: Camden House.

Kehinde, Ayobami. 2010. 'Ability in Disability: J. M. Coetzee's *Life & Times of Michael K* and the Empowerment of the Disabled.' *English Academy Review* 27 (1): 60–72. DOI: 10.1080/10131751003755948.

Kernberg, P. F. 1989. 'Narcissistic Personality Disorder in Childhood.' *Psychiatrics Clinics of North America* 12 (3): 671–94.

Kierkegaard, Søren. 1946. *Either/Or: A Fragment of Life*, vol. 2, translated by Walter Lowrie. Princeton: Princeton University Press.

Kierkegaard, Søren. 1948. *Purity of Heart is to Will One Thing*, translated by Douglas V. Steere. New York: Harper & Row.

Kierkegaard, Søren. 1978. *Søren Kierkegaard's Journals and Papers*, translated by Howard V. Hong and Edna H. Hong. Bloomington and London: Indiana University Press.

Kierkegaard, Søren. 1983. *The Sickness unto Death: A Christian Psychological Exposition for Upbuilding and Awakening*, edited by Howard V. Hong and Edna H. Hong. Princeton: Princeton University Press.

Kierkegaard, Søren. 1989. *The Concept of Irony: With Continual Reference to Socrates. Together with Notes of Schelling's Berlin Lectures*, translated by Howard V. Hong. Princeton: Princeton University Press.

Kierkegaard, Søren. 1993. 'The Gospel of Sufferings.' In *Upbuilding Discourses in Various Spirits*, edited by Howard V. Hong and Edna H. Hong, 217–341. Princeton: Princeton University Press.

Kierkegaard, Søren. 2000. '*Faedrelandet* Articles and *The Moment*.' In *The Essential Kierkegaard*, edited by Howard V. Hong and Edna H. Hong, 424–48. Princeton: Princeton University Press.

Kierkegaard, Søren. 2004. *The Sickness unto Death*, translated with an

Introduction and Notes by Alastair Hannay. London and New York: Penguin Books.
Kierkegaard, Søren. 2009. *Concluding Unscientific Postscript*, edited and translated by Alastair Hannay. Cambridge: Cambridge University Press.
Kleege, Georgina. 1999. *Sight Unseen*. New Haven and London: Yale University Press.
Kleege, Georgina. 2010. 'Dialogues with the Blind Literary Depictions of Blindness and Visual Art.' *Journal of Literary & Cultural Disability Studies* 4 (1): 1–16.
Kleege, Georgina. 2013. 'Blindness and Visual Culture: An Eyewitness Account.' In *The Disability Studies Reader*, edited by Lennard J. Davis, 447–55. London and New York: Routledge.
Koch, Jerzy, and Paweł Zajas. 2006. '"They pass each other by, too busy even to wave": J. M. Coetzee and His Foreign Reviewers.' In *A Universe of (Hi)Stories: Essays on J. M. Coetzee*, edited by Liliana Sikorska, 111–15. Frankfurt am Main: Peter Lang.
Kolarov, Radosvet. 2021. *Repetition and Creation: Poetics of Autotextuality*. New York and London: Routledge.
Koopman, Eva Maria, and Frank Hakemulder. 2015. 'Effects of Literature on Empathy and Self- Reflection: A Theoretical-Empirical Framework.' *JLT* 9 (1): 79–111.
Kossew, Sue. 1993. '"Women's Words": A Reading of J. M. Coetzee's Women Narrators.' *Journal of the South Pacific Association for Commonwealth Literature and Language Studies* 37. Accessed 29 August 2019. www.mcc.murdoch.edu.au/ReadingRoom/litserv/SPAN/37/Kossew.html.
Kossew, Sue. 1996. 'The Anxiety of Authorship: J. M. Coetzee's "The Master of Petersburg" (1994) and André Brink's "On the Contrary" (1993).' *English in Africa* 23 (1): 67–88.
Krentz, Christopher. 2022. *Elusive Kinship: Disability and Human Rights in Postcolonial Literature*. Philadelphia: Temple University Press.
Kreuz, Roger. 2020. *Irony and Sarcasm*. Cambridge, MA, and London: MIT Press.
Kudlick, Catherine. 2018. 'Social History of Medicine and Disability History.' In *The Oxford Handbook of Disability History*, edited by Michael Rembis, Catherine Kudlick and Kim E. Nielsen, 105–24. Oxford: Oxford Handbooks.
Kusek, Robert. 2017. *Through the Looking Glass: Writers' Memoirs at the Turn of the 21st Century*. Kraków: Jagiellonian University Press.
Kusek, Robert, and Wojciech Szymański. 2015. 'An Unlikely Pair: Berlinde De Bruyckere and J. M. Coetzee.' *Werkwinkel* 10 (1): 13–32. https://doi.org/10.1515/werk-2015-0002.
Lakoff, George, and Mark Johnson. 2003. *Metaphors We Live By*. Chicago and London: University of Chicago Press.
Lambek, Michael. 2003. 'Introduction: Irony and Illness – Recognition and Refusal.' In *Illness and Irony: On the Ambiguity of Suffering in*

Culture, edited by Michael Lambek and Paul Antze, 1–19. New York and Oxford: Berghahn Books.

Leatherbarrow, W. J. (ed.). 1999. *Dostoevsky's 'The Devils': A Critical Companion*. Evanston: Northwestern University Press.

Leist, Anton, and Peter Singer. 2010. *J. M. Coetzee and Ethics: Philosophical Perspectives on Literature*. New York: Columbia University Press.

Lessing, Doris. 2006. *Time Bites: Views and Reviews*. New York: Harper Perennial.

Lévi-Strauss, Claude. 1976. *Tristes Tropiques*. London: Penguin Books.

Linett, Maren. 2017. *Bodies of Modernism: Physical Disability in Transatlantic Modernist Literature*. Ann Arbor: The University of Michigan Press.

Lopez, Maria J. 2011. *Acts of Visitation: The Narrative of J. M. Coetzee*. Amsterdam and New York: Rodopi.

Lyotard, Jean-Francois. 'Defining the Postmodern.' In *The Norton Anthology of Theory and Criticism*, edited by Vincent B. Leitch et al., 1465–8. New York: W. W. Norton and Company.

MacLeod, Lewis. 2006. '"Do We of Necessity Become Puppets in a Story?" or Narrating the World: On Speech, Language, and Discourse in J. M. Coetzee's *Foe*.' *Modern Fiction Studies* 52 (1): 1–18. DOI: 10.1353/mfs.2006.0034.

Macmillan Dictionary, 'Care for', accessed 30 October 2022. www.macmillandictionary.com/dictionary/british/care-for.

Marais, Mike. 1998. 'Writing with Eyes Shut: Ethics, Politics, and the Problem of the Other in the Fiction of J. M. Coetzee.' *English in Africa* 25 (1): 43–60.

Marais, Mike. 2009. *Secretary of the Invisible: The Idea of Hospitality in the Fiction of J. M. Coetzee*. Amsterdam and New York: Rodopi.

Marinkova, Milena. 2011. *Michael Ondaatje: Haptic Aesthetics and Micropolitical Writing*. London and New York: Continuum.

Marks, Laura U. 2002. *Touch: Sensuous Theory and Multisensory Media*. Minneapolis and London: University of Minnesota Press.

Masłoń, Sławomir. 2018. *Père-versions of the Truth: The Novels of J. M. Coetzee*. Katowice: Wydawnictwo Uniwersytetu Śląskiego.

McCabe, Kevin Patrick. 2017. 'The Wound That Heals: Disability and Suffering in the Thought of Søren Kierkegaard.' *Journal of Disability & Religion* 21 (1): 43–63.

Mcleod, Deborah Susan. 2014. 'The "Defective" Generation: Disability in Modernist Literature.' PhD diss., University of South Florida. Accessed 30 October 2022. http://scholarcommons.usf.edu/etd/5272.

McNicol, Sarah. 2018. 'Theories of Bibliotherapy.' In *Bibliotherapy*, edited by Sarah McNicol and Liz Brewster, 23–40. London: Facet Publishing.

Medin, Daniel L. 2010. *Three Sons: Franz Kafka and the Fiction of J. M. Coetzee, Philip Roth, and W. G. Sebald*. Evanston: Northwestern University press.

Mehigan, Tim. 2011a. 'Introduction.' In *A Companion to the Works of J.*

M. *Coetzee*, edited by Tim Mehigan, 1–8. Rochester and New York: Camden House.
Mehigan, Tim. 2011b. '*Slow Man* (2005).' In *A Companion to the Works of J. M. Coetzee*, edited by Tim Mehigan, 192–207. Rochester and New York: Camden House.
Metz, Christian. 1982. *The Imaginary Signifier: Psychoanalysis and the Cinema*, translated by Celia Britton, Anwyl Williams, Ben Brewster and Alfred Guzzetti. Bloomington and Indianapolis: Indiana University Press.
Mitchell, David T. 2000. 'Body Solitaire: The Singular Subject of Disability Autobiography.' *American Quarterly* 52 (2): 311–15.
Mitchell, David T. 2015. 'Mute Speech: Literature, Critical Theory and Politics by Jacques Ranciére.' *Journal of Literary & Cultural Disability Studies* 9 (3): 368–71.
Mitchell, David T. and Sharon L. Snyder. 2000. *Narrative Prosthesis: Disability and the Dependencies of Discourse*. Ann Arbor: The University of Michigan Press.
Mitchell, David T. and Sharon Snyder. 2015. *The Biopolitics of Disability: Neoliberalism, Ablenationalism, and Peripheral Embodiment*. Ann Arbor: The University of Michigan Press.
Mitchell, David, Susan Antebi and Sharon L. Snyder. 2019. 'Introduction.' In *The Matter of Disability: Materiality, Biopolitics, Crip Affect*, edited by Mitchell, David, Susan Antebi and Sharon L. Snyder, 1–36. Ann Arbor: The University of Michigan Press.
Mitchell, W. J. T. 2002. 'Showing Seeing: A Critique of Visual Culture.' *Journal of Visual Culture* 2 (1): 165–81. DOI: 10.1177/1470412902 00100202.
Mosse, Richard. 2021. '*Waiting for the Barbarians* and the Origins of Incoming.' In *J. M. Coetzee and the Archive: Fiction, Theory, and Autobiography*, edited by Kai Easton, Marc Farrant and Herman Wittenberg, 213–18. London, New York and Dublin: Bloomsbury.
Murray, Stuart. 2012. 'From Virginia's Sister to Friday's Silence: Presence, Metaphor, and the Persistence of Disability in Contemporary Writing.' *Journal of Literary & Cultural Disability Studies* 6 (3): 241–58.
Murray, Stuart J. 2014. 'Allegories of the Bioethical: Reading J. M. Coetzee's *Diary of a Bad Year*.' *Journal of Medical Humanities* 35 (3): 321–34.
Murray, Stuart. 2018. 'The Ambiguities of Inclusion: Disability in Contemporary Literature.' In *The Cambridge Companion to Literature and Disability*, edited by Clare Barker and Stuart Murray, 90–103. Cambridge: Cambridge University Press.
Nashef, Hania A. M. 2009. *The Politics of Humiliation in the Novels of J. M. Coetzee*. New York and London: Routledge.
Nashef, Hania A. M. 2010. 'Becomings in J. M. Coetzee's *Waiting for the Barbarians* and Jose Saramago's *Blindness*.' *Comparative Literature Studies* 47 (1): 21–42.
Neimneh. Shadi, and Nazmi Al-Shalabi. 2011. 'Disability and the Ethics

of Care in J. M. Coetzee's *Slow Man*.' *Cross-cultural Communication* 7 (3): 35–40.

Newton, Adam Zachary. 1997. *Narrative Ethics*. Cambridge, MA, and London: Harvard University Press.

Nocella II, Anthony. 2017. 'Defining Eco-ability Social Justice and the Intersectionality of Disability, Nonhuman Animals, and Ecology.' In *Disability Studies and the Environmental Humanities: Toward an Eco-Crip Theory*, edited and with an Introduction by Sarah Jaquette Ray and Jay Sibara, 141–67. Lincoln, NE, and London: University of Nebraska Press.

Nünning, Ansgar F. 2005. 'Reconceptualising Unreliable Narration: Synthesizing Cognitive and Rhetorical Approaches.' *A Companion to Narrative Theory*, edited by James Phelan and Peter J. Rabinovitz, 89–107. Oxford: Blackwell.

Nussbaum, Martha C. 1990. *Love's Knowledge: Essays on Philosophy and Literature*. New York and London: Oxford University Press.

Nussbaum, Martha C. 1995. *Poetic Justice: The Literary Imagination and Public Life*. Boston, MA: Beacon Press.

Nussbaum, Martha C. 2001. *Upheavals of Thought: The Intelligence of Emotions*. Cambridge: Cambridge University Press.

Ong, Walter. J. 2000. *Orality and Literacy: The Technologizing of the Word*. London and New York: Routledge.

Online Etymology Dictionary, 'Image', accessed 24 November 2017, www.etymonline.com/index.php?allowed_in_frame=0&search=image.

Oser, Lee. 2009. *The Ethics of Modernism: Moral Ideas in Yeats, Eliot, Joyce, Woolf, and Beckett*. Cambridge: Cambridge University Press.

Oxford Dictionary of English Etymology. 1994. Edited by C. T. Onions. Clarendon: Oxford University Press.

Oxford English Dictionary, 'Prosthesis', accessed 16 October 2018. https://en.oxforddictionaries.com/definition/prosthesis.

Oxford English Dictionary, 'Silence', accessed 16 October 2022. www.oed.com/view/Entry/179646?rskey=fLq0BH&result=1#eid.

Oxford Paperback Thesaurus. 3rd ed. 2006. Edited by Maurice White, Lucy Hollingworth and Duncan Marshall. Oxford and New York: Oxford University Press.

Parker, Kenneth. 1995. 'J. M. Coetzee: The Postmodern and the Post-Colonial.' In *Critical Perspectives on J. M. Coetzee*, edited by Graham Huggan and Stephen Watson. London: Macmillan Press.

Pawlicki, Marek. 2013. *Between Illusionism and Anti-Illusionism: Self-Reflexivity in the Chosen Novels of J. M. Coetzee*. Newcastle upon Tyne: Cambridge Scholars Publishing.

Penner, Dick. 1986. 'Sight, Blindness and Double-Thought in J. M. Coetzee's *Waiting for the Barbarians*.' *World Literature Written in English* 26 (1): 34–45.

Penson, Richard T., Lidia Schapira, Kristy J. Daniels, Bruce A. Chabner

and Thomas J. Lynch JR. 2004. 'Cancer as Metaphor.' *The Oncologist* 9 (6): 708–16.
Pett, Sarah. 2014. *Reading and Writing Chronic Illness, 1990–2012: Ethics and Aesthetics at Work*. PhD diss., University of York, accessed 16 August 2021. https://etheses.whiterose.ac.uk/6645/1/Sarah%20Pett_Thesis%20Corrections_3.0.pdf.
Poyner, Jane. 2016. *J. M. Coetzee and the Paradox of Postcolonial Authorship*. London: Taylor & Francis.
Preston, Alex. 2016. '*The Schooldays of* Jesus by J. M. Coetzee Review – Obscurely Compelling.' *The Guardian*, 18 September 2016. www.theguardian.com/books/2016/sep/18/the-schooldays-of-jesus-jm-coetzee-review-david-Simón-ines-estrella-ana-magdalena-arroyo-dmitri-juan.
Preston, Alex. 2019. '*The Death of Jesus* by J. M. Coetzee Review – a Barren End to a Bizarre Trilogy.' *The Guardian*, 31 December 2019. www.theguardian.com/books/2019/dec/31/the-death-of-jesus-jm-coetzee-review.
Probyn, Fiona. 1998. 'Cancerous Bodies in the Apartheid.' In *Critical Essays on J. M. Coetzee*, edited by Sue Kossew, 214–25. New York: G. K. Hall and Co.
Propp, Vladimir. [1968] 2003. *Morphology of the Folk Tale*, translated by L. Scott. Austin: University of Texas Press.
Puar, Jasbir K. 2017. *The Right to Maim*. Durham, NC, and London: Duke University Press.
Quayson, Ato. 2007. *Aesthetic Nervousness: Disability and the Crisis of Representation*. New York: Columbia University Press.
Quintana, Pablo Ricardo. 2014. *The Comprehensive Dictionary of Patron Saints*. Bloomington: iUniverse.
Rabaté, Jean-Michel. 2017. 'Coetzee and Psychoanalysis: From Paranoia to Aporia.' In *Beyond the Ancient Quarrel*, edited by Patrick Hayes and Jan Wilm, 180–96. Oxford: Oxford University Press.
Rancière, Jacques. 2011. *Mute Speech: Literature, Critical Theory, and Politics*, translated by James Swenson and with Introduction by Gabriel Rockhill. New York: Columbia University Press.
Raskin R, Novacek J. 1991. 'Narcissism and the Use of Fantasy.' *Journal of Clinical Psychology* 47 (4): 490–9.
Riordan, R. J., and L. S. Wilson. 1989. 'Bibliotherapy: Does it work?' *Journal of Counseling & Development* 67 (9): 506–8.
Rockhill, Gabriel. 2011. 'Introduction: Through the Looking Glass – The Subversion of the Modernist Doxa.' In Jacques Rancière, *Mute Speech*, translated by James Swenson, 1–29. New York: Columbia University Press.
Rodas, Julia Miele. 2009. 'On Blindness.' *Journal of Literary & Cultural Disability Studies* 3 (2): 115–30.
Rody, Caroline. 1994. 'The Mad Colonial Daughter's Revolt: J. M. Coetzee's *In the Heart of the Country*.' In *The Writings of J. M. Coetzee*, edited by Michael Valdez Moses, 157–80. Durham, NC: Duke University Press.

Rorty, Richard. 1993. *Contingency, Irony and Solidarity*. Cambridge and New York: Cambridge University Press.

Roth, Philip. 2001. *The Dying Animal*. Boston, MA, and New York: Houghton Mifflin Company.

Roth, Philip. 2008. *Exit Ghost*. London Vintage.

Rutherford, Jennifer. 2021. 'Curating Coetzee: From Austin to Adelaide.' In *J. M. Coetzee and the Archive: Fiction, Theory, and Autobiography*, edited by Kai Easton, Marc Farrant and Herman Wittenberg, 219–24. London, New York and Dublin: Bloomsbury.

Samolsky, Russell. 2021. 'Shades of the Archive: J. M. Coetzee, the Paradox of Poetic Sovereignty and the Lives of Literary Beings.' In *J. M. Coetzee and the Archive: Fiction, Theory, and Autobiography*, edited by Marc Farrant, Kai Easton and Hermann Wittenberg, 197–210. London, New York and Dublin: Bloomsbury.

Sass, Louis A. 2001. 'Schizophrenia, Modernism, and the "Creative Imagination": On Creativity and Psychopathology.' *Creativity Research Journal* 13 (1): 55–74. DOI: 10.1207/S15326934CRJ1301_7.

Savarese, Ralph. 2010. 'Toward a Postcolonial Neurology: Autism, Tito Mukhopadhyay, and a New Geo-poetics of the Body.' *Journal of Literary & Cultural Disability Studies* 4 (3): 273–89.

Schalk, Sami. 2018. 'Disability and Women's Writing.' In *Literature and Disability*, edited by Clare Barker and Stuart Murray, 170–84. Cambridge: Cambridge University Press.

Schor, Naomi. 1999. 'Blindness as Metaphor.' *Differences: A Journal of Feminist Cultural Studies* 11 (2): 76–105.

Shakespeare, Tom. 2006. *Disability Rights and Wrongs*. New York: Routledge.

Shakespeare, Tom. 2015. 'Different Ways of Seeing.' *Perspectives* 9993 (386): 521. https://doi.org/10.1016/S0140-6736(15)61464-7.

Shakespeare, Tom. 2017. 'The Social Model of Disability.' *The Disability Studies Reader*. 5th ed., edited by Lennard J. Davis, 195–203. New York: Routledge.

Shakespeare, Tom. 2018. *Disability: The Basics*. London and New York: Routledge.

Shelley, Mary. [1818] 2018. *Frankenstein*. New York: Penguin Books.

Shulevitz, Judith. 2020. 'J. M. Coetzee's Jesus Sees the World as Don Quixote Does.' *The New York Times*, 26 May 2020. www.nytimes.com/2020/05/26/books/review/coetzee-death-jesus.html.

Siebers, Tobin. 2010. *Disability Aesthetics*. Ann Arbor: The University of Michigan Press.

Sikorska, Liliana. 2006. 'Michael K's Odyssey: Displacement and Wandering in the Context of the Medieval Concept of Homo Viator in J. M. Coetzee's *Life and Times of Michael K*.' In *A Universe of (Hi)Stories: Essays on J. M. Coetzee*, edited by Liliana Sikorska, 87–109. Frankfurt am Main: Peter Lang.

Silvani, Roman. 2012. *Political Bodies and the Body Politic in J. M. Coetzee's Novels*. Zurich and Berlin: Lit Verlag.
Small, Helen. 2007. *The Long Life*. Oxford: Oxford University Press.
Sontag, Susan. 1978. *Illness as Metaphor*. New York: Ferrar, Straus and Giroux.
Stanton, Katherine. 2006. *Cosmopolitan Fictions: Ethics, Politics, and Global Change in the Works of Kazuo Ishiguro, Michael Ondaatje, Jamaica Kincaid, and J. M. Coetzee*. London: Routledge.
Sterponi, L., Kenton de Kirby and Jennifer Shankey. 2015. 'Subjectivity in Autistic Language: Insights on Pronoun Atypicality from Three Case Studies.' In *The Palgrave Handbook of Child Mental Health*, edited by Michelle O'Reilly and Jessica N. Lester, 272–95. Palgrave Macmillan: London. https://doi.org/10.1057/9781137428318_15.
Stevenson, Robert Louis. 2003. *The Strange Case of Dr Jekyll and Mr Hyde*. London and New York: Penguin Classics.
Tanc, Apanra Mishra. 2020. *Pedagogy in the Novels of J. M. Coetzee: The Affect of Literature*. London and New York: Routledge.
Tegla, Emanuela. 2015. *J. M. Coetzee and the Ethics of Power. Unsettling Complicity, Complacency, and Confession*. Leiden and Boston, MA: Brill Rodopi.
Todorov, Tzvetan. 1971. 'The Two Principles of Narrative.' *Diacritics* 1 (1): 37–54.
Touhy, Theris A., and Kathleen F. Jett. 2013. *Ebersole and Hess' Gerontological Nursing & Healthy Aging*. St. Louis: Elsevier Health Sciences.
Trotter, David. 2008. *Paranoid Modernism: Literary Experiment, Psychosis, and the Professionalization of English Society*. Oxford: Oxford University Press.
Tweed, Hannah. 2020. 'Challenging the Neurotypical: Autism, Contemporary Literature, and Digital Textualities.' In *The Routledge Companion to Literature and Disability*, edited by Alice Hall, 366–77. London and New York: Routledge.
Uhlmann, Anthony. 2020. *J. M. Coetzee: Truth, Meaning, Fiction*. New York and London: Bloomsbury.
Van Bever Donker, Vincent. 2016. *Recognition & Ethics in World Literature: Religion, Violence, and the Human*. Stuttgart: Ibidem-Verlag.
van der Merwe, Chris N, and Pumla Gobodo-Madikizela. 2007. *Narrating Our Healing: Perspectives on Working through Trauma*. Newcastle upon Tyne: Cambridge Scholars Publishing.
Vidali, Amy. 2010. 'Seeing What We Know: Disability and Theories of Metaphor.' *Journal of Literary & Cultural Disability Studies* 4 (1): 33–54.
Warner, Michael. 1999. *The Trouble with Normal*. New York: Free Press.
Wasson, Sara. 2010. *Urban Gothic of the Second World War Dark London*. Basingstoke: Palgrave Macmillan.
Wasson, Sara. 2017. 'Haunted Selves, Fractured Identities: Writing Chronic

Pain in the Gothic Mode.' Presentation at the Discourse of Identity Conference, University of Santiago de Compostella, 8–9 June.
Wasson, Sara. 2020. 'Spectrality, Strangeness, and Stigmaphilia: Gothic and Critical Disability Studies.' In *The Routledge Companion to Literature and Disability*, edited by Alice Hall, 70–81. London and New York.
Watson, Stephen. 1986. 'Colonialism and the Novels of J. M. Coetzee.' *Research in African Literatures* 17 (3): 370–92.
Wedgwood, Hensleigh. 1872. *A Dictionary of English Etymology*. 2nd ed. London: Trübner.
Weigl, Engelhard. 2011. '*Life and Times of Michael K* (1983).' In *A Companion to the Works of J. M. Coetzee*, edited by Tim Mehigan, 76–90. Rochester and New York: Camden House.
Wheatley, Edward. 2018. 'Monsters, Saints, and Sinners: Disability in Medieval Literature.' In *The Cambridge Companion to Literature and Disability*, edited by Clare Barker and Stuart Murray, 17–31. Cambridge: Cambridge University Press.
Wheeler, Elizabeth A. 2017. 'Moving Together Side by Side: Human–Animal Comparisons in Picture Books.' In *Disability Studies and the Environmental Humanities Toward an Eco-Crip Theory*, edited and with an introduction by Sarah Jaquette Ray and Jay Sibara, 594–622. Lincoln, NE, and London: University of Nebraska Press.
Wiegandt, Kai. 2019. *J. M. Coetzee's Revisions of the Human: Posthumanism and Narrative Form*. Cham: Palgrave Macmillan.
Wilm, Jan. 2016. *The Slow Philosophy of J. M. Coetzee*. London, Oxford, New York, New Delhi and Sidney: Bloomsbury.
Wilm, Jan. 2017. 'The J. M. Archive and the Archive in J. M. Coetzee.' In *Beyond the Ancient Quarrel*, edited by Patrick Hayes and Jan Wilm, 215–32. Oxford: Oxford University Press.
Woessner, Martin. 2010. 'Coetzee's Critique of Reason.' In *J. M. Coetzee and Ethics*, edited by Anton Leist and Peter Singer, 223–48. New York and Chichester: Columbia University Press.
Woessner, Martin. 2017. 'Beyond Realism: Coetzee's Post-Secular Imagination.' In *Beyond the Ancient Quarrel*, edited by Patrick Hayes and Jan Wilm, 143–59. Oxford: Oxford University Press.
Wojtas, Paweł. 2021a. 'Crippling Commitments: Charting the Ethics of Disability in Forster and Coetzee.' In *The World of E. M. Forster – E. M. Forster and the World*, edited by Krzysztof Fordoński and Anna Kwiatkowska, 115–34. Newcastle upon Tyne: Cambridge Scholars Publishing.
Wojtas, Paweł. 2021b. 'Disability and the Modalities of Displacement in the Early Fiction of J. M. Coetzee.' In *Mobility and Corporeality in Nineteenth- to Twenty-First-Century Anglophone Literature: Bodies in Motion*, edited by Jaine Chemmachery and Bhawana Jain, 113–30. Lanham, Boulder, New York and London: Lexington Books.
World Health Organisation. 2018. 'Blindness and Vision Impairment.'

Accessed 11 October 2018. www.who.int/news-room/fact-sheets/detail/blindness-and-visual-impairment.

Worthington, Kim. L. 2011. '*Age of Iron* (1990).' In *A Companion to the Works of J. M. Coetzee*, edited by Tim Mehigan, 113–31. Rochester, NY: Camden House.

Wright, Laura. 2006. *Writing 'Out of All the Camps': J. M. Coetzee's Narratives of Displacement*. New York and London: Routledge.

Zahra, Saloua Ali Ben. 2021. 'Masculinity, Disability, and Empire in J. M. Coetzee's *Waiting for the Barbarians*.' In *Disability in Africa: Inclusion, Care, and the Ethics of Humanity*, edited by Toyin Falola and Nic Hamel, 228–38. Rochester, NY: University of Rochester Press.

Zimbler, Jarad. 2014. *J. M. Coetzee and the Politics of Style*. New York: Cambridge University Press.

Zimbler, Jarad. 2020. 'Stories and Narration: *In the Heart of the Country*, *The Master of Petersburg*, *The Childhood of Jesus*.' In *The Cambridge Companion to J. M. Coetzee*, edited by Jarad Zimbler, 45–63. Cambridge: Cambridge University Press.

Index

Achebe, Chinua, 30
aesthetic nervousness, 2, 36, 118, 122, 194–5
affect, 3, 66, 71, 232, 238, 240, 266–7, 271
Agamben, Giorgio, 193
apartheid, 3, 4, 7, 29, 53, 76, 86, 126–30, 135, 138–9, 142, 205, 216, 255
  and disability, 80
Attridge, Derek, 13, 18–20, 27, 29, 30, 32, 39, 66, 69, 76, 86, 112, 142–3, 146n, 161, 178, 180, 182, 188, 196n, 197n, 212, 219, 229n, 232, 271
Attwell, David, 12, 26, 27, 30, 35, 40n, 65, 95–6, 99n, 115–16, 123n, 128, 142, 146n, 154, 158, 162, 164, 179–80, 187–8, 198, 206, 220, 241, 253, 263, 268
Auster, Paul, 123, 262
autism, 3, 7, 8, 31, 79, 108, 246–8, 257–8, 265n
  Asperger's syndrome, 245–6, 257, 259, 265n
autobiography, 3, 4, 12, 14, 15n, 56, 110, 128, 130, 146, 174n, 188, 219–20, 265n, 272
  disability, 208, 253–64; *see also* Coetzee, John Maxwell, life
autogerontography, 4
  ironic, 11, 218–27

Barker, Clare, 24–5, 40, 126, 189
Barth, John, 87

Baudrillard, Jean, 166, 186
Beckett, Samuel, 76, 87, 99, 145, 180, 196n, 220, 229n
Bellow, Saul, 220
Benjamin, Walter, 185
Bérubé, Michael, 2, 8, 37, 114
bibliotherapy, 11–12, 14n, 230–43, 250–2
Black, Sheila, 245
Blatty, William Peter, 169
blindness, 21, 27, 43–7, 49, 50–62, 67–8, 119–20, 167, 173, 216, 259
  metanarratives of, 44
  see also metaphor of blindness / vision loss; modernism / modernity; vision
Bloomfield, Leonard, 105
Bolt, David, 9, 43–4, 47, 73n
Breytenbach, Breyten, 5
Brink, André, 5
Brontë, Charlotte, 151–2
Bruyckere, Berlinde de, 1–2
Byatt, A. S., 220

cancer, 3, 4, 10, 125, 126–30, 131, 135, 140, 138–9, 191, 196n, 205, 208, 211, 217, 234, 263
care, 11, 14n, 81, 131–2, 143–4, 176, 181–2, 184–7, 190–4, 196n, 203, 206, 212, 215–17, 225–6, 235
Chaucer, Geoffrey, 90
Christie, Agatha, 169
Clarkson, Carrol, 39n, 91, 108, 146n
Coetzee, David, 147n, 262, 265n

Coetzee, Gisela, 131–2, 158, 208
Coetzee, Jacobus, 27, 40n
  portrayal in *Dusklands*, 19–20, 23–8, 50, 203, 270
Coetzee, John Maxwell, life
  102, 130–2, 140, 147n, 154, 158, 163, 206–9, 219–20, 241, 253–64, 264n
Coetzee, J. M., writings
  Age of Iron, 3, 4, 5, 10, 53, 109, 125–46, 199, 205, 211, 216, 237, 264n, 270–1; drafts, 129, 132, 138, 140; notebooks, 127, 129, 132, 138, 145, 271; correspondence, 131
  'As a Woman Grows Older', 11, 15n, 199, 201, 207, 209, 228–9n
  Boyhood, 140, 147n, 253, 255–7, 261–2; drafts, 255, 257, 261, 265n; notebooks, 254, 255
  'Burning the Books', unfinished novel, 51, 268–9
  Childhood of Jesus, The, 11, 41, 72, 110, 123n, 230, 238–44, 246–50, 253, 255–7, 262–3, 265n
  Cripplewood/Kreupelhout, 1–2, 229n
  Death of Jesus, The, 3, 11, 110, 230, 238, 239, 246, 248–50, 257, 259, 261–2, 263, 272
  Diary of a Bad Year, 5, 7–8, 11, 59–60, 72, 103, 123, 199–200, 207–9, 212, 215, 218–227, 236, 238, 241, 254, 262, 267, 271, 228n, 241, 267
  Disgrace, 11, 15n, 107–8, 148, 172–3, 183, 199, 205–6, 227n, 236, 237; notebooks, 16n, 173
  'Dostoevsky: The Miraculous Years', 174n
  Doubling the Point, 4, 10, 26, 36, 77, 87, 95–6, 98, 102–3, 105, 116, 123n, 142, 147n, 164, 167, 174, 180, 183, 187, 196n, 253–5, 266, 269, 289
  Dusklands, 3, 5, 9, 19–28, 38–9, 50, 203, 270; drafts, 26, 39n, 235, 264n
  Elizabeth Costello, 11, 33, 123n, 124n, 199, 207, 209–12, 217–18, 226, 227n, 228–9n, 231, 254, 264n, 267n
  'Farm Novel and "Plaasroman" in South Africa', 99n
  Foe, 6, 10, 53, 102, 110–23, 203, 228n; drafts, 114–17, 123n, 267; notebooks, 114–17, 269
  'Glass Abattoir, The', 229n
  Good Story, The, 123n, 231, 236, 244
  'He and His Man', 123n
  Here and Now, 123n
  'Hope', 229n
  'House in Spain, A', 199, 227n
  'Humanities in Africa, The', 191, 206, 228n
  Inner Workings, 220
  In the Heart of the Country, 3, 5, 6, 9, 28–38, 39, 152, 174n, 204, 264n, 270; drafts, 33–4, 40n, 269; notebooks, 1–2, 34, 36–7
  Late Essays 2006–2017, 220
  'Lies', 199, 207–8, 212, 215, 229n
  Life & Times of Michael K, 5, 9–10, 30, 53, 76–99, 103, 108, 174n, 203, 216, 227–8n, 270; drafts, 89–90, 100n, 259; notebooks, 88, 90–1, 266
  Lives of Animals, The, 228n
  Master of Petersburg, The, 3, 10–11, 54–5, 109, 148, 153–73, 183, 237, 271; drafts, 154–6, 158–9, 162–4, 168, 169, 172, 174n
  'Old Woman and the Cats, The', 11, 209–10, 213–15, 226, 229n, 235, 241
  Pole, The, 3
  Scenes from Provincial Life, 12, 55, 101, 219, 241, 253
  Schooldays of Jesus, The, 11, 123, 230, 238, 242–3, 246, 249, 256, 259
  Slow Man, 3, 5, 7, 11, 56–9, 87, 109, 184–96, 207, 209, 215, 217, 228n, 241, 255, 264n, 271; drafts, 185, 191, 194, 197n, 216
  Stranger Shores, 220
  Summertime, 101, 125, 199, 209, 211, 219–20, 229n, 236, 241,

Coetzee, J. M., writings (*cont.*)
   256–7, 260, 266; drafts, 258, 261; notebooks, 257, 265n
  Waiting for the Barbarians, 5, 9, 43, 50, 51, 53, 60–9, 70–2, 109, 270; drafts, 65, 68, 267, 269; notebooks, 37–8, 62–3, 65, 267–8
  'What is Realism?', 199, 228n
  Youth, 55–6, 241, 253, 255, 260, 265n
Coetzee, Nicolas, 130–1, 154, 158
Coetzee, Vera, 130–2, 198–9, 262
Coetzee, Zacharias, 130–1
Collins, Wilkie, 152
Conrad, Joseph, 175
Cooper, James Fenimore, 90
crip ex machina, 170–3
cripped environmentalism, 9–10, 83

Davidson, Michael, 24, 31–2, 171, 177, 178
Davis, Lennard J., 7, 11, 18, 29, 95, 98, 175–7, 181–4, 193, 248, 271
deafness, 49, 54, 105
  metaphor of, 119, 159
Defoe, Daniel, 76, 110–12, 114, 115
dependency, 11, 14n, 58, 176, 181–2, 184, 190, 192–6, 209, 217, 225, 229n
Derrida, Jacques, 10, 66–7, 75n, 105, 146n, 148, 160, 164–7, 170, 186
Desai, Anita, 30
disability
  and colonialism, 30–1
  and gender, 30–1, 33–4
  and Gothic form, 149–53
  and impairment, 5
  and metaphor, 8, 25, 27, 31–2, 34, 54, 73n, 97–8, 119, 126, 165, 169, 170–1, 177, 179, 183, 255, 259–60
  and modernism, 31–3, 177–9
  see also models of disability
disabled textuality, 2, 9, 13, 37–8, 272
dismodernism, 7, 11, 176–7, 181–4, 186, 194–6
Dostoevsky, Fyodor Mikhailovich, 76, 89, 154–5, 158–9, 161–2, 164, 172, 174n, 238, 263
  portrayal in *The Master of Petersburg*, 8, 54–5, 109, 153–64, 167–73, 183, 236, 271

epilepsy, 3, 8, 89, 154, 158–62, 174n, 208, 263, 271

falling, 3, 148, 158–62, 249, 263
  sickness, 158–62, 271
Faulkner, William, 33, 180
Foucault, Michel, 64, 68, 91–2, 123n, 149–50, 192–3
Freud, Sigmund, 156, 237

Galton, Francis, 32
Garland-Thomson, Rosemarie, 7, 39n, 176
Goffman, Erving, 79–80
Gordimer, Nadine, 5, 87, 98, 129, 196n
Gothic, 10, 21, 145, 148–73; *see also* disability and Gothic form
Grass, Günter, 90

Hall, Alice, 5, 6, 14n, 17, 20–1, 46, 49, 58, 60–1, 73n, 98, 180, 187, 189, 195, 208, 217, 219, 220, 254
haptic metaphor, 72
haptic perception, 50, 53–4, 58, 61, 66–7
haptic reading, 42, 60, 70
haptic visuality, 3, 9, 60–1, 65–6, 68, 70
Harris, Thomas, 153
Harry Ransom Center, The, 12, 13n, 15n, 131, 254
haunting, 148, 155, 159–60, 164–7, 170, 172; *see also* spectre
hauntology, 10–11, 148, 165
Hamsun, Knut, 90
Hegel, Georg Wilhelm, 149, 185
hermeneutical impasse, 93, 122, 189
Highsmith, Patricia, 169
Hill, Joe, 153
Hutcheon, Linda, 26, 179, 200

illness, 7–12, 23, 125–45, 149, 152, 158, 161, 164, 199, 218, 230–63, 270

metaphor, 4, 125–8
  narrative, 3, 11, 231, 239, 243, 245, 250, 252, 254, 271–2
inclusionism, 5, 83, 98, 112, 224–5, 271
injustice
  epistemic, 15–16n, 45–7, 150–1, 173, 270
  hermeneutical, 45–6, 53
  testimonial, 10, 45, 63, 77, 88, 92, 98, 132
  see also narrative violence
ironic defamiliarisation, 211–12
ironic dialogism, 11, 200, 210–13, 218, 271
irony, 11, 22, 199–227
  confrontational, 211–12, 214
  embodied, 210
  ethical, 201, 205, 206–18
  formal, 11, 200
  historical, 209
  liberal, 210
  overt, 11, 200
  romantic, 215
  senile, 200–6
  situational, 207

Jackson, Shirley, 157
James, Henry, 171
Jonk, Abraham, 99n

Kafka, Franz 76, 90, 93, 100n
Kannemeyer, John Christoffel, 72, 130–1, 208, 229n, 265
Keats, John, 14n, 244–5, 248, 272
Kesey, Ken, 24
Kierkegaard, Søren, 10, 35, 126, 134–46, 146n–7n, 159–60, 200
King, Stephen, 153, 157, 169, 171
Kleege, Georgina, 44, 46, 65, 69–71, 73n, 75n
Kleist, Heinrich von, 90
Koontz, Dean, 153
Kurtz, Arabella, 123, 231, 236, 244
Kühn, Christoffel Hermanus, 99n

La Guma, Alex, 5
Lapper, Alison, 195, 197n
Lawrence, David Herbert, 32, 180

Leroux, Gaston, 151
Lessing, Doris, 169, 220
Levinas, Emmanuel, 65, 146, 174n
Lévi-Strauss, Claude, 103, 119
Levin, Ira, 157
Lyotard, Jean-François, 186

McCarthy, Cormac, 155, 157
madness, 31–7, 54–5, 139–40, 162, 269; *see also* psychiatric disorder; mental disorder
Malherbe, Daniël Francois, 99n
Marks, Laura, 3, 9, 61, 70
Masterton, Graham, 153
mental disorder, 28–31, 151, 232, 246; *see also* psychiatric disorder; madness
metafiction, 22, 26–8, 40n, 58, 71, 76, 95–6, 179, 184, 187–90, 196, 207, 210, 217, 219, 229n, 243, 250, 268–9
  situational, 27
  see also self-reflexivity
metaphor
  of blindness / vision loss, 27, 43, 45, 50, 54, 74
  of cancer, 4, 10, 125, 126–30, 138–9
  visual, 41–2, 43, 45, 53
  see also disability and metaphor
Mitchell, David T., 6, 15n, 22, 57, 71, 86, 88, 90, 104, 172, 187, 224
models of disability
  social (constructionist), 5–6, 17, 141, 150, 174n
  medical, 5, 7, 17, 150, 174n
modernism / modernity, 11, 19–20, 31–2, 48–9, 177–96
  and vision, 47–9
  see also disability and modernism; dismodernism; postmodernism / postmodernity
Morrison, Toni, 155, 169
Murray, Stuart J., 14n, 24–5, 85, 185–6, 227
mute letter, 102–6, 109, 112–13; *see also* mute speech
muteness, 3, 10, 102–6
mute speech, 10, 102–6, 108, 110, 112, 115, 121–2; *see also* mute letter

mutism *see* muteness

Nabokov, Vladimir, 87
narrative
    ethics, 9, 18–23
    prosthesis, 13, 22, 28, 57, 71, 88–90, 118, 172
    violence, 10, 77, 87–8, 90–1, 94–6, 98; *see also* injustice
negative capability, 244–5, 248, 250, 252, 272
neomaterialism, 6, 86
normate, 7, 17, 150
Nussbaum, Martha, 178, 231–2

Oates, Joyce Carol, 153, 156, 171
ocularcentrism, 9, 41–9, 51, 53–4, 57–8, 70, 72, 73n, 105
ocularnormativism, 9, 44, 46, 49
Ong, Walter, 104–5

Parkinson's disease, 7–8, 220–1
Perkins Gilman, Charlotte, 152
phonocentrism, 53, 73n, 103, 105, 115, 120, 122
physical impairment, 3
plaasroman, 76, 99n
poetics of failure, 10, 36, 77, 87, 95–9, 196n
postmodernism / postmodernity, 7, 9, 11, 87, 95–6, 98, 105, 157, 176, 179–4, 186–7, 196n; *see also* disability and modernism; dismodernism; modernism / modernity
Pound, Ezra, 32
Propp, Vladimir, 88
psychiatric disorder, 3, 31, 36; *see also* mental disorder; madness
Puar, Jasbir K., 4, 223–4, 255

Quayson, Ato, 2, 8, 30, 32, 36–7, 40n, 93, 108, 118, 189, 271

Rancière, Jacques, 10, 104, 109
realism, 3, 18, 21, 27–8, 58, 90, 149, 177, 179, 187–9, 229n, 244, 255, 257, 264n

Rhys, Jean, 152
Rorty, Richard, 200, 210, 229n
Roth, Philip, 15, 162, 220
Rushdie, Salman, 30

Sapir, Edward, 105
Saussure, Ferdinand de, 105
scopic regimes, 24, 41, 44, 46, 49, 54, 60, 65–7
senescence, 3, 11, 17, 180, 200–2, 207, 213, 220, 254, 260, 271; *see also* irony; senility
self-reflexivity, 9, 13, 16n, 19, 22, 26–8, 36, 50, 71–2, 87, 91, 99, 104, 110, 178, 179, 182–3, 187, 190, 233–4, 242, 253, 255, 257, 268, 270
senility, 11, 198–227; *see also* irony; senescence
sight *see* vision
silence, 10, 53, 55, 93–6, 102–6, 118–22, 210–11, 235, 270
    and writing, 106–16
    elective, 17n, 96, 108, 112, 114, 121
Schreiner, Olive, 99n
seizure *see* epilepsy
Seltzer, David, 169
Serote, Mongane Wally, 5
Shakespeare, Tom, 6, 79, 84, 92, 98, 245
Shelley, Mary, 151, 157
slow reading, 14n, 43, 233–4
Smith, Pauline, 99n
Snyder, Sharon L., 15n, 22, 57, 86, 88, 90, 172, 224
Sontag, Susan, 126, 128
Soyinka, Wole, 30
spectre; *see also* spectrality, 10–11, 185, 148, 165–70; *see also* haunting
Stein, Gertrude, 32
Stevenson, Robert Louis, 151–2
stillness, 69, 239–43, 252

Todorov, Tzvetan, 88
Twain, Mark, 90

unreliable narration, 20–2, 28, 29, 32, 35, 37, 52, 235

Van Bruggen, Jochem, 99n
Van den Heever, Christiaan Maurits, 99n
Van Meile, Johannes, 99n
vision, 50–60, 119
  and colonial oppression, 61–5, 68
  peripheral, and reading, 69–71
  see also blindness; metaphor of blindness / vision loss; modernism / modernity

Wilde, Oscar, 151–2
Wilm, Jan, 12, 14, 15, 43, 69, 71, 229n, 233–4
Woolf, Virginia, 32

Yeats, William Butler, 32

EU representative:
Easy Access System Europe
Mustamäe tee 50, 10621 Tallinn, Estonia
Gpsr.requests@easproject.com

www.ingramcontent.com/pod-product-compliance
Lightning Source LLC
Chambersburg PA
CBHW050203240426
43671CB00013B/2234